A Reflective Image

Margaret Alty

Published 2016 by arima publishing

www.arimapublishing.com

ISBN 978 1 84549 681 4
© Margaret Alty 2016

Printed and bound in the United Kingdom

Typeset in Garamond

Swirl is an imprint of arima publishing.

arima publishing
ASK House, Northgate Avenue
Bury St Edmunds, Suffolk IP32 6BB
t: (+44) 01284 700321

www.arimapublishing.com

Chapter One

ENGLAND

At first he was only one of the many colourless shapes reflected in the window until he moved away to stand against a stone pillar outside the museum. Although she couldn't make out his features it was the set of his shoulders and the way he was tilting his head slightly to one side which reminded her of Anthony. The resemblance was so disturbing, that the display of ceramic plates she had been admiring no longer held any appeal. She turned round to get a clearer view of him and to prove to herself how mistaken she had been, only to find he had gone. In less than a minute he had simply vanished. He hadn't come out on to the pavement, nor was he among the group of people milling around the front entrance, therefore, she reasoned, he must be inside the museum and, impulsively, she crossed the road.

Once in the museum, Kate looked around, but there was no sign of any man in a light-coloured trench coat and trilby. She was on the verge of giving up and returning to the street when she spotted him on one of the balconies, standing quite still with both hands on the rail and looking directly down at her, but she still couldn't see his face properly; he was in the shadows up there, the brim of the trilby making his features even more indistinct.

She had to find out; she had to, and walked quickly towards the stairs, but by the time she reached where he had been, she was too late. Once again, she'd lost him and there were too many rooms to search any further, making up her mind by now that it had been foolish to even try. It couldn't have been Anthony. He had just looked like him, that's all, trying to convince herself, but for a few moments back there she really believed it had been him.

It wasn't until later she began to wonder why he had been watching her, because whoever it was, certainly had been. Was he merely some weirdo who went around London making an occupation of staring at women? A weirdo who happened to resemble Anthony, her husband, who had been killed in a car crash ten years earlier?

At the time of the accident Kate had been in Scotland spending Christmas with her daughter and aunt. The call had come from the managing director of the company Anthony had worked for in Samriboi, a small town on Zambia's Copperbelt and where they had been living for eight years. Apparently, Anthony had been driving along the road on the outskirts of the town when his car must have skidded on the laterite surface and, going out of control crashed through the undergrowth and careering over the edge of the ravine. Although the car had been sighted, there had been no sign of him. It was officially agreed, mainly because the driver's door had been wrenched off its hinges, he had been thrown clear of the vehicle into the fast-flowing river below. Kate hadn't needed to be reminded that those waters were crocodile-infested. She knew exactly where that ravine was and the picture in her mind of how it must have been for him had stayed with her for a long time.

She had returned only once to Samriboi, but there was very little she had to attend to in the way of any formalities, the company having taken care of those. Her main task had been to sort out their belongings and have them crated up and transported back to London. Anthony had no family which meant she was spared having to break the news of his death to any of them. She'd already told Dawn before leaving Scotland and although she had been upset, Kate didn't think her grieving would have any long-lasting effect on her. She had seen so little of her father; he had never offered to accompany her back to Britain when she was able to spend some of the school holidays with Dawn, Kate had realised from when their daughter had been a baby, Anthony had been devoid of any paternal instincts, but had learned to live with this fact. Dawn had only been three when they went out to Samriboi and although she did attend the small church school there, by the time she was eight, it became clear she would soon have to go to boarding school. Kate had found this a difficult decision to make and made even more so by Anthony's attitude. "We're expatriates, Kate," he had said, "and most children from Dawn's age spend a good part of their education as boarders. It's the norm and unless you want your daughter to grow up useless academically, you have no choice." Harsh words and they had hurt, but what he had said was true. It had been her aunt who had softened the situation for both Dawn and herself by suggesting they send Dawn to the boarding school close to where she lived on the east coast of Scotland. Seeing that man this afternoon had brought all of these sad old memories back and ones she had firmly believed were tucked well away at the back of her mind. She'd tell Steven this evening, she decided; that's what she would do. With his keen lawyer's brain he would help her to come up with a rational explanation.

***

Steven was already home when she arrived back at the apartment and pre-empting her, had opened a bottle of wine and filled a dish with a selection of savoury appetisers. And, as always at the end of the day, putting the glasses and nibbles on the kitchen table, rather than in the lounge.

'You're early, darling,' she said, kissing him, 'but I'm glad.'

'What's wrong, Kate?' he asked, touching her lightly on the cheek.

'How well you know me.' she smiled.

'I should do by now, sweetheart, so why not sit down and tell me.'

'I don't really know whether there is anything wrong,' she said slowly and waiting until he had filled their glasses, 'but something strange happened this afternoon.'

'Yes?' he prompted, sitting down opposite to her.

'I was in Great Russell Street, Steven. You know where the Contemporary Ceramics Centre is, don't you?'

'Opposite to the British Museum.'

'Yes, that's right; well I was looking in the ceramic shop's window when I saw the reflection of someone who looked uncannily like Anthony – '

' – go on.' he urged gently.

'He was leaning against one of the pillars outside the front entrance to the museum, but when I turned round to get a clearer view of him, he'd gone.'

'Gone?'

'Yes, just like that. In less than a minute, Steven.'

'Was he looking in your direction?'

'I think so; in fact now I'm sure he was.'

'Why?'

'Because as he wasn't around, not even on the pavement, I thought he may have gone into the museum.'

'That seems likely,' he agreed, 'were there many people about?'

'Quite a few, but no-one dressed as he was; he was in a light-coloured trench coat, also he was wearing a trilby.' she added.

'So what did you do?'

'I went across to the museum to try and see if he was in there. And he was, you know; standing on one of the balconies and this time he was looking directly at me –'

'- weird.'

'It was, but by the time I went up the stairs to where he was, once again he'd gone.'

'That place is a labyrinth of nooks and crannies; he could have gone anywhere.'

'That's what I thought, so I decided I was wasting my time.'

'Were you able to see his face properly?'

'Not really. I suppose it was his overall appearance which struck me as so similar; same height, build and the way he stood, that sort of thing.'

'He could have been a crank; there are plenty of them about. Nothing better to do but admire a pretty woman.'

'And he just happened to look like Anthony.' she put in, but smiling.

'Kate?'

'Yes?'

'You've told me about Anthony's accident, how it probably happened. I've never asked you before, but when you went back to Samriboi did you actually see him?'

'No, that wasn't possible. They were unable to recover his body.'

'Given the seriousness of the accident and where the car ended up, that wasn't all that surprising, but bodies, in the water I mean, do have a habit of turning up eventually.'

'That ravine is infested with crocodiles, Steven.'

'Yes, I remember you telling me and the last thing I want to do is upset you, darling.'

'You're not, Steven, honestly, but for the first time I'm beginning to question that accident. Naturally, I didn't then. There was no reason for me to. The authorities had reached their verdict and I accepted it.'

'Indeed and why shouldn't you have done? You had already gone through enough and to start asking questions would only have made things worse.'

'I'm trying to convince myself that I imagined the man I saw earlier was Anthony, but –'

' - but you're finding it difficult.'

'A bit, yes.'

'You have two choices here, Kate.'

'I have?'

'Yes, you can put it down to an overactive imagination or you could start asking some questions.'

'Oh, dear.' she sighed.

'Listen, darling,' he said, standing up and walking round to her side of the table and placing an arm around her shoulders, 'I'm with you and I always will be. Don't forget that.'

'I know; I know, but if I do believe it was Anthony I saw, where on earth do I begin?'

'This could be painful,' he warned, his expression serious, 'but I believe you will need to think back and analyse, not only Anthony's personality, but your marriage. And before you say anything, I do want to help. Now,' he went on, 'unless you want to talk more about this, why don't we decide where we're going to eat this evening?'

'You really are a lovely man,' Kate said, 'and of course you're right; it is Saturday after all.'

'So, darling,' he smiled, topping up her glass, 'what is your preference; Chinese, Italian, Mexican or English?'

'A wide choice,' she laughed, already feeling better; that awful blanket of impending and unexplainable disaster evaporating.

They chose Giovanni's, one of their favourite Italian restaurants and within easy walking distance from the apartment. Giovanni greeted them, a wide smile on his plump face: 'Bonjourno, Senor, Signora.' and without asking, led them to their usual table by the window. It was still light and warm for late September, many of the pedestrians strolling along the pavements stopping to look at the menus outside the restaurants, all acting as if they had nothing further from their minds, Kate thought, than the evening ahead when they could enjoy a good meal over a bottle of wine. In an ideal world that is exactly how Saturday nights should be, realising she was allowing herself to indulge in useless and uncharacteristic philosophizing.

'A penny for them;' Steven asked, a quizzical smile hovering on his lips, 'you were miles away.'

'Sorry,' she said, 'I was just thinking how carefree everyone out there looks.'

'Don't you believe it,' he answered, 'you can call me a cynic, but they're only human, Kate. Only toddlers and very young children can be carefree.'

'True, I suppose. It's sad though, isn't it,' she went on, 'that by the time you are an adult you can't remember ever being in that idyllic state?'

'There are compensations, you know.'

'Are there?'

'Of course, darling; adults have choices, children don't.'

'How profound you're being this evening.'

'Perhaps I am, but sometimes it's difficult to switch off.'

'You mean about what I've been telling you?'

'Yes; I know we've agreed to give the subject a rest for now, but I've been thinking.'

'You don't believe that man I saw and thinking it could have been Anthony was a figure of my imagination, do you, Steven?'

'Well, I know they say, whoever *they* are, that everyone has a double, also that you are the least fanciful of women, the chances of him being Anthony are pretty strong. Of course I never met him; therefore I'll have to rely on your description of the type of person he was. For instance,' he went on quickly, obviously warming to his theory, 'if he had contrived the accident, we have to ask ourselves whether he would have had the necessary temperament and courage to carry it out, and if so, why.'

'The answer at the moment,' she said and wishing she had his ability to be as succinct when her own thoughts were in a jumble, 'is, I don't know. But, if he did, he would have needed help. I don't see how he could have arranged the accident and been able to leave the country on his own.'

'Ah,' Steven said, 'perhaps we're getting somewhere.'

'You're thinking there could have been another woman?'

'Not necessarily. We would have to find out why he wanted to disappear, which brings me back to wanting to learn more about his personality; what made him tick, I mean. How honest was he and remember, Kate, everyone has his price.'

'Well,' she said thoughtfully, 'he wasn't terribly good with money. He always earned high salaries, but he liked spending; if Anthony wanted something, he merely went out and bought it, regardless of whether he could actually afford it.'

'Was he a gambler?'

'When he got the opportunity, yes.'

'He could have got into financial difficulties.'

'Perhaps, but if he had, he took rather drastic steps to avoid his creditors.'

'Depends on how high the stakes were. Anyway, perhaps we should draw a halt here; otherwise we're in danger of going round in circles and getting nowhere.'

'You're right,' passing the menu over to him, 'I've decided already.' she added.

'*Tagletelli Carbonara.*'

'Mind reader!'

'You've probably guessed what I'm going to have.'

'*Pizza Margarita.*'

'Spot on!'

***

They were about to leave the apartment the following lunchtime, having made arrangements to meet up with a couple of friends, when the phone rang.

'It's for you, Kate,' Steven said, handing the receiver over to her, 'a Mr Anderson.' he added, covering the mouthpiece with his hand.

Robert Anderson, her aunt's lawyer, knowing in advance what he had to tell her couldn't be good news. She had known him for years; he had been more of a family friend and had acted for the family for as far back as she could remember.

'Hello, Mr Anderson.' she said.

'Hello, Kate,' he said, the Scottish accent taking her back; it had been a long time since she had spoken to him, more than ten, fifteen years, but he sounded exactly the same, 'I'm sorry to phone you on a Sunday,' he went on, 'but I have some sad news for you –'

'– it's Aunt Eileen, isn't it?'

'Yes, my dear, she passed away late yesterday afternoon; quite peacefully.' he added gently.

'Oh, dear. I only spoke to her at the beginning of last week, Mr Anderson and she sounded fine.'

'Your aunt was a very plucky lady, Kate, but then you don't need me to tell you that. She didn't want to worry you.'

'And I had no idea.'

'No, and that was the way she wanted it, my dear. She knew she didn't have much longer, but being the type of woman she was, she had ignored the symptoms for quite a while, but in the end I'm sorry to say she lost the battle and, I might add, not without a struggle. Even last week she said to me she refused to accept her heart would let her down, but, alas, it did. I'm sorry, Kate.'

'It's so sad, Mr Anderson. I'd known her all my life. She was a wonderful person.'

'I know, Kate, I know.'

'When is the funeral?'

'On Wednesday; rather short notice for you, I know.'

'Not at all, that will be alright.'

'I don't really know how many people will be attending.' he went on, 'The captain of your aunt's golf club has offered to provide a luncheon for a number of us.'

'How kind.'

'She was much respected, Kate; quite a legend in fact among the golfing fraternity and not only in the town, but further afield.'

'I know,' she agreed, 'both Dawn and I were so proud of her.'

'We all were, Kate; we all were. Now,' he said, 'would you like me to meet you –'

'– no, I wouldn't dream of asking you to do that. I'll take a taxi from the station and book into the Braemar Hotel.'

'If you're sure, Kate.'

'I am, Mr Anderson.'

'Very well, then. I'll see you at the funeral of course and afterwards perhaps you and I can have a talk about the bequests your aunt has made.'

'Of course.' Kate said. The thought of having been left anything had never occurred to her; the sadness of losing her was too intense.

Eileen Campbell, her father's younger sister had been an indomitable character, and as she replaced the receiver, Kate could remember so much about the woman who had been such a strong influence on her during her teens after both her parents had died. It had been her aunt who had encouraged her to follow a literary career, although she had never tried to hide her disappointment when that career path came to an abrupt end once she and Anthony decided to move out to Africa. Eileen hadn't taken to Anthony, although she hadn't said as much, but then as far as Kate was concerned knowing her so well, she didn't need to. On the rare occasions when Anthony had been with her in Scotland, her aunt's body language was sufficient. Kate had often wondered whether Anthony sensed the thinly veiled hostility, but he had never said.

Eileen had not married, having devoted most of her life to being a professional golfer and even after her retirement worked as a coach for one of the golf clubs in the town where she had lived since a child. Her bungalow was as close as any property could be to the golf course and from her kitchen window there was a perfect view of the eighteenth green. Latterly, she would spend a good part of her time looking out at what at one time would have been so familiar to her, but there was no maudlin sentimentality about her; she was far too down to earth to waste time looking back. Yes, Kate thought, she was going to miss her and not looking forward to the few days she would be spending up there. The funeral would be a strain, having to meet and talk to those people who had been her friends, but going through her aunt's personal effects would be far worse. Kate had been an only child; therefore she had no brother or sister who could have shared the responsibility with her.

'I wish I could come with you, Kate,' Steven said when she told him, 'I really do, but I'm going to be in court for most of the week.'

'I understand.' she said quickly and she did. He had already told her of the major court case scheduled for the next week; being a lawyer, she had discovered over the years she had known him, could be demanding. 'I'll manage, Steven; don't worry about me.'

'But I do, darling. What about Dawn,' he asked, 'do you think she'll be able to get away?'

'I'm not sure, but I won't be too disappointed if she can't; she might find it difficult to get the time off at such short notice, but we'll hear what she has to say when we phone her later; being a Sunday, there isn't much she can do today.'

'More to the point perhaps,' Steven said, 'how about Justin?'

'He won't be pleased of course; you know how he hates his routine disturbed, but this time he will just have to accept that I'm going to be away for a few days.' not looking forward to the following morning when she would have to tell him. She had worked for Justin Mellows for more than nine years, not long after she returned from Samriboi. It hadn't taken her long to pick up the threads of her career, having found that being involved in book publishing suited her, less stressful than before when she had worked for a bi-monthly magazine publisher where deadlines had been crucial and although Justin was a hard taskmaster and short on patience she didn't dislike him, respecting his professionalism and had learned how to ward off any initial flash of annoyance when something, invariably quite trivial, didn't please him. These outbursts had always, up to now, not lasted long, but tomorrow might prove to be the exception.

Chapter Two

ENGLAND

John Brookes had been meaning to clear out the desk for years, ever since Pamela had gone, but somehow had never got round to it. If it hadn't been for the lack of space in the room he used as his office, he doubted whether he would have taken the trouble, but with the increasing volume of paperwork generated in the running of the estate, it made sense for him to use what had always been recognised as Norman's private domain. Even when they had been boys, and because of Norman's seniority, John had never, unless invited, the temerity to encroach on his brother's space. Old habits die hard, he thought, tipping out the contents of one of the top drawers. After Norman's death, Pamela had commandeered not only the room, but also Norman's desk. His sister-in-law had not been the tidiest of women and, looking now at the heap of what he could only describe as fairly useless stuff: scraps of paper, old receipts, dried up biros, pencil stubs, theatre tickets and defunct railway timetables, only reinforced what he thought about her. She had even left an old passport, the photograph showing a much younger Pamela; the way she had looked when Norman brought her home to meet them all: a froth of blonde curls, heavily fringed cornflower blue eyes and shiny pink-painted lips. John could remember his mother's reaction when Norman had introduced Pamela to her. "So, at last I'm being permitted to meet the young lady who apparently has bowled my son off his feet." she had said, languidly shaking hands with her, but there was no real welcome in his mother's expression as she looked at the younger woman; she simply did not approve of Norman's choice, but to John, being an impressionable fifteen year-old at the time, Pamela epitomised glamour. It was as though Marilyn Monroe had miraculously been transported from Hollywood to their home in the Cotswolds and, young though he was, he wondered why she had been attracted to Norman, his stick-in-the-mud brother.

He had almost finished emptying the drawers when he found beneath a pile of theatre programmes, a copy of the coroner's report with Zambia's national emblem printed at the top of the single sheet of paper. Surprised she hadn't kept this along with the rest of Norman's papers, he smoothed out the creases. It was a strange feeling to read for the first time about the way Norman had died. The gist of the report was more or less as Pamela had told him when she had returned to England the day after the inquest; namely, that an intruder had gained entrance to their bungalow in Samriboi in order to steal anything of value when they had been disturbed by Norman, his body having been found later that night by her, but it was the concluding section which struck him as odd, in that the weapon used had been a British Service pistol, a nine millimetre Browning. Although Norman had not been in the services, John knew he had owned just such a gun. A couple of years before he had married Pamela, he had shown it to him but he didn't say how he had come by it and John never thought to ask. Was it the same weapon he wondered and if so, had it been stolen at some time. But, continuing to try and fathom it out, perhaps it hadn't been like that; Norman could have confronted the intruder and been over-powered. In that case, though, surely there would have been signs of a struggle? If so, there had been no mention of this at the inquest.

John spent the remainder of the morning rearranging the room and bringing in all his files and computer equipment, but all the time his mind was preoccupied with what he'd read, wishing there was someone he could talk to, but he couldn't think of anyone. Ursula, he knew, wouldn't be interested, no doubt telling him that it must have been a coincidence and reminding him that as it happened ten years ago, there was nothing he would be able to do and of course she would be quite right. His wife was a practical down-to-earth type of woman and in many respects not dissimilar to how his mother had been. If she had still been alive that was exactly the response he would have received from her.

By lunchtime he was reaching the realisation that he could be concerning himself with something which really didn't have such an importance; Norman had been shot by someone who had broken into the bungalow, but all the same, and not knowing why, he continued to fret, wanting to find out more. Had no-one in Samriboi asked any questions? It sounded to him the police had automatically assumed the crime had been committed by one of the local gangs. He had read that break-ins were prevalent in that part of the world where most of the expatriates were more wealthy than they were, also that they were often armed. All of which brought him back to Norman's pistol. In other words, a dead end. If it had happened in this country, John decided, he would have been able to go to the area where it happened, but in this case it was not possible. Even if he did go to the extreme and fly out to Zambia and talk to those expatriates in Samriboi, it was more than likely they would no longer be living there and then he remembered someone Norman had mentioned once when he and Pamela had been home on leave. He had been called Harry; Harry Knight and he had been seconded by his bank out to Samriboi and, coincidentally, came from nearby Norwich. He would very likely have completed his contract in Africa by now, John reckoned, and it was possible he had returned to Norwich.

A long shot, but worth a try, he thought, picking up the telephone directory and flicking through the pages until he came to the section he wanted. There were three Harold Knights in the Norwich area and, without taking the time to deliberate further, dialled the first number. After a couple of seconds a woman answered and he couldn't believe his luck when she said her husband had worked in Africa and it had been in a place called Samriboi and if he could wait a moment she would bring him to the phone.

John apologised for bothering him on a Sunday, going on to briefly explain why he was phoning. As soon as he mentioned Norman's name and said he wanted to speak to someone who had been friendly with him and could they meet sometime, he didn't raise any objection, hadn't even sounded surprised at the call and was quick to agree to see him in Norwich the following lunchtime, suggesting "The Old Vine", one of the pubs in the same street where he worked.

***

You look like your brother,' Harry Knight said, shaking hands with John, 'so I had no trouble recognising you when you came in.'

'Not many people have said that. Anyway,' he went on, 'it's good of you to agree to see me. We'll get a couple of beers, shall we?'

'Good idea.'

'How long have you been back in England?' John asked.

'Almost six years now. I have to admit it took me a while to settle back here.'

'I expect it did. Norman told me quite a lot about life in Samriboi. I've been going through a few of his papers recently,' he said, stretching the truth slightly, but wanting to avoid any mention of the pistol, 'and I now regret not asking more about how he was killed; that is,' he added, 'if there is anything further from what Pamela told us when she came back.'

'Ah, Pamela,' Harry said slowly, 'what is she doing these days?'

'I haven't seen or heard from her since she re-married; also she and her husband are living in the West Country.'

'What's he like, John; anything like Norman?'

'The total opposite I would say. Apparently she had known him for years, shortly after she and Norman were married in fact.'

'I just wondered that's all. As you know, your brother was a fairly laid back sort of guy. Also, too trusting; didn't seem to notice what was going on right under his nose.'

'In what way?'

'With Pamela, I mean. Oh, I expect at first when they arrived in Samriboi she made an effort to mix with the other wives, but then she probably became bored and started playing around.'

'Anyone in particular?'

'There had been a few, none of them lasting very long, but she'd been having an affair with Anthony Johnson for a while, right up to the time Norman was killed.'

'I had no idea.'

'I don't suppose you did, John, but all I can say is, if you had been there, in Samriboi I mean, you would have noticed alright. Neither of them was exactly discreet.'

'Poor Norman; do you think he had any idea?'

'He may have done and had chosen to ignore it, hoping the affair would be short-lived like the others had been. Mind you, as it turned out, Anthony was killed in a car crash and by some quirk of fate this happened on the same day as Norman died.'

'A coincidence.'

'Must have been.'

'Wasn't that considered a bit odd though?'

'Well, we expats, who were aware of what the pair of them were up to, did think that at the time, but as far as the authorities were concerned they would have had no idea and, unlike in Britain, there was no way they were likely to find out.'

'What about this Johnson chap; was he married?'

'Oh, yes. Kate, a lovely woman, far too good for a cad like him.'

'She must have been upset when she heard about the accident?'

'She was,' Harry agreed, 'but she was away on leave at the time. She came back to Samriboi naturally, when she heard, but didn't stay long; packed up their possessions, that sort of thing.'

'And attended his funeral?'

'There wasn't one,' he said, 'you see, they never found his body.' and going on to describe the accident. 'His company, who took care of the various formalities, arranged a small memorial service for him, which we attended but more to support Kate than anything else.'

'Did she know about the affair?'

'I don't think she did. You know what they say, don't you?'

'The wife is the last to know.'

John didn't ask many more questions. The enormity of what was taking shape in his mind was too serious to contemplate anything further for the time being, also, he didn't know what he should do. Ignore the implications or speak out, regardless of the consequences? If he did, he had no doubt there would be. John had been fond of his brother, but it went further than that; it would involve the family. But, if there had been anything suspect about the way Norman had died, wasn't it his duty to expose whoever had been responsible? Also, there were other people here; such an exposure could very well tarnish their reputations also. What Harry had told him about Pamela had shocked him.

He had always thought she had been good for Norman; his brother being a shy and serious type, Pamela had brought him out a bit. She was a party animal; vivacious, with a devil-may-care attitude to life which John secretly thought had amused Norman, but men couldn't help be drawn to her, although the effect on women was quite different; most of them didn't like her very much. His mother had been quick to voice her opinion and he could remember what she had said shortly before Norman and Pamela went out to Zambia: "A flighty miss, I'm sorry to say, John," she'd said, "I only trust she won't have too much time on her hands when she starts mingling with the expatriate community out there." It would now appear that in her wisdom his mother had been right.

***

'It appears, John,' Hugh Bannister said on Friday afternoon, 'your suspicions were correct. Since you phoned me on Tuesday I've had some feedback from passport control and they've confirmed that Anthony Johnson arrived at Heathrow from Lusaka on Thursday, the nineteenth of December.'

'Really? I don't know whether to be surprised or not.' John said, wondering now where this investigation would lead. Hugh had been more Norman's friend, both of them having been at school at the same time. Norman had often brought him home for the weekend and in the warmer weather they would play tennis, the foursome made up by one of their cousins. It had been some time since John had seen him, but having exhausted his own conjecturing, Hugh seemed to be the obvious person to talk to, although at the same time realising that in Hugh's position as a senior officer with New Scotland Yard, should there be something sinister behind Norman's death he would have no choice but to go along with the ensuing and in-depth enquiry which would inevitably become official.

'There's more, John,' Hugh said, leaning slightly forward in his swivel chair, 'the following day he took a flight to Paris, but there is no record of him returning to Britain; also,' he added, 'his passport had not been used since then and it would have expired two years later which has not been done.'

'Strange.'

'Perhaps, but I believe it's more than likely he changed his name. It would have been extremely difficult for him to exist without any formal means of identity and, of course, have the ability to move elsewhere.'

'He must have had contacts, then.' John suggested slowly, having no experience of such underhand behaviour, only what he'd read or seen in television movies.

'Yes, you're right. I've had a check done on his background and a part of it is somewhat obscure.'

'In what way?'

'Well,' Hugh answered, picking up the sheet of paper from his desk, 'the early years are fairly straightforward: born in Cambridge in 1965; his father being one of the porters at the university meant the family had staff living quarters on the campus. He was educated at Histon and Impington Junior and Secondary schools; the villages, as you probably know, lie north of the city. After leaving school, he spent the following four years as an articled clerk with Webster and Jackson, a firm of chartered accountants in Cambridge and upon qualifying took up an accountant's position with Douglas Banks Limited in Nigeria, returning to England two years later, but there is no trace of him until he returned to Africa, this time to Zambia in 1992, although he did marry before then in 1988.'

'That would be the woman Harry Knight mentioned; he said she was called Kate.'

'Yes,' Hugh nodded, 'Katherine Campbell, originally from Scotland, but she had been working in London at the time of her marriage to Johnson up until the time they moved to Zambia.'

'He must be somewhere,' John remarked, 'he can't just have

disappeared.'

'He'll be somewhere alright and we'll find him; that is, if he's alive.'

'You say he was born in 1965; that would make him forty-seven now and presumably still working.'

'Should be and it remains to be seen exactly what, doesn't it?'

'Whether he's honestly employed, you mean?'

'Yes. He sounds to me as though he's a bit of a chancer; well,' he continued dryly, 'he must be. He must have faked the accident with the car and to do that and make his way to the airport in Lusaka he would have needed assistance.'

'I'd thought of that.'

'I think the next step is for us to approach Norman's wife. Have you an address for her, John?'

'All I know is that Pamela moved to Taunton when she re-married. This was in the spring of 2003.'

'Provided you know the name of the husband, it shouldn't be a problem tracing her.'

'He's called Gregory Smythe-Jones.'

'There can't be many Smythe-Jones in Taunton.' Hugh smiled.

'I shouldn't think so.'

'It may well turn out that those two cases; Norman's death and Anthony Johnson's accident, will have to be re-opened, but at this stage, John,' he explained, 'we first have to find out as much as we can before approaching the authorities in Samriboi. Whether you and I think there is any credence in Pamela's involvement cannot come into the equation, at least not at present. What you were told by Harry Knight about their affair is hearsay; it has no real substance.'

'What a conundrum.'

'One way of describing it;' Hugh agreed, 'what came first, John; the chicken or the egg?'

'You mean the accident or what happened to Norman.'

'Quite. And this is one of the reasons why Pamela has to be questioned. She was there, John, she discovered his body.'

'That's about all we do know. She didn't tell me much more when she came back here; in fact,' John added, 'she hardly said anything; just that she found him when she returned to the bungalow late that night and that he had been in his study when he was shot.'

'According to the coroner's report you showed me,' Hugh said, 'he had been seated at his desk which presumably was positioned facing away from the door and hadn't even had time to turn round and see his assailant.'

'So, there couldn't have been a break-in, otherwise he would have heard.'

'The logical explanation being either the front or back doors to the bungalow had been unlocked or the intruder had a key.'

'That hadn't occurred to me,' John admitted, 'I'm pretty certain they would have been locked; Norman told me how security conscious they all were in the town with break-ins and robberies being considered quite common place.'

'The joys of the expatriate life, eh?'

'Wouldn't appeal to me, but Norman seemed to have adapted very well. He only had a few months left on his contract, you know, before he would have been back and as much as he liked Africa, I think he was looking forward to coming home.'

'A bad business, John; a very bad business and incidentally I believe you were right in airing your concerns.'

'It's the least I can do for him.'

'I know, old chap.' Hugh agreed, shaking his head, 'So,' he continued, 'all the more reason to meet with Pamela. I want to find out more about the pistol. Was it in the bungalow when she packed up and had she known of its existence? Also, I'd like to learn more about times. The coroner's report only mentions the estimated time of death. When had she last seen him and how did she spend the evening and with whom? Perhaps those answers may link up with Anthony Johnson's accident which of course now appears to have been fixed by him and someone else, that person remaining unknown at present.'

'You were saying that Anthony Johnson left from Lusaka.'

'Yes.'

'Well, Samriboi is a long way to Lusaka; mostly, people take the domestic flight from Ndola; that's the nearest airport to Samriboi. Check-out would have viewed his credentials in Ndola, so he would have been taking a risk by taking the plane which meant the only other way would be by road.'

'That's right,' he agreed, 'and unless he had another car, he would have needed help. Either someone drove him to Lusaka or he acquired a second vehicle and, if so, where did he park it when he arrived at the airport?'

'Ten years is a long time ago.'

'Yes, and that's a drawback, John,' he said, 'and indicates we will probably have to get in touch with the Zambian authorities. They are not going to like it, but we'll delay that move until we have exhausted our search for Anthony Johnson. We don't know yet when the car was discovered. All we do know is that the crash happened on the Wednesday night and by the following night he was back in England.'

'Harry Knight would know.' John suggested tentatively.

'No doubt he would, but I think we should hold back on that until we have some information on Anthony Johnson's whereabouts; we don't want to alert anyone to the fact we suspect anything is amiss. It's too soon in our enquiry.'

Chapter Three

ENGLAND

Kate had little time during the following days to dwell on what Steven and she had been talking about; both of them agreeing that for the present the possibility of her having seen Anthony and what she was going to do, would have to wait until she got back from Scotland.

It turned out she had been worrying needlessly about Justin's reaction; for once, he had sounded genuinely sympathetic, even when she had said there was every likelihood she may have to spend a couple of days up there.

'I do understand, Kate,' he had said, 'you've mentioned your aunt a number of times over the years and I realise you must have been very fond of her.'

'I was, Justin.'

There had been several mourners at the funeral, most of them old friends of her aunt; although Kate didn't remember having met many of them before and as everyone left the church each one of them expressed their condolences, all going to prove how respected Eileen Campbell had been. The cold buffet luncheon in the club house was ideal for the occasion and, once again, she was reminded of the warmth of these people who had known her aunt. Mr Anderson had greeted her solemnly as she went into the church, the kindness in his eyes as he shook hands exactly as it had always been from when she had been a child.

'A sad day, Kate,' he had said after the meal and they were in a small ante room, 'but she wouldn't want you to grieve too deeply or for too long. I have lost count,' he had gone on, 'how many times I have heard her say to me, "Life is for the living, Robert".'

'I know, Mr Anderson,' Kate smiled and at that moment feeling the strong presence of her aunt, 'I've heard her say that as well.'

He had gone on to outline Eileen Campbell's last wishes, 'I have a copy of the will here for you,' he said, 'but perhaps you would prefer to read it later when you're on your own, so I'll just give you the salient points, shall I?'

'Please.'

'It is a simple will, Kate, which was as she wanted.' he explained, 'There are a number of small bequests to a few of her friends whom she had known for most of her life and the bulk of her estate, including the bungalow and all the contents, to you and Dawn.'

'How very generous.' Kate said quietly.

'You and Dawn were her only relatives; a pity she isn't here to be with you today.' he added.

'She wasn't able to;' Kate said, remembering how upset Dawn had been when she had phoned her, 'she's working for the British Consulate in Paris now and having only been with them since the beginning of August couldn't get permission to take any leave, but in many respects I think it is best she isn't here. She loved her aunt very much; also, Mr Anderson, she's never been to a funeral before. I believe she would have found it distressing. There's time enough for her, as I'm sure you would agree, to learn and experience the harsh realities of life – and death.'

'Of course, Kate.'

And now, in the train on the way back to London, she was able to sit back and think; not about Anthony and whether or not he was still alive or not, but about her aunt who had been such a mainstay in her earlier years. She had spent the previous day going through the personal papers, and as expected everything had been meticulously documented. There wasn't much for her to attend to, although realising she had to make a decision about the bungalow, but first she wanted to discuss this with Steven. Did she really want to hold on to it? And, if not, perhaps Dawn would like it and as for the furniture and a rather fine collection of china, that was another question, but for now she was unable to come up with any solution. She had only brought a photograph album back with her and one which her aunt had been using for years. Kate couldn't explain why she had this urge to delve back into the past, realising it could make her even more nostalgic than she was already and had been since she heard about her death.

The album, leather-bound, was full with each photograph neatly annotated. She had started it in 1989, the year Dawn was born. Kate had many of the baby ones at home, but later, those from the time they went out to Africa, she could scarcely recall seeing before; those eight years spent in Samriboi seemed such a long time ago. There were several when they had been with a group of friends they had made there. She looked at them closely trying to remember their names. There was Martha Underwood and her husband, Luke; Peggy and Terry Price, Norman and Pamela Brookes and Harry Knight. Some, she had taken, although Anthony was in them all and for the first time she noticed that always he was either sitting or standing next to Pamela with his arm round her; even when she herself had been in the photograph. In one of them, taken at the bar in the sports club, she had been on Anthony's right-hand side, but again it was Pamela he was focusing on and she hadn't even noticed. How on earth could she have been so blind? It could have meant nothing; he was merely being friendly and posing for the camera. Was she reading too much into this, she wondered, looking at them again, seeing that they covered most of the years she had spent in Samriboi. What about the others who had been there; had any of them thought his behaviour extreme, but more importantly what had her aunt thought? If she had noticed, this could explain her dislike for Anthony. It had not occurred to Kate to have asked her to explain her coolness towards him, but perhaps this was because she hadn't wanted to know and being an honest woman her aunt would have told her. Too late now, she sighed; she would have to work it out for herself.

Soon they would be approaching London and, eager to get home, she put the album back in her bag, regretting now the decision to bring it with her. It wasn't always wise to dwell on the past, recalling Steven had said she may have to and analyse, not only Anthony's personality, but her marriage. He had also warned that it could be painful, all of which brought her full circle to last Saturday outside the museum.

The last time she had spoken to Anthony had been on the morning she had left for the airport. He hadn't taken her, saying it was impossible for him to get away from work and had arranged instead for Pamela to drive her there. Now, ten years later, it occurred to her to wonder why, of all their friends, he had asked her. It wasn't as though Pamela had been a personal friend and prior to that morning during the fifteen mile drive it had been the first time Kate had anything remotely resembling a conversation with her, although it had been somewhat one-sided with her making obvious remarks which mostly received monosyllable responses, but Kate had put it down to her being preoccupied with driving.

Pamela hadn't come inside the airport building with her which had rather surprised her at the time, but she remembered feeling relieved. It had become apparent that Pamela and she had little in common and she had already run out of anything further to say. Perhaps Kate thought as she remembered the coolness in Pamela's manner as she briefly wished her a good flight before driving away, she had felt the same way and wondering what she was doing now. It had been Luke Underwood who had told her about what happened to Norman; this had been when she returned to Samriboi after Anthony's accident. She had always liked Norman and had been shocked by the news, but by the time she had arrived Pamela had already returned to England which meant she wasn't able to offer her any condolences. It did occur to Kate she could have written to her, but her own life being in such a turmoil she never got round to it.

Her train was pulling into Kings Cross Station and, picking up her travel bag, she followed the other passengers on to the platform. Steven was waiting for her, waving from where he was standing at the barrier. How good it was to see him, she thought, hurriedly walking towards him.

'Kate,' he said, kissing her and taking the bag from her, 'I'm so happy you're back; it's been a long week without you.'

'Me too.' smiling up at him and linking her arm with his, 'is your case finished?'

'Yes; we wrapped it up at four this afternoon. Defence put up a hard fight, but the lad, a mean looking character if I ever saw one, got fifteen years, so he'll be out of harm's way for a while.'

'That's good and does this mean you'll have the weekend free?'

'It certainly does and I thought as the weather forecast looks fine for the next couple of days we should take advantage and drive down to the West Country in the morning and spend the night at The Smugglers in Taunton.'

'That's a brilliant idea.'

'Now, darling,' he added, 'if you're not too weary, shall we walk along to Tony's for a drink, followed by one of his splendid tandoori king prawn masalas?'

***

The Smugglers Hotel, a traditional country inn, situated on a cliff and looking out to sea: stone-built, an overhanging roof, low lintels above the doors and a spacious stone-flagged terrace. A peaceful and picturesque spot and as Thomas Hardy would have described it, 'far from the maddening crowd'. At least that was how it appeared to Kate as they pulled into the inn's car park. The drive down from London had been an easy one, with very little congestion and, for once, no road works on the main stretch of motorway leading towards the West Country to delay them.

'Happy, darling?' Steven asked, leaning over to kiss her.

'Very.'

They had stopped off in Salisbury on the way for lunch and it was still early, not yet five o'clock. There was a soft balmy breeze accompanied by the familiar tang of the sea and the only sound to break the stillness of the late afternoon was the plaintiff cry of the seagulls as they swooped above their heads, all reminding Kate of her childhood, most of it spent in Carnoustie, on the east coast of Scotland. An Indian summer she thought, following Steven inside; the deep sadness she had been feeling for most of the week was lessening and as far as her earlier concern about what she described to herself as her museum experience, that had retreated to the back of her mind. It had been a good idea of Steven's to come here, needing this time to relax and perhaps be more prepared to give Anthony a little more thought.

Steven had booked a table for eight-thirty, asking especially if they could have one next to a window. By now, the light was beginning to fade, but once the string of miniature lanterns on the terrace had been switched on it didn't matter; their deep pink glows spreading out and illuminating the whole area.

'How lovely,' she said, taking a menu from him, 'it doesn't seem real somehow, does it?'

'You mean like a dream,' he smiled, 'and one you hoped wouldn't come to an end.'

'I know,' she laughed, 'but it is all very –'

' – romantic?'

'I do mean that, but you have to admit, cynic that you are, Steven, they have managed to create a perfect setting.'

'So I'm a cynic, am I?' but he was teasing her.

'Well –'

She was prevented from finishing what she was going to say by the arrival of Pamela. This is positively surreal she thought, unable to take her eyes off the woman she had known in Samriboi. Here they were; Steven and herself, in the heart of the West Country and who should turn up but Pamela Brookes; the woman she was beginning to suspect had been more than friendly with Anthony. She wasn't alone and the two of them were standing in the open doorway waiting to be shown to a table. Pamela hadn't changed all that much; the same ash-blonde hair and the voluptuous figure, although perhaps a bit more curvy than it used to be and wondering whether she had noticed her. She didn't have long to find out; as luck would have it, the waiter was directing them past where they were sitting.

'Kate Johnson! What are you doing here?' Pamela asked, leaning over to her and giving her a couple of air kisses.

'I would ask the same of you, Pamela?'

'Oh,' she waved a hand dismissively, 'I live down here now, in Taunton actually. By the way,' she added, 'this is my husband, Gregory Smythe-Jones. Gregory, darling,' she drawled, 'Kate was in Samriboi at the same time as I was.' pulling him forward.

'Hello, Gregory.' Kate said and not missing his indifference. The man didn't want to know, he just wasn't interested in anyone his wife once knew and turning towards Steven to introduce him to them both she guessed by his quizzical expression he was remembering what she had told him about those photographs.

'Anyway, Kate,' Pamela said, immediately the introductions had been made, 'nice to have seen you again.' and taking Gregory's arm, walked over to where the waiter was patiently standing at their table and as she watched them, Kate was instantly reminded of another time. It was the way Pamela was moving; slowly, provocatively, her body close to his as she looked up into her husband's face and for a second it felt to Kate that time stood still. Unbidden, the memory, long dormant, surfaced:

They had all been in the club one night; it must have been a Saturday because there had been a dinner dance. The club didn't run to any live band and they had to be content with CDs, one of the men acting as the disc jockey for the night. She remembered the song; it had been "Killing Me Softly with His Song", although she didn't know the name of the singer. Anthony and Pamela had been dancing; it wasn't as though they were all that close,, but it had been in the way they were moving on the dance floor; in perfect harmony and with the intimate familiarity only a couple who knew and loved each other could. Lines of the almost forgotten lyrics were coming back to her: "..... I heard he sang a good song; I heard he had a style. He sang as if he knew me in all my dark despair. And then he looked right through me as if I wasn't there. And he just kept on singing ....." Anthony had looked across at her that night, but she realised now he wasn't focusing on her. Perhaps if I had been truthful with myself, Kate thought, I should have admitted that from that precise moment my marriage was over.

'Seeing her has brought back some sad memories, darling, hasn't it?' Steven asked, taking one of her hands in his.

'It's made me remember, Steven,' she said, 'but they are no longer sad.'

'Good. So,' he smiled, 'that was Pamela and one of life's coincidences she should be here this evening.'

'What were your impressions of her?' she asked him.

'Well, apart from her being obvious in an over-sexed sort of way, I would describe her as cold.'

'Cold?'

'Yes; I've met a few woman not dissimilar to her in my career, Kate and they do seem to have one characteristic in common.'

'Yes?'

'They are schemers, will do anything to achieve what they want from life. They are also excellent actresses, but there's an expression in their eyes which I've learned not to trust. It's as if they are saying one thing, but really they mean something entirely different. Oh, they're clever,' he went on, 'but only up to a point and I don't believe Pamela Smythe-Jones is any different.'

'We weren't going to talk about any of this.' she reminded him, wanting to retrieve the ambience of earlier.

'And we won't, Kate,' he promised, 'this is our weekend. Seeing her has broken into that, I know, but maybe it should be considered in some respects as fortuitous.'

'How?'

'Because it's helping you to put together a picture of what your life was like in Samriboi.'

'It has actually.'

'We'll leave it at that, then;' he said, 'now to important matters. What are we going to eat this evening?'

***

By the end of the week both cases had been re-opened and because of the new evidence emerging to disprove the official verdicts, the enquiry was now being handled by MI6. Philip Spencer, one of their officers who had been with the Foreign Office for the past six years, having been transferred from the London Metropolitan Police, was leading the enquiry. He was thirty-seven, thoroughly professional with a sharp analytical brain and during those six years had gained considerable accolades for the way he conducted the assignments in which he had been involved.

Philip had read through the reports from New Scotland Yard, familiarising himself with the background of Norman Brooke's murder and Anthony Johnson's accident, taking into account the inescapable fact they had both occurred simultaneously and on the same night in Samriboi ten years previously. His initial brief was to interview Norman Brooke's wife and glean as much as he could from her.

He drove into Taunton shortly after ten on Monday morning. The Old Manor was on the outskirts of the town, set well back from the road. Expensive, he thought, not that he expected anything else. Philip had looked up Gregory Smythe-Jones on the internet the day before; not only did his profile carry a photograph of him, but a comprehensive précis of his career to-date. He was fifty-three years of age and, after leaving Cambridge University graduating with an honours degree in fine arts, he had worked for Christies in London before opening his own antique business in Bournemouth. Over the last ten years this business had flourished, so much so, he had moved the premises to Bond Street in London, trading under the name of Smythe-Jones Limited, Antique dealers, Restorers and Valuers.

He pulled up alongside a brand new Mazda MX-5 sports car parked in front of the sweep of steps leading up to the front door. He had one foot on the bottom step when the door opened and a blonde-haired woman came hurrying out, stopping abruptly when she saw him.

'I'm sorry,' Philip said, 'I didn't mean to startle you.'

'You didn't really,' she said, 'but I hadn't heard any car coming up the drive.'

'You are Mrs Smythe-Jones?' he asked her.

'Yes.'

'My name is Philip Spencer, Mrs Smythe-Jones,' Philip said, handing her one of his cards, 'from the Foreign Office.'

'The Foreign Office,' she repeated, glancing at the card, 'I don't understand.'

'If you can spare the time, I'll explain.'

'Well,' she began, 'I was going out, but -' hesitating as she looked at him, more closely this time, '- I suppose it wasn't all that important. Perhaps we should go into the house,' she added, 'better than standing out here.'

Philip followed her inside, once more being reminded by the understated elegance of the hall just how wealthy the Smythe-Jones were. The hall; parquet flooring, dark wood panelling and high ceiling; the only furniture being a long table in walnut and in the centre a tall crystal vase of late summer roses; their reflection being mirrored on the polished top of the table.

'We'll go into the library,' she suggested, walking further along the hall and opening one of the doors on the right, 'would you like some coffee, Mr Spencer?' she asked, obviously making an effort to be sociable, although when he refused it wasn't difficult to recognise the relief in her expression.

'I'll be as brief as I can,' he said, once they were seated, 'I don't want to take up too much of your time.'

'That's alright.' she said politely.

'How well did you know Anthony Johnson, Mrs Smythe-Jones?'

'Anthony?' her eyes widening in surprise.

'Yes, I understand he was in Samriboi at the same time as you were and, like yourself, being an expatriate in the town would have meant you would very likely have known him.'

'It's true, all of us knew Anthony and his wife, but as to how *well* I knew him,' she emphasised, 'he wasn't really a personal friend. In fact, in Samriboi, although all we expatriates would see each other regularly in the club, any friendship we had was bound to be extremely short-lived. We were all on contracts, you understand, and Anthony was no different. In time, he also would have had to leave Samriboi.'

'Which he did.'

'How do you –' stumbling over the words, '– what makes you say that? I'd always believed he died in a car crash out there.'

'When did you leave Zambia, Mrs Smythe-Jones?'

'I expect you know what happened to my husband, Mr Spencer?'

'We do know, yes.'

'I left soon after that. I attended the inquest the following day and flew back to England the next night which was a Friday. I can't remember the date, only that it was shortly before Christmas.'

'Did you keep in touch with anyone from Samriboi?' changing tack.

'No – no, I didn't. Why do you ask?'

'I was wondering how you heard about the car accident. It is our understanding Anthony Johnson's car wasn't found until the Friday afternoon and, as you've told me, you left the country that night.'

'Oh, I see what you mean. It was Terry Price who told me, actually. He drove me to Ndola Airport as I had to take the domestic flight to Lusaka.'

'Did he mention how he'd heard?'

'No, he didn't.'

'And you didn't ask him?'

'Mr Spencer, I had recently lost my husband and quite honestly I was in no fit state to think about anyone else. I just wanted to get back home.'

'I understand,' and what she had said was credible, but there was something in her attitude which didn't ring true, 'I would like to move now to the night your husband was shot, Mrs Smythe-Jones.'

'Why?' a tiny frown appearing on her forehead. Was her question purely an automatic one; had she no idea where he was coming from or was she stalling for time; the time she needed to mentally prepare herself for what he might say next?

'In the last few days, Mrs Smythe-Jones,' Philip said, 'new evidence has come to light concerning your husband's murder and Anthony Johnson's accident, which has resulted in us, namely the Foreign Office, in having to re-open both cases. We need, therefore, to examine the background of each case as far as we can.'

'I don't understand. I know nothing about Anthony's accident and as far as what happened to Norman, all I can tell you is that I was the one to find him on the night he was shot.'

'We were already aware of this,' Philip said, 'but I would like to talk about the murder weapon.'

'How on earth do you think I can help you, Mr Spencer?' a flash of indignation this time, 'There was a break-in at our bungalow and the intruder was armed, that was it!'

'Were you aware that your husband owned a pistol?'

'I was, yes. He told me ages ago.'

'Did he show it to you?'

'Goodness me, of course not! Why should he have? I have no interest in guns, Mr Spencer.'

'When you packed up your belongings prior to leaving the country, was there a gun among your husband's possessions?'

'There wasn't, as it happens.'

'Didn't you wonder where it could be?'

'To be honest, Mr Spencer,' she said, 'I'd completely forgotten about it.'

'And he took the gun with him when you went out to Africa?'

'Yes; he told me it was for our protection when we were there. Ironic really,' she added, 'when he needed the gun, it was no longer there.'

'The weapon used by his assailant, Mrs Smythe-Jones, was a British Service Browning pistol, an identical make to the one owned by your late-husband.'

'How do you know?'

'We have it on good authority.' Philip said briefly, not prepared to elaborate.

'Does this form part of the new evidence you were talking about?' she asked, a smile hovering on her lips; an expression he didn't like very much.

'The night your husband was murdered, Mrs Smythe-Jones,' choosing to ignore her question, 'apparently, it was late when you returned home.'

'It was, I suppose; well after midnight I'm sure. I'd been in the club, a place where none of us bothered about time. We were there to enjoy ourselves, Mr Spencer.'

'Can you remember then what time it was when you went there that evening?'

'Not really. It started off as any other evening, actually. Norman and I would have eaten early as we were in the habit of doing; about six-thirty I think, and afterwards I went along to the club.'

'He didn't mind?'

'Not at all. Norman wasn't exactly a club person, preferring to spend the evenings in his study, besides,' she added, 'I would have gone crazy if I had to spend every evening in the bungalow. There was a certain pattern to my life in those days, you understand; I had to fill my days somehow or other, mostly playing either tennis or badminton in the mornings, the afternoons spent around the swimming pool at the club and in the evenings having a drink with those people I've mentioned.'

'I realise it was ten years ago, Mrs Smythe-Jones,' he asked her, 'but can you recall who you were with that night?'

'Oh, dear,' she sighed dramatically, 'that's difficult, Mr Spencer. You see, as I've said, that evening was no different from any other I spent in the club and I wasn't always talking to the same people.'

'You've mentioned Terry Price; was he there?'

'Yes, he and his wife were there, but I don't think I spoke much to them. I remember they were sitting at the end of the bar talking to another couple I knew fairly well, Martha and Luke Underwood. Martha was one of the women I used to play tennis with.' she explained, 'I spent a good part of the evening talking to Harry Knight and later on we were joined by Bill and Mary Richardson.'

'Was Anthony Johnson there?' Philip asked, watching her expression closely, but it didn't change.

'No, he didn't come in that evening.'

'Was this unusual?'

'I suppose now you come to mention it, it was.'

'When you left the club,' Philip pressed on, 'did you go straight back to the bungalow?'

'Of course I did; there was nowhere else to go!'

'It occurred to me you may have been invited for a coffee by one of your friends before you went home.'

'Oh, I see; well, I didn't.'

'You mentioned a few minutes ago, Mrs Smythe-Jones,' sensing by now she'd had enough, 'that your bungalow had been broken into; did you see any physical signs of this?'

'None at all.'

'What about the doors; were they all locked?'

'Well,' she said, 'the front door was, but I didn't think to check the back one, but the police would have done that.'

'How many keys did you and your husband have?'

'There were three sets, actually; Norman had one set and I had one of course.'

'The third set;' prompting her, 'where were they?'

'Norman kept them in one of the drawers of his desk.'

'And were they there when you finally packed everything up?'

' – I think so,' hesitating for a second, 'I can't remember, but they must have been.'

'You would have handed over the keys to someone though, wouldn't you?' Philip asked her, wondering why, for the first time, she sounded as though she was prevaricating. Up until now she had been quick to answer all of his questions.

'I gave them to Terry; he worked for the same company as Norman and he said he would hand them into the office the following morning.'

'When was the last time you saw Anthony Johnson, Mrs Smythe-Jones?' not missing the almost imperceptible flicker of an eyelid, followed by the way her eyes narrowed; only seconds, but it was enough to convey to him the question had not only surprised her by his sudden deviation, but there was a look of wariness in her manner now.

'Oh,' she drawled, making he felt sure, a pretense of remembering, 'it would have been the evening before but I can't be certain. I don't actually remember talking to him, but both Norman and I were in his company on the Saturday night. I can remember that quite well.'

'I see.'

'Mr Spencer,' she asked, 'why are you asking me all these questions about Anthony?'

'Because,' he replied, 'we are not satisfied with the official verdicts of your husband's death and Anthony Johnson's accident.'

'And *this* is because of the new evidence you mentioned earlier?'

'Primarily, yes. Were you aware, Mrs Smythe-Jones,' he asked, 'that both incidents happened on the same night?'

'Did they really; I had no idea. Surely, Mr Spencer that must have been a coincidence?'

'When two members of an extremely small expatriate community should have died suddenly and unexpectedly our first criteria must be to make absolutely certain how and perhaps why this was. It would be too easy, Mrs Smythe-Jones,' he added, 'to overlook any possible significance and use the convenience of coincidence.'

'All of this is beyond me.' she shrugged, 'Are you implying there is something *suspicious* about what happened?'

'I'm not implying anything,' he said, 'I'm examining everything I am able to glean and hopefully build up a picture of events that night and this can only be accomplished by speaking to as many people as possible who were there at that time. However,' he went on, 'I believe I've asked you all I wanted to know for the present, but before I leave, I would be grateful if you would give me the names again of those friends you've mentioned.'

'Of course, but I'm sure they won't still be out there, Mr Spencer.'

'I don't expect them to be, but nevertheless, we should be able to locate them without too much difficulty."

'Incidentally,' she asked him as he was leaving, 'how do you know that Anthony crashed his car on the Wednesday when it wasn't found until the Friday?'

'Anthony Johnson was in the habit of always going home each day after he finished work, but on the Wednesday, he didn't. In fact, he wasn't in his bungalow at all that night.'

'But,' she insisted, 'how do you know?'

'His servant informed not only the police when he was questioned, but one of the directors from Anthony Johnson's company called at the bungalow on Thursday afternoon and the man told him the same.'

'His servant?'

'Yes, apparently he always had a meal ready for him and as he lived on his own compound at the rear of the bungalow, he would have known if Anthony Johnson had returned.'

'Servants!' a look of haughty disdain on her face, 'What on earth do they know!'

'I think you might be surprised, Mrs Smythe-Jones, exactly how much these people do know. Servants, or houseboys as I believe they are called in that country, talk to each; they gossip, they tittle-tattle. Would you not agree?'

'I have absolutely no idea, Mr Spencer.'

'Presumably you had a houseboy working for you?'

'Naturally, but fortunately I was never around when he was in the house and by the time I came back from swimming in the afternoons, he was working in the garden, also he would already have prepared the food for our evening meal, he didn't have to cook it, I did that, and that's the way I preferred it. Unlike some of the women, I didn't spend more time with him than I had to and I certainly did not engage in any conversation. He knew what to do and he got on with it.'

***

After Philip Spencer had gone, Pamela returned to the library. She stood for a while at the open window overlooking the drive and long after his car had reached the gates and turned on to the road, she remained there. She wasn't seeing the lush greenness of the well-tended garden and beyond, to where the trees were beginning to change their colour. Instead, she was remembering Samriboi, where the only road leading into the town was tarmac, the others, dusty red laterite with many treacherous potholes; the town itself had always reminded her of those wild west towns she'd seen in movies: all the buildings were on one level, wood-built with orange corrugated tin roofs; the one super-market where there were more empty shelves than full ones, shortages being considered by the expats as normal; the Indian-owned bread and cake shop and their speciality, somosas; spicy hot and surprisingly good. Their bungalow was one of many owned by the mining company, Norman's employers. Each building was identical to its neighbour, the only difference being in the individual choice of soft furnishings; the main furniture, utility but functional, had belonged to the company. Talking about Samriboi and those people she had known had brought everything back to her; memories she wished she could forget, but this morning she was finding it impossible. The man from the Foreign Office had opened the Pandora box and all she was left with was a feeling of unease. Who was he, she fretted. Her knowledge of police procedure was limited, but being attached to the Foreign Office must mean he held a fairly high position with some authority. Could he be MI6, she wondered, the thought suddenly occurring and with this possible explanation the breath caught in her throat as she considered what this could mean.

Seeing Kate the other evening at The Smugglers had been quite ironic, she thought. Was she aware that questions were now being asked about Anthony's accident? Would Philip Spencer also be calling on her? If he did, he would be wasting his time; Kate hadn't even been in Samriboi then.

Pamela had first met Anthony Johnson more than ten years ago; it had been not long after she and Norman had arrived there. She was in the club bar having a cold drink after her morning game of tennis and he was there, half a pint of lager in front of him. No-one else had been around and she remembered being surprised to see him; it was seldom any man would be in the club at that time of the day except at weekends. Samriboi was predominantly a mining town, copper being the country's main export, and the majority of expats worked for the mining company.

Those who didn't were either with the bank, like Harry, lecturers at the local technical college or for the ministry of public buildings and works.

She had noticed him around the club, but up to that morning had never been in his company before. He had been quick to introduce himself and they spent almost an hour talking; he had been charming and flattering which she had enjoyed. He neglected to tell her he was married, which she thought later hadn't been too sensible as he must have realised she would have soon found out for herself. In fact, one of the women who'd been playing tennis in the second court earlier had come into the bar, minutes after Anthony had left. She wasted no time in informing her, trying now to remember her name, but she couldn't, not that it mattered all that much, although she could recall what the woman had said to her and the scathing cattiness of those words: "Anthony Johnson is a married man, you know," she'd said, "his wife is called Kate and *extremely* attractive, also they have a little girl."

"Oh," taken aback, "I hadn't realised; he didn't say."

"Well, he wouldn't, would he, my dear."

"What do you mean?"

"Anthony Johnson is what would have been described when I was young as a *philanderer!*"

"How do you know?"

"Because I use my eyes, that's why. You haven't been out here long, have you?"

"No," reluctant to get into conversation with the woman, "a few months."

"Any family?"

"No."

"That's a pity, my dear; a couple of toddlers would keep you occupied."

"I am quite occupied, actually," finding the temerity to speak up for herself, "anyway, it's time I went."

"Just as you wish, but I'm only saying this for your own good, you know. Beware of men like him. They'll only bring you grief."

"I *am* a married woman." she'd heatedly responded.

"Of course you are, my dear; we're all married women here and all the more reason to conduct oneself correctly. When you've been out here as long as I have, you'll know exactly what I mean."

Even now, after all these years, the woman's words still had the power to rankle and how unfair they had been. She had only just met Anthony, for goodness sake! She hadn't even considered him as someone she might want to have an affair with, but it had been as though the woman had triggered off a little demon in her brain and she started to view him differently and decided not long after that to develop their relationship. Call it curiosity or boredom, but when she next saw him she recognised by the way his eyes lingered on her lips as she spoke that he was sexually attracted to her and from then onwards it wasn't long before they were sleeping together. Pamela Brookes, as she was then, was above all, a realist. She was also a snob and even at the beginning she was aware Anthony was not her social equal and never could be. His background, even without him elaborating on it, was totally different to what hers had been, but she was living in Africa, in a small nondescript apology for a town, and had had to accept that the choice of men was extremely limited, therefore if she did decide to have an affair, Anthony would have to do. The fact he had a wife didn't come into the equation. As far as Pamela was concerned that wasn't a problem. All she wanted to do was to fill her days until Norman's contract came to an end and she could be back in the territory she was used to. At least in England she had space; space to get into her car when she felt like it and drive off somewhere civilised, but in Samriboi it was tantamount to living in a goldfish bowl.

Anthony and everyone else she knew in Zambia were history now, mentally dismissing them all and turning away from the window. She would forget about the man from the Foreign Office; there was nothing more she could tell him. Even if he was able to get in touch with those people she had told him about, it was unlikely they would say anything different. Norman was dead and as far as she was concerned so was Anthony.

Chapter Four

ENGLAND
(The week before)

He had only been in London for forty-eight hours and with time to spare before his meeting with Lenny Yeung, decided to have a walk round the British Museum; not for any real interest in anything historical or of an aesthetic nature, but it was close to the Hotel Russell where Lenny had suggested they meet. He didn't spend long inside; finding the place too sombre for his liking and after only a cursory glance at the exhibits on the ground floor went back outside, appreciating the warmth of the September sun. He was standing by one of the pillars in the courtyard of the museum when he saw Kate across the road.

Although she had her back to him, having stopped to look into one of the shop windows, he could tell by the way her shoulders stiffened she had seen him, and sensing she was about to turn round, he moved behind the pillar. At the same time, a coach load of tourists arrived and he was able to merge with them as they walked up the steps to the main door of the museum. Once inside, he walked quickly towards the stairs. He didn't know whether she would follow him or not, but he was taking no chances. It was ironic he thought, as he reached the gallery, that he would see her again after all this time.

Anthony Johnson was devoid of any feelings of guilt or remorse; he had never considered the way he had treated Kate to be wrong. He had felt stifled by his marriage and his belief at the time that being married could mean he would be like any other loving and faithful husband just didn't happen. In an effort to re-capture his former lifestyle which he missed, he embarked on a number of brief affairs, but the hard fact remained; he was married and no longer free to behave as he wished. Anthony was a gambler, not so much at the gaming tables, but with his life and if there was an element of risk attached to his various negotiations all the better. It's true, that in the end Pamela had disappointed him, but since then he had come to the realisation that for them ever to have had any sort of future together had been unrealistic. He had an inferiority complex and what she'd said to him when they last met only exacerbated this weakness in his nature.

Anthony had been aware from an early age, no matter how hard he tried to blend in with anyone from a more privileged background than his own, this was not possible. Living as he had been within the cloistered environment of Cambridge University and constantly seeing the relaxed confidence of the students had acted as a constant reminder that he was only a boy who attended a state school and whose father was one of the university porters. These had been envious thoughts which, by the time he had reached his teens, had taken a strong hold, resulting in him becoming bitter and self-destructive and, by the time he was in his twenties and before he met Kate, his life had evolved into an irreversible pattern, and one, although he did try to change when they were first married, he found impossible. Perhaps if he had stayed in England and not chosen to live and work overseas, he may have felt differently, been able to settle down and conform to the regularised lifestyle of the average British male, but in his cynical moments he didn't believe this. Marrying Kate had been an impulsive act and one which didn't take him long to regret. Even when his daughter was born he didn't feel any closer to Kate and had quickly discovered he had no paternal instincts towards the child.

He had been enchanted by Pamela from the moment he had first met her in Samriboi. Unlike other women he had known she didn't ask questions; she was utterly incurious and he had found this refreshing. When she told him that Norman's contract was almost at an end and they would soon be returning to England they talked about the possibility of them having a future together, but not in any great depth. He did consider resigning and going back, but at the same time realising it would be virtually impossible to continue their affair which up to then had been relatively uncomplicated. He didn't even think about a divorce; Kate, being a catholic would, he knew, never agree and Pamela, in her frank way, had already said she wouldn't divorce Norman for the simple reason she couldn't afford to. Norman's father, a wealthy landowner, had recently died and had left him his entire estate, which she had stressed was quite considerable.

"No, darling," Pamela had said, "I have no option but to remain married to Norman. Unless," she had added, an unreadable expression on her face, "he was to die."

"That's hardly likely," he had answered, not fully understanding what she meant, "he's still in his forties, isn't he?" and then she had to spell it out to him; at first he didn't like what she was suggesting, but the more he thought about it all, especially when she had said Norman had made out his will and she would inherit a substantial sum, the idea she had put into his head took shape and refused to budge. It might just work, he had thought; risky, but then he was used to that.

Together, they had worked out the plan and as they had agreed, met up again in Paris. He had already acquired another passport under the name of Clive Edwards; a new name, a new identity and the bonus being Pamela. They had discussed at length what they would do; she had told him that Norman and she owned a villa in the South of France and this could be a starting-off point for them. Big plans. A new life to look forward to, but it wasn't to be. Pamela had other ideas. She hadn't wasted any time when they met; she made it abundantly clear there was no future for them together. Even ten years later, he still mentally cringed when he remembered her words.

"It would never have worked, you know, Anthony."

"What are you saying?" he'd asked.

"I'm trying to make this easier for you, but the fact is I've changed my mind."

"What do you mean; you've changed your mind? We had all of this worked out in Samriboi if you remember."

"Oh, I remember alright," she'd said, "but the situation has changed."

"Do enlighten me." anger and frustration starting to set in. Who was this woman, he had thought, feeling physically sick as the full impact of what he had done hit him. She had deliberately tricked him into believing he would be with her. She had known all along, right from the beginning of their relationship perhaps exactly what she wanted from him in order to gain her own personal freedom.

"Not to put too fine a point on it, Anthony," she had said, "you couldn't possibly fit into my world. Living an expatriate life means one must associate with absolutely anyone!"

There it was again, he had thought, mentally reeling; he, Anthony Johnson from a humble background, was being excluded from joining the privileged classes. It had taken him some weeks to put the whole disastrous business behind him, and to pick up the threads of where he left off before going out to Zambia and it was very rare he ever thought of Pamela, but seeing Kate had brought it all back again.

She was down there now, standing in the open doorway of the museum and looking up to the balcony. She had seen him, but he didn't think she would be able to make out his features properly and glad he was wearing his hat, hoping the wide brim would help. She started to walk towards the stairs, but before she had reached them he had moved away from the balcony. It had now become imperative for her not to spot him again and quickly walked in the opposite direction until he reached another set of stairs leading back down to the ground floor. Once outside, he quickened his step, taking a short cut through the gardens in Russell Square and within five minutes was approaching the hotel. By the time he pushed through the glass swing doors he had convinced himself he had nothing to worry about, reckoning if Kate did mention to anyone that she'd seen him it was extremely unlikely they would believe her. Anthony Johnson had died in a car crash in Africa ten years ago. He was confident he had covered his tracks well, knowing that Pamela would never talk. To do so would only endanger her own position and she would never do that.

Lenny was already in the bar waiting for him.

'Hello, Clive,' he said, shaking hands, 'how are you?'

'I'm fine, Lenny. Sorry, I'm a bit late; it took longer than I thought getting here.'

'It didn't matter; as you can see I've already ordered a beer. I wasn't sure what you would want.'

'Oh, I'll have the same.'

After the polite formalities were over and the waiter had brought Anthony's beer to their table, Lenny became the suave businessman Anthony was more accustomed to. He had known Lenny Yeung for almost ten years and during that time had acted as his personal courier. The countries Anthony visited on his behalf were as varied as the contents of each consignment. Lenny paid him well; fifty per cent in advance and the balance upon delivery. Anthony was satisfied with the arrangement. They worked well together; they recognised each other's professionalism and the risks involved if at any time one of them should slip up, but so far they hadn't. Lenny's base was in Hong Kong where he had his own company, trading under the ambiguous description of "Exporters of Fine Arts", but he also leased a suite of offices in Regent Street, although, because of the part Anthony played in his other business activities, they always conducted their meetings in London away from the office. In Hong Kong, when Anthony was there, it was the same; Lenny would, as he had this time, select where they would meet.

'This assignment, Clive,' he was saying, 'will be slightly different from the others in that it will be in two stages.'

'Yes?'

'First, there are some documents I want you to take over to Amsterdam with you and when you've done that to visit one of my contacts in the city who will give you three small pouches of uncut diamonds. These,' Lenny added, 'I want you to bring out to me in Hong Kong. Secondly,' he explained, 'I'll give you a package to bring back to London with you; I'll provide you with delivery details when I see you in Hong Kong.'

'Sounds straightforward enough.' Anthony commented.

'There is something you should be aware of, Clive.'

'Yes?' and here comes the snag he thought, stifling a sigh, but really not all that surprised. Lenny, from time to time, had presented him with this sort of task, which undoubtedly would mean he would have to be extra vigilant.

'The address you'll be going to,' he explained, his expression as inscrutable as any Chinaman Anthony had ever known, 'is in the warehouse quarter of the town near the docks; not one of Amsterdam's tourist attractions, especially after dark.'

'And I suppose that's when I'm to be there.'

'You suppose right, Clive; so you've been warned. The transaction will only take minutes; Jan Jansen will be in the warehouse waiting for you and I would suggest if you're planning on taking a taxi you leave it some distance away.'

'Right.'

'I have your flight tickets here,' he said, taking them from his jacket pocket and handing them over, 'as you'll see, you should arrive at Schipol Airport shortly after midday on Monday; your first call can be made at any time during the afternoon; they have their offices in the Vijzelstraat, but I'll give you one of the company's cards before you go. Your meeting with Jan Jansen has been arranged for eight that night and your onward journey to Hong Kong, the following night, is at twenty-three hundred hours, arriving nineteen hundred hours, Hong Kong-time, on the Wednesday. As usual, Clive, everything has been taken care of.'

'Hotels?' Anthony asked.

'No problem; a room has been reserved for you at the Carlton in Amsterdam and the Intercontinental Hotel in Hong Kong, Kowloon-side.'

As Lenny had said, everything had been taken care of, just as it usually was. He couldn't fault him either on the choice of hotels; they were of a high standard, although he would have preferred not to be at the Carlton. Amsterdam had well over three hundred hotels and, of all of them, he would be staying there. It's true it had been several years ago and it was more than likely the staff had changed since those days when he had been a frequent guest; back to the time when he had been known as Anthony Johnson, but it couldn't be helped; the reservation had been made and even if he were to move to another hotel, chances were that Lenny would find out.

'Alright, Clive?'

'Yes, fine.'

'Good. Afraid you won't have much time to enjoy Amsterdam's highlights, though.'

'You mean the famous Red Light district?'

'Where else, Clive,' Lenny chuckled, 'indeed, where else?'

***

AMSTERDAM

The British Airways flight touched down at Schipol Airport at ten minutes past midday and, only having a cabin-approved travel bag, Anthony walked straight through to Immigration and less than fifteen minutes later he was in a taxi and heading for the city centre. Always, in the initial stages of a project, he was experiencing the flow of adrenalin at what could lie ahead. The unlikely event of being recognised no longer concerned him; as far as he was concerned Anthony Johnson no longer existed and in less than forty-eight hours he would be on his way once more. This leg of the trip, he decided, seeing the familiar landmarks of the city, was going to be a piece of cake. Lenny had done all the groundwork; all he had to do was deliver the package personally to Alexander Van Ommeron, one of the directors of the shipping offices in the Vijzelstraat and tonight meet up with Jan Jansen.

Within twenty minutes his taxi was turning into the Vijzelstraat and pulling up outside the Carlton Hotel. Paying off the driver, he walked up the few steps and on into the hotel. Filling in the reservation card took only minutes, the transaction carried out courteously and with the usual efficiency. He was presented with the key to his room, noting that it was on the sixth floor and probably one of the best-positioned in the whole hotel; overlooking the Singel Canal and the floating flower market. He was not disappointed, appreciating as he had done before, that the constant roar of the traffic on the highway below was considerably muted up here.

So far, he hadn't recognised any of the staff on reception and it was the same when he went into the bar. Anthony had an excellent memory for faces and the man who served him his Heineken definitely hadn't been working there before. Taking his beer over to the open window, he sat down. Strains of the "Cuckoo Waltz" reached him from a street barrel organ on the pavement immediately outside the hotel, followed by the "Hellbaardier March"; a welcome respite from the bustling city he thought, taking a long and satisfying sip of his beer. The bar wasn't busy: a young couple at the table next to him, holding hands and oblivious to anyone else but each other; a woman on his other side, in her late forties he guessed: dark hair with blonde highlights, cut short and elegantly dressed in a lilac two-piece with a silk scarf in a deeper shade draped across her shoulders, and by the way she repeatedly looked at her watch it would seem she was waiting for someone. There were half a dozen customers standing up at the bar; all male, wearing business suits and white shirts. None of them gave any hint of being interested in him and, indeed Anthony thought, why should they? He was dressed as many other tourists were: light-coloured trousers and an open-neck sports shirt giving, he hoped, the impression of having nothing better to do than spend time relaxing over a glass of beer prior to doing a little sightseeing in the afternoon.

He had just bought another Heineken and was returning to his table when he saw that the woman had been joined by the man she had presumably been waiting for. Anthony couldn't see his face, only his profile, but there was something familiar about him, only vaguely, but enough to make him search through his memory. It hadn't been recently, he knew that much, but he continued to feel he had seen him before and the more he concentrated on the possibility, without making his scrutiny too obvious, the memory continued to elude him. He felt it had been somewhere abroad, but then that was really like looking for the proverbial needle in the haystack; he had, during the last twenty years or so, done a considerable amount of travelling and had long lost count of the number of countries, some of which he had only spent two or three days; in and out, not dissimilar to this visit to Amsterdam, and a few where he had been on contract, and during those times he had been in the company of dozens of men. And then, there were many whom he may have seen regularly, but never been in conversation with. He gave up after a while. There was no point in continuing to scratch through his past, dismissing the resemblance now as unimportant and he certainly wasn't going to worry about that time in Samriboi; that would be too much of a coincidence. They were going now in any case he noticed; neither of them looking in his direction and with their backs turned to him were walking through the open doorway towards the lobby.

The shipping offices were only three blocks away from the hotel and once he had handed over the package Lenny had given him, he spent the remainder of the afternoon occupying his time as so many others appeared to be doing; sightseeing. It was late afternoon when he finally returned to the hotel; the barrel organ was still there and continuing to churn out a medley of old international favourites. Two middle-aged women were getting carried away with the strains of "Boogie Woogie Baby" and attempting a Charleston on the grass verge of the canal. Not for the first time he wondered cynically why it was that some people had this inbuilt ability to openly enjoy life regardless of drawing attention to themselves. Something, even as a young boy, he had never been able to do. Too inhibited he supposed, always trying not to make a fool of himself. All of which reminded him of those early years when he would enviously watch the antics of the students on the campus in Cambridge.

Dusk was beginning to fall when he left the hotel later, allowing plenty of time to walk to where he was meeting Jan Jansen, deciding against taking a taxi as Lenny had suggested. Even if he was to only take it a couple of streets from the warehouse he considered it would still be too conspicuous. Anthony had neglected to tell Lenny on Saturday that he knew Amsterdam well, the warehouse quarter in particular. He needed no directions and, handing his room key in to reception, went out. The barrel organ was still playing and as he had often thought each time he came to

Amsterdam whether these old boys ever slept. To him, they had always been old, and not much to distinguish one organ grinder from another as they operated their ancient and ornate barrel organs for hours at a time for what must be a pittance.

Walking briskly, he turned into the Dam, the city's main square with its historical buildings, but tonight he had no interest in aesthetics; his energies and concentration focused on what lay ahead.

The square was behind him now and carrying on down a side street he was passing the Hotel Krasnapolsky towards the docks, along the Oudezijds Voorburwal canal, turning right into a labyrinth of narrow streets with poor lighting and penetrating the warehouse district of the city.

This was familiar territory to him, and hugging the wall of the buildings and avoiding what lights there were, he finally reached the street, narrower than the others, where Jan Jansen had his warehouse. Here, the gabled roofs leaned so far out to the others the space between them couldn't be much more than a hand's breadth.

Climbing the flight of steps, the soft soles of his shoes making little sound on the worn out wood, he turned the handle on the door facing him and went inside the warehouse.

A tall thickset man moved out of the gloomy shadows at the far end and walked towards him.

'Please close the door,' he said quietly, 'and then introduce yourself.'

'Clive Edwards.'

'And I am Jan Jansen.' making no attempt to shake hands, 'Please come with me; my office is on the floor above.'

A man of few words, Anthony thought, and apparently lacking in any of the characteristic Dutch courtesies, following him across to the stairs; steep with a far from steady handrail. His office appeared to occupy the whole of the upper floor, although that description was somewhat exaggerated; one large table with an untidy heap of box files and a half-full ashtray, no computer or even a telephone, but he probably used a mobile. Along one wall behind the table was a steel safe and with his back to Anthony, he dialled the combination. The two doors of the safe swung open and within a matter of seconds he had taken out three leather pouches from the top shelf and, turning round to face him handed them over.

'Give my regards to Lenny, Mr Edwards.' was all he said as they retraced their steps back down to the ground floor, leaving Anthony to make his own way to the door. Putting the pouches into the inside pockets of his jacket, he silently let himself out.

He had almost reached the entrance of the Hotel Krasnapolsky, the light from the foyer illuminating the pavement in a wide arc. The streets were busier now, with the late night revellers making their way towards the red light district. A group of people were coming out of the hotel, but one of them who didn't appear to be with them held back at the top of the steps until they had moved away. He reached the pavement at exactly the same time as Anthony drew level with the steps, where he stood for a fraction of a second before walking towards him.

'Hello, Anthony,' he said, 'it's been a long time since we last saw each other, hasn't it? I suggest we have a drink for old time's sake.'

***

HONG KONG

Lenny waited until after eleven on Wednesday night to phone Jan. The arrangement had been that Clive would call him shortly after he arrived in Hong Kong, but he'd heard nothing from him and, according to the Intercontinental, he had not yet booked in. A further call to someone he knew at Immigration confirmed Clive Edwards had not been on the flight from Amsterdam and it was this which promulgated him in doing what he could to find out where he had gone.

'Hello, Jan,' he said, 'it's Lenny.'

'Lenny? I did not expect to hear from you so soon.'

'I'm worried, Jan,' Lenny said, side-stepping any preambles, 'Clive hasn't turned up.'

'Oh, dear.'

'You don't sound all that surprised.'

'Well, it's obvious, isn't it?' Jan pointed out calmly, 'he's done a runner.'

'I wouldn't go so far as to say that, Jan. Clive's been working for me for a number of years and he's never let me down.'

'There is always a first time.'

'That aside,' Lenny said, irritated by his matter of fact manner, but Jan Jansen was always like this; looking on the obverse was normal with him, 'something may have happened to him.'

'It's always possible, of course, but when you think about it logically, Lenny, why should it?'

'You tell me, Jan; that whole area is not what you would describe as salubrious.'

'That's true,' he agreed, 'anyway, you may be interested to hear that he met someone after he left here.'

'How did you find that out?' surprised. Clive was a loner, except for his womanising, but it was extremely unlikely he would have brought a woman to Amsterdam with him. Lenny had made it his business to find out as much as he could about him before he decided to take him on and what he had learned he had kept to himself in the event Clive ever tried to double-cross him. He also knew Clive Edwards wasn't his real name and, more importantly, why he may have changed his identity. So far, as he had just said to Jan, Clive hadn't let him down. He was efficient, always delivered on time and didn't ask any unnecessary questions; Lenny liked that.

'Because,' Jan explained, 'I had one of my men following him from the moment he left the warehouse. I did this more for my own peace of mind you understand; I didn't want anyone snooping about and showing too much interest in any visitor.'

'Makes sense, I suppose.'

'I think so.'

'This person he met,' Lenny asked, 'am I right in saying it was a man?'

'You are, Lenny.'

'And this was on his way back to the city centre?' prompting him impatiently; there were times Lenny thought that trying to get information from Jan was one hard slog.

'Yes, that's right. He got as far as the Hotel Krasnapolsky; you know where that is, don't you?'

'In one of those side streets off from the Dam; I've been in there a few times.'

'I thought you may have been. Well,' he continued pedantically, 'he was just passing the hotel when this man came down the steps and walked up to him.'

'A chance meeting do you think?'

'Hard to say, Lenny. My man was too far away from them both and of course couldn't hear what was said. However,' he continued, 'they went into the hotel.'

'Clive must have known him then.'

'Sounds like it.'

'What did he look like?'

'Forty-six, or thereabouts, clean-shaven, dark brown hair, cut short, quite tall, about six foot.' he reckoned.

'A good description.' wondering how he was able to get so much detail, especially as it must have been fairly dark in the street.

'My man followed them inside; they were both in the bar by this time. He hung about for a few minutes, but getting the impression they seemed to be in no hurry to move anywhere else, he phoned me to report.'

'And that was that?'

'Afraid so, Lenny. It's obvious to me that he had no intention of taking that flight out to Hong Kong the following day. I don't need to remind you that the street value of those diamonds is very high, very high indeed.'

'I know, I know.' unable to shrug off a feeling of premonition, 'You could be right about what you say about Clive, but all the same it appears out of character. Clive Edwards knew when he was on a good deal and I can't believe he would throw it away –'

'– unless he received a more lucrative offer and one he couldn't refuse.'

Jan interrupted, 'Remember, Lenny, everyone has his price.'

And with that little homily, Lenny had to be satisfied. He was the one who had lost; the money he had already paid Jan and the diamonds he hadn't received. There wasn't a great deal more they had to say to each other and, promising to keep in touch, Lenny rang off.

He spent most of the following morning in the gym in the hope that exercise would help to relieve the build-up of stress which had taken a grip of him over the last couple of days. He'd had a disturbed night, tossing and turning, until finally, around six, he was able to sleep, but waking only a couple of hours later by sun streaming through the bedroom window, reminding him he had forgotten to draw the blinds before going to bed. He was in no mood for work, putting to the back of his mind the accumulation of emails and correspondence. They would have to wait, he decided, at least until the afternoon. Laura, his secretary, was good but not that good and there was much about his business she was not privy to which inevitably meant only he could handle it.

He took the Star Ferry back to Hong Kong Island and had reached the Yung Kee restaurant in Wellington Street when his mobile rang.

'You're early, Jan,' he said, immediately recognising the number of the caller, 'something wrong?'

'You could say that,' Jan said, his voice crackling with static, 'but your man's turned up.'

'Tell me more.'

'The police pulled his body out of the Oudezijds canal on Tuesday morning -'

' – and they recognised him?' Lenny interrupted quickly, not liking what he was hearing; not necessarily for the demise of Clive Edwards, but more for what this could mean for himself.

'Not until late yesterday.' Jan said, 'After I spoke to you, Lenny, I did some discreet phoning around in the off chance that Clive may have had an accident; I have some reliable contacts among the police, no questions no pack drill, if you know what I mean?'

'I know what you mean; go on.'

'Well,' Jan said, 'strangely, or perhaps not so strangely, he had no means of identity on him; it wasn't until they received a call from the Carlton. They had become concerned when he hadn't returned; anyway,' he added, 'his passport and travel documents were in his room.'

'I see,' Lenny said, 'no mention of the goods he was carrying, I suppose.'

'No, afraid not, Lenny and believe me they would have if there had been. One consolation, though.'

'What?'

'That lets me out of the picture.'

'I wouldn't be so sure, Jan.'

'What do you mean?'

'What I mean is, whoever dumped his body in the canal must have taken them and, whoever it was, could have followed him to the warehouse on Monday night.'

'True, perhaps, but they would have a job proving anything.'

'So,' Lenny said, 'presumably his death will now be treated as an international matter; as you know, he was a British subject.'

'Don't forget the man he met after he left here.'

'I'm not forgetting him, Jan.'

Chapter Five

ENGLAND

Gregory was at home when Lenny called and, not wanting Pamela to hear, he took the mobile through to his study. This timing is wrong he muttered to himself; up to now, he had always managed to conduct any communication with Hong Kong well away from her natural inquisitiveness, but realised Lenny must have a very good reason for phoning him so late in the day when he must have realised he would have finished work.

'Yes, Lenny,' he said sharply, 'what's up?'

'Don't sound so alarmed, my friend. It's nothing that can't be resolved, but a recent occurrence means your next consignment won't reach you this weekend.'

'What do you mean by a recent occurrence?' he asked frowning; there were times when Lenny could be exasperating. For a businessman of his particular calibre this side of his nature of appearing to be deliberately obtuse never failed to surprise.

'To put it as succinctly as possible, Gregory,' he said, 'Clive won't be able to make the delivery because,' he added slowly, 'he has met with – shall we say – an accident.'

'What sort of accident?' he pressed him, at the same time mentally considering what he was going to do about this unprecedented delay because he already had a customer for the two items of jewellery and he was not going to be at all pleased when he broke the news to him.

Lenny and he went back a long way; since their prep days when Lenny's father, a wealthy industrialist from mainland China, had sent him to England to be educated. Even at such a young age, Lenny Yeung had shown an extraordinary scheming and devious mind and later, when by chance they had met up again at Oxford University, those earlier trends in his personality had become intensified, making him a formidable character. It hadn't taken Gregory long to suss him out. Not being entirely squeaky-clean himself, he had been quick to recognise someone not averse to side-stepping the law. Their partnership had proved to be a lucrative one with Lenny sourcing and delivering to him selected pieces of jewellery and artefacts from the Far East. Gregory had never asked him exactly where or how they had been acquired, always maintaining it was best he didn't know, working on the premise that it was Lenny who was taking that initial risk especially, as he suspected, those sources were in the least suspect. Similarly, Lenny didn't question him about the customers who were sufficiently wealthy to make the purchase. As in all partnerships, there has to be a strong element of trust, and theirs was no exception; they shared all relevant costs and the proceeds of each sale on a fifty-fifty basis and in spite of the basic difference in their backgrounds and where they were based geographically, the partnership worked, providing them both with tax-free incomes.

'I had a call from someone I know in Amsterdam a short while ago,' Lenny was saying, 'to tell me Clive's body had been dragged out from one of their canals.'

'Hardly an accident, Lenny.' he commented dryly.

'No –' Lenny admitted slowly, '- but I suppose it is feasible he may have fallen in.'

'Come on, Lenny, both you and I know that would be pretty extreme, especially for someone as cautious as Clive.'

'I know, I know.'

'I take it he was in Amsterdam on your behalf?'

'He was, yes and,' he added, 'he should have flown out here on Tuesday. Regrettably, I have lost a considerable amount of money over this debacle, Gregory.'

'Debacle,' Gregory repeated, 'I guess that's one way of describing it, but there's nothing you can do about it, is there?'

'No, and that's the frustrating part.'

'Are you expecting any comeback?'

'You mean from the authorities?'

'Of course; as he was British, I expect the matter will be handed over to Interpol, or someone like that. The Dutch police won't be all that interested.'

'I'm sure they won't,' Lenny agreed, 'to them he was only another foreigner ending his life in one of their canals and let's face it, Gregory; Amsterdam has a fair number of them.'

'How discreet do you think Clive Edwards really was, then? You knew him a lot better than I did.'

'You mean, how well did he cover his tracks?'

'Yes.'

'He was skilful in watching his back, that's for certain. Mind you, he'd had a lot of practice.'

'Was that his real name; I've often wondered and you've never said.'

'Didn't think there was any need, but as you ask, his real name was Anthony Johnson and I made a point of finding out all I could about him before I agreed to take him on.'

'And?'

'Ten years ago he was living in Africa and arranged a rather dramatic disappearance by staging a car crash out there and the authorities, even although they couldn't find his body, officially declared him as dead, probably because of the terrain where it happened. From what I've been able to glean, they assumed he had been jettisoned from the vehicle and perished in the ravine which incidentally, and no doubt conveniently for him, was infested with crocodiles.'

'What surprises me,' Gregory said, 'is how you've been able to find out all of this when apparently everyone else believes this Anthony Johnson is dead.'

'I've been waiting for you to ask me that,' he chuckled, 'but it's quite simple, you know. I had never heard of Anthony Johnson before; it was Clive Edwards I knew, so after a considerable amount of back-tracking, asking the right questions to the right people, arrived at the name of Anthony Johnson who it transpired wasn't dead at all.'

'Clever, Lenny and as you say, dramatic, but it sounds as if there's no cover-up this time; he really is dead.'

'True.'

'This is all very well, you know,' Gregory went on, 'but when do you reckon I can expect this delivery? Have you got anyone else you can send over with it?'

'I could have, but it will take time.'

'Couldn't you bring them over yourself?'

'I don't want to put my head in that particular noose, Gregory; far too risky. I know we've been partners for a long time and I realise how disappointed you must be, but all I can suggest is for you to think of a credible excuse to explain the delay to your customer. Sorry; I really am.'

'I know you are. It's a damnable situation. It wouldn't be so bad if he wasn't so unreasonably impatient. You know the type, I'm sure; a blustering autocrat; self-opinionated and loud-mouthed with it. Thinks money can buy anything.'

'Which it can't of course, Gregory and on that philosophical note I'll bring this call to a close.'

After Lenny rang off, he sat for a while contemplating on what they'd been talking about. Somehow, he would be able to pacify his customer, realising he would have no alternative but to wait; those items he was purchasing were too unique for him to cancel the order. Also, Gregory knew he would always be able to find another buyer if it became necessary. The gemstones were a rare design and although Lenny had only shown him photographs he trusted his judgement; the emerald and gold pendants had been cut and polished in Thailand and individually they were worth a considerable amount, but selling them as a pair as he was to an avid collector of precious and semi-precious stones, increased their value. He was confident Lenny would be able to find a replacement for Clive, appreciating whoever it was, would have to be vetted.

He had only met Clive Edwards a couple of times; this had been on trips he had made to Hong Kong, and then only briefly. Gregory's initial reaction was that he found Clive a difficult kind of man to know or, if he was being truthful, to even like. And now, learning about the faked accident, he couldn't say he was all that surprised. He hadn't thought to ask Lenny whereabouts in Africa this had been. It wasn't as though it was all that important; Africa was immense and the chances of it being anywhere near where Pamela used to live would surely be remote, he thought, getting up from his desk and walking over to the window.

He had known Pamela before she and Norman went out there, remembering back to those stolen afternoons they would spend together in his apartment in London. Then, he hadn't considered there would have been any real permanency to their relationship and had believed Pamela felt the same and had therefore been surprised when she continued to keep in touch and on those occasions when she came back to London for short visits, they managed to see each other and pick up from where they had left off. Later, when he had learned about Norman's death and by this time she was back in England, although he had been shocked to hear about the way in which he had died, that had been the extent of any grief he may have felt for a man he hardly knew.

***

AMSTERDAM

The demise of one of the Hotel Carlton's guests caused scarcely a ripple in the smooth running of the hotel. As far as the management was concerned, the incident had occurred outside their establishment and therefore could not possibly affect their untainted reputation.

Only a brief mention had been made in that morning's *De Telegraaf* of an English tourist's body having been dragged from the Oudezijds Voorburwal canal on Tuesday morning although they had been unable to identify him until late the following day.

'I wonder how that happened.' Christine Ford commented, pointing to the single column half-way down one of the inside pages of the newspaper. 'Did you read it, Guy?'

'Only the headline, Christine. As you know, my Dutch comprehension is poor and as usual when I'm here, I take the easy route and buy one of the English papers. So,' he added, 'what does it say? I don't suppose it would have given the person's name.'

'No, too soon, I expect. There wasn't much,' she said, 'only a few lines: "The body of an English tourist was discovered close to the side of the Oudezijds Voorburgwal canal by a passerby on Tuesday morning." she read out to him, "The man, in his late forties, had been immersed in the water for approximately twelve hours and at this stage the police are not disclosing whether they are suspecting foul play.".'

'The Oudezijds Voorburgwal canal,' Guy said thoughtfully, 'that's towards the warehouse quarter, isn't it?'

'Yes, that's right; not one of Amsterdam's prettiest sights,' she said, pursing her lips in distaste, 'particularly at night. It does make you wonder though, doesn't it, why he should have been walking along there?'

'Naturally curious, I suppose.' he suggested, visualising that part of the town. He could be totally off beam of course, but in his career as an investigative journalist he had learned not to immediately accept coincidences. Anthony Johnson had been down there on Monday night and he certainly hadn't been sightseeing.

On that Monday lunchtime when he had met up with Christine in the lounge bar of the hotel he had spotted him instantly and had deliberately chosen to sit with his back to him in the hope he wouldn't be recognised. The one and only time he had seen Anthony Johnson was in Paris twenty-five years ago. He had been there to follow up on a fresh lead into the disappearance of Lord Lucan which, as many of them before, proved to be negative. Shortly after the well publicised scandal there had been what was considered at the time by the police to be a definite sighting but to no avail, therefore with so many disappointments and red herrings covering the thirteen years since the murder in Lower Belgrave Street in London, Guy was not too hopeful of succeeding where other journalists before him had failed.

He had made his way to the Mercure Paris Monty Opéra Hotel in a relatively quiet street between Lafayette and Grands Boulevards where, according to a number of sightings his paper had received, Lord Lucan had, for the past four weeks or so, been in the habit of visiting for an early evening drink. The lounge bar had been packed and standing in the open doorway Guy had looked round the room. They were mostly couples and a few men on their own, but he couldn't see anyone who bore any resemblance to Lord Lucan and then, as he had been on the point of ordering a drink, he noticed at one of the tables by the window two men deep in conversation, one of whom could have been said to look like the missing earl. He would have been fifty-three by that time, those intervening thirteen years having taken their natural toll; the hair, still dark, hadn't the same lustre Guy had remembered from those earlier photographs when he had made his disappearance and to add to any doubts he may have had, the man he was looking at didn't have a moustache, but then Guy had concluded, to shave it off may have been the first thing he would have done as a preliminary disguise.

As he continued to watch him, spinning out his beer and making up his mind what he should do next, they both stood up and walked across the room to the door leading back into the lobby. Disappointed, but not unduly so, Guy ordered another drink and remained where he was. It could only have been minutes later when the man he had been with returned and, instead of going back to where he had been sitting, came over to stand next to him.

'*Un whisky, s'il vous plait, monsieur.*' he asked the barman in an English accept, Guy recognising the flat tones of the fen country, moved slightly to make room for him at the bar.

'Excuse me.'

'That's alright,' Guy said, 'I saw you a few moments ago,' he went on, deciding to come straight to the point, 'but I was more interested in the man you were with, actually; he looked remarkably like -'

'- the infamous Lord Lucan.' he finished for him, an unfathomable expression on his face.

'Well, yes.'

'Are you with the police by any chance?'

'No, I'm not.'

'You must be press, then.' he said quickly, his expression unchanged as he looked at Guy.

'I'm a journalist,' Guy explained, handing him one of his cards, 'optimistically following up on another lead into the disappearance of Lord Lucan. This case continues to be a fascinating mystery for the British people, resulting in both the police and the press following up sightings in various countries around the world. In fact,' he went on, 'not since the Profuma scandal in 1963 has there been such a keen public interest.'

'Lord Lucan disappeared in 1974, didn't he?'

'Yes, that's right.'

'I would still have been at school then, but I can remember hearing about it. Nobody seemed to be talking about anything else and couldn't wait to get the next day's papers.'

'Going back to your companion this evening,' Guy asked him, wanting to move the conversation forward and to find out whether he was wasting his time or not, 'how well do you know him?'

'As well as you will ever know someone you see now and again in a bar, I suppose.' he shrugged. He was lying. Guy wasn't fooled by the attempt to appear indifferent; the man wasn't a good actor. It's rare, he thought, for two mere acquaintances to choose to sit at a table rather than remain at the bar. Also, he concluded, there was rather a big age difference. Lord Lucan would be a good thirty years older, wondering what they could have in common.

'When did you first see him,' Guy asked, 'can you remember?'

'Oh, about a month ago. I've been working in Nigeria for the last three years and decided to treat myself to a well-deserved holiday in Paris.'

'And the man you were with,' Guy persisted, 'has he told you anything about his background?'

'Not much, except that he had been living in California, sounded quite idyllic over there.'

'Did he mention what he did for a living?'

'No, and I didn't bother to ask him. He's an interesting man, though,' he added, 'been around a bit I would say.'

Realising he was getting nowhere, but deciding he would come back to the hotel the next day, he finished off his beer.

'I think you could be right, you know,' he said, surprising him, 'he may very well be the man you're looking for.'

'What makes you say that?'

'Listen,' he said, lowering his voice, 'I know where he used to live when he was in England. One evening, he'd had a few more whiskies than usual and was fairly talkative. It sounded like bragging really, but perhaps he was trying to impress me.'

'And where did he live?'

'Any chance for being reimbursed for this snippet of information?' he asked, evading an answer, 'If he does turn out to be Lord Lucan and you run the story for your paper, it will increase your own personal status which in the end will no doubt come down to money, I would say.'

'You haven't told me your name?' being equally evasive and stalling for time. He did have funds available for positive information, but his head would literally be on the block if they were deliberately false.

'It's Anthony Johnson.' he said.

***

Christine had mixed feelings about returning to Amsterdam. She had been away for a long time, having moved to London in the early 1990s, and since both her parents died had seldom thought about the country where she had spent her younger years, yet, even then, her mother being English meant there were regular visits to see her grandparents. It had been Guy's idea for them to spend a few days in Amsterdam. For once, a parallel lull had occurred in their careers; Guy had just wound up a three-month investigation into a political scandal, while she had come to the end of a long run at The Garrick Theatre. Rehearsals for a Tom Stoppard play were not due to start until the first week in November and, apart from having to learn her lines, which she could do anywhere, there was no reason why she couldn't take some time off, but Christine suffered from an actor's superstition; uneasy about not being in the hub of things, namely the theatre.

Guy and she had been here for almost a week and she had to admit that she had enjoyed herself; it had been fun showing him all her old haunts. Even although he was familiar with the city, there were places he had never been to before and it was gratifying to see the short holiday was doing him good; she knew he worked too hard, but during the last few days he had become less tense and more like the man she had married fifteen years ago.

After breakfast they had spent the remainder of the day by first shopping in the Pijp district; wandering through the Albert Cuypmarkt, reputed to be one of the busiest outdoor markets in Europe with over three hundred stalls, and then drinking mugs of hot chocolate in one of the surrounding cafés, the weather being warm enough to sit outside. They found a delightful sea-food restaurant in Waterlooplein Square and after a leisurely lunch of oysters on spinach with Mornay sauce washed down with a bottle of chilled Merlot, spent a couple of hours at The Rembrandt Museum.

'Have you had enough culture for today, Guy?' she asked him as they emerged from the museum and into the sunshine of the late afternoon.

'I would say so,' he laughed, taking her arm, 'I think it's time for an aperitif. Do you agree?'

'What do you think?' smiling up at him, 'It's been a lovely day; I felt like a tourist.' she added, realising it was exactly how she had felt; those earlier years, on looking back and remembering, seemed in many respects quite surreal.

They chose one of the bistros opposite to the Bloemenmarkt.

'Did you know,' Christine asked, 'that the Bloemenmarkt is the only floating market in the world?'

'No, I didn't,' he grinned, 'but if you say it is, my darling, it must be right.'

'You wouldn't be making fun of me, would you Guy Ford, because -'

' – no, no,' he interrupted, holding his hands up in mock surrender, 'although I can't help thinking it is rather a tall statement. The world is a big place and who's to say that somewhere, some small practically unknown country, doesn't have one?'

'Touché'

'Ah, here's the waiter; what would you like?'

'Something different this evening, I think;' she said, 'a campari and soda, please.'

'That sounds good; I'll have the same.'

'Guy,' she said slowly, once their drinks had arrived, 'I've been meaning to mention this to you; since Monday in fact.'

'Yes?'

'When we were in the hotel bar at lunchtime, there was a man sitting by the window close to where we were, but you may not have seen him; you had your back to him.'

'I did see him, Christine.'

'Oh.'

'Why do you ask?'

'Because he kept staring at you as if he knew you.'

'He knew me alright.'

'You never said anything, though.'

'It was a long time ago,' he said and she could tell by his grim expression that what he was going to say wasn't going to be pleasant, 'and I never expected to see him again. The memory isn't one I wished to be reminded of, but I suppose like all bad pennies they have a habit of turning up.'

'Are you going to tell me?'

'Of course, darling; I have nothing to hide from you.' taking a sip of his campari, 'It was twenty-five years ago and I was in Paris for my paper following up on a lead we'd received of a sighting of Lord Lucan. I went along to the bar where he had apparently been spotted and sure enough there was a man there who did look like him. He wasn't on his own as perhaps one might have expected him to be, but in conversation with the same person we saw here on Monday. Remember, Christine, I was an eager young reporter in those days, but that was no excuse for being so gullible as to pay him for what I thought at the time was authentic information.'

'Oh, dear,' she said sympathetically, 'and it wasn't?'

'Well,' he sighed, 'he was more clever than that; he said after the man had gone, that he had told him a few things about his past which agreed with what I already knew. For example, Lord Lucan's address in Belgravia; his three children; his wife's name, even her family. He also mentioned he had spent some time in California playing golf, racing power boats and generally swanning around. All of this is quite true, you know, Christine; it tied in exactly with Lord Lucan's background, but the man I saw that evening in the bar was not the missing earl.'

'How could you have been so sure he wasn't?'

'Because, after I'd given him some cash, he went and I stayed on and managed to get into conversation with the barman and he told me the man I was beginning to believe was Lord Lucan was a Frenchman and had lived on and off in the area for at least fifteen years. I had been well and truly duped; it wasn't a nice feeling, but it taught me a lesson. I was lucky in that my editor was a reasonable man and I didn't get the roasting I deserved.'

'Don't you think you're being a bit hard on yourself, Guy; it was over twenty years ago after all and as you said you were very young.'

'True, I suppose, but it has rankled all the same and seeing him again this week brought it all back to me.'

'They still haven't found Lord Lucan, though.' she prosaically pointed out.

'No, and it's unlikely anyone ever will. However,' he went on, 'there's something else.'

'Yes?'

'I saw him again on Monday.'

'Really, I'm surprised I didn't.'

'You weren't with me, that's why. After you had left to meet up with your old college friends that evening, I decided to walk along to the Krasnapolsky Hotel for a drink. Apart from being so unbelievably elegant in an old-fashioned way, they have an extremely comfortable bar; also it's perfect for people-watching. Anyway,' he went on, 'I had a couple of drinks and when I was walking down the front steps of the Krasnapolsky, who should be coming along the pavement but Anthony Johnson.'

'Anthony Johnson?' frowning.

'Sorry, that's what he'd told me his name was.'

'Oh, I see.'

'He was walking up from the warehouse quarter and as I reached the bottom step he became level with me. It was eye to eye contact, Christine, there was no way he could ignore me.'

'What happened next?'

'I suggested we go into the Krasnapolsky and have a talk. As you can imagine he wasn't keen, but, if nothing else, he is well-mannered and followed me meekly back into the bar.'

'Did he appear apologetic?'

'Not in the slightest; quite the reverse in fact. He had the audacity to say that he hadn't actually said that the man he'd been with was Lord Lucan, only that he knew all the gen about him.'

'Cool customer.'

'One way of describing him, I suppose. He's a conman, Christine. Anyway, I was too disgusted by his attitude; I didn't want to spend any more time in his company, so I left and went straight back to The Carlton.'

'Leaving him in the bar.'

'That's right. I turned round to take a last look at him when I reached the door and he had taken out his mobile and had started to dial. No doubt, up to more mischief.' he added wryly.

'Poor love,' she smiled gently, 'an unpleasant encounter. You should have told me before.'

'Perhaps, but it's history, really, Christine and hardly important now.'

'You're right. Shall we have another drink before we go back to the hotel?'

'Good idea.' beckoning over to the waiter.

'What you've just told me, Guy,' she said, 'has made me think. Perhaps you'll think this is crazy, but you know about the body of the man they found in the canal -'

'- I think I know what you're going to say,' he interrupted, 'you're wondering whether it was Anthony Johnson.'

'Is it a crazy notion?'

'No, I don't. It had also occurred to me. It did happen on Monday night and when I saw him he must have come from the warehouse quarter; there is nowhere else he could have been, is there?'

'No,' she agreed, 'and certainly not a part of the city for any tourist, besides,' she added, 'the lighting is practically non-existent in parts; there would be nothing for him to see.'

'You're right, of course. I have been along there although it was during the day and as you said this morning, not a pretty place.'

'Guy,' she asked, 'if it was Anthony Johnson, what will you do?'

'Professionally, you mean?'

'Well, yes, there could be a story in it.'

'How well you know me, darling,' he smiled, leaning across the table to kiss her lightly on the cheek, 'but we are supposed to be on holiday, remember.'

'I know.'

'First of all, I need to try and find out more about this drowning, if it was a drowning. They found the body on Tuesday morning, didn't they?'

'Yes.'

'Why the delay in reporting it? By rights, it should have been in yesterday's paper.'

'I don't know; perhaps it took them some time to find out who he was.'

'You could be right,' he agreed, 'I'll give my editor a ring when we get back to the hotel and get his agreement to cover any possible story. Unless someone isn't on to it already. The man was English after all, a tourist; therefore he may have had an address in England.'

'Why do you say may have?'

'I was thinking about Anthony Johnson; he told me back in Paris he'd been working in Nigeria for three years. How many Englishmen actually live in England, Christine?'

'That's an impossible question!'

Chapter Six

ENGLAND

Philip was back in London by the middle of the afternoon after his meeting with Pamela Smythe-Jones. He had telephoned through to Headquarters before leaving Taunton passing on the names of those expatriates she had given him and was gratified to find the results of a preliminary search already on his desk. Margaret and Terence Price, he read, were living in Winchester, their address and telephone number included in the report. William and Mary Richardson, now retired, had recently moved to Old Portsmouth. Harold Knight was back in Norwich working for the same bank he had been with before taking up the contract in Zambia. Luke and Martha Underwood were now divorced and had been for the last eight years, shortly after returning to England. So far, the office hadn't been able to locate her, but Luke Underwood lived in Guildford, but worked in London. It would give him something to go on he thought, making a note of the contact numbers and wondering whether any of them had kept in touch.

The internal phone rang as he was about to make the first call and picking up the receiver without any preamble he heard the gravelly voice of his superior.

'Can you spare a few minutes, Philip,' he said, 'something interesting has turned up.'

'Of course, Charles; I'm on my way.'

It took quite a lot to penetrate the habitual matter of fact manner of Charles Hastings which Philip recognised as a front he affected deliberately. He had a razor-sharp brain and had never been known to jump to conclusions or to pre-judge a person whether officers or someone they were treating as a suspect. He relied on hard facts and as far as Philip was aware didn't resort to hunches. However, he concluded, walking along the corridor to Charles' office, whatever he had to tell him must be something of importance, perhaps in connection with this current case.

'Ah, Philip,' he said as soon as he saw him, 'take a seat, won't you? As I said, this is interesting, also more than a little surprising, but I've just had a call from Hugh Bannister.'

'Yes?'

'New Scotland Yard had been contacted by the Criminal Investigation Department in Amsterdam last Friday. Apparently, earlier in the week, the body of a British male was dragged out of one of their canals, the Oudezijds Voorburgwal to be precise, and they hadn't been able to trace any next of kin. In a nutshell, Philip, the people in Amsterdam have passed the matter over to us.'

'The Criminal Investigation Department you say?'

'Yes, they have been treating the man's death as fairly low-key, no doubt not wanting to create ripples in their tourist trade.'

'I take it he didn't trip and fall into the canal?' Philip asked.

'No; he'd been stabbed before being pushed in. In the meantime, they've been trying to locate his next of kin, but without any success.'

'I see.'

'There was one contact name in his passport, but it would seem he doesn't exist. New Scotland Yard have, of course, done a double check and they were quite right. However,' Charles went on, 'here comes the intriguing part, Philip; the passport was in the name of Clive Edwards and had been renewed in 2005 and when this was processed it was noted that in the previous one there had been names of two next of kin. New Scotland Yard have been able to get in touch with them both, the brother and sister as it happens, and they have confirmed that Clive Edwards was murdered in a mugging while he was in Paris in October 2002. His passport was never found by the police, which indicates it may have been absorbed into the black market and presumably sold to someone who resembled the murdered man.'

'2002,' Philip said quickly, 'that was the year Anthony Johnson returned to England, followed practically immediately by him flying on to Paris.'

'Quite,' Charles said, 'and you know how much I dislike coincidences.'

'I know. It would be ironic though, wouldn't it,' Philip pointed out, 'that after fixing his accident out in Africa, that now, ten years later his life comes to an abrupt end?'

'It would indeed.' he agreed, 'I don't know whether this development, if we are right that is, will assist us in this case or not.'

'It could.' Philip said slowly, figuring out what this would mean. If Anthony Johnson had been using Clive Edwards' identity, whether he was now dead or not made no difference to their investigation; the case still remained unsolved with nothing so far to substantiate their suspicions. There were only two solid facts: Johnson had fixed the car crash and Norman Brookes had been murdered, both on the same night. 'All the more reason to speak to those who had also been there at the time,' he concluded, 'also, there's the question of identity, isn't there?'

'Which brings us to the one person who would be able to do that.'

'You mean Kate Johnson of course?'

'Yes, reluctant although I am to inflict this unpleasant task on to her, but perhaps we'll have no choice.'

'There are a few who could, Charles, but at this stage, I wouldn't be altogether confident about their honesty.'

'Ah,' he smiled, 'you made some headway today with Pamela Smythe-Jones.'

'Not much,' Philip admitted, 'she didn't tell me any more than we had learned already, although she did give me the names of those expatriate friends she and her late-husband had made. The office has managed to put together contact numbers for them and I intend to follow up on that as soon as I can.'

'What did you make of her?'

'Very aware of her social status, somewhat autocratic,' he said, remembering her scathing comments in respect to servants as she had labelled them, 'attractive,' he added, 'in a rather obvious way. Probably accustomed to getting her own way, I would say.'

'Too much money, Philip,' he said, shaking his head, 'I'm surprised she had anything to do with a man like Anthony Johnson; apart from already being married, he was hardly a financial catch and certainly not someone she would consider as her social equal. Strange that.

'Perhaps she was bored,' Philip suggested, the idea occurring to him for the first time, 'living out in Africa, a small predominantly mining town with a handful of other expatriates for company. On the other hand, Charles, she may have deliberately led him on.'

'Meaning?'

'Well, she was quick to re-marry and, according to the report we received from Hugh Bannister, 'she already knew Smythe-Jones prior to going out to Zambia.'

'I see, Philip; a clever hypothesis.'

'But that's all it can be.'

'Having met the woman, would you say she would have been capable of doing that?'

'In one word, yes. Her manner changed as soon as I started asking questions about Anthony Johnson; tried to tell me she hadn't realised his accident and her husband's murder had happened on the same night.'

'She must have known.'

'Yes, I agree, so we'll see how she fares when I next question her, which I will do once I've spoken to the others.'

'Returning to the question of the formal identification,' Charles said, 'this should really be carried out as early as possible.'

'Of course.'

'The body is being flown back to London late this afternoon which shouldn't pose a problem for Mrs Johnson, therefore, Philip, from what we've been saying, we'll have to ask the lady to do this for us.'

'I understand, Charles, of course. It's almost five now,' he said, glancing at his watch, 'she should be on her way home from work fairly soon. I think it's only fair for me to see her, rather than ask her over the phone. What do you say?'

***

'Kate, darling,' Steven said, taking both her hands and pulling her towards him, 'I would have given anything for you not to have gone through that.'

'It was grim, Steven, of course it was, but it was something I had to do. There was no-one else.' she added.

'You're a brave woman, Kate,' he said, kissing her, 'it couldn't have been easy for you.'

'No,' she smiled, leaning her head against his chest, 'and if you hadn't been there with me I don't know how I would have coped.'

She hadn't been exaggerating. Her reactions, and her feelings, from the moment the pathologist pulled back the sheet to reveal the face of the man she had been married to, had been weird. Anthony had died ten years ago and she had always believed this to be true, but today she had been told his death only occurred a week ago. She was finding this difficult to absorb. Becoming more certain each day that if it had been Anthony in the museum did nothing to lessen her impression of incredulity and she had needed Steven's solid presence to remind her that everything in her life was free from the frightening encroachment of disorder. Too much had been happening in such a short time: seeing Anthony that Saturday; hearing of Aunt Eileen's death and attending the funeral; gradually realising the extent of Anthony's unfaithfulness and now, learning he was being suspected of murder. Knowing she may have been married to a murderer was dire enough, but it was Dawn who really concerned her.

'I'll have to tell Dawn, won't I, Steven?'

'I think it would be best.' he agreed, 'From the way Philip Spencer was talking, it would seem there's a lot more to this case than what happened in Amsterdam.'

'Samriboi.' she sighed.

'Afraid so, darling. Both those cases have now been re-opened and it's probably only a matter of time before news leaks out about him changing his name. The press will have a field day in other words, Kate.'

'I know, and if Dawn should read about it, well –' hesitating for a fraction of a second, inwardly shuddering at the thought, '- it doesn't bear thinking about.'

'It won't come to that, darling,' he said gently, 'it's just a pity she isn't here in London. Suddenly Paris seems so far away.'

'You're right.'

'Listen, Dawn is a sensible and level-headed young woman and I believe a lot tougher than you think.'

'She's far more resilient than I am.'

'I wouldn't say that exactly,' he smiled, 'but perhaps fortunately for her, Dawn doesn't have your vivid imagination. Why don't you give her a call, it's not too late, and I'll open a bottle of wine.'

Kate dialled the number of the phone in Dawn's apartment in Paris and waited apprehensively, not having any idea of how she was going to explain. Steven had been absolutely right in the way he had described her. Growing up the way she had, Dawn had learned at a very early age how to be self-reliant; the years at boarding school had taught her that and then, later, spending more years away from home when she'd been at university had probably fine-tuned this side of her personality.

'Mum, this is a surprise.' Dawn said as soon as she heard her voice.

'I've been meaning to ring you since I came back from Scotland, but -' faltering and realising she was handling this badly, '- sorry, Dawn —'

'- Mum. What's wrong; is it Steven?'

'No, dear,' she answered quickly, 'Steven is fine and sends you his love. The main reason for phoning you is to tell you something we both think you should know.'

'Go on, Mum; I'm listening.'

'Well,' taking a deep breath, 'it's about your father, Dawn. Oh dear, I'm finding it so difficult to explain, but this evening I was asked by someone at the Foreign Office to identify the body of someone they believed to be him.'

'What a ghastly experience that must have been for you; no wonder you're so upset.'

Dawn's immediate response was not what she expected, but then she had hardly known Anthony and it was typical that her concern would be for her rather than asking the obvious question.

'Fortunately Steven was with me which helped enormously. Anyway, we're back home now, but we thought you should know.'

'I'm glad you did of course, but this is all a bit confusing. Have the authorities any idea of what happened all those years ago in Samriboi?'

'They're putting the pieces together and it appears he faked the accident and came back to Britain. Also, he had been using another name.'

'But why, Mum? Why did he do that? Make a new life for himself I mean. Perhaps he had another woman,' she suggested, 'although it does seem rather extreme. Did they say?'

'Philip Spencer didn't elaborate, but this could be because they don't really know yet. However, Dawn,' she said, 'there is something else.'

'Yes?'

'On the night of the crash, one of our friends in Samriboi was shot dead -'

'- and they think he did it.'

'I believe they do. I'm sorry to be so blunt, Dawn.'

'I did ask you though, didn't I? But you mustn't worry about me, Mum; it's you I'm concerned about. You are alright, aren't you?'

'I'm fine; just a bit dazed, that's all. You see,' she added, 'the other Saturday, the day before I heard about Aunt Eileen, I thought I saw him outside the British Museum. I thought at first he was just a man who happened to look like your father, but I've had time to think since then and had come to the conclusion it must have been. I mentioned this to Philip Spencer and I got the impression he agreed with me. At least he didn't dismiss it out of hand.'

'Some story.'

'And that brings me to the other reason for telling you all of this, Dawn; once the press get an inkling of what has been happening, that is exactly how they will treat it.'

'Does that worry you?'

'Strangely, not unduly. After all, I have nothing to say.'

'What does Steven think?'

'We haven't got round to talking about that aspect of the case yet, but I'm sure he'll agree with me.'

'Mum,' and she recognised the concern in her voice, 'don't let these reporters pester you.'

'I won't dear. I'll just say "no comment".'

'You've been watching too many movies.' and Kate knew she was smiling; her down-to-earth daughter and much older than her years, was trying to cheer her up.

***

'Mr Price,' Philip said, 'what I'm trying to do is, as far as possible, to recreate the evening when Norman Brookes was shot.'

Terry Price had shown no real surprise when he had phoned him in the morning. Wanting to keep these initial interviews informal, rather than asking him to call into one of the offices at Winchester Police Headquarters, he had suggested they meet in "The Old Vine" in Great Minster Street which was near to where Terry worked. Being lunchtime, the pub was busy, but they managed to find a table on the terrace and took their drinks out there.

'I don't quite understand.' Terry said slowly, frowning, 'I know you said on the phone the case had been re-opened, but the authorities in Samriboi led us to believe that Norman had been a victim of a local gang and nothing to do with the expat community.'

'We, at the Foreign Office, Mr Price,' Philip explained, 'have learned differently since then. New evidence now shows that Norman Brookes' murder had been premeditated and carried out by someone who knew him; therefore we have to start our enquiry from the beginning. We are, as you probably realise, hampered by the fact that not only did it happen ten years ago, but in a country some considerable distance from Britain.'

'Not an easy task, Mr Spencer.'

'I don't expect it to be,' Philip commented dryly, 'however, I'm confident that with diligence we will arrive at the truth and that's why anything you can remember specifically about that evening could well be helpful to us.'

'I see,' he nodded, 'well, all I can remember is that my wife and I were in the club where we went most evenings. Expats, as we were then, needed our own social meeting place. The same as your local here, I suppose.' he added.

'Were the usual crowd in there that evening?' Philip asked him.

'I think so,' he said thoughtfully, 'Peggy and I arrived around eight, perhaps eight-fifteen, I can't remember exactly. We would have had our meal at seven as we usually did and then driven along to the club shortly after we had eaten. The Richardsons were already there when we arrived, also Luke and Martha. Harry Knight came in a bit later; I think it was just after half past eight and followed shortly afterwards by Norman's wife.'

'Were they together?'

'Oh, no, Harry was on his own and so was Pamela, not that that was unusual,' he added, 'Norman preferred to spend his evenings during the week at home.'

'Did you talk to her?'

'No, I don't think we did. We joined Luke and Martha who were at the other end of the bar from her.'

'Was Anthony Johnson in the club that evening?'

'You know about him?' he asked, the frown returning, 'About his accident I mean.'

'We know of the car crashing into the ravine, yes.' Philip said, 'Also, that it happened on the same evening as Norman Brookes was shot.'

'None of us saw him in the club that evening, Mr Spencer, and later we heard that he hadn't returned home from work.'

'Was this common knowledge among you all, then?'

'Oh,' he chuckled, 'call it the African grapevine! There wasn't much that occurred in the town, especially concerning us, that the servants didn't know about.'

'I see,' Philip nodded, 'at least I think I do.'

'Anthony's servant was a brother of Silas; that was the name of our houseboy as they are more usually called in Zambia,' he explained, 'and when Anthony didn't turn up at the bungalow for his evening meal, or return home at all that night, his houseboy began to get concerned and mentioned it to Silas the following morning who, in turn, passed the information on to Peggy. We hardly needed a telephone out there!'

'It's our understanding,' Philip said, 'that the car wasn't discovered until two days later.'

'Yes, that's right,' he agreed, 'I heard in the afternoon as I was leaving work. A couple of local schoolboys were on their way back to their village which is about a couple of miles along that stretch of road past the ravine, and spotted it wedged halfway down the embankment. The pair of them promptly ran back to Samriboi in a state of great excitement to report what they'd seen.'

'By this time Norman Brookes would have been dead for two days,' Philip commented, 'did his wife hear about the car crash do you know?'

'She hadn't until I told her; you see, earlier on the Friday Norman's body had been airborne back to England and I mentioned the accident as I was driving her to the local airport to catch the night flight from Lusaka to London.'

'Did she appear upset by the news?'

'Not really, but I thought at the time she was probably still suffering from the shock of finding Norman the way she had.'

'Have you kept in touch with any of the people you've mentioned?'

'Only Luke. He's living in Guildford now, although he works in London and when we get the chance we meet and have a chat, mostly about the Samriboi days I might add.'

'And his wife?'

'He and Martha split up almost as soon as they returned to England. He doesn't mention her name very often which I suppose is only natural as he did tell me once that the divorce was fairly acrimonious.'

'Have you any idea where she's living now?'

'Sorry, I haven't; Luke never said.'

'I appreciate you taking the time to talk to me, Mr Price, especially during your lunch break. I'm beginning to get a clearer picture of what it must have been like, in particular, living in such a close community.'

'It's the least I can do,' Terry said, 'we all liked Norman.'

'I won't take up any more of your time,' Philip said, 'unless you'd like another beer?'

'No thanks, better not; I have a busy afternoon ahead of me. Mr Spencer,' he went on, 'there's something I'd like to ask you.'

'Yes?'

'Why have you been asking about Anthony Johnson?'

'Mainly because we don't like coincidences, or I should say, we don't trust them and when two people are reported as having been killed on the same night in a town in central Africa with a relatively small white population, we begin to ask questions. Also, last night I had confirmation from a reliable source that Anthony Johnson did not die in a car accident.'

'You mean -' stumbling to express himself, 'it was rigged?'

'It must have been, Mr Price. There is no other explanation because of this new evidence, which is irrefutable; Anthony Johnson made his way back to England and assumed another identity.'

'My God! That is incredible,' he gasped, automatically lowering his voice, 'but why? Why on earth did he do such an extraordinary thing?'

'That is what we have to find out. As far as these last ten years are concerned, his life had been a virtual blank.'

'*Had been*,' he emphasised, 'does this mean he's dead?'

'Yes, this happened in Amsterdam last week. Up to now, Mr Price,' Philip said quickly, having decided he had said enough for the time being, 'no mention of his death has been mentioned in the press, only, we understand, in the Dutch newspapers, but even and when it does, hopefully there will be no connection with Anthony Johnson.'

'Hopefully?'

'Yes,' Philip nodded, 'there is always the chance that some eager and over-zealous journalist may arrive at the truth. We can't prevent this happening, but we would prefer the space we have at the moment to continue conducting our investigation. We must also consider the privacy of Mrs Johnson.'

'Of course. Poor Kate, she doesn't deserve this sort of intrusion; she's been through enough already. I take it she does know?'

'She does, yes, but she hasn't been told the name Anthony Johnson had been using; that is something for the present we will be withholding.'

'I'm glad about that.'

'Incidentally, Mr Price,' Philip said, glancing at his watch; they had been there for almost an hour and it was time to bring the questioning to an end, 'and this is no doubt something you will arrive at yourself, which is, how he was able to get to the airport, presumably leaving Samriboi on the Wednesday night.'

'I see what you mean,' quickly picking up on his line of thought, 'well, either someone took him there or he drove there himself.'

'Did he have another car?'

'Not as far as I know.'

'Finally,' Philip asked, 'what time did you and your wife leave the club?'

'Around eleven-thirty; Luke and Martha left much earlier and then Harry joined us; this was after his snooker game with Bill Richardson. The Richardsons went soon after that and when we'd had another drink with Harry, the three of us left the club and drove back home at the same time.'

'You have a good memory.'

'Our evenings, Mr Spencer, especially during the week, were very much the same; it was only on Saturdays they were any different; some of us would eat in the restaurant and then there would be a bit of a dance. Sundays were quieter, although there was always a curry at lunchtimes which was inclined to carry on into the afternoon.'

'You describe very well what life must be like out there.'

'It did get a trifle monotonous, but then we had our leaves to look forward to when we would return to England and have a spell of normality.'

'I can imagine. You obviously saw a great deal of each other. Did you live in the same area?' he asked him.

'We did, yes; they were all bungalows, alright although somewhat mediocre in furnishing, not easy to give them an individual touch, if you know what I mean, although Peggy and the other wives did their best.'

'Were they near the centre of the town?'

'About a five minute drive away. If you have a piece of paper, Mr Spencer,' he suggested, 'I'll make a rough sketch of the residential quarter where the majority of expats lived.'

Philip tore a sheet from the notebook he always carried with him and watched as Terry quickly first drew the outline of the main Kitwe-Ndola road, with a narrower road leading off and into Samriboi.'

'No more than a mile,' Terry explained, 'this tarmac road didn't lead anywhere else; after it reached the centre of the town, it became a laterite one, with dozens of potholes, going on in the direction of the yacht club, which made a pleasant change from the club on a Sunday. This was a couple of miles from the centre of the town, a good part of the terrain being taken up by the copper mines, together with the administration section, plus squash courts, owned by the mine company. Beyond the mines were the townships, but,' he went on, 'the residential part started here,' drawing a line half the way along the last stretch of tarmac road, 'and on the right-hand side was where the bungalows began, in avenues like this,' making a horse-shoe shape and sketching in a handful of houses, 'the first bungalow you came to on the right, Mr Spencer,' he said, 'was where Norman and Pamela lived, Harry Knight had the second, followed by Bill and Mary Richardson's; Peggy and I were next door to them and on our other side, Luke and Martha; Anthony and Kate had the last one in the crescent.'

'This is going to prove a great help, I'm sure.' Philip thanked him, folding the sheet of paper and slipping it into his notebook.

'I have to say,' Terry said, 'it has made me feel quite nostalgic talking about the place, but,' he added philosophically, 'one can't remain isolated from real life indefinitely.'

***

Philip took his time driving on to Old Portsmouth to see the Richardsons. He had phoned them earlier in the day before leaving London and they assured him they would both be in at four that afternoon. Joining the M27 at the Chilworth roundabout outside Romsey, he stopped off at the first service station on the motorway for some coffee and a sandwich. He wanted to go over the content of the conversation he'd had with Terry Price, pick out the relevant points and collate his findings. He wasn't dissatisfied with what he had learned; Terry had been forthcoming and hadn't given the impression of holding anything back. So far, there was one glaring discrepancy in what Pamela Smythe-Jones had told him yesterday, taking out his notebook to check on what she had said in respect to when she had arrived at the club on that Wednesday night, flicking through the pages until he came to the right one:

"Norman and I," he'd written, "would have eaten early as we were in the habit of doing; about six-thirty, I think, and afterwards I went along to the club."

Terry Price had been quite precise about the time he and his wife had arrived there, adding that Harry Knight came in around half past eight and followed then by Norman's wife. Philip calculated that it would be unlikely she and her husband would have spent more than an hour over their meal which meant she should have arrived at the club by eight, but it must have been nearer to nine. It would be too easy to assume at this stage which he had no intention of doing, but it was an anomaly all the same and required checking out as thoroughly as possible. Presumably the Richardsons who had, according to Terry, already been in the club would be able to corroborate Pamela's arrival. It wasn't as though he doubted what Terry had told him, but he had to be certain before he next spoke to Pamela. Before then, he wanted to speak to the others and would be circumspect with his questioning to avoid giving any of them the impression he was concentrating on anyone in particular, primarily Norman Brookes' wife. He was not discounting the sharpness of Terry's intelligence, remembering the report Hugh Bannister had sent through to

Charles when the point had been made that the affair between Anthony Johnson and Pamela had been common knowledge among those expatriates in Samriboi. It would seem that neither of them had exercised any discretion, therefore Philip reasoned, it was more than likely Terry would reach the same conclusion that the woman was under suspicion. A little bit like walking on eggs, he thought, finishing his coffee and going back to the car.

Bill and Mary Richardson lived in Bath Square with the old Spice Island Inn as a neighbour and already at that time in the afternoon there were a number of customers sitting outside on the wooden benches enjoying a pint and making the most of the late afternoon sunshine. Bill Richardson was quick to introduce himself to Philip, gesturing expansively for him to come in.

'We'll go into the kitchen, Mr Spencer; as you can see,' he said, pointing to half a dozen packing cases in the hall, 'we are in the throes of moving into our new abode.'

'It's good of you to take the time to see me,' Philip answered, stepping over a pile of crumpled tissue paper.

'Not at all, not at all,' nimbly walking ahead and opening a door on the right, 'meet my wife, Mr Spencer;' adding somewhat unnecessarily, 'Mary, dear, this is Mr Philip Spencer from the Foreign Office.'

'I'm sorry about the mess,' she apologised, shaking hands, 'but I expect you know what it's like moving house, although this time, it is a great deal more challenging as we only arrived from Zambia a short time ago.'

'That's right,' her husband put in, 'I'm retired now, so theoretically, I should have more time on my hands.'

'I won't keep you for long,' Philip assured them and wondering whether he would make much headway with these two; talkative to the point of being unstoppable, 'but as I mentioned to you on the phone this morning, the Foreign Office have re-opened the case of Norman Brookes' murder and in order to substantiate certain facts which have now emerged, I need to talk to some of the people who knew him in Samriboi.'

'So, he wasn't shot by one of the locals, then?' Bill Richardson asked sharply.

'We don't believe he was.'

'Can't say I'm all that surprised,' he said, his eyes narrowing as he peered short-sightedly at Philip.

'Why do you say that, Mr Richardson?'

'Why do I say that,' he repeated, 'because the verdict was too pat, that's why. If it had been a local, the place would have been ransacked and anything of any value would have been taken, but according to Pamela nothing was missing, also the locks on the front and back door hadn't been forced. Norman would have made sure the doors were locked; we were all security-conscious out there, Mr Spencer. He could have known the killer, or whoever it was, could have had a key to the bungalow.'

'That's neat thinking,' Philip complimented him, 'but apparently his wife went out after their evening meal to the club; she may have forgotten to lock the door.'

'It's possible, I suppose,' he grudgingly admitted, but it was clear to Philip he didn't think so, 'but it seems more likely to me that Norman knew who it was.'

'Have you any suspicions of whom it may have been, Mr Spencer?' Mary Richardson asked, the keen intelligence equalling her husband's.

'These new investigations have only just commenced, Mrs Richardson; it's too early to suggest anyone specific.' Philip said, deliberately avoiding a direct answer and knowing he hadn't fooled either of them.

'We hope you find this person, Mr Spencer.' Bill Richardson said, 'We really do. He was a good man, Norman. Some might have described him as a bit of a stick-in-the-mud, but I didn't think of him in that way. He wasn't keen on too much socialising, although occasionally he would come along to the club for a drink and he always attended the Saturday night supper dances. He could be very amusing in his own quiet way.'

'A pity he didn't keep a closer eye on his wife, though,' Mary put in, 'giving her so much freedom –'

'– Mary,' Bill interrupted, 'there's no need to go into all of that.'

'There might be, Bill.' she retaliated, 'Dear me, what must you be thinking of me, Mr Spencer,' she said, turning again to Philip, 'I'm not usually so catty, but well -'

'Yes, Mrs Richardson?' Philip prompted. This further insight was exactly what he wanted to hear although he had a pretty good idea what she was leading up to, but it didn't matter.

'Oh,' she sighed, 'everybody knew what Pamela was like and I did warn her when she and Norman first arrived in Samriboi when I saw how attracted she was to that scoundrel and I wasn't the only woman either,' she went on, 'who tried to tell her how unwise she was in having anything to do with the man – '

' – Mary, please! The man's dead.'

'Anyway, it's true, Bill. You knew that; we all knew. Pamela wasn't the first woman who fell for his so-called charms. You see, Mr Spencer,' obviously determined to make her point, 'Bill and I were in Samriboi for well over twenty years. It wasn't all that unusual for some of the expatriates to have the odd little fling, but if they did, at least they made an attempt to be discreet. Not those two, oh, no. Anthony Johnson was attracted to a pretty face and there's no denying that Pamela wasn't a lovely looking woman, rather on the vampish side I have to say, but she was bored, Mr Spencer. She didn't have anything to occupy her during the time she was out there, but most of us made an effort. Also, Norman and she didn't have any family. I always thought that was a pity.'

'If we could go back to that Wednesday evening in the club.' Philip suggested, having made a mental note of her candid portrayal of the woman, also filling out what they had learned about Anthony Johnson's character.

'Of course,' Bill Richardson said, 'I'm sure you're not interested in tittle-tattle, of which I'm afraid we were all rather guilty.'

'You and your wife were in the club that evening?'

'Yes, we were, and being a Wednesday when Mary played Bridge with her friends in the afternoon, we ate in the restaurant,' he explained, 'nothing grand you understand, but we had an excellent chef; Chinese he was and we always looked forward to the ritual of our meal in the middle of the week, didn't we dear?'

'Bill is absolutely right, Mr Spencer,' smiling benignly at her husband, 'and that evening was no exception; the sweet and sour pork I remember was cooked to perfection and his Cantonese rice was the best I've ever tasted.'

'Sounds good,' Philip said politely, by this time becoming increasingly impatient with their nostalgic meanderings, trusting he could bring them both to the present, 'however, when you'd finished your meal, would I be right in saying you went into the bar, unless the club's restaurant was part of the bar area.'

'My goodness no, Mr Spencer;' he said quickly, his voice edged with righteous indignation, 'while our club facilities could never be compared with western standards, there was a certain old world colonial charm about it all. We had an excellent swimming pool; tennis and badminton courts; a recreation room where we men could enjoy a game of billiards or snooker and the restaurant adjoining also boasted a very good dance floor and, of course, the *pièce de résistance*, the bar; the hub of our social life and where we could relax at the end of the day and over the weekends. And,' he went on, pausing only to catch his breath, 'you were quite right, after our dinner we took our drinks with us into the bar. This was at eight o'clock,' he added, 'and why I remember that particularly is because Luke and Martha Underwood arrived exactly as the clock, an old British Railways one, I might add, was striking the hour.'

'Did you sit with Mr and Mrs Underwood?'

'Not that night, no; we got into conversation with a young couple who had recently arrived in Samriboi and later, we went over to talk to Pamela and Harry and when Pamela left I had a game of snooker with him.'

'Can you remember when Pamela Brookes arrived at the club?'

'Yes, I can as it happens; she came in about quarter to nine, but she didn't stay very long, only about an hour.'

'And Anthony Johnson?'

'No, he didn't turn up, but then, he wouldn't have done, would he?'

'Probably not.' Philip agreed, 'When did you last see him?'

'I don't think we saw him at all that week, it must have been the previous Saturday night, although he could have been there the next day. We gave the club a miss on the Sunday, didn't we dear?' turning to face his wife.

'That's right, but I saw him on the Wednesday, Mr Spencer,' she said, 'it must have been about six; we'd just finished playing bridge and I spotted him going into the bar.'

'Alone?'

'I think so; at least I didn't see anyone with him and by the time Bill had arrived and we went in there for a pre-dinner drink, he'd gone.'

'There is only one more thing I would like to ask you.'

'Yes?'

'The road where the accident happened, Mr Richardson, where does it lead?'

'Ah, you're wondering where he could have been off to, I suppose. Well, it carries on past the ravine and the first town is Ndola. It's just one long straight road, with nothing to break the monotony of the journey but the odd straggling village, otherwise it is just bush, with the rusty remains of crashed vehicles, minus their wheels and any other recyclable part the locals could make use of, lining the route as a grim reminder of what happens when one drives too fast.'

***

Luke Underwood had spent most of the afternoon in the conference room parrying with, in his jaundiced opinion, a barrage of irrelevant questions from his board of directors and not for the first time regretting his decision to work for a conglomerate the size of Heineman & Van Dijk, Importers, Exporters. Life had been simple in the Samriboi days, he grumbled to himself, clearing his desk of a pile of unanswered mail. He was on the point of switching off his computer when the phone rang.

'Yes, Jilly?' surprised she was still here. His secretary was not in the habit of working a minute after five unless on rare occasions.

91

'There's a call for you, Luke,' she said, 'a Mr Philip Spencer.'

'Philip Spencer?' he repeated, 'who's he?'

'He didn't say; so shall I put him through?' recognising the poorly disguised impatience in her voice.

'Alright, Jilly,' stifling a sigh of irritation, 'put him through.'

'I'm sorry to disturb you at work, Mr Underwood, but would it be possible to meet, possibly this evening?'

'I'm sorry, but –'

'– I'm from the Foreign Office,' he explained quickly, 'I didn't mention this to your secretary; I've found that when most people hear this, they generally jump to the wrong conclusions.'

'I see,' Luke said, but not seeing at all, 'and how can I help you, Mr Spencer?'

'We, at the Foreign Office have re-opened the case in respect to Norman Brookes' death in Africa ten years ago.'

'Norman Brookes? How extraordinary, after all this time.'

'We are trying to re-construct a picture of that night in particular and to do this we need to talk to as many people as possible who were living in Samriboi at the time.'

Little more was said before Philip Spencer brought the call to a close, arrangements having been made for them to meet at six-thirty in the "Sherlock Holmes", a five-minute walk from the office.

Taking the lift down to the ground floor Luke had mixed feelings about the forthcoming meeting; curiosity as to why the authorities were no longer satisfied with the verdict of Norman's murder, plus an inborn reluctance to uncover the past. Whenever he thought about him these days, which wasn't often, he remembered what else happened that night although Anthony's car hadn't been found until two days later and for the second time that week a second inquest was held. They had been so shocked by the news it was some days before any of them at the club had voiced an opinion about the coincidence of both tragedies. It had been Bill Richardson, Luke remembered, now walking round the corner into Northumberland Street. Bill, older than the rest of them and never slow to air his opinions had probably voiced what they'd all been thinking, recalling practically word for word the somewhat one-sided conversation: "Surely," Bill had said, "it has occurred to you all that there is something glaringly obvious here? First, Norman is shot, and then that fellow Johnson crashes his car;" he had gone on and on, relentlessly, giving no-one the chance to either agree or disagree with him, "it's like some damn stage-setting and an amateurish one at that!" Terry had been the only one to make any attempt to reason with him by reminding him that, although Anthony hadn't been all that well-liked, perhaps he was being wrong to jump to conclusions. But, Luke wondered, had there been more than a grain of truth in what Bill had said. Perhaps he was soon to find out, he thought, pushing open the door of the pub and going inside.

He had no preconceived idea of what Philip Spencer would look like. He had sounded quite young on the phone and probably didn't look much different to the other men standing at the bar; the regimental dark city suit and white shirt, with only the choice of tie to distinguish one from the other, but he need not have concerned himself as one of them who had been standing at the far end of the bar waved over in his direction.

'Luke Underwood.'

'How on earth did you work that out?' Luke smiled, shaking hands.

'Years of practice,' he grinned, 'but perhaps not so surprising; whenever a man goes into a pub, all he's interested in is going directly up to the bar for a drink, unless he's meeting someone and in your case, Mr Underwood, although you were looking for someone, it was apparent that whoever it may have been wasn't here.'

'I'm impressed.'

'Don't be; all part of the training.'

They found a free table and took their drinks over. An easy man to talk to, Luke thought, sitting down. He was still in his thirties, he reckoned, a good five or six younger than he was; about the same height, five-ten, and looked as though he worked out; all in all, Luke concluded, in pretty good shape.

'On that Wednesday night I understand you and your wife were having a drink in the club?'

'That's right, we were.'

'Can you remember what time you arrived and left, Mr Underwood?'

'We got there about eight I think. We didn't stay as long as we usually did; perhaps it was because it was the middle of the week with still two more working days when I had to be up ridiculously early each morning, I don't know, anyway we went home at ten.'

'I've already spoken to three of the people who were in Samriboi at the same time as you were, Mr Underwood.'

'I was wondering whether you might have done. Who were they?'

'Terry Price and Bill and Mary Richardson;' raising his glass to him, 'Mr Price told me that you and he have continued to keep in touch.'

'That's quite true; whenever we get the chance and when Terry manages to come to London.'

'I've already mentioned to you that we have re-opened the case regarding Norman Brooke, but we are also investigating Anthony Johnson's car crash on the same night and his subsequent disappearance.'

'What do you mean by disappearance? I realise his body was never found, but –'

'– sorry for sounding so cryptic; it wasn't intentional, but Anthony Johnson wasn't killed in Samriboi. Evidence has now emerged that he flew out from Lusaka on the Thursday morning and although he arrived in London, he flew on to Paris the following day. At this stage of our enquiry, there appears to be no record of what he'd been doing since then.'

'Good Lord!' Luke gasped, 'What a convoluted exercise, but he must have had help, Mr Spencer. He couldn't possibly have arranged all that without any.'

'Quite,' Philip nodded, 'and that is why our enquiry has to continue until we locate that person and get to the truth of the whole business.'

'So,' Luke said slowly, 'Bill Richardson was right.'

'In what way?'

'Well,' he explained, 'he always believed Norman's death and Anthony's accident were connected. He was quite adamant, actually. Said the verdict about Norman was too pat, that if it had been a local who had shot him, the bungalow would have been ransacked, that sort of thing. We tried to reason with him, but it was a waste of breath; mind you, Bill was like that and I don't think any of us took him all that seriously.'

'I got more or less the same impression when I was talking to him.' Philip remarked, 'Apparently, Anthony Johnson wasn't very popular.'

'The man's a womaniser, Mr Spencer. He could be very charming and quite a number of the women fell for that.' he added quietly, his lips tightening.

'Including your wife, Mr Underwood?' It was a long shot, but he was trying to move the conversation forward. So far, from the few he had talked to about the general set-up in Samriboi, an undercurrent was beginning to emerge and he had to get to the bottom of it.

'My ex-wife,' he corrected, 'but you're right; Martha was no exception, not that she ever admitted it, but she didn't have to. I knew she was having an affair with him, or perhaps more accurately, I knew when the relationship ended.'

'How did you know?'

'By her manner; I thought at first she was ill, but she wasn't. This was when he started his affair with Pamela. Norman and she had just arrived in Samriboi and it was obvious to most of us she was bored stiff and I think Anthony, being the type of man he is, homed into this pretty quickly, resulting in him finishing with Martha. There were other signs; I began to notice the way she would go out of her way to avoid his company, not easy in an environment as small as ours was. And, as far as Pamela was concerned, she didn't actually ignore her, which would have been impossible, but I don't remember the pair of them talking to each other. Not very pleasant.'

'I appreciate your frankness; it couldn't have been easy.'

'Expatriate life, Mr Spender.' shrugging dismissively.

'Have you an address for her?'

'I did have her London address, but after the divorce I understood she moved to Amsterdam.'

'We'll find her, Mr Underwood,' Philip said more confidently than he felt, 'but it's important to speak to her. Incidentally,' he added, 'do you know whether she went back to using her maiden name after the divorce?'

'I really have no idea, she may have done. In fact, I would say, she probably did.'

'Which is?'

'Jacobsen.'

'With an e?'

'Yes, her father was Dutch,' he explained, 'and rather ironic I always think when I'm now working for a group of Dutch companies, but I can assure you that is coincidental.'

'Was she brought up in Holland?'

'Yes, although her mother was English. This means she has always been able to speak both languages.'

'She may have re-married, but if she has we shouldn't have much difficulty in locating her.'

'You consider it sufficiently important to talk to her?'

'It could be. You see, this enquiry of ours, or double enquiry would better describe it, has now extended beyond Samriboi which theoretically should make things easier for us, but that remains to be seen.'

'Yes?'

'A few moments ago I mentioned Anthony Johnson's disappearance. When he reached Paris, he changed his identity and returned to England. We have still not filled in all of those ten years, but yesterday, we received a report from the Amsterdam authorities to say the body of a British male had been discovered and as they have been unable to locate any next of kin they passed the whole business over to us in London. Last evening,' Philip continued, conscious of Luke's heightened interest, 'the body was formally identified as Anthony Johnson.'

'How bizarre; how positively bizarre!'

'You could say that.'

'What an impossible task you have, Mr Spencer.'

'At times it does appear like that, but usually we get there in the end.'

'Amsterdam,' he said thoughtfully, 'I wonder what he was doing there?'

'It may have been something as simple and innocent as a holiday.'

'You don't think Martha is involved in any way, do you?'

'At this stage, I don't think anything. Quite frankly, Mr Underwood, I can't afford to; it's hard facts we deal with and a great deal of our work is sifting various pieces of information from anyone who knew the victims. At times, one hard slog, I'm afraid.'

'And I thought my job was stressful.'

'To me,' Philip smiled, 'it most certainly would be.'

Chapter Seven

AMSTERDAM
(The week before)

Guy got the go-ahead he wanted from his editor on the Friday morning. There had been no mention in the English newspapers of the death of any English tourist in Amsterdam, at least not so far, all of which gave him a head-start. He and Christine were due to fly back to England the following morning, but he reckoned a day should be long enough to do some ground work in sussing out anything he could, at least to establish how the man had died and with a bit of luck find out his name. Christine had mentioned at breakfast the fact that neither of them had seen Anthony Johnson around the hotel since Monday. It had been a valid point, but it could be he hadn't been staying in the same hotel. This was something else he should be able to find out.

It was only eleven-thirty and, as he had hoped, he was the only customer in the bar. The barman, whom he had learned was called Frederick, was giving the optics their morning polish when he walked in.

'Good morning, sir.'

'Good morning, Frederick; I'd like a Heineken, please.' and watched as he expertly poured it.

'Are you and your wife enjoying your stay in our beautiful city?' he asked, passing the glass over to him.

'We certainly are, but we'll be going back to London tomorrow. Both of us start work again on Monday.' Guy added.

'London,' he smiled, 'another beautiful city.'

'It is indeed,' Guy agreed, trying to veer the conversation to where he wanted it to be without giving him the impression he was no more than mildly interested in the death of an English tourist, 'however, sadly, there will be one less tourist returning to England.'

'Oh, yes,' he said quietly, 'you are referring to that poor man they pulled out of the Oudezijds Voorburgwal canal on Tuesday. Terrible. He was a guest, you know, sir.'

'Really?'

'He only arrived on Monday. Elspeth, one of our chambermaids, told me his room hadn't been slept in and as he was due to book out of the hotel on Tuesday, she immediately reported this to the housekeeper. We even had a police officer here, but he didn't stay long. Just long enough to collect Mr Edwards' possessions.'

'That's dreadful,' Guy said, 'Edwards you say?'

'Yes, that's right, sir; Clive Edwards he was called.'

'Oh, the paper didn't say.'

'No, I know. In fact, sir, you may remember seeing him.'

'Why?'

'Because he was in here on Monday, around lunchtime, when you and your wife were having a drink. A very smart gentleman he was; a cream linen jacket and a blue and white striped shirt. He was seated by that window over there.' he added, pointing to where Guy had seen Anthony Johnson.

Fortuitously, more customers arrived, bringing their brief, but productive, conversation to an end. Both he and Christine had been right; it had been Anthony Johnson. Why, he wondered, did he change his name and equally as important perhaps, when. Conversely, Guy reasoned, if he discovered when this had been, it may very well give him the reason.

Finishing off his lager, he left the bar, deciding the next step should be to go back to the Hotel Krasnapolsky.

He was in luck; the same barman who had been on duty before was there again. Guy ordered another Heineken, hoping he would be as forthcoming as Frederick. Why was it, he wondered, barmen the world over always seemed eager to have a chat and this one, Arnold, according to the badge on the lapel of his jacket, was no exception; he hardly needed any prompting.

'The gentleman you were with last week, sir; I've been puzzling over when I had last seen him. Mind you,' he went on quickly, 'this wasn't recently, it must have been more than ten years ago, but he used to come in here quite regularly back then. He never stayed in the hotel, I know that, but he often ate in our restaurant.'

'I knew Clive used to visit Amsterdam,' Guy fabricated, 'but he didn't mention he'd been in here before. I don't know him all that well, more of an acquaintance than a friend.'

'Did you say his name is Clive, sir?'

'That's right,' Guy nodded, 'Clive Edwards.'

'I think I must have been mistaken then; the gentleman I'm talking about wasn't called Clive Edwards; it was Anthony Johnson. He often used to settle his bill by credit card and I remember the name quite well.'

'Well, they say everyone has a double.' Guy commented. So, he thought, experiencing the first frisson of excitement which signalled the breaking of a story, I was right. Anthony did change his name. Somehow, he must find out more. Could be an even bigger story, he thought, his journalist's antenna on full alert and as it had done on Monday when he'd seen Anthony Johnson, remembering back to when he had first met him.

He had said very little about himself, only that he had recently returned from Nigeria and was having a holiday in Paris which presumably indicated he didn't live there, although when he had ordered a drink at the bar he had spoken in French; fluently, although with an English accent and Guy had thought at the time he probably originated from around the Cambridgeshire area. Not a great deal to go on, but it was a start and wondering whether he had stayed in England or moved back abroad and, if so, where. There was something missing here, but the more he puzzled over what it could be, the more elusive the memory became. It was when he had mentioned working overseas and then Guy remembered; he had asked him whether he planned to stay in Europe or was the pull of Africa too strong. "It probably will be," Anthony Johnson had laughed, "it is quite true what people say, you know, Africa does get in your blood. I've actually been offered another job out there, in Zambia this time, working for one of their copper mines, but I think I'll put it on hold for a while; see what turns up at home."

There wasn't a great deal more he could accomplish in Amsterdam, being hampered by not having the authority to glean information from any official authority, but then, he shrugged, what was new; Guy was accustomed to relying on any feedback from other sources, just as he had done with the two barmen. He had learned over the years how to phrase his questions without resorting to actually asking a direct one and very often, as it had done today, it paid off. There was a keen competitive edge to Guy's personality; he wanted to be first with this story and he didn't want to fall back on speculations and veiled innuendoes which in the end carried no substance; he needed proven facts to support what he was going to write. His editor expected nothing less; neither would any reader of the newspaper.

***

Christine spent most of the afternoon in the Magna Plaza shopping centre; an impressive old building behind Dam Square. As well as being a rarity for her, this shopping expedition was sheer indulgence. She knew only too well that once she was back home and involved in rehearsals, followed by what she hoped would be another long run at The Garrick, she would have little time for much else.

She bought a fine cashmere sweater for Guy in Pringles and in Gieves & Hawkes, a cream and navy striped silk tie, which she knew he would like. Perhaps like many men of his age, he was not over-keen on wandering around shops, having told her more than once that to him it seemed an aimless occupation and only became necessary when there was an item of clothing he specifically wanted to buy. She lingered for several minutes admiring a Stella McCartney creation; a two-piece in variegating shades of lilac, a mixture of lace and chiffon and staggeringly expensive, but decided it was not for her, preferring instead, the classic lines of Dior and Chanel.

By three she had reached saturation point; enough was enough, deciding to have a coffee before returning to the hotel. She remembered seeing a coffee shop next door to Pringles and retraced her steps, gratified to find there was a free table by the window and looking out on to the mall.

'Excuse me, but would you mind very much if I shared this table with you? It's terribly busy – Good Lord, Christine!'

'Martha, what a surprise.' suddenly recognising her; Martha Jacobsen, someone she hadn't seen for years. 'Do sit down,' she added, 'I've just ordered a coffee; would you like one?'

'I'd love one,' Martha smiled, placing an assortment of glossy carrier bags on the floor by her chair, 'shopping! It's so exhausting! Anyway,' she went on breathlessly, 'I didn't expect to see you here, in Amsterdam. I thought you lived in England now.'

'And I thought you did also, Martha. I'm trying to remember when we last saw each other, but I can't.'

'It was about six months before I got married,' she said, 'twenty years ago.'

'A long time ago.' Christine remarked and seeing no wedding ring reluctant to ask whether she had returned to Amsterdam or not.

'You haven't changed a bit, Christine,' she said, 'you always were so tactful, even at school. Not like me; many a ticking off I used to get for talking out of turn. Luke and I were divorced eight years ago and you were right, I did go to England, that's where I met Luke. We spent a couple of years there and then went out to Zambia to live; he had an accountancy job with one of the copper mines out there.'

'And now?'

'Well, after the divorce, I came back here, found myself a reasonably good job with a shipping company, all of which I must admit I don't regret and I certainly don't miss Samriboi.'

'Samriboi?'

'That's the name of the town where we lived,' she explained, 'it's on what is called the Copperbelt; a small town, rather like those in Wild West films. You know, wooden buildings with red corrugated tin roofs and verandas running along the length of them and, no doubt in the old days, some people who were rich enough to own a horse, would have tethered them to the posts while they went inside to make their purchases.'

'It sounds fascinating; very different to life in Europe.'

'How right you are; life in Samriboi, and in any other town where there are expatriates living, revolves around the clubs. I heard that years earlier these clubs were called European Clubs, but once the country gained its independence, that changed to Sports Club.'

'And don't you miss the friends you must have made while you were there?'

'Not really, Christine;' she answered, 'we're all inclined to be a transient breed. I think it must be because we know we'll only be out there for a relatively short period, at least most of us were, and it was not exactly conducive to making long-term friendships. Being foolish, I thought it would be different with Anthony, but I was wrong -'

' – I thought your husband was called Luke?' puzzled; she had forgotten Martha's habit of going off at a tangent. When they'd been schoolgirls she had found it amusing, but not now; it was merely irritating, wondering whether she did it on purpose.

'It was,' she said, 'but Anthony was someone I met in Samriboi and we had a bit of a fling. I was serious about our relationship, but it turned out he wasn't. As I said, I was foolish.'

'I don't know what to say.' embarrassed, not being accustomed to hearing confidences of such a personal nature.'

'There's nothing *to* say; 'it's all done and dusted now.' she sighed, 'But, Christine, what about you. I have been going on about my misdemeanours and I haven't asked what you've been doing.'

They spent the next half hour or so catching up with the intervening years, but apart from those early days, Christine was finding they didn't have a great deal in common and she couldn't help feeling slightly relieved when Martha said she had to go, something about catching up with some paperwork, but she didn't elaborate.

Guy was already there when she got back to the hotel and after she had taken her purchases to the room and freshened up, he suggested they have a walk to the same little bistro they were in the other day for a drink and, as then, talked about Anthony Johnson. When she had mentioned to him about bumping into Martha and what she'd had to say, his eyes instantly sparkled, the way they did when he was excited.

'Well, well, how extraordinary!' he gasped, 'And,' he added, 'what a stroke of luck.'

'Do you think the Anthony she mentioned could be the same Anthony?'

'Possibly, but it's a bit more than that;' he started to explain, 'what you've just told me, my love, is music to my ears.'

'It's a long time since I've seen you so animated.' she laughed.

'It bet it is, but it isn't often when luck, or pure chance if you like, turns up when you need it.'

'Meaning?'

'Sorry, Christine,' waiting until the waiter had placed their drinks on the table, 'but part of my brain is struggling to put today's findings in some sort of order and the other part, the impatient side, wants to formulate my piece for the paper. First of all,' he went on, raising his glass, 'I know that the body they pulled out of the canal was that of Anthony Johnson, also,' he added and she recognised again the controlled excitement in his voice, 'he was called Clive Edwards.'

'How did you find that out; it wasn't mentioned in the paper?'

'Frederick told me. Apparently, Anthony Johnson had been staying at The Carlton and Frederick had heard from a chambermaid about his room not being occupied on the Monday night, and as they knew he had booked in under the name of Clive Edwards, including the description Frederick gave me of him, was all the confirmation I needed.'

'So, Anthony Johnson must have changed his name.'

'It looks like it and the next step is to find out why.'

'How are you going to accomplish that, Guy? It sounds an impossible task.'

'Ten minutes ago, my love, that's what it seemed, but you've given me the lead I want. You see,' he continued quickly, 'and I don't want to jump to conclusions here, but when your friend, Martha, mentioned about having this fling with a guy called Anthony, little bells started to ring in my head. The fact that this boyfriend had been called Anthony wasn't sufficient, but there was something else somewhat more significant.'

'Yes? This sounds intriguing; was it something to do with the fact she mentioned Zambia?'

'It was, especially as when I first met him he told me he'd been offered a job in Zambia for one of the country's copper mines, but didn't intend to take it, but now, I'm beginning to wonder whether he did return to Africa. Surely it's far too much of a coincidence that Martha's husband worked on the Copperbelt and she had an affair with a man called Anthony?'

'Of course I agree with you, but I still don't see how you'll be able to take this further.'

'I'm going to try,' Guy smiled at her, 'and I have a gut feeling I'm going to succeed, Christine. After I'd finished talking to Frederick I walked along to the Hotel Krasnapolsky and, fortuitously, the same barman was on duty and he was remarkably forthcoming.' going on to explain how he recognised the man he was talking to on Monday night, but he had known him as Anthony Johnson.'

'Yes, go on.' admiring his logical train of thought. She could never be as rational; what a clever man she had married.

'Well,' he said, 'this affair, fling, or however you want to describe it, must have happened more than eight years ago. Anthony had spent some time here, according to the barman at the Krasnapolsky, calling himself Anthony Johnson. Therefore, if he was in Samriboi at the same time as Martha, something significant must have happened in his life around then and that is what I want to find out.'

'How?'

'First, contact Reuters and see what they come up with, if anything, and take it from there. I know a little about that part of Zambia, in particular the various towns on the Copperbelt. The expatriate community is relatively high in relation to other countries in central Africa, primarily because of the copper. From what Martha has told you, it would seem Samriboi, although a mining town is not large, unlike Kitwe, Ndola and others in that area, which should make my search easier.'

'I expect you can't wait to get back to London now?' she asked him, but not minding too much. They'd been here for a week; it felt time to go home and she, too, was going to be fully occupied preparing for the first rehearsals at the beginning of next week.

'How well you know me, my darling;' he grinned, not looking in the least shame-faced, 'now, let's decide where we're going to eat this evening.'

'Somewhere quite elegant;' she smiled, 'I bought a dress this afternoon, a Jasper Conran in fact, and I can't wait to wear it.'

'I thought you may have done. In that case, we'll book a table at The Ciel Bleu -'

' – The Ciel Bleu,' she interrupted, 'impressive!'

***

What Martha said to Christine about having some paperwork to do hadn't been the truth. She felt if she had stayed one moment longer in her company she would have said too much, wondering now, as she walked through to the end of the mall and into Dam Square, what Christine had thought of her being so outspoken about her relationship with Anthony. She didn't believe she would have even mentioned it if she hadn't seen him the other night, regretting now the impulse to call into the Krasnapolsky for a drink, but she'd been working late, preparing the documents for a large shipment due in at seven the following morning, and was reluctant to return to an empty apartment with only her confused and troubled memories for company. Normally, living on her own, which she had been since coming back to Amsterdam, was no problem to her, but she was still mentally reeling from the impact of seeing Anthony earlier when he had called into the office. He hadn't noticed her and not wanting to speak to him, she had walked back along the corridor towards her own office, but not before overhearing the receptionist say his name; not Anthony Johnson as she had expected, but Clive Edwards. She needed to have people around her; not necessarily to talk to, but to remind her she was not entirely isolated.

Martha had been about to go into the bar when she saw him for the second time that day. This is positively uncanny, she thought; twice in one day and after all this time. He hadn't been on his own, but was standing at the far end of the bar talking to someone; not one of Krasnapolsky's regular customers, otherwise she would have recognised him. She had returned to the lobby, positioning herself by the newsagent's kiosk from where she could still see him, wondering what she should do next. Unlike in the afternoon, she did want to talk to him; ask why he had gone to such extreme lengths to disappear.

She didn't have long to wait; within five minutes or so the man he'd been with had finished his drink and without any exchange of words between them, quickly turned on his heels and left the bar, passing her within inches of where she had been standing. This was what she had been waiting for and without hesitating she had replaced the magazine she had been holding and walked on into the bar.

She had remained in the open doorway for a second and for the first time for more than ten years looked at him properly. He hadn't changed all that much; he didn't even look older and wondering why she had ever been attracted to him. Who was the real man? The elegant smooth-talker she had once known or the one only a few feet away from her: a replica of his former self or the shady character who had taken on a different name, a new persona. He had seen her, but he made no sign of recognition, neither did he make any attempt to turn away; the cool, slightly amused expression on his face which at one time she had found irresistibly attractive, remaining as she had slowly walked up to him.

"Hello, Martha," he had said quietly, "this is a surprise. What are you doing here?"

"I would ask you the same question, Anthony, but I won't. Why all this – this charade?"

"Charade?" a quizzical lift of one eyebrow.

"Yes, charade;" she had repeated, "why go to such lengths, Anthony?"

"I felt at the time it was necessary."

"And now?" immediately picking up on the nuance.

"What do you mean?"

"I didn't come in here to play games, Anthony."

"Why did you then;" he'd asked, "you must have a reason? I trust you're not thinking of blackmailing me because if you are you'll be wasting your time."

"The thought never crossed my mind; I'm not the blackmailing type."

"Good," the smile not reaching his eyes, "and I'm not the type to be blackmailed. Now you are here, Martha, would you like a drink?"

"A white wine, please," waiting until he had ordered, "so," she had continued, "what happened between you and Pamela?"

"Pamela is history."

"You surprise me, you really do. Someone must have helped you that night and the only person I can think of is Pamela. Did she, Anthony?"

"You don't honestly think I'm going to answer that, do you? You can think whatever you like, Martha; it makes no difference to me."

"You always did have an answer. How long will it be, I wonder, when the authorities catch up with you?"

"Who's to say?" shrugging, "Where's Luke by the way? Still in Samriboi?"

"Luke and I are divorced and as to where he is, probably in England somewhere. Obviously we don't keep in touch."

"Obviously."

"You continue to amaze me, Anthony; here you are, putting on this act of nonchalance which all goes to prove that I never knew you at all."

"Probably not, Martha. Anyway, I'm leaving tomorrow and you can forget bumping into me; not that anyone would believe you if you did decide to mention you'd seen me this evening."

"Don't count on it, Anthony," she had said, "and remember, I don't owe you any favours."

"*Touché!*"

She hadn't stayed much longer, having no wish to pursue a useless one-sided conversation. There had been no point, and when she had said she was going, there had been no change in his expression, only perhaps one of mild amusement, as he watched her finishing her drink and turning her back on him.

Since that Monday he had been constantly on her mind, but maybe seeing Christine again and recalling how sympathetic she always was, had acted as the possible safety valve she needed. There was no-one else in whom she could confide, but all the same she had said enough. Poor Christine, she had looked really uncomfortable, feeling slightly guilty for attempting to share the hurt memories she had been carrying for so long. If she was an American, Martha thought cynically, she would have consulted her shrink years ago, although she knew it wasn't in her nature to divulge her innermost thoughts to a stranger or to anyone really. All she could sensibly do was to forget she had ever known Anthony and sure, trying to rationalise, the chances of ever seeing him again were remote.

Chapter Eight

ENGLAND

Guy Ford's piece in 'The Times' reached the news stands on Wednesday morning. Philip had been on his way to an early meeting at Headquarters with Charles Hastings to discuss the outcome of the previous day's discussions with the handful of people who had known Anthony Johnson, when the headline two-thirds of the way down the front page caught his attention:

"MURDERED MAN WAS IMPOSTER"

"When, over a week ago, the body of a British visitor to Amsterdam was dragged out of the Oudezijds Voorburgwal canal, the authorities, on checking through his travel documents, were able to name him as Clive Edwards, but new evidence has now come to light to discount this identification. The dead man had been Anthony Johnson who had, resulting in a car crash in Zambia some ten years previously, been declared officially dead although his body had never been found. This had been considered at the time to be a credible and acceptable deduction, given the wild terrain of where the 'accident' occurred.

"For ten years Anthony Johnson succeeded in avoiding being recognised and up to the present time it is understood that there is no valid explanation why he should have rigged the crash. It could be said there was certain relevance in the murder of Norman Brookes which occurred within the small expatriate community where Anthony Johnson had lived and on the same night, Norman Brookes' assailant remaining undetected.

"Understandably, the rumours surrounding what happened, not only in Africa, but more recently in Amsterdam, will be in abundance, although only hard provable facts can be put forward by this newspaper, together with straightforward questions requiring honest answers.

"It is hoped," the journalist had wound up, "that these questions will now be asked in an effort to solve this case before it falls into the annals of history, namely 'Unsolved Mysteries'."

'Well,' Charles said, 'I suppose it was only a matter of time before this leaked out.'

'He's done his homework,' Philip commented, 'but what I would like to know is how did he get on to the change of identity in the first place.'

'Who can say,' Charles smiled ruefully, 'the journalist's nose for anything newsworthy, plus chance, perhaps.'

'He's reliable though, Charles.'

'Guy Ford, you mean?'

'Yes, he's been in the business for a long time.'

'I know and as far as I'm aware he's never been known to fudge his facts. Also, he's never been known to use underhand tactics like some of them I could mention.'

'It's early days yet.'

'How right you are, Philip. Just wait, Fleet Street will grab this story and milk it for all it's worth.'

'It's Kate Johnson I feel sorry for.'

'Can't be helped,' he shrugged, 'although from what you were saying the other evening, she sounds the resilient type, also she has the support of her boyfriend, Steven Robertson. He won't put up with her being badgered by the press. Meanwhile, let's get on, Philip; how much were you able to glean yesterday?'

'A couple of discrepancies came to light concerning what Pamela Smythe-Jones had told me when I saw her on Monday,' starting to explain, 'and these were in respect to timing.'

'Ah;' leaning forward in his chair, a look of eager expectancy on his face, 'are you going to tell me the lady had been lying?'

'It would seem so; both Terry Price and the Richardsons said she had arrived at the club on the Wednesday evening around eight forty-five and she had made a point of telling me that she had left for the club as soon as she and her husband had finished their meal, also that they always ate early, about six-thirty. Assuming they wouldn't have taken much more than half an hour over their meal, and the drive to the club was apparently only minutes away, there is a space of time here unaccounted for.'

'At least an hour and a half.' Charles put in quickly.

'That's right and equally importantly; it's possible there is an even more significant space of time later that night although we don't have the actual time she phoned the police. All she told me was that it had been late, definitely well past midnight. That may in fact be true, but according to Bill and Mary Richardson, she only stayed at the club for an hour.'

'So,' Charles said, 'how long are we talking about; two and a half hours, three?'

'It sounds like it, yes. You're thinking about Johnson being able to get from Samriboi to Lusaka, aren't you?'

'I was, but she couldn't have got there and back in that time, could she?'

'No,' Philip said, doing a quick mental calculation, 'but she could have taken him halfway. We know he took the eight o'clock flight out on the Thursday morning; he would have had to spend the night somewhere.'

'Kabwe, maybe,' Charles suggested, 'that's the only place of any note along the route and he would have had no problem in reaching the airport the following morning, either by taxi or hiring a car from whichever hotel he spent the night. It's all circumstantial of course, Philip, but we have to start somewhere; the main problem being it happened such a long time ago and made even more difficult by distance.'

'The undisputed fact does remain, though; Johnson couldn't have achieved what he did on his own, right from the moment he rigged the accident and reached the relative security of somewhere within easy access to Lusaka Airport. It wouldn't have been possible.'

'I know and she is the obvious choice, but it still isn't enough, is it?'

'Not yet, but it does give me a little more ammunition when I see her again.'

'That should be interesting,' Charles smiled, 'and then we'll just see how smart she is. She's bound to trip up at some stage. They invariably do.'

'You're quite right and usually it's because they say too much, but before I get in touch with her, Charles, there is something else I would like to check out.'

'Yes?'

'I managed to meet up with Luke Underwood when I got back to London yesterday. He was quite frank with me, actually; this was when we began talking about his ex-wife. Apparently, she also had been having an affair with Johnson -'

' – busy chap.'

'Exactly. Well, this was before he started his relationship with Pamela Smythe-Jones and from what Luke was saying it would seem as soon as she came on the scene Johnson was quick to ditch Martha Underwood. Also,' Philip added, 'she took it quite hard and interestingly, after the divorce, he thought she had returned to Amsterdam where she had been brought up.'

'Amsterdam.' a frown appearing on his forehead, 'I don't like the sound of that.'

'Neither do I.' Philip admitted, 'It's perhaps rather a long shot, but on the other hand it might not be and this is why I think I should fly over there as soon as possible and try to find out more about what happened to Johnson. Up to now, we don't have any motive for his murder.'

'You think we may have a potential suspect?'

'A woman scorned, you mean?'

'Stranger things have happened, Philip, not that you need me to tell you that.'

'I feel it's time this Samriboi case started to make some sort of sense and whether Johnson's death has any connection remains to be seen.'

'When are you thinking of going?'

'The sooner the better, Charles; I'll try and get a flight sometime this afternoon.'

'That's fine by me,' he agreed, 'and with this latest development,' pointing to the newspaper on his desk, 'it could make a few people a trifle edgy, which is not altogether a bad thing. By the way, I haven't mentioned this to you yet, but the Amsterdam authorities sent through Johnson's travel documents and a few other items he had left in his hotel room.'

'Anything of interest?'

'I don't know,' he answered slowly, deliberately, 'there might be. I have them here.' he added, taking out a manila envelope from his desk drawer and handing it over to him.

Philip spread out the contents in front of him. As Charles had said, there were only a few other items apart from the passport: his flight ticket from Heathrow to Amsterdam for Monday, the seventeenth, an ongoing flight to Hong Kong the following day and a return to Heathrow three days later, including in a separate envelope, another flight on the same day to Singapore and with a return to Heathrow on Sunday the 23rd. There was his wallet, containing twenty-odd euros and fifteen pounds sterling; two credit cards: a Barclays Visa and a HSBC Gold, and a photograph of a young auburn-haired woman.

'His wife, Philip?' Charles asked, watching as he picked up the snapshot to have a closer look.

'No, it's not Kate Johnson,' he said, 'neither is it Pamela Smythe-Jones.' not knowing whether to be disappointed or not; it was too much to hope that he had kept any photograph of an ex-lover, especially prior to the time he left Samriboi. Lucky breaks only happened infrequently, he thought cynically, putting the photograph back into the wallet.

'It could be Martha Underwood, although probably unlikely considering the circumstances of that particular relationship. No doubt the man had a number of girlfriends.'

'It sounds as though he did,' Philip nodded, picking up the last item on the desk, 'an address book. Is this what you thought might be interesting, Charles,' he asked, thumbing through the pages.

'It could be. As you can see there aren't many entries. In fact, I wonder why he bothered to keep it; it's for the year 2003.'

'People do out of character things sometimes, don't they. Johnson didn't strike me as the sort of man to be sentimental. Probably quite the reverse.' he said, attempting to rationalise; perhaps this was intentional if he had wanted to rid himself of any reference to his old self. Therefore, Philip frowned, why keep the photograph. He took it out of the wallet again, trying this time to work out just how long he must have had it. It was only a head and shoulders one, but he could tell by the style of jacket the woman was wearing it dated back at least twenty years, if the padded shoulders were anything to go by. It was always possible he hadn't even known her, using it merely as a prop to support his acquired identity. He continued to look through the address book, wondering whether any of the names entered could mean anything relevant to their investigation, but it was impossible at this stage to tell. He was about to close the book when the business card slipped out, falling on to the floor.

'Did you see this, Charles?' he asked, bending down to pick it up.

'No, I didn't.'

'Now, here we may have something,' Philip said, curbing a tiny tingle of excitement and one he was familiar with whenever a likely breakthrough occurred, 'Bakker & Bakker, Shippers and Distributors,' he read out loud, 'Vijzelstraat, Amsterdam. Only the telephone number and the names of the two directors,' Philip said, 'but just a minute, one of them, Lenny Yeung he's called.'

'Yes? Obviously Chinese.'

'Sounds like it, but, Charles, Johnson had written his name in the address book, 'flicking through the pages again until he found the one he was looking for, 'yes, here it is: Lenny Yeung, Apartment thirty-three, Garden Road, Mid Levels, Hong Kong, no telephone number though, but there's a pencilled note in the margin.' screwing up his eyes to read what was no more than a scribble, 'I can just about make it out, there's a date; Saturday fifteenth, followed by H. Russell one o'clock.'

'That must be the Hotel Russell.' Charles said immediately.

'Of course. Do you know, Charles, I believe this is what we've been looking for; what I mean is a link up with what Johnson may have been up to.'

'You could be right;' he said, this time with a broad smile on his face, 'it all comes to he who waits, eh, Philip?'

'I hope we are working along the right lines, but Kate Johnson told me she had seen him outside the British Museum on that day and it is literally only a stone's throw away from the Hotel Russell. What do you think he'd been doing hanging about there?'

'Could have been too early for his appointment with this Lenny Yeung and felt like a spot of culture. What do you think, Philip?'

'I believe that is very possible,' Philip smiled, sharing his elation, and for the first time since the re-opening of this case, beginning to think they were getting somewhere, 'at last we may have found something tangible to follow up on.'

'Right,' Charles said, getting to his feet, 'I suggest you make your travel arrangements, Philip and meanwhile I'll put some feelers out in respect to Lenny Yeung, the Hotel Russell being the starting point. Also, I'll get in touch with Immigration about Martha Underwood -'

' – Luke seemed to think she would have reverted to her maiden name, by the way, which is Jacobsen.'

'Fine, Philip, that's all we need and hopefully by the time you arrive in Amsterdam I'll have something definite for you. We may be lucky that she is indeed living in Amsterdam, but if not, somehow I don't think your visit there will be wasted.'

***

AMSTERDAM

Philip arrived at Schipol Airport at five-thirty and Charles' call came through to him as he was waiting at the carousel for his bag to arrive.

'Good flight, Philip?'

'Yes, thanks. I'm just waiting for my baggage to make its appearance.'

'I won't stay on the line for long, then,' he said, 'I've got the feedback we wanted, although it did take a little longer than I expected, but Lenny Yeung did stay in the Hotel Russell on the night of Saturday the fifteenth and one of the waiters, with a remarkable talent for remembering faces, recalled seeing one of their guests, namely, Mr Yeung from Hong Kong, having a drink in the bar with a man closely resembling Johnson. And,' he went on, scarcely taking a breath, 'in respect to Martha Underwood, or I should say Martha Jacobsen, I received confirmation less than hour ago that she is indeed living in Amsterdam and has been for the past eight years. We have her address, Philip and telephone number which I'll give you, but even more interesting, we know where she's working.'

'This is excellent,' Philip said at the same time spotting his bag emerging from the rubber flap at the end of the carousel, 'why is it I'm getting the impression there is more to come?'

'Astute as ever,' Charles Hastings laughed, 'and you're not wrong. She's working for a shipping company called Bakker & Bakker.'

'Brilliant, Charles,' leaning over to drag his bag from the conveyor belt, 'this has given me quite a bit to work on.'

'I know, Philip. Anyway, I'll ring off now. If there is anything else at this end I'll give you a ring and meanwhile I'll be interested to hear what transpires with you over the next couple of days.'

Within twenty minutes Philip had booked into his hotel, intentionally deciding on The Carlton which he'd reckoned would be the base for his initial enquiries, although from what he had learned from Charles meant he could more or less immediately extend these enquiries, far more than either of them had envisaged less than a few hours ago when it had felt they were literally going round in ever-decreasing circles and getting nowhere. It was already almost seven, too late to make any positive start, but he could at least formulate a plan of how he was going to proceed from tomorrow morning onwards, although he had already decided as soon as he had finished talking to Charles what his first priority would be which was to contact Martha Jacobsen.

Philip dialled the number Charles had given him for her shortly after eight the following morning, trusting that she wouldn't have left for work, but after a couple of rings she answered. There was only a trace of a Flemish accent in her voice which surprised him slightly, especially as she had been living in her homeland for the past eight years.

'I apologise for phoning you so early, Mrs Jacobsen -' he started to say before she interrupted him indignantly.

'- it's *Miss* Jacobsen, actually;' she emphasised sharply, 'but you have me at a disadvantage. I don't believe I know you.'

'I was about to introduce myself;' he responded; he, too, could be equally as sharp, being reminded for a fleeting second of Pamela Smythe-Jones' frosty reception, 'my name is Philip Spencer,' he went on, 'from the Foreign Office in London.'

'Foreign Office;' she repeated, 'why on earth are they getting in touch with me?'

'Rather than go into any lengthy explanation over the phone,' he said, 'I would like us to meet sometime today.'

'I do work, you know!'

'I realise that, Miss Jacobsen, but what I would like to discuss with you is a matter of some importance. I am only in Amsterdam for a few days, primarily to further our enquiries into the murder of Norman Brookes whom I believe you once knew and to do this as thoroughly as we can, it is crucial I contact anyone who was living in Samriboi at the time of his death. At this stage,' Philip added, 'this is a matter of routine, you understand.'

'I see,' she said quietly, 'but after all this time; it all sounds very mysterious, Mr Spencer. However,' she carried on grudgingly, 'I suppose I could meet you during my lunch break, but it would have to be somewhere near my office; I do have an extremely heavy workload, also a demanding boss.'

He arranged to meet her at the "La Tosca Brasserie" at twelve-thirty, a two-minute walk from the offices of Bakker & Bakker. After he'd had breakfast he was able to see the Carlton's manager, Walter G Smit, according to the brass plaque on the door to the left of the reception desk.

'This is a surprise, Mr Spencer,' he said, glancing at the card Philip had given him, 'and you say you are here in connection with the death of one of our guests?'

'Yes, Monsieur,' Philip nodded, matching the manager's cordial manner, 'while we, at the Foreign Office, realise that Mr Edwards didn't die in the hotel, nonetheless, we have to make an endeavour to retrace the man's movements during that day.'

'I still don't see how any of our staff can assist you,' he said, peering short-sightedly at him through rimless spectacles, 'but naturally, we'll do our best.'

'Thank you.' wondering whether this conversation was going to get anywhere. Monsieur G Smit's whole demeanour was the epitome of a practiced stiff protocol which gave nothing away; rather like penetrating the proverbial brick wall. 'Did you happen to see Mr Edwards when he was here?'

'I may have seen the gentleman walking through reception, but of course I wouldn't have known who he was. I manage a large hotel, Monsieur Spencer,' he explained pompously, 'and it is impossible for me to know and remember any of our guests who are staying here.'

'Of course, I understand; except perhaps, Monsieur, if they were regular visitors?'

'I see what you mean, but I don't recall ever having heard the name before and,' he added, 'I pride myself in having a good memory.'

'You are fortunate,' complimenting him, 'if I were to mention the name of someone we believe had been staying in your hotel on more than one occasion, you may very well remember.'

'It is possible.'

'He was called Anthony Johnson, Monsieur.'

'Johnson. Johnson.' he repeated, 'I must admit it does sound familiar and I believe I do remember him. It was a long time ago, though, but yes, a Monsieur Anthony Johnson did stay here a number of times.'

'You say it was some time ago,' Philip prompted, surprised his little ploy had paid off. This could go towards filling in those missing years in Johnson's background, 'can you remember just how long?'

'Well –' obviously making an effort to remember, also to prove his infallible memory, Philip thought cynically, 'it must have been at least twenty-five years ago, Monsieur,' he said at last, 'it couldn't have been more than that, because I didn't take up my position as manager until

1987, the first of February to be precise.'

'That is quite a while ago,' Philip commented, 'what about your restaurant and bar staff, Monsieur Smit; have they also been here for as long as you have?'

'Dear me, no.' without any hesitation this time.

'You've been extremely helpful.' Philip thanked him. What he had discovered may or may not be significant, although it could help to explain perhaps why Johnson had come back to Amsterdam, also the type of work he had been doing. His had been an accountancy background, Philip recalled, which didn't necessarily mean he'd followed the same career path once he had returned from Zambia. There was an idea formulating in his mind what this may have been, but first he wanted to speak to Martha Jacobsen.

The "La Tosca" was beginning to fill up with lunchtime customers, but he was able to find a table in an area for those who only wanted a drink and facing the open door. There were no women sitting on their own, therefore it would seem he had reached the brasserie before her. Having no idea of what she would look like, but deciding he would use the same deductions as he had with Luke Underwood on Tuesday. As it happened, he didn't need to; the woman walking swiftly and unhesitatingly towards him, beat him to it.

'Hello,' she said, 'you *are* Philip Spencer?'

'A good guess;' he said, 'won't you sit down?'

'Oh, I wasn't guessing,' she said, pulling out the chair opposite, 'I live in Amsterdam, remember, and most of the customers come in here each lunchtime, unless they're tourists, of course, but you don't look like one. Besides,' she went on, 'you are the only man on his own I hadn't seen before.'

'Would you like a drink, Miss Jacobsen?' he asked, slightly disconcerted by her manner and wondering whether she had always been so brash and forthright, recalling how Luke had described their divorce.

'I'd like a Chardonnay; well chilled.'

'I will come straight to the point,' Philip said when their drinks had arrived, 'I realise you haven't much time.'

'I wish you would.'

'I would like you to think back to the day Norman Brookes was shot; I understand you were in the club that evening.'

'We used to go to the club every evening,' she said quickly, 'but I suppose you know that already. You've been talking to Luke, haven't you?'

'Yes, also to some of your friends who were living in Samriboi at the same time.'

'And what did Luke tell you, Mr Spencer?'

'Only what everyone else has said, Miss Jacobsen,' he answered, deciding for the moment to go along with the way she apparently wanted the conversation to go, 'the various times people arrived in the club, also -' deliberately pausing, giving her the chance to interrupt.

'- also what?' her head tilted to one side, 'That Anthony Johnson was killed in a car crash on the same night?'

'We were already aware of that.'

'Oh.'

'You sound surprised.'

'I suppose I am. Anyway,' she went on, 'there's something I don't understand here; why, after all this time, are you questioning what happened to Norman? Everyone knew it was one of the local gangs who killed him.'

'Not everyone, Miss Jacobsen.'

'What do you mean?'

'One or two of the people I've spoken to recently stressed they didn't believe the verdict.'

'Well, that's their prerogative.' shrugging dismissively, 'Is this why you've re-opened the case?'

'No, we have received strong evidence to support that Norman Brookes was shot by someone he knew.'

'I can't think who that could have been.'

'That is precisely what we have to find out;' he told her, 'now, if we could go back again to that evening.'

'Very well.'

'We have already learned that Anthony Johnson hadn't been in the club that evening, although he had been in earlier.'

'How do you know that?' for a fraction of a second the colour draining from her cheeks, but long enough for him to work out why.

'Anthony Johnson was seen going into the bar about six that evening. Was he meeting you, Miss Jacobsen?'

'Yes.' sighing deeply, 'I expect Luke told you I had been having an affair with Anthony,' but not waiting for him to answer before going on, 'mind you, we were always very discreet; besides it didn't last long. As soon as Pamela Brookes arrived in Samriboi he quickly decided to move on to someone else, but I expect you know about their affair. Neither of them were in the least circumspect, as they should have been of course, but Pamela isn't like that.'

'You say your relationship with him was over,' Philip reminded her, 'therefore what was the reason for seeing him again?'

'That's a little difficult to answer, actually.' she said, faltering for the first time, 'It was a ridiculous idea of mine, but you see I was crazy about the man and I knew the Brookes would be leaving Samriboi soon and I thought Anthony would then forget her and we could have picked up from where we had left off. It wasn't too sensible, but you know, Mr Spencer, living in Africa is a weird experience for us westerners, especially the women: not enough to occupy ourselves with; no job; no housework; even if we had children they were soon packed off to boarding school; too much sun; too much to drink. Oh, the list is endless.

'And was that the last time you saw Anthony Johnson?'

'Yes.' she said, lowering her voice. She had taken so long to answer; he had been beginning to think she hadn't heard the question.

'You're sure?'

'Oh, dear, you're putting me in a very awkward position, Mr Spencer. The last thing I want is to be considered spiteful, or vindictive either if it comes to that, but I did see him again.'

'Here, in Amsterdam?'

'Yes,' sighing again and taking a deep breath before continuing, 'it was a week past Monday. He called into the office where I work, although he didn't see me, and again at night; I'd been working late and had decided to have a drink in the Hotel Krasnapolsky before going home; the hotel is quite close to my apartment and seeing him again and realising he must have faked the accident in Samriboi had upset me. I needed some time to get my thoughts together. Anyway,' speaking more quickly now as though anxious to come to the end of what she had to say, 'he was in there, in the bar, talking to a man standing next to him. By this time, I had decided to confront him and ask why he had planned his disappearance, so I waited in the hope that whoever he was with would leave before him.'

'Did you recognise the man, Miss Jacobsen?'

'No, I had never seen him before.'

'Could you give me a description of him, perhaps; height, hair colour, age, that sort of thing?'

'He was about your height; dark brown hair, cut short; a chiselled jaw and a high forehead, a bit like Harrison Ford. As to age, that's hard to say, but perhaps in his late forties. Why do you want to know?'

'As you say,' sidestepping a direct answer, 'Anthony Johnson didn't die in the car accident, which means we have to find out where he's been for the last ten years, any friends or associates he may have, also what sort of work he's been doing.'

'He's an accountant, like Luke, but then you probably knew that also.'

'Yes, we did.' realising she didn't know that Johnson was dead and he had no intention of enlightening her. No doubt, if the media had anything to do with the latest news, it would only be a matter of time before it reached the European newspapers.

***

There were only a few customers in the bar in the Krasnapolsky which suited Philip fine; he wanted to have a word with the barman, hoping he would be the same one who was on duty when Johnson had been in there. He ordered a lager and remained at the bar, waiting until the barman had dealt with a couple who had just come in, before saying anything further.

'I'm from the Foreign Office in London,' Philip told him, 'and the reason I'm in Amsterdam is to make a few enquiries regarding the murder of a British subject called Clive Edwards.'

'I read about it last week in *Der Telegraaf*, although they didn't give his name.'

'No, they wouldn't have,' Philip said, 'that was likely because his next of kin hadn't been informed.'

'Oh, I see.'

'I understand Mr Edwards was in here on the night he was killed, this was a week ago last Monday.'

'Well – well, yes, he was.'

'You sound doubtful.'

'I'm more puzzled than anything else, sir,' he said, frowning, 'and we must be talking about the same man, but you mentioning his name reminded me of a gentleman who came in here for a drink last Friday. He had been in before, on the Monday night, and as I was sure I recognised the person he had been talking to as having been, at one time, one of our regular customers called Anthony Johnson, I mentioned this to him, but he said I must have been mistaken as his friend was Clive Edwards, not Anthony Johnson.'

'Can you describe the man you've just mentioned to me?'

'He had dark hair, tall, almost six foot I would have said and probably in his late forties or very early fifties. I'm sorry, sir, not much of a description.'

'On the contrary,' assuring him, 'it matches very well the one I heard earlier today. By the way, did you happen to notice when Mr Edwards left here on the Monday?'

'As to the exact time, I couldn't; we started to get busy as the evening wore on, but it must have been about nine o'clock; a good half hour after Miss Jacobsen went. She's one of our regular customers and she'd been having a drink with him; this was after the other man had gone.' he added, all of which tied in with what Martha Jacobsen had told him. It didn't look as though he was going to gain a great deal more, but between the time Johnson left the Krasnapolsky and ended up in the canal, he must have met someone. Philip was finding it hard to accept that Johnson had been a victim of a mugging which had gone out of control. That would be an easy solution and he firmly believed there was considerably more to Johnson's death than that. The man he had been talking to in the bar may have been waiting for him outside; a possibility, but he needed to delve deeper. The main question he felt lay behind the reason why Johnson should have been in Amsterdam. Surely not merely to call into Bakker & Bakker and speak to someone there; something that couldn't as easily have been said over the phone or emailed to them. The obvious deduction being he was delivering or collecting something of such a delicate or sensitive nature it had needed a courier which led him back to that germ of an idea he'd had since arriving in Amsterdam. Was that what Johnson had been doing for the last ten years under the name of Clive Edwards; acting as a courier? Always on the move. No permanent address, at least so far they hadn't been able to trace one. And perhaps the crucial question was how legitimate had his work been? Johnson had been crooked, very likely a murderer; there wasn't much further he could have gone down the slippery path.

After leaving the Krasnapolsky, Philip made his way back to the hotel, but before going inside he walked the couple of blocks to where Bakker & Bakker had their offices, pausing only momentarily to decide what his approach was going to be. He was aware he could be creating a disturbance here, given that Lenny Yeung was one of their directors, and by the time he had finished saying what he had to, would no doubt immediately be informed of his visit. On the other hand, he reasoned, it might not be a bad thing to 'rattle a few cages'; it could act as a catalyst in opening up this whole case, which up to now wasn't far removed from being static. There were far too many undercurrents; too many secrets and too many people, if not exactly lying, evading the truth.

Philip introduced himself to the girl on reception, asking if it was possible to see their managing director and after a surprisingly short time was shown into Alexander Van Ommeron's office; a spacious wood-panelled room, the plate-glass window overlooking the Singel Canal at the rear of the building and a massive highly-polished oval desk in the centre of the room. Mr Van Ommeron stood up to greet him with no hint of surprise or even curiosity on his face as to why anyone from London's Foreign Office should wish to see him.

'Good afternoon, Mr Spencer,' gesturing Philip to take a seat, 'my secretary has told me you are from the Foreign Office; it is not often we, at Bakker & Bakker, have the privilege of meeting someone from the high echelons of the British Government.'

'Thank you, Mr Van Ommeron,' equally matching his stiff cordiality, 'it is good of you to spare the time to see me, but we have been trying to locate a man called Clive Edwards for some time and recently we received word that he had come to Amsterdam.'

'Yes?'

'Does the name mean anything to you, Mr Van Ommeron?'

'I'm not sure; I would have to think about it. You see, Mr Spencer, in the course of each day I talk to many people, some of whom I can easily remember, while others are, shall we say, not so memorable.'

Was he stalling for time? It certainly seemed like it. There was coolness now in his manner which hadn't been apparent before. Unprepared to play any cat and mouse game, he decided to change tack.

'I understand, Mr Van Ommeron,' Philip said, choosing his words with care and all the time watching to see whether there was any change in the man's expression, 'that Clive Edwards called into these offices on the afternoon of Monday, the seventeenth of September.'

'The seventeenth.'

'Yes, that's right.'

'Oh, yes, I remember now; that would have been the courier. The reason for my apparent forgetfulness, Mr Spencer,' he said smoothly, 'is that I had never met him before, but yes, he was here.'

'Did you see him, or one of your staff?'

'No, no. You see, Mr Spencer, the package he was bringing here was addressed to me personally, highly confidential you understand. He was only in my office for minutes; just long enough to hand the package over.'

'I'm not going to ask you to divulge the contents of this package, but I would like to know the name of the person who instructed Clive Edwards to deliver it to you. We will of course respect the confidential nature of the matter.'

'Well – I don't -'

'I regret having to take this line, Mr Van Ommeron, but finding out as much as we can about Clive Edward's friends and associates who may have seen him recently has become crucial to us in the Foreign Office.'

'I understand.'

'Alright,' Philip said quickly, 'I'll put it like this; are you in the habit of having items delivered not by an internationally recognised firm of carriers, but by a man apparently working on his own?'

'No, this was the first time, but as he was coming to Amsterdam anyway, the sender took advantage of this fact.'

'May I have the name of the sender, Mr Van Ommeron?' Philip persisted, feeling at last he might be getting somewhere.

'It was from my co-director, Mr Yeung.'

'He is Chinese?'

'Yes, Lenny Yeung. We have another shipping company in Hong Kong, Mr Spencer; I manage this one in Amsterdam and Mr Yeung controls the Hong Kong end.'

'Is he resident in Hong Kong?'

'Oh, yes; naturally he does a fair amount of travelling, but his home is there.'

'You've been very helpful,' Philip said, standing up and formally shaking hands with him, and I appreciate you taking the time to talk to me.'

Walking back to his hotel, passing one of the flower markets on the banks of the canal and inhaling the heady perfume of the early autumn blooms, he went over what he had been able to find out so far, most of which they had known before, although there had been surprises; namely, the positive tie-up with Lenny Yeung. Van Ommeron's comment that Johnson was coming to Amsterdam anyway meant the call at Bakker & Bakker hadn't been his sole reason for being in Amsterdam. The fact he had been booked to fly straight on to Hong Kong the following day instead of returning to London further substantiated this. It was also feasible to reason that Lenny Yeung would have given Johnson these further instructions, otherwise why did Van Ommeron mention it? At this precise moment he was unable to work out how he was going to go about tracing Johnson's movements. There was also the man he'd been talking to in the Krasnapolsky. Had he merely been someone at the bar that evening Johnson had never met before and the conversation they had had, the normal exchange between strangers having a drink at the end of the day? Too many unanswered questions, he sighed. Far too many.

He picked up a copy of *Der Telegraaf* someone had left behind in the lounge bar. His comprehension of the Dutch language, while it fell far short of A Level standards, was sufficiently adequate to enable him to understand the double column of print in the centre of the front page. Mentally translating the piece, he stumbled his way through until he reached the end; the gist of the report being that there had been another stabbing. This time, the name of the victim had been given. Martin Joosten, aged twenty-nine, had been stabbed several times, his body being discovered by police after forcing an entry into his apartment in the warehouse quarter of the town. Apparently, a neighbour becoming disturbed by sounds of a fight in the early hours of Monday morning, rang them, but by the time they arrived it was too late to save him, also no sign of the assailant.

Philip had two options, having decided he could not afford to ignore this killing. He could contact police headquarters, make himself known to them or he could continue as he had been doing since arriving the day before, trying to find out what he needed to know by asking questions to those he thought could provide the answers. He preferred to work on his own, especially as the whole background to this convoluted case did not focus entirely on Amsterdam. Already, there were a number of people involved, whether criminally or not still had to be established, therefore he didn't have much of a choice.

'This is not good.' he said to the barman whom he now knew was called Frederick, and pointed to the article.

'Indeed it is not, sir,' he said, 'not good for poor Martin and not good for our fine city.'

'Did you know the man, then?'

'Oh, yes; we were at school together and I, too, have an apartment close to where he lived.'

'Have you any idea of what happened, Frederick?'

'No, I don't. Martin was what you would have described as a loner. Even when we were kids he was like that. It's some weeks since I last saw him and even then we only exchanged a few words.'

'Was he a barman like you?'

'No. No.' he said, 'Martin always liked to be on the move. He loved cars you know, but I don't think he could ever have afforded to buy one, but I suppose you could say he made up for this by getting a job as a driver. He probably thought it was the next best thing.' he added, smiling sadly.

'A steady job.' Philip remarked casually in the hope he would be able to draw him out without having to ask too many questions.

'He worked at Jansen Enterprises, they're in the warehouse quarter of the city, had been with them for two or three years, I'm not sure exactly, but I reckon you could say it was steady enough. I will say this, sir,' he added, leaning over the bar and lowering his voice, 'I know some of the crowd he mixed with and well -'

' Dubious?'

'I don't know about that,' he answered quickly, 'but put it like this, sir, they're not the type of people who would be welcome in the Carlton.'

More customers came into the bar at that moment and he moved away to serve them. Philip finished his drink and made his way through to the restaurant. He had got what he wanted, hardly able to believe how easy it had been. Jansen Enterprises. Was it possible, he wondered, there was a connection between the company and Johnson's other reason for being here. Tomorrow, he would do his best to find out.

Chapter Nine

HONG KONG

Two days earlier, on the Tuesday, Lenny had a call from Jan Jansen to tell him the diamonds had turned up.

'No doubt this surprises you, Lenny?'

'It does, yes. Where the hell have they been all this time?'

'You may well ask,' Jan chuckled, 'you may well ask.'

'Come on, Jan, what's been going on?'

'I don't think anyone knows, Lenny, but I had a visit from the police yesterday –'

'- I expect that alarmed you.' he interrupted, wanting to puncture his smugness. There were times Lenny grumbled to himself, when he found Jan's self-satisfied manner insufferable.

'Not unduly; you see, I had been becoming more than a little concerned about the absence of Martin Joosten –'

' – who's he?'

'Give me time, my impatient fried; that's the guy I had following Clive the other night, Martin had been on my payroll for a couple of years.'

'Ah,' Lenny said, beginning to know where the conversation was leading, 'you're using the past tense.'

'Yes, the police raided his flat in the early hours yesterday after receiving an irate call from a neighbour complaining about the noise coming from Martin's place. Apparently, they were quick to arrive on the scene, but not quick enough to break up the fight; that was how the neighbour described it: shouting, crashing of furniture and so on. Anyway,' Jan went on, 'when they broke in they found him; he'd been stabbed, several times. Naturally no sign of the killer, but it didn't take them long to find the diamonds.'

'Presumably the intruder didn't have time to make a search of the flat.'

'I think that's the way it must have been.'

'So, Jan, your theory that Clive had taken them was wrong.'

'True. It's the old story, isn't it; the temptation was too great. Martin must have had an outlet for them, although why he'd still been hanging on to them is anyone's guess. It could have been he was still trying to find an outlet and someone tried to beat him to it.'

'So your man must have killed Clive.'

'Looks like it,' he agreed, 'he could have been waiting for him to come out of the Krasnapolsky that night, but whichever way you look at it, it had to have been unpremeditated; Martin would have had no way of knowing I was going to ask him to keep an eye on Clive when he left here.'

'An opportunist.'

'Most of them are, my friend; but this one wasn't too bright.'

'Tell me, Jan; how were the police able to trace the diamonds to you?'

'Aha,' another chuckle, 'I was waiting for you to ask me that, but it is really quite simple.'

'Well?' prompting him impatiently.

'As I've said,' he explained, 'Martin worked for me; quite legitimately I might add, which meant there were papers to support this.'

'What sort of papers?'

'My word, what a worry guts you've become, Lenny. Income tax returns, old timesheets from when he clocked on and off, but most importantly, his contract of employment signed by yours truly.'

'I see,' continuing to smart from his amused criticisms, but he couldn't help worrying; not for the wellbeing of Jan Jansen, he could look after himself, but for his own. The last he wanted was any hint of his involvement to surface, 'I take it you were able to prove to the police the diamonds *were* your property?'

'Of course, no problems there. Call it professional fudging, my friend, but as far as they are concerned, all my figures are in perfect order, so you can relax; there won't be any unpleasant comebacks. For either of us.' he added.

'That's a relief.'

'Thought it might be.' he answered glibly, 'Now, back to business.

Have you a replacement for Clive yet?'

'I have as a matter of fact. I'll be making the necessary arrangements for her to fly out to Amsterdam, hopefully at the end of the week.'

'A woman?'

'Yes. You haven't any hang-ups about that have you?'

'No; why should I?'

'Good, I'm glad to hear it,' Lenny said, 'and this time, Jan, please do not have anyone follow her when she leaves your warehouse.'

***

By the Thursday when he hadn't any further calls from Jan, he began to relax. Perhaps he had been worrying needlessly and wondering now whether Jan had been right, but he was incapable of acting any differently. He couldn't mentally shrug off and store away at the back of his mind anything which could ultimately affect him and erode the structure he had taken years to build. It was his nature, his upbringing, to look on the obverse, to recognise or even imagine potential problems. Jan was different; he lived for the moment which meant not much penetrated that thick outer skin of indifference the man had more than likely been born with.

'Alright, Cecelia,' he said to the woman sitting across the desk from him, 'here's your brief; I've spoken to your contact in Amsterdam. He's called Jan Jansen; of Jansen Enterprises.' he added, 'The arrangement is that you will call at the warehouse at midday on Friday; there should be plenty of people around at that time, therefore you're not going to look conspicuous. He'll give you three small pouches; they'll contain a total of thirty uncut diamonds. I suggest you put the pouches among any of your own jewellery you'll be taking with you. I don't anticipate problems, Cecelia,' he said, 'it would be unusual for any search to be made among a woman's personal belongings. I have your tickets here,' he said, taking the Cathay Pacific folder from a drawer and passing it over to her, 'as I've already said, you're booked on the five o'clock flight this afternoon, arriving at Schipol Airport at eleven local time tonight. This ticket,' he explained, pointing to the second one, 'is for an onward flight to Heathrow on Saturday morning at eight, returning here the following afternoon at two, estimated time of arrival on Monday morning at ten. I've made a booking for you at the Hotel Russell in London for the Saturday night and the Carlton in Amsterdam for the Thursday and Friday.' wondering for a fleeting second about the wisdom of her staying in the same hotel, but Lenny Yeung was a rare breed of Chinaman; he wasn't overly superstitious. It isn't as though Clive was killed there, or even in close proximity, so why shouldn't it be perfectly reasonable for her to do the same; besides, the Carlton was an excellent hotel and one he had visited frequently over the years.

'This is the first time you've mentioned the London visit, Lenny.'

'I know,' he nodded, 'but I thought it made sense. You've met Gregory Smythe-Jones, haven't you?'

'Yes, it must have been a couple of years ago when he came here.'

'That's what I thought. Clive had always handled the London end of the courier business, Cecelia, but I'd like you to take over now. No objections, I trust.'

'None whatsoever.' she assured him quickly.

'Good. I have a package I want you to take to him. Not to his office, he'll meet you in the lounge bar at the Hotel Russell at four on Saturday afternoon. I suggest you pack this in the luggage you'll be booking through rather than in your hand luggage in the event an over-zealous customs officer becomes too curious.' handing the package to her.

'That's fine, Lenny,' she said, making to stand up, 'is that everything?'

'Yes, for the moment,' appreciating the woman's down to earth approach. He had known Cecelia Cunningham for a number of years, the last ten of which she had been working for him; mainly on short courier trips within the pacific rim and in that time she had never let him down. As with Clive, she never asked too many questions and he paid her well, sufficient to prevent her looking elsewhere. When he had put this assignment to her she had shown no surprise, or even nervousness, especially when she was aware that Clive had done the journey before her, 'all I will say is, watch your back and don't,' allowing himself a rare smile, 'talk to any strange men.'

'Most men are strange, Lenny.'

'You are a cynic, Cecelia.'

'I know.' she smiled sweetly.

Lenny worked later than usual that day. He was on the point of leaving the office when one of the phones on his desk rang and wearily leaning over towards it, lifted up the receiver.

Any sense of euphoria, however slight, he may have had earlier in satisfactorily solving the imminent problem of replacing Clive's services, rapidly dispersed when he listened to what Alex Van Ommeron had to say.

'Just a moment, Alex,' he said, 'before you go any further; you're telling me this guy – what was his name again?'

'Philip Spencer,' Alex told him, 'from the Foreign Office –'

' – yes,' Lenny interrupted; his brain going into overdrive, 'that's exactly what *is* concerning me. You know what that means don't you?'

'I don't believe I do.' His answer came slowly and Lenny could tell he was out of his depth; in other words Alex had no idea what he meant.

'As if that wasn't dire enough,' Lenny said, doing his utmost to curb the rising panic, 'and it isn't like you to be so obtuse, Alex, but when I hear the words Foreign Office, I immediately read MI6.'

'Sorry, Lenny, I have to admit that hadn't occurred to me. It should have done, I suppose, but it didn't. Sorry.'

'Okay. Okay.' regretting his outburst; there was no point taking his reactions out on him, 'It's always possible I may be jumping to conclusions, although that's too much to hope for. We have to consider the possible affect this –' pausing, not wanting to alarm him too much; there wouldn't be much sense both of them spiralling into panic mode, '- this intrusion into our business activities. Do you see what I'm getting at now?'

'I'm beginning to; what do you suggest we do, then?'

'Apart from making sure our books are kosher, there's not much else we can do. You didn't tell him you knew Clive was dead, I hope?'

'Give me credit, Lenny, for having a modicum of commonsense. I, too, can exercise discretion when it's necessary.'

'Sorry, Alex, but I'm trying to get my head round this unexpected turn of events.'

'So,' he asked, 'why do you think they were trying to find Clive?'

'A good question, Alex, and believe it or not, I think I know the reason.'

'Obviously something to do with his past.'

'You're getting warm, very warm in fact, but not Clive Edwards' past, Alex –'

'– Anthony Johnson's?'

'Ah, you've remembered his name and yes, you're right. You see, when I told you he'd changed his name, I didn't explain the very likely reason for this.'

'Which was?' and Lenny knew he had his full attention when he didn't interrupt, as he would normally, as he reached the end of what he had discovered when he'd checked out Clive Edwards.

'So, the man was a murderer.'

'I would say so,' Lenny agreed, 'everything I've been able to unearth indicates this. There was too much stacking up against him: he fixed the car crash on the same night his lover's husband was shot dead and somehow, obviously with help, managed to leave not just Samriboi where he was living then, but the country, change his name and start a new life undetected, possibly right up until recently.'

'And all that time his luck held out.' Alex commented.

'Yes,' Lenny went on, 'something or someone has turned up to attract the attention of the British authorities; ultimately as in this case, MI6. Philip Spencer would have known damn well Clive Edwards and Anthony Johnson were one and the same. There is something which is puzzling me, though.'

'Yes?'

'How did they know Clive had called into your office?'

'I've no idea.'

'Think about it, Alex, think about it.'

'I am; believe me, I am.'

'Someone must have told Philip Spencer.'

'I suppose so.' sounding doubtful.

'How else?' Lenny persisted, 'Apart from you, me and Clive of course, there was no-one else, was there?'

'Absolutely not; I hadn't even told Martha.'

'Perhaps you'd made a note in your desk diary; she would have seen that, wouldn't she?'

'Even if I had, which as it happens, I hadn't, I trust Martha implicitly. As you know, she's been my P.A. for years. In fact, Lenny, I've never had anyone working for me who is so professional, and discreet.' he added, his voice rising in righteous indignation.

'Alright; look at it this way, then; if the information did come from your office and somehow this Spencer guy just happened to know Clive was going to turn up, he or she could have told him.'

'But, Lenny, I've just told you. Nobody did know in advance of Clive's visit.'

'I'm not talking about *before*, Alex,' he emphasised, impatient now, believing he might be close to knowing how MI6 were alerted, 'I mean someone Clive had known could have seen him when he arrived.'

'Oh, of course, that is possible.'

'It's an idea though, isn't it?'

'Yes, a clever deduction, Lenny.'

'Thank you,' accepting the compliment, 'however, if that did happen they, whoever it was, must have known Clive several years ago.'

'As Anthony Johnson.'

'Exactly and passed this information on to Philip Spencer.'

'Except,' Alex was quick to point out, 'the British authorities were looking for Clive and not Anthony Johnson.'

'Oh, Alex, please,' mentally exhausted by this time, feeling as though he'd climbed down from the Big Dipper, 'what you've said brings us right back to where we started this conversation.'

'Something has just occurred to me.'

'Has it?' Lenny answered wearily, and it's about time too, he grumbled under his breath. Up to now it seemed he had been doing all the thinking.

'Yes, it was when you mentioned the name of the town where Anthony Johnson used to live in Zambia; I knew I had heard the name before.'

'Go on; this sounds as though it could be interesting.'

'I believe it is. You see,' Alex explained, 'that was where Martha lived when she and her husband were out there. I remember she mentioned it at the time I interviewed her.'

'Well, well, you could call that a coincidence, unless Philip Spencer already knew she was working here.'

'What do you mean?'

'When I was checking through Clive's background and first heard about this place, I did some further checking and found it was a mining town on the country's Copperbelt with an extremely small expatriate community. It's my guess MI6 will have sussed that out for themselves; also, if Martha had been there at the same time, have learned where she is now.'

'Even if this hypothesis of yours is right, Lenny, it doesn't really concern us, does it?'

'No, perhaps not, but at the very least it does provide us with an explanation of why Philip Spencer should arrive unannounced on your doorstep, Alex. You know the old adage: "Better the devil you know"?'

***

AMSTERDAM

Philip had set himself one final task before leaving Amsterdam, which was to test his hunch that Johnson had been to Jansen Enterprises on the night he was killed. He may be wasting his time, but if he was, he would mentally write it off as worth a try. Frederick at the Carlton had mentioned that Martin Joosten worked as a driver for them, but perhaps more importantly, although Frederick hadn't elaborated on the type of person Martin Joosten was, he had mentioned the people he had mixed with and that, Philip felt sure, ruled out the man Martha had seen with Johnson at the Krasnapolsky. Also, Philip was familiar with the warehouse district and that it was within easy walking distance from the hotel, therefore he reasoned, if Johnson had come from that area, the Krasnapolsky would be the first likely venue on the way back towards the Carlton for either a drink or as a meeting place.

He was reluctant to make himself known to anyone at Jansen Enterprises, but he didn't see how else he was going to take his hunch any further, deciding this time he would avoid mentioning the Foreign Office.

Jansen Enterprises scarcely differed from any of its neighbours with only a painted sign at the top of the flight of steps leading up to the main door of the warehouse to tell him who they were. "JANSEN ENTERPRISES", he read, "IMPORT/EXPORT". No frills; no name of the proprietor, not even a telephone number, glancing up from where he was standing at the bottom of the steps to the narrow windows on the first and second floors; almost opaque with the grime of years. The paintwork on the wooden structure had also been long neglected; faded dark green paint and peeling in places. The silver-grey open-top convertible parked alongside the front of the warehouse was in stark contrast. Must be money in the import/export business, he thought cynically, placing his foot on the first step.

There was no bell and turning the handle, surprised to find it wasn't locked, went inside. It took several seconds for his eyes to re-adjust from the brightness outside, the only light which penetrated the ground floor filtering weakly down from the floor above. Philip slowly walked over to another flight of wooden steps at the far end of the warehouse, noticing that the whole floor area was empty, devoid of anything which he would have expected to be there; no boxes, crates, no equipment of any kind and no activity either. His footsteps, echoing loudly in the heavy and airless silence, he reached the stairs and looked up.

'Good morning, can I be of some assistance to you.' a disembodied voice floated down to him, to be followed by its owner, his large broad frame filling the space at the top of the stairs momentarily blocking out the meagre light.

'Good morning,' matching his formality, 'I hope you can. I am in Amsterdam to look into the recent death of a British subject.'

'May I ask, why have you come here?'

'Do you think it's possible if either you come down to the ground floor, or if you prefer, I will come up to where presumably you have your office.'

'Very well,' he said but with obvious reluctance, 'you had better come up and be careful with the steps; they are a little worn.'

Gingerly, and holding on to an equally worn handrail, Philip did as he suggested. The room he was in was slightly more habitable, at least it bore some resemblance to an office, although the furnishing was spartan: a long table, devoid of anything else except a laptop, the blue screen flickering and providing considerably more light than from the filthy windows; an ancient utility-type grey filing cabinet behind the desk; a swivel chair and only one other, a plain wooden one, to which he gestured, walking round to the other side of the desk and sitting down.

'You are English.'

'Yes,' Philip said, passing his passport over to him.

'Thank you,' he said stiffly, glancing at the last page, 'you are Philip Spencer.'

Again, it wasn't a question. How pompous can one get, he thought. The man's manner was almost as archaic as his surroundings.

'And, Mr Spencer, who are your employers?'

'I am working for myself on this assignment, Mr –'

'My name is Jan Jansen.'

' – Mr Jansen. The man's family want me to find out as much as possible; for their own peace of mind, if you know what I mean.' continuing to fabricate, 'you could describe me as a freelance investigator.'

'You are a newspaper reporter I think.'

'No, Mr Jansen, I'm not with the press.' noticing a folded copy of *De Telegraaf* on the top of the briefcase leaning against the filing cabinet.

'That is good. In my experience, when they appear, especially uninvited, it usually means trouble. However, as I have already asked you; why are you here?'

'In the course of some enquiries I have made I was informed that the man I mentioned had an appointment to visit your warehouse on the day he was killed.'

'I can assure you, Mr Spencer, Clive Edwards did not come here.'

'You knew about the murder?'

'Naturally; everyone who read the newspaper report in *De Telegraaf* would have known about it, and as he had been British I remembered; it is not often,' he added, 'foreigners, from Britain you understand, are murdered in our splendid city.'

'Well, Mr Jansen; it would seem I have had a wasted journey this morning. I apologise for disturbing you.'

'Not at all,' he said, standing up, but remaining where he was, making no offer to escort him from the premises, 'this has given me a chance to practice my English.'

A likely tale, Philip thought, letting himself out of the warehouse and gratefully breathing in fresh air; the man was a liar. As soon as he had said he'd read Clive Edward's name in the paper Philip had known, remembering exactly what the barman at the Krasnapolsky had told him: "I read about it last week in *De Telegraaf*, although they didn't give his name." What he had to do was find out whether *De Telegraaf* made any further mention of the murder. Perhaps it might be worthwhile having another talk with the barman.

When he reached the end of the road where it turned left in the direction of the city centre, he looked back, half-expecting to see Jan Jansen watching him, but instead, was in time to see a tall, auburn-haired woman emerge from the taxi which had drawn up outside the warehouse, watching as she climbed the steps and without hesitating went in, closing the door behind her. Seconds later, the taxi with its 'for hire' sign illuminated passed him. Who was she, Philip wondered, walking more briskly now, wanting to reach the Krasnapolsky before the bar became busy. Jansen's girlfriend? Somehow, although he only had a fleeting glimpse of her, he didn't think so, realising as he memorised what she looked like that he had seen her before; she had been in the restaurant at breakfast that morning, on her own he remembered, therefore like himself, she was a guest at the Carlton and it was possible he may see her again. She could be in Amsterdam on business, except he wouldn't have thought the premises of Jansen Enterprises was really conducive for somewhere to meet any customer, prospective or otherwise.

The clock above the reception desk was striking the half-hour when he pushed through the glass swing doors of the Krasnapolsky, gratified to see the same barman on duty again.

'Good morning, sir. It's a pleasure to see you again.' he smiled, 'What would you like to drink?'

'A lager, please.' and watched as he poured it, deciding to come straight to the point before they were interrupted, 'Do you remember telling me yesterday that you had read about Clive Edward's death in *De Telegraaf*?'

'I do, yes.'

'What day was this?' Philip asked.

'It was in last Thursday's paper, sir.'

'Would you happen to know whether any further mention was made; the following day perhaps?'

'I'm sure it wasn't. You see,' he went on, 'I always buy a copy on my way to work each morning and I know I would have noticed if there had been.'

So, Philip thought, taking a sip of his beer, my hunch paid off, although realising it wouldn't be wise to assume too much; there remained considerable work to be done yet, but as far as Amsterdam was concerned, he considered he had accumulated sufficient information to extend the enquiry, which could be done back in London, deciding to book a flight back the next day. Meanwhile, he would make a start on his notes which meant he would have a head start when he saw Charles.

Finishing off his beer, he began to think once again about the article in Wednesday's edition of 'The Times' and now he knew that the Dutch press had made no mention of Clive Edward's name, he was wondering how the journalist had known. Guy Ford had been the first journalist to mention, not only the name, but the murder in Amsterdam. They, at Headquarters, hadn't known until the Monday when the Yard contacted them, so how was Guy Ford able to find out so quickly? Only one explanation occurred to him, which was he may have been in Amsterdam around the time of Johnson's murder. Given the content of the article, it seemed feasible to believe he had met Johnson at some time, presumably when he had still been Anthony Johnson. If that was the case, had he deliberately misled the barman by telling him he must have been mistaken in thinking the man he had been with on that night was Anthony Johnson? No wonder the poor fellow was confused. It was beginning to sound as though Guy Ford had been pursuing his own line of enquiry which had resulted in his column in 'The Times'. There was of course the other killing, the stabbing of one of Jansen Enterprises' employees. There had to be a link here. There had to be. It looked very much as though he would have no choice but to get in touch with the police here in the hope they may be able to provide some answers, the main one being what, in their opinion, was the motive. Not so much, perhaps, who was responsible for Martin Joosten's death, but why. At last, there appeared to be some cohesion with the numerous aspects of this case, although he had to admit they remained to be fairly scattered and would need considerably more tidying up before they could reach a credible and satisfactory conclusion.

Chapter Ten

He was told by the desk sergeant that Inspector Horst Brendaan was leading the murder enquiry and after buzzing through to his superior, escorted Philip along the corridor to his office.

'Good afternoon, Mr Spencer,' the Inspector said, standing up and coming round to the front of his desk to shake hands with him, 'it is not often we have the pleasure of meeting someone from Britain's Foreign Office. Do take a seat,' he added, pointing towards a small conference table in the centre of the room, 'less formal than sitting facing each other across a desk.'

'I am hoping, Inspector Brendaan,' Philip said, 'to learn more about the murder of Martin Joosten.'

'You think there may be some connection with the death last week of the British tourist?'

'I have reason to believe there could be,' Philip admitted slowly, 'although it is too early in the enquiry to come to such a positive deduction.'

'I see.' a look of keen intelligence in the dark blue eyes, 'I was the one who spoke to the officer at New Scotland Yard when we felt we had exhausted our search in trying to find the man's next of kin. Am I correct in saying you had more success?'

'With more than a little luck,' Philip told him, 'we discovered, Inspector, that he had only been using the name of Clive Edwards for the past ten years. Once that was established, it wasn't too difficult to find out who he really had been.'

'There was something dubious about his past, Mr Spencer?'

'There certainly was and we've been concentrating these last few days on how he had been conducting his life since that time and if you hadn't informed New Scotland Yard of his death, it would have taken us somewhat longer. Evidence is building up, Inspector,' he continued, 'to suspect he was involved in something of a criminal nature, possibly large scale.'

'In Amsterdam?'

'Partly, perhaps, but before following up on the leads we have already, I want to make an attempt to find out as much as possible about the people he had contacted during the brief time he was here.'

'And you believe that Martin Joosten may have been one of them?'

'I need to know more about him, of course, but I think he was small fry in the scale of what Anthony Johnson had been up to.'

'Anthony Johnson, so that's what he was called.'

'Yes. Regrettably, certainly prematurely, the news has leaked out about the change of identity. Up to a few days ago, mention has only been made in one English newspaper, but we are sure it will only be a matter of time before it becomes more widespread, reaching possibly your own press.'

'At least we will have been prepared for when that occurs.'

'Of course you and I know that there is nothing your country or mine can do about any unwanted press coverage; newspapers are printed, people read them as they always have, but just as quickly forget about what was perhaps front page news one day as soon as it is replaced by whatever happens next.'

'Reporters, journalists and the people who produce our newspapers all have to earn a living.'

'That's true. However, if you could tell me anything you know about Martin Joosten, I would be grateful. All I've gathered so far,' Philip added, 'is where he worked, but not much more.'

'You would know that when my officers reached the apartment, Martin Joosten was already dead?'

'Yes.'

'Well, after the body had been removed, a search was made of his apartment.'

'Were they looking for anything in particular?'

'No, but as the property had the appearance of having been ransacked, not only the room where the stabbing occurred, but the other rooms also, this alerted us to a possible reason why it happened; the assailant may have been searching for something.'

'And was anything found?' Philip asked.

'Oh, yes, three pouches of uncut diamonds. He had cunningly taped them under the lid of the toilet cistern.'

'They had been stolen?'

'Apparently from his employer.'

'And were you able to establish this, Inspector?'

'We were as a matter of fact; it didn't take long. The fact Martin Joosten worked for Jansen Enterprises who are importers and exporters of, among other items of marketable value, precious and semi-precious stones, gave us the lead we were looking for, therefore,' he added, 'I went along there, taking the diamonds with me. Jan Jansen, the proprietor, was able to verify they were part of his stock, producing the necessary papers to substantiate this.'

'Did he say when they went missing?'

'Unfortunately, no, but he suggested Martin Joosten could have been taking a small amount out of the warehouse over a period, making it more difficult for him to notice.'

'Possible, I suppose.' Philip agreed, but not believing this for one minute. Those diamonds had been handed over to Johnson on the Monday night, the plan being for him to taken them on to Lenny Yeung in Hong Kong, but how to prove it. Not easy. Neither, so far, could he prove Johnson had called into the warehouse that night. If he had, and Martin Joosten had known why, it meant that at some point after Johnson had left the Krasnapolsky he had been waylaid by him, all of which meant that Martin Joosten had killed him, taken the diamonds and pushed Johnson's body into the canal. Because of the complexities of this case, he was not in the position to say anything further to the Inspector. The murder of Martin Joosten, as far as the Dutch authorities were concerned, would have to remain on their records as unresolved, unless they were able to find the person responsible. It would appear from how the Inspector spoke about Jan Jansen they had no suspicions about his activities. Up to now there was one common denominator, namely Lenny Yeung, and if it should transpire there was also something suspect about either Jansen Enterprises or Bakker & Bakker, inevitably, Inspector Horst Brendaan would then have to be informed.

This short trip to Amsterdam had not been unproductive he decided, walking back to the Carlton. Seeing the Inspector this afternoon had provided him with something further to add to his report in that, possibly, they may have a motive for Johnson's murder. He couldn't help feeling more than a little surprised that the Inspector appeared not to have had any hesitation in accepting the explanation given by Jansen on how the diamonds had been stolen. Jansen hadn't struck him as a careless man, quite the reverse; neither did Philip think he was the trusting kind. According to the barman, Martin Joosten had been employed as a driver which would imply he wouldn't have been privy to any first-hand knowledge of stock of such a high value, surely this would be in a safe and one which only Jansen would know the combination. From the cursory glance around the room which purported to be his office, there had been no evidence of any safe, but it didn't mean there hadn't been one in there.

It was almost six when he reached his hotel. Time to switch off Philip thought; also time for a beer. A different barman was on duty, presumably this was Frederick's night off he concluded, ordering a lager.

There was no sign of the woman, but it was early yet; she could still come in. When he had first noticed her she had reminded him of the woman in Johnson's photograph, but had dismissed what was no more than a fleeting resemblance as being a coincidence; a woman Johnson had known, possibly intimately for him to have carried the photograph around with him, and that she should turn up in Amsterdam, book in at the same hotel and paying a visit to Jansen Enterprises as he may have done. If he could have a closer look at her he would know whether it was a coincidence or not. Could he be so lucky, Philip thought wryly, taking his beer over to a table, deliberately choosing one close to the bar which would place him in a better position should she appear.

He had almost finished his beer when she came in. She had changed from the cream two-piece she'd been wearing earlier, the emerald green shift remarkably the exact shade of green worn by the woman in the photograph. It wasn't enough though, watching her as she walked further into the room and going, as he had hoped, up to the bar.

This was the moment he had to decide whether to approach her with a hastily put-together concoction of why he wanted to talk to her, or do nothing; merely remain where he was, which he knew would be a total waste of time and would achieve nothing. As so often, he had no real choice, standing up and taking his empty glass with him, went back to the bar to stand next to her.

'I believe we've met before.' he said.

'Do you really?' she answered, slowly, turning to face him, 'I don't remember.'

'It was some time ago,' he fabricated, 'in the late nineteen-eighties it would have been, in London, but I can't remember the name of the pub. You were with an old friend of mine, Anthony Johnson. We knew each other out in Nigeria.' he added.

'I did know Anthony around that time,' she said, 'but I'm afraid I still don't remember seeing you.'

'Perhaps I'm not the memorable type.' affecting casualness. So far, his gamble had played off. He had already worked out from the photograph that it must have been taken about then; before he changed his name to Clive Edwards and possibly before his marriage to Kate in nineteen eight-eight, although given Johnson's reputation, that was debatable, but from the style of jacket she had been wearing he had made a guess it would have been out of fashion from the nineteen-nineties onwards.

'Oh, I wouldn't say that;' she laughed spontaneously, a deep throaty chuckle, 'what a ridiculous conversation this is.'

'I suppose it is,' he admitted, 'but I never forget a face, especially of an attractive woman.'

'Well, thank you,' accepting the compliment with a slight shrug, 'anyway,' she went on, 'as it appears I have a poor memory for anyone I met over twenty years ago, perhaps you'll tell me your name again.'

'Actually,' he said, padding out the fiction, 'Anthony didn't introduce us.'

'How remiss of him.' she commented lightly, and giving the impression she hadn't believed a word of what he'd said.

'Not really,' ignoring the impression. He wasn't concerned whether she believed him or not; already and no doubt without her realising it, he had found out more than he had expected: she didn't know that Johnson was dead. If she did, she was a damn good actress. Also, and probably more importantly, it was likely she had known, or known of, Clive Edwards and had been instructed to pick up where he had left off, all of which brought him back again to Lenny Yeung, 'the bar was packed that evening and you and Anthony didn't stay long. So,' he smiled at her, 'I'm Peter Prescott.'

'Cecelia Cunningham.' returning his smile and formally shaking hands with him.

'After all that, Cecelia,' he said, 'can I buy you a drink?'

'I'd like a wine please.'

'And do you live in London?' he asked once the barman had taken their order.

'Not anymore; I moved out to Hong Kong, it must have been shortly after the time you saw me and I've been there ever since. What about you, Peter,' she asked, 'where do you live?'

'London mostly; that is when I'm not travelling.'

'Exciting job?'

'Not particularly; I'm in the property investment business.'

'Interesting.'

'It can be.' matching her enigmatic responses.

'You're in Amsterdam on holiday?'

'Partly.' coming to the end of the game she was playing. He hadn't been fooled by her line of small talk, most of which could have been considered normal between a man and a woman who had just met. Here was a woman, Philip thought, who was well used to looking after herself; there was no real warmth in those amazingly cat-like green eyes. She had a purpose behind everything she had said, but he still wanted to know more about her before he made his excuses to leave. 'And what about you, Cecelia,' he asked, 'what made you decide to live in Hong Kong and to have stayed there for so long?'

'I wanted a change,' giving another shrug, 'and I always had itchy feet.'

'Yet you've lived there for over twenty years?'

'I have a good job, Peter,' she smiled, 'and the money is excellent. I could never earn as much in England.'

'I have heard salaries are high there.' was all he said, waiting for her to elaborate.

'I'm with a publishing firm, guide books actually; on the sales and marketing side.'

'Which obviously involves travelling?'

'Yes, that's right. We've recently brought out a hard-backed guide book on Amsterdam and I'm here to promote customised editions to the hotels.'

'Now, that does sound interesting.' he said, at the same time thinking that Jansen Enterprises and the district where it was positioned would scarcely have any appeal to the average tourist, wondering why she felt the need to go to such lengths to fabricate any reason for being in Amsterdam and, realising it was unlikely there would be any truth in whatever else she was going to come out with, he saw no point in continuing the conversation. Normally, he may have asked her to join him for dinner, but he didn't. Cecelia Cunningham, apart from not being the type of woman he was attracted to, was he felt not to be trusted. Also, he had no wish to prolong the evening being subjected to a pack of lies. He could be wrong; she may know Jan Jansen personally and her visit to the warehouse could have had nothing to do with the publishing business, but he didn't think so. All in all, he decided, as he made to leave, he didn't trust her and the fact she had once had a relationship with Johnson went a long way to reinforce this view.

Only the slight raising of an eyebrow indicated surprise when he told her he was going to have an early meal, but she made no comment. He was conscious of her cynical expression as he drank the remainder of his beer and walked away towards the restaurant.

***

Cecelia saw him again the following morning. He was near the front of the queue to book in for the eight o'clock British Airways flight to London. He hadn't seen her, but once they were in Departures, it was inevitable. She wasn't sure she wanted to talk to him again. She couldn't make up her mind about him; he had been friendly enough; handsome in a rugged kind of way and he had bought her a drink, but there was just something, a niggling at the back of her mind, which hadn't quite rung true. One thing for sure, she was positive she had never met him before, not when she had been with Anthony; she would have remembered, and why was it, she wondered, when he could recall seeing them both, he couldn't remember the name of the pub. No, she decided, moving a few steps forward and watching as he took his boarding card and passport from the girl at the desk. Who was Peter Prescott anyway, and why did he approach a woman he didn't know, not even her name. If he had been an old friend of Anthony's Cecelia felt certain Anthony would have introduced her, but he hadn't. He hadn't been making a pass at her either, even although he had been quick to offer her a drink, because if that had been his intention, surely he would have invited her to join him for dinner, but he hadn't. In fact, he had given her the impression he wanted to end the conversation as speedily as possible and it was only now she was beginning to understand why; he had found out what he wanted from her. By this time she had almost reached the desk, deciding to put her speculations on hold until later.

She was gratified to find on boarding the aircraft their seats were sufficiently far apart to make any sort of communication impossible, although he had spotted her, acknowledging this with a slight nod. Well, Cecelia thought to herself, if that's the way he wishes to play it, it suited her fine. She didn't see him again until she was waiting at the carousel at Heathrow for her baggage to come through the flap and then when it did, as was often the way, having to lean right over to grab the handle before it trundled past.

'Allow me.' he said, effortlessly lifting her travel bag from the conveyor belt and placing it on the floor beside her.

'Thank you,' she acknowledged. 'I had visions of it disappearing through the flap and having to wait for it to emerge again and make another attempt to grab it.'

'You would have thought with all this technology today someone could have come up with a less arduous system.'

'At least it was only a short flight; I always find on the long haul ones by this stage of the journey people's patience is at its lowest ebb.'

'A bit like the increase in road rage at the end of the working day.'

'I've never thought of it like that, but you're probably right.'

More inconsequential exchange of words, she thought, as they walked side by side towards Customs; neither of them all that interested in what they were saying and wondering why she should be thinking like this. She wasn't normally so critically perceptive, but there was something about him she didn't like, but whatever it was, continued to elude her.

'I'll be taking a taxi to Trafalgar Square, Cecelia,' he said when they went through 'Nothing to Declare' to emerge on to the Arrivals concourse, 'If you happen to be going in the same direction, we could share one.'

'No thank you, Peter,' relieved she wouldn't be sharing a taxi with him, 'but I'm going in a different direction. Russell Square actually.' she added.

'Too bad,' he smiled, shaking hands with her, 'another time, perhaps.'

It wasn't until she was in her taxi and heading towards Bloomsbury that the possible implication of why Peter Prescott had gone out of his way to talk to her. It hadn't registered at first, but as he was only carrying a relatively small travel bag, there would have been no need for him to be anywhere near the carousel, therefore, she reasoned, he had deliberately come over to where she had been standing. For those few moments in his company she had naively believed that his offer for her to share his taxi had been genuine and it was only now, with the time to analyse his manner towards her, she knew why. He had wanted to know where she was going and she had fallen right into the trap by practically giving him the address! It was true that the Hotel Russell wasn't the only hotel in Russell Square, but if it was sufficiently important for him to find out, it would only be a matter of elimination until he did. She had been careless, annoyed with herself for letting her guard down. She had nothing to substantiate her suspicions that Lenny's business was less than squeaky-clean, it was more by instinct than anything else, but she had always worked on the premise so long as she didn't know any details, she had nothing to worry about, but now she wasn't so sure. This man, Peter Prescott concerned her, but perhaps she was making too much out of it all. What if he did find out which hotel she was staying in? Was that so dire? Once she had handed over the package to Gregory in the afternoon, her work on this assignment would be completed and by tomorrow afternoon she would be on her way back to Hong Kong.

***

Bill Richardson was later than usual going out to buy a copy of 'The Times' on the morning after Philip's visit; the delivery of a new washing machine disrupting the daily routine he had set himself since Mary and he had returned to England. He still had to flatten out the empty cartons and find a space to store them in the garage, but that would have to wait until later, he decided; first he would read the main pieces of news, determined not to permit this interminable task of settling-in to prevent him from catching up with what was happening in the world.

He got no further than the front page, the stark heading immediately catching his attention and, without taking the time to sit down, remained where he was, in the middle of the kitchen, avidly reading every word of what the journalist had written. 'My word!' he gasped as he came to the end of the article.

'Mary!' he called upstairs to her, 'Come and read this!'

'What is it, Bill? Has there been another major disaster?'

'Not exactly earth-shattering, my dear,' he said, thrusting the newspaper at her, 'it's about Anthony Johnson.'

'Anthony -' wrinkling her brow, at the same time as putting on her reading glasses, '- in 'The Times'?'

'Yes,' he nodded impatiently, urging her to read it for herself, 'it looks as though he really *is* dead this time.'

She seemed to take an age to reach the end of the column and when she did it was several seconds before she said anything, but he waited, realising she needed time to fully absorb this latest revelation.

'After all this time, Bill; it is really incredible. Do you think Philip Spencer knew that Anthony had been found?'

'I would say it was extremely likely. Do you remember him telling us yesterday that new facts had emerged?'

'I do, yes, but I thought he was referring to Norman's murder.'

'That's probably what he wanted us to think, Mary. You know, I've been thinking about that visit he made especially to talk to us, but it looks as if the press had somehow or other pre-empted him.'

'It's Kate I feel sorry for; I really do. What on earth is she going to think when she reads this?'

'I don't know of course, but I would say she's already been contacted by the Foreign Office. If they knew about it, they would realise there was always the chance the news would leak out.'

'I hope you're right, but all the same it must have come as a dreadful shock to her; learning that her husband had deceived her and had actually been alive all these years. I wonder what she's doing now. She may have re-married, Bill!'

'Now, Mary, don't go worrying about that. If she had, she would have married in the knowledge that Anthony had been officially declared dead by the Zambian authorities. All above board, you know, my dear.'

'You're right, of course,' she agreed, 'but you have to admit, it all sounds somewhat -'

'- far-fetched.'

'That is exactly what I meant. Far-fetched.'

'Well, in the end you could say the man finally made front-page news!'

***

154

When Pamela read Guy Ford's article on the Wednesday morning she was appalled. Not for the sudden death of a man she used to know, nor to the reference of how he rigged the car crash, but the suggestion of a comparison with Norman's murder, and picking out the way it had been expressed: "........ It could be said," the journalist had written, "there was a certain relevance in the murder of Norman Brookes which occurred within the small expatriate community where Anthony Johnson had lived and on the same night ...."

She wanted to crumple the newspaper and throw it away; to pretend she hadn't read the article, even pretend it hadn't been written, but she couldn't. She had to think this through logically, her main criteria being to convince Gregory none of it had anything to do with her. She hadn't told him about Philip Spencer's visit on Monday, realising now she should have done. She had been following her natural instincts of being secretive, not wanting to alarm him, give him the slightest inkling she was under any suspicion. She knew he loved her, he had told her often enough, but being a realist, she couldn't help wondering just how strong that love was and unprepared to have it tested.

Rather than wait until the evening to speak to him, she decided to phone him at the office, knowing she would find it impossible to get through the remainder of the day in this suffocating apprehension. Dialling the number, she waited for his secretary to put her through to him.

'Pamela, darling,' he said, sounding exactly as he had done at breakfast and for a fleeting second she wondered whether he had seen 'The Times' yet, but realising as he always bought a copy at the station, he must have done, 'I thought you might call. In fact,' he went on, 'I was on the point of giving you a ring.'

'You've read it, Gregory?'

'I have, yes. You sound a bit agitated, darling; did the article upset you?'

'I'm not exactly upset,' she said, 'more concerned than anything else. It was when the journalist implied the inference between the two deaths: Norman's and Anthony Johnson's. I didn't know what your reactions would have been, Gregory. Although he didn't actually spell it out in so many words, he may as well have done.'

'Surely you're over-reacting, Pamela. Let people think what they like; it would only be those people you and Norman knew in Samriboi after all and they may not even have read the article.'

'Perhaps I am being,' she admitted slowly, 'but there's more to all of this, I think.'

'In what way?'

'On Monday, I had a visit from someone from the Foreign Office; he was asking questions about both Norman's death and the accident Anthony Johnson was meant to have had.'

'You should have told me.'

'I meant to,' uttering her first lie, 'but honestly, Gregory, I didn't put all that much importance on his visit.'

'What sort of questions did he ask you?'

'Oh,' taking a deep steadying breath, recognising she was fast approaching the point of no return; what she said to him from now on had to be balanced between an affected surprise at why someone from the Foreign Office should have called to see her and her disinterest, again affected, in Anthony's accident. Not easy, but she had to if she wanted to preserve her marriage and this was something, more than anything else, she wanted to do, 'more or less the same questions I was asked by the Zambian police, actually; that I had spent the evening in the club and had found him when I returned to the bungalow late that night. I had nothing more to add, Gregory.'

'I'm sure you didn't, darling,' trying to reassure her, for which she was grateful, but aware she still had a long way to go yet in trying to describe that night in Samriboi, 'but what about this guy, Anthony Johnson, were you asked about him?'

'Only if I knew him, and of course I told him I had. All our crowd knew Anthony; I was no different from any of them. He was an expatriate like the rest of us.'

'Well,' Gregory said quickly, 'it's plain from what you've said this man from the Foreign Office was carrying out some routine questions into both the shooting and the car crash.'

'I think so. I'm sorry, Gregory,' she went on, 'I should have told you about Philip Spencer being here on Monday.'

'Don't worry about it, Pamela; you've told me now and that's all that matters. This is all history now and quite frankly I don't see what can be gained by making any attempt to get to the bottom of what really happened to Norman in Samriboi. It would be best, I think, for you to put all of this out of your mind; nothing can be achieved by dwelling on what might or might not have been going on. It's not good to rake up the past, you know, darling;' he added, 'it will only bring you grief.'

'I'll try, Gregory,' she said, 'but it is not easy and reading that article has only brought the whole unhappy business back to me.'

***

When Gregory replaced the receiver, he remained at his desk while he tried to absorb what she'd told him. In spite of his attempt to reassure her, stress that she was worrying needlessly, he hadn't meant it. Instinctively, without applying any reason to the way his thoughts were going, he knew there was far more to what Pamela had said. He had intentionally not asked her the questions he desperately wanted to know the answers and at that precise moment as he sat there, he wasn't sure what he felt. Pamela was his wife and had been for almost ten years and up to now there had been no outside interferences to disturb what he had believed was a loving and trusting relationship. He had never asked her about her life before he'd met her and, apart from knowing she had been married to Norman Brookes, that was all he had ever wanted to know and as for the way he conducted his various business activities were concerned, this was something he had never shared with her.

Reading the piece in 'The Times' hadn't bothered him unduly, but when Pamela had mentioned the visit she'd had from the man from the Foreign Office, Philip Spencer, she had said he was called; well, that did concern him. As she had suggested, the questions he had asked her could have been routine ones; part of the procedure he would have to follow if, as it seemed likely, the two cases in Samriboi had been re-opened, wondering for the first time why, after the long lapse of time, this should have happened. Perhaps there was a simple solution, he thought; it could be because Anthony Johnson's reappearance had acted as a catalyst and the implications of any connection with Norman's death had no substance. A coincidence? Both events occurring on the same night and in the same town? As much as he wanted to accept that, Gregory couldn't. There had to be a connection. Nothing altered the fact that Clive Edwards, or as he now knew him to be Anthony Johnson, was bad news. Gregory remembered telling Lenny not long after he met Clive in Hong Kong that he didn't like the man and it would seem now that he had been right.

Somehow, he and Pamela would get through this business, feeling fairly certain Philip Spencer would be back. If the Foreign Office were involved, this indicated the whole business was being investigated on an international scale; they would be making every effort to find out why Clive had been in Amsterdam and this could lead them down the path which at that precise moment Gregory didn't feel up to contemplating. There was far too much at stake here. It wasn't only Lenny who could be in a compromising situation; he was the one who had sent Clive out to Amsterdam after all, but with his long-standing liaison with Lenny, he also could be at serious risk of exposure. He had thought, as soon as Pamela had told him about Philip Spencer and who he was with, that he could be MI6 and now, as the full realisation hit him, a cold shiver went down his spine. They were thorough these guys and if they were able to pick up the trails leading from Lenny in Hong Kong to his dealings with him, the outcome didn't bear thinking about.

The dilemma which faced him now was whether to mention all of this to Lenny, but decided for the time being it might be best to say nothing. He expected to hear from him any day to tell him when Clive's replacement would be arriving in London, considering it wise not to add to the current aggro he was going through. Time enough if and when there were any developments which may have any serious bearing on their business activities, to mention any potential problems which may occur, Lenny, he knew, was a shrewd businessman and would have covered his tracks meticulously. Gregory felt that if there were to be any serious repercussions they wouldn't be from him, but it remained to find out exactly where they would come from.

***

Philip's meeting with Charles had been arranged for two in the afternoon on the Saturday which gave him sufficient time to freshen up, have a bite to eat, before making his way to Headquarters. Charles was already in his office when he arrived.

'Hello, Philip,' he greeted him, 'glad to see you are back.'

'It's good to be back, Charles,' Philip smiled, 'Amsterdam was becoming somewhat claustrophobic.'

'I can imagine,' Charles chuckled, 'but from what you've been saying on the phone, you seem to have unearthed quite a lot since Wednesday. Your emailed report made interesting reading.' he added.

'I thought you might think that,' he said, 'and what has emerged so far is that it appears apart from Johnson being murdered by Martin Joosten for the acquisition of the diamonds he had been carrying, there is a much bigger issue here; namely, the dubious activities of Lenny Yeung in conjunction with his co-director, Alexander Van Ommeron of Bakker & Bakker, and Jan Jansen who was the source for the diamonds intended for transportation to Hong Kong by Johnson. The case, or I should say the cases, from Samriboi onwards have now oscillated to develop into something of probably an international level.'

'I think you're right, Philip,' he agreed, 'and now we have this additive.'

'Cecelia Cunningham.'

'Exactly. I believe it would be credible to say she has replaced Johnson, having perhaps collected the diamonds from Jansen and now, instead of returning directly to Hong Kong has another assignment in London.'

'It is always possible this leg of her journey is to visit any friends she may still have here.'

'That remains to be seen, Philip. However, a report should soon be coming in about what she is up to and more importantly, if she is meeting anyone who may be of special interest to us.'

'Were you able to discover which hotel she's in, Charles?'

'Oh, yes, that was easy; the Hotel Russell.'

'The same one Lenny Yeung stayed in the other week.'

'Quite. The officer was able to take a photograph of her this morning at Heathrow which should prove helpful. It now remains to hear whether she has in fact arranged to meet anyone at the hotel. According to Reservations, she's booked to fly back to Hong Kong tomorrow afternoon, arriving there at nine on Monday morning and I've been in touch with Derek Insole, who as you know is based out there, instructing him to keep tabs on her from the time she arrives. The chances are her first contact will be Lenny Yeung; she'll have to offload those diamonds as soon as possible, but if Derek loses her when she leaves the airport, we know where she lives, so it shouldn't be too difficult for him to pick up her traces once she gets home. On the off chance she goes directly to his office he will have someone covering the place. It's not an ideal situation, but as we are more intent on her leading us directly to the man she's working for without alarming him, it's probably the best we can arrange for the present. We don't want to warn him prematurely as I'm sure you will agree.'

'I do, yes. And Guy Ford, Charles; was he in Amsterdam last week?'

'He was indeed; I rang him up yesterday and he told me he and his wife were staying in The Carlton and that's where he saw Johnson. He recognised him immediately and interestedly he'd met him years ago in Paris and got the vibes then that the man was something of a charlatan; he managed to extract some money from Guy for supplying him with some cock and bull story that he knew where Lord Lucan was staying in Paris.'

'Lies?'

'Yes, apparently Johnson had been in the bar of the same hotel where

Guy had been drinking and had been in the company of a man who had looked like the infamous Lord Lucan, but later, when Guy sussed it out he found he wasn't Lord Lucan at all. I got the distinct impression Guy was still pretty miffed about that.'

'I expect he was. So, Johnson was what you could describe as a conman.'

'That's right. Among other things.'

One of the phones rang on Charles' desk and he leaned over to pick up the receiver.

'Yes, Tim, fire ahead......'

'...... so, is she still there?' he asked after a few seconds.

'......you say you know who she was meeting ....'

Philip watched as Charles, pulling his pad towards him, wrote down a couple of words before ringing off.

'Well, Philip,' he said, leaning back in his chair, 'the plot thickens. Cecelia Cunningham met up with someone in the lounge bar of the Hotel Russell –'

'- and?' Philip prompted, impatient to hear more and sensing this was that moment in an investigation of this size when they could be approaching, not exactly to wrapping it up, but making, hopefully, significant progress towards discarding extraneous irrelevancies to penetrate to the core of the whole business.

'Gregory Smythe-Jones.'

'Pamela Brookes' husband.' Philip commented dryly, 'Where does he fit into the picture, I wonder.'

'You may well ask.'

'These last few days have seen us returning to the name of Lenny Yeung, wouldn't you say, Charles?'

'Yes, the Hong Kong connection,' Charles nodded, 'his tie-in with Bakker & Bakker, also with Jansen Enterprises, both of them visited by Johnson whom, we believe, was employed by Yeung and now Cecelia Cunningham, first calling into Jansen Enterprises and now meeting up with Gregory Smythe-Jones. I can't believe this was a social meeting,

Philip, can you?'

'Not really; it would be too much of a coincidence. If Yeung had arranged for her to see him, it must mean he knows the man. Perhaps,' Philip suggested, 'if there is any coincidence it would be the fact that Gregory Smythe-Jones is now married to Pamela Brookes, but who can say at this stage.'

'There's a certain irony in this investigation,' Charles said, 'a murder in Africa ten years earlier, Johnson, whom we strongly suspect as being responsible, being murdered in Amsterdam, followed by the death of one of Jan Jansen's employees, Martin Joosten, taking us along to uncover something possibly on a much larger scale.'

'A chain of events.'

'Yes, Philip,' he agreed, 'and chains can be broken.'

Chapter Eleven

Peggy Price had a free afternoon and being a Saturday Terry was playing golf. The weather was warm and sunny for late September and she decided for a change she would drive to Southsea. The last person she expected to see was Mary Richardson as she came out of Debenhams in the shopping precinct and by Mary's expression, it was obvious she was just as surprised as she was.

'Peggy!'

'Hello, Mary; are you and Bill on leave?'

'No,' she answered, 'Bill retired a couple of months ago, so we're back for good and have just bought a house in Old Portsmouth.'

'How lovely. Have you time for a coffee; we've probably got a lot to catch up on.'

'Of course. Bill is watching motor racing and, quite frankly, I'm glad to get a reprieve from all the unpacking which has been something of a nightmare.'

'Tell me about it,' Peggy laughed, 'it took us an age to get settled.'

'How is Terry, and the children of course?'

'He's fine, also the girls who are no longer children; they're both at university now.'

They managed to find a table in Demarco's coffee shop which, at that time in the afternoon, was bustling.

'Did you read about Anthony Johnson?' Mary asked her as soon as their espressos had been brought over to them.

'I most certainly did. Honestly, Mary, I don't know what to think. To have gone to such lengths; that was a wicked thing to do.'

'The man was a scoundrel and that's exactly what I told the man from the Foreign Office on Tuesday when he called to see us.'

'Philip Spencer?'

'Yes, that's right; did he see you and Terry as well?'

'I didn't meet him, but Terry did; this was in Winchester during his lunch break on the same day.'

'Bill thinks he's with MI6.'

'Does he?'

'It sounds as if he must be talking to those who were in Samriboi around the time poor Norman was shot.'

'Probably, but after all this time, I don't know what he can expect to find out.'

'Well,' Mary said thoughtfully, 'he told us they had re-opened the case of Norman's murder as some new facts had emerged, although he didn't elaborate.'

'I don't suppose he would and now there's another murder enquiry, even although Anthony was killed in Amsterdam.'

'I wonder what he was doing there.'

'I doubt if we'll ever know.' Peggy answered.

'Didn't Martha come from Amsterdam?'

'Yes, she was born there; her mother was Dutch.'

'Oh, I wasn't aware of that. Have you kept in touch?'

'Not since Luke and she were divorced; I'm not sure where she's living now. Terry sees Luke now and again, but apparently the divorce was rather acrimonious and he seldom mentions her name.'

'Oh, dear,' Mary sighed, 'that's sad.'

'It is, Mary, but,' shrugging her shoulders and wishing she hadn't mentioned anything about the divorce, 'these things happen.'

'They always seemed such a happy couple, or so I thought.'

They had finished their coffee by this time and Peggy, reluctant to pursue a subject which only depressed her, made her excuses by saying she had to be back in Winchester. She had forgotten how inquisitive Mary Richardson was, grateful Bill hadn't been with her. If he had been he would have certainly monopolised the conversation and would not have been slow in putting forward his caustic opinions.

She couldn't get Martha out of her mind and memories of the Samriboi days stayed with her all the way to Winchester; one in particular refused to budge, even when half an hour later she was pulling up outside the house.

She was back in Samriboi. It was Wednesday, the day Norman was shot. She spent most of that afternoon by the swimming pool and had been so engrossed in a book she had borrowed from the club's library, she had lost track of the time. She had hurriedly gathered together her towel and swimsuit before making her way to the car park, passing the open door to the bar. Expecting it to be empty at that time of day she was surprised to see Martha and Anthony in there. Normally, she would have called out to her, but for a reason she couldn't really explain, had held back and, instead, carried on to where she had left the car.

Later, when they had met up with Luke and Martha in the club bar, naturally enough she didn't mention seeing her earlier. Instinctively, she sensed that would have been a mistake. There had been something about Martha's manner which had slightly disturbed her although that evening she looked exactly as she always did; openly friendly, relaxed and giving every impression of looking forward to the evening ahead when they could all enjoy a couple of glasses of wine, but when she had been talking to Anthony there had been an intensity about her; the way she had been leaning towards him, only inches away from where he was standing at the bar.

Peggy had almost forgotten about the incident, but it wasn't until Terry and she had heard about the divorce about eight years ago, shortly after Luke and Martha left Samriboi, that she began to question how well she had known Anthony. He was still having the affair with Pamela then and as the rest of them had always agreed the pair of them made no effort to hide what was going on. Had Martha been another of his lady friends? If she had been, Peggy thought now, she had given no hint, not even to confiding in her. And what about Luke; had he known? There was something else she was trying to remember, but it was eluding her and it wasn't until she was in the shower and, for once, not thinking about anything in particular, she remembered. Again, in Samriboi; it had been not long after Pamela and Norman had arrived. The usual crowd had been in the club one evening with the exception of Martha. All Luke said when she had asked him if she was alright was that she wasn't feeling too well. Nothing else, just that. Martha hadn't been at the club the following morning to play tennis, although Peggy remembered she'd been with Luke in the bar as usual in the evening and she had been quite insistent that she was fine, but she hadn't looked fine; there were dark shadows below her eyes which she had obviously made an attempt to camouflage with make-up. It was some days before she was back to her old self again, although now and again Peggy would catch a faraway look in her eyes, as though she was thinking of something different to what was being said around her.

'This was a good choice for tonight, Terry.' Peggy said as they were being shown to their table in the *Los Amigos* in St. George's Street; the atmosphere a delightful mix of Italian and Spanish and without a doubt one of her favourite restaurants.

'I thought you would approve,' he smiled, 'and no more than you deserve. We'll have a drink before we order, shall we?'

'That would be lovely. You know, Terry, each time we come here I'm always reminded of those summer holidays we used to have when the girls were still toddlers and before we went out to Zambia.'

'Talking about Zambia,' Terry said, 'I had a call from Luke this afternoon.'

'How is he?'

'He sounded fine; just the same. He'd read the piece in 'The Times' by the way; I think that was the main reason why he called. Also, Philip Spencer had been in touch with him on Tuesday, therefore he wasn't too surprised to read how Anthony fooled us all.'

'Probably like us pretty disgusted. I drove into Southsea this afternoon, Terry, and you'll never guess who I bumped into.'

'Pamela Brookes.'

'No, thank goodness; Mary Richardson.'

'Have they left Samriboi, then?'

'Yes, but only fairly recently. They've bought a house in Old Portsmouth and are still in the throes of getting everything straight.'

'I suppose she'd heard about Anthony?'

'She was full of it, but you know Mary; she always did like to get to the core of things. I expect she means well, but I always get the strong impression she wants to know too much and, quite frankly, I didn't feel like encouraging her. I find this whole business so depressing and I see no point in thrashing it to bits.'

'I know what you mean and as you say pointless to go on and on. Leave it to the experts; Philip Spencer seems a very capable chap and I bet he'll be thorough.'

'Mary told me he had been to see Bill and her this week.'

'There you are then, Peggy. He'll get to the bottom of what's been going on I'm sure.'

***

AMSTERDAM

Martha didn't hear about Anthony's death until the Saturday evening when she called in to the Krasnapolsky Hotel for a drink. This was the first time she had been in there since the evening she had spoken to him over a week ago. It was the barman who unwittingly broke the news to her, having assumed she knew already and once the initial shock had dissipated, she was left feeling utterly drained and recognised in advance that, as before, when she believed he had died in the car crash, it would be days before she would be able to get her emotions back on an even keel.

'I'm sorry, Miss Jacobsen,' Arnold's voice reaching her as though from a great distance, 'I thought you were aware of what had happened to him.'

'No, Arnold,' she managed to speak, her voice sounding strange, 'you have no need to apologise. He was someone I used to know years ago, but I must admit to feeling shocked. When did – did this happen?'

'It must have been sometime later on the night you were talking to him in here and after he left. Presumably it was on his way back to his hotel when he was attacked. Stabbed to death and his body thrown into the Oudezijds Voorburgwal canal. It was in *De Telegraaf,* but not until three days later although they didn't disclose his name. Also, Miss Jacobsen,' he went on, 'you might not want to read this, but there was an article in the English newspaper one of our guests left behind on Thursday. You could find it distressing.' he added.

'I feel I must,' she said, 'this is all so dreadful and to think I had no idea.' was all she would allow herself to say, taking the folded newspaper from him and putting it in her bag. She would read it later when she got home. So, she sighed, she had finally lost him. Who was to blame, she wondered. Not the assailant, but the person who took him from her in the first place. Part of her brain was trying to tell her, warn her, that these were crazy thoughts, but the other part, the one which was in danger of running out of control, was urging her to ignore rational thinking. Above all, she was seeking a form of revenge. How she was going to achieve this, she didn't know yet, but she would think of a way.

Somehow, Martha managed to get through the evening, wishing she hadn't agreed to meet up with her work colleagues, but it was becoming important for her to appear exactly as she always did. It was Saturday and they would very likely end up at the Chinese restaurant along the road from the Krasnapolsky.

Already, a plan was beginning to formulate in her mind of what she was going to do. First, she had some telephone calls to make, but they would have to wait until the following morning and then on Monday she would ask Alex for some leave, hoping he wouldn't raise any objections, but as she hadn't had any time off since earlier in the year, she didn't think so.

Martha slept badly that night, awake until well into the early hours of Sunday morning and even then, what little sleep she had, was continually interrupted by vivid dreams of Anthony: Anthony as he had looked when she first met him in Samriboi; a kaleidoscope of shifting images of what it had been like when she had been with him, right up to those last moments when he spoke to her in the Krasnapolsky. Always, Anthony had been in them, but like a shadow on the periphery of each dream there had been Pamela; voluptuous, sexually provocative and utterly selfish.

When she finally woke shortly before eight, those dreams were still present, hovering in her brain and remained for most of the day, strengthening her resolve, making her more determined than ever to deal with Pamela Brookes for once and for all.

***

John Brookes, while not exactly worried, was puzzled. Norman had been dead for ten years; also it was ten years since Pamela had left Zambia and returned to England. In all that time there had been no telephone calls for her from anyone she had known out there, up until now. The woman who had rung on Sunday told him her name was Pat James and had been a friend of Pamela's in Samriboi; the name meant nothing to him and thinking back to the time Norman and she had lived there, the only person he could remember hearing was that of Harry Knight and probably Norman only mentioned him because he came from Norwich. She had gone on to say she was only going to be in England for a few days and thought it would have been good to meet up with Pamela and when he said Pamela no longer lived here she had sounded genuinely disappointed, especially when John had added that he didn't have an address for her, only that she had moved to Taunton in Somerset when she had re-married.

He wasn't normally given to questioning the truth of what he was hearing, but since learning about the sinister undercurrents surrounding Norman's death he had become mentally more aware of anything which sounded to him as being away from the normal. He had been unable to place the woman's accent, not even certain she was English. The more he thought about her and why she had decided after all these years to get in touch with Pamela and not coming up with a credible answer, the more confused he became. The thought did occur she may be a newspaper reporter, but it was almost a week since the article in 'The Times' with, as far as he knew, no further mention made, at least not in 'The Times', all of which he had taken as a sign there was no continuing interest in the case, but he could be wrong. It had taken him until the following day to make up his mind to give Harry Knight another ring; he would surely be able to tell him whether Pat James had been in Samriboi at the same time as Pamela and if she had been he could forget about the call. And if she hadn't? Well, he sighed, he would have no option but to get in touch with Hugh.

John waited until the evening to phone and as before Harry's wife answered and within minutes he was talking to him.

'Hello, John, how are you?'

'I'm fine, thanks. The reason I'm phoning, Harry, is because I had a call from a woman called Pat James yesterday, she told me she was friendly with Pamela when they were in Samriboi. Without trying to come over as being a doubting Thomas, I can't help feeling a bit –' floundering, reluctant to put his suspicions about the woman into words.

' – suspicious?' Harry put in.

'Frankly, yes.'

'I think you have every right to be, John,' he said, 'I've never heard of anyone called Pat James. She certainly wasn't living in Samriboi either before Norman and Pamela arrived or after she had left.'

'She could belong to the press, I suppose.'

'That's a possibility. That piece in 'The Times' was fairly descriptive of what happened out there, wasn't it?'

'You can say that again.'

'Are you going to take this any further?' Harry asked him.

'I think I ought to. I'll have a word with someone I know at New Scotland Yard.'

'You're not worried, are you?'

'Not particularly, but whether she's with the press or not, I think they may consider it relevant.'

They didn't stay on the phone for much longer and promising to keep in touch, John brought the call to a close. At least now, he thought, he had something positive to tell Hugh. The last thing he wanted to do was waste police time. Although he had suggested to Harry that Pat James could be a member of the press, he was not all that convinced; even with his limited knowledge of how such people were able to contact anyone they wanted to interview, John found it had to believe they would go to such lengths. If any of them wanted to talk to Pamela, he reasoned, there must be more direct ways of finding out where she lived, also, the idea occurring to him for the first time, how were they able to discover his telephone number? Years ago, even before Norman had gone out to Zambia they had, because of irritating cold selling calls disrupting the running of the estate, decided to go ex-directory. Even the most tenacious reporter wouldn't be able to penetrate British Telecom's system; therefore, Pat James had acquired it from someone who had known it. John remembered her saying on Sunday that she was only going to be in England for a few days; this may not have been the truth of course, but this was something the police should be able to find out.

***

HONG KONG

The Cathay Pacific flight from London touched down at Hong Kong's Chek Lap Kok airport at precisely nine o'clock on Monday morning and within seconds of coming through from Customs and into the Arrivals hall, Cecelia's mobile rang. As she had expected, it was Lenny, presumably to confirm the time of their meeting.

'Good morning, Cecelia,' Lenny said, 'welcome back.'

'Thank you, Lenny.'

'Cecelia,' he went on quickly, 'there's been a slight change of plan.'

'Yes?'

'I'm acting on the cautious side here; I've nothing to substantiate my suspicions, but I think it's possible there may be someone from London's Foreign Office interested in your movements. I don't wish to alarm you unduly, but I want you to act as naturally as possible. Whatever you do, don't start looking round.'

'Alright, Lenny, I understand.' a tiny flutter of apprehension of what this could mean, thinking of Peter Prescott. She would have to tell Lenny of course, but now wasn't the moment. It would have to wait until she met him.

'Good, I thought you would. Now, this is what I would like you to do.'

'Yes.'

'Take the Airport Express as you normally do. When you reach Central, there will be a car waiting for you, a white VW Golf; the driver will take you to the Mandarin Oriental. I'll be upstairs in the Clipper Lounge.'

'Alright, Lenny. I should be able to get the train at ten.' she added, looking at her watch.

It was quarter to eleven when she walked through the foyer of the Mandarin. As she had said, he was already in the Clipper Lounge on the first floor of the hotel.

'Hello, Cecelia;' he said, standing up as she approached his table, 'not too tired after the journey?'

'No, I'm fine. I managed to get some sleep.'

'You were lucky; I never can. Also, I'm a chronic sufferer from jetlag. Anyway,' he went on briskly, 'first things first, what would you like to drink? As you can see I've already ordered mine.' pointing to the steaming mug of hot chocolate, reminding her of the Chinese penchant for sweet beverages. As they waited for her coffee to arrive, she told him about her two encounters with Peter Prescott, both in the Carlton in Amsterdam and on Saturday morning at Heathrow airport. He listened without interrupting, a slight frown appearing on his forehead when she mentioned Anthony's name and becoming more pronounced when she came to the bit about telling Peter Prescott she was going to Russell Square.

'You never met Clive, did you?' Lenny asked her.

'No, I didn't.' wondering what he was leading up to. Apart for the fact that she had been in Amsterdam and London as Clive's replacement, she couldn't think how he fitted into what she had just told him.

'What I'm going to say, Cecelia, will probably come as a shock to you, but it appears you didn't know that the man you knew as Anthony Johnson changed his name about ten years ago to Clive Edwards –'

'– that is incredible!'

'No doubt it does sound like that to you, but nevertheless, I can assure you it is true.'

'But why, Lenny? Have you been able to find out?'

'Not exactly why he should have taken such steps to change his identity, except that prior to that time he had been living in Zambia and decided to fake a car crash out there and make his way back to Europe. There's obviously considerably more to this, but so far, I haven't managed to learn what it was. And now listening to what you've told me, it would appear that the Foreign Office was on to him.'

'Peter Prescott.'

'I would say so. You see, after you left for the airport last Thursday, I received a call from my co-director in Amsterdam; he'd had a visit from someone from London's Foreign Office asking questions about Clive. What is puzzling me, though, is why Peter Prescott should have gone out of his way to talk to you and, of course, mentioning Anthony Johnson's name.'

'I don't know, Lenny. I really don't.'

'How well did you know Anthony Johnson?'

'We were lovers, if that's what you mean, but the affair didn't last long, just long enough for me to discover he was married and that his wife was pregnant with their child.'

'Not nice.'

'Not nice at all, Lenny, but I got over it; that was when I decided to come out here. Living in London had gone sour on me.'

'Understandable. I think there must have been something among Clive's papers which linked up with him knowing you, although somewhat careless of him, considering he had so much to hide.'

'Do you know,' she said, suddenly remembering the snapshot Anthony had taken of her, 'I believe I know what that was.'

'Do you?'

'Peter Prescott said he had recognised me, but I'm one hundred per cent sure it hadn't been how he said. I have a good memory for people I've met, Lenny; even years ago and I had never seen Peter Prescott before.

But he had recognised you?'

'Yes, very likely, but it could only have been from a photograph; Anthony took one of me about the time when we first met and in those days he used to keep it in his wallet.'

'That could explain Prescott's interest in you. It sounds very much as though the Foreign Office knew Clive's real identity, but what concerns me slightly is they may have known why Clive was in Amsterdam.'

'Do you think I was being followed when I was there, Lenny?'

'Not necessarily, but you may have been once you arrived in London.'

'What about here?'

'I hope not, but there is a possibility. Let's say if Peter Prescott is who we suspect, they will have other officers stationed in major cities around the world, Hong Kong being no exception. Rather like a relay race.' he added cynically.

'What do you suggest we do next?'

'We continue to be circumspect,' Lenny said, 'we meet away from the office as and when necessary. I'd like you to fly out to Singapore later in the week; similar to a number you've made before. Considering what we've been talking about, Cecelia, does this worry you?'

'Not unduly. I'll cope, Lenny.'

'Good, and once you've handed over the package Jan Jansen gave to you, no-one can connect you with anything remotely untoward which may or may not have been going on, either here or in Europe.'

***

LONDON

'Good afternoon, Mrs Johnson; do come in.' Reginald Hutton said, coming round to the front of his desk to shake hands with her, 'I was delighted to hear from my old friend, Robert Anderson, this morning, but deeply saddened to hear about your aunt. She was a fine lady,' he added, 'Robert introduced her to me on one of my rare visits to Scotland.'

'Thank you,' Kate said, 'I still can't quite believe I'll never see her again.'

'I can understand exactly what you mean,' he sympathised, 'my wife passed away five years ago and it took me a while to realise she wouldn't be waiting for me when I got home from work each evening.'

Steven and she had spent the weekend in Carnoustie making sure everything was in place in the house for the auctioneers to pick up. There had been very few of the contents she wanted to keep, only the Queen Anne canteen of cutlery and the cheval wall mirror which Dawn had always admired. Apart from Aunt Eileen's collection of oriental figurines, everything else would be sold at auction. It had been Steven's idea for the figurines to be valued when she had told him they had never appealed to her.

"It's a fine collection," he had said, picking up one of the ivory pieces to examine more closely.

"I suppose it is," she had admitted, "although I always found them rather too austere and menacing, reminding me of the inflexible regimes of the ancient dynasties, but Aunt Eileen liked them. I think they symbolised for her order and discipline; she didn't like what she called 'sloppiness'."

She had mentioned the figurines to Robert Anderson when Steven and she had lunch with him on Saturday and he had suggested she took them to Huttons of Haymarket in London, offering to give Reginald Hutton a ring and arrange an appointment for her to see him.

"Reginald and I were at University together, Kate," he had told her, "and surprisingly we have managed to keep in touch all these years. He has made a lifetime study of Far Eastern artefacts and fine arts and has become something of a specialist."

She took them out of the small case, pulling away the tissue paper and placing each one on the desk in front of him.

'Most impressive,' Reginald Hutton said and as Steven had done, picked up one of them, holding it in the palm of his hand, 'Robert mentioned on the phone, Mrs Johnson, that your aunt had been collecting them over a period of many years.'

'Yes, I think she must have been. I remember some of them from when I was a girl, but to be honest, Mr Hutton, I never paid very much attention to the collection.'

'Not to your taste?' he smiled.

'Sorry, no.'

'Oh, don't apologise, Mrs Johnson. To a collector, they would be much sought after.'

She watched as he keyed in an entry to the computer, quickly scrolling down the screen.

'Here we are,' he said, swivelling the screen round towards her, 'as you can see,' he explained, 'the photographs are identical to most of your figurines.'

'Not all of them?'

'No, these four,' he went on, 'are listed in a different category.'

'I don't understand,' puzzled; to her, they all looked identical, 'they look the same to me.'

'Just a moment,' he said, 'I'll go to another screen.' and within a couple of minutes came up with an image of the four pieces he had separated from the others; two in ivory, one of them inlaid with jade and edged with narrow gold beading, the remaining two porcelain. 'I'm afraid to say, Mrs Johnson,' he said, giving her an apologetic smile, 'they once formed part of a private collection and -' hesitating, ' - and they were stolen -'

'- stolen!' she interrupted, 'This is dreadful. My aunt would never have known that, Mr Hutton.'

'No, no, I'm sure she wouldn't.' he said calmly, 'From time to time, Mrs Johnson,' he explained, 'this sort of thing does happen and it is for this reason we, valuers, are officially informed in the event they may turn up.'

'What do I have to do now?' she asked, appalled at the news, only thankful her aunt would never know.

'There is nothing you need to do, Mrs Johnson. When you were sorting through your aunt's papers did you find any bills of sale, authenticated receipts perhaps for such purchases she made?'

'I did, actually,' she said, 'although I haven't looked at them properly.' taking out an envelope from the case, 'My aunt kept all the figurines in one display cabinet and this was in the bottom drawer.' she explained, handing the envelope to him.

'Thank you; this indeed may be helpful.' he said, taking out a handful of receipts, separating each one from the other until he came to the one he wanted. 'This is it, Mrs Johnson,' showing the slip of paper to her; 'you will see your aunt bought these four figurines at the same time. I will of course make a double check to ensure they are the missing pieces, but I'll have to keep them here, you understand, until the matter is concluded.'

'I don't want them, Mr Hutton.'

'Please don't distress yourself; I can assure you that you have nothing to worry about. Naturally,' he went on, 'I'll write out a receipt for them and in respect to the other eight figurines, I will be in a position to give you a written valuation within the next couple of days.'

She thanked him and he helped her to rewrap the pieces she would be taking home with her. In spite of his reassurances, she was concerned and she had meant what she had said; she didn't want them. The very thought of touching anything which had been stolen was abhorrent to her. To think her aunt had proudly displayed those four pieces alongside the rest of her collection made her feel even worse. She remembered the date on the receipt; it had been the 1st of May, 2006, but there had been something else about that receipt which hadn't registered at the time. Her aunt had bought them from a firm of antique dealers, Gregory's Antiques, they had been called, but it wasn't that which practically brought her to a standstill on the pavement packed at that time of the day with people finishing work and making their way home; it was the name of the proprietor printed along the bottom of the paper; Gregory Smythe-Jones.

Chapter Twelve

The report from Reginald Hutton reached Hugh Bannister of New Scotland Yard on Tuesday morning confirming the retrieval of four items stolen six years previously from a private collection belonging to Sir Desmond Bevington who had been working for the British Consulate in Singapore at the time. Normally Hugh wouldn't be involved, which at this stage would be a purely routine procedure and dealt with by one of his officers, but the circumstances surrounding the way the goods had been recovered were considered to be worth bringing to his attention.

So, Hugh thought, reading through the report, another twist in an already convoluted enquiry. Fate, as he had often discovered, did move in a very circuitous way and, lifting up the receiver, dialled Charles Hastings on his private line.

'I'll email the report through to you, Charles,' he said after giving him the gist of what he'd been reading, 'but I thought you should be aware of this as soon as possible.'

'I'm glad you did;' Charles answered, 'we'll pick up what threads we can from hereon, although I can't help but feel it is all rather weird. Even if you ignore for the minute the question mark over Norman Brookes' murder and what still remains obscure about Anthony Johnson's dubious past, we now have the added factor that Kate Johnson's aunt had purchased those four figurines, presumably in good faith, from Gregory Smythe-Jones who just happens to be married to Pamela Brookes. Incidentally, Hugh,' Charles went on, 'it would appear that Smythe-Jones is a man of some considerable substance if the property he owns in Taunton is anything to go by.'

'Apart from him being in the antiques business, do you know anything else about him?'

'Up to now we have been concentrating more on Anthony Johnson, but Smythe-Jones' name has recently cropped up, suggesting there could be a much wider element to this whole investigation and, hopefully, this latest surprising turn of events could go towards leading us in the right direction.

'I had a call from John Brookes yesterday which may or may not bear some relevance. He was saying he'd had a telephone call from someone called Pat James asking to speak to Pamela.'

'Really?'

'She told John she had been friendly with her when they were in Samriboi.'

'But they hadn't kept in touch.'

'That's right, so he rang Harry Knight to ask whether he remembered her.'

'And I suppose he didn't.'

'No; this was why John was concerned, but I suggested to him the woman could have been a journalist trying to pad out what had already been printed.'

'Very possible, Hugh; on the other hand, she could have had another reason.'

'I have wondered about that, but I haven't been able to come up with one.'

'We'll put out a check on her; if it turns out she is a bona fide member of the press, we can disregard her. Also, we'll get British Telecom to trace the call if it's possible. Did John mention when she phoned?'

'Around ten on Sunday morning. Also, there was something else he mentioned.'

'Yes?'

'Two things, as a matter of fact; the woman told him she was only going to be in England for a few days and he had been unable to trace her accent and couldn't be sure that she was English.'

'Still could be press, Hugh. Anyway, that phone check may help.'

***

Kate's mobile rang as she was leaving the office. She wasn't all that surprised to hear Philip Spencer's voice; she had been half-expecting to hear from him after seeing Reginald Hutton the day before, although perhaps not so soon.

'Mrs Johnson,' he said, 'is it possible to see you when you finish work today?'

'Is this something to do with my aunt's collection, Mr Spencer?'

'I have read Reginald Hutton's report,' he answered, 'but that's not why I would like to talk to you; it's concerning your late-husband's background. We thought you may be able to assist us in filling in a few gaps.'

'Of course I will if I can;' she said, 'where shall we meet, Mr Spencer? I was just about to the leave the office when you rang.' she added.

Philip suggested the 'The Lord Moon of the Mall', knowing it was only a short distance from where she worked and even at that time of the day they should still be able to find a table.

'What we are trying to do,' he said to her once he had brought their drinks over to where she was sitting, 'as I mentioned, is to fill in a few gaps.'

'And you think I'll be able to help?'

'You might be,' he said, 'from when he returned from working in Nigeria in 1987 up until he went to Zambia with you and your daughter. From the information we have gathered so far there appears to be no record of where he was living or working. We know you and he were married in London in 1988, but not much else.'

'Missing years.' she commented.

'Yes,' Philip nodded, 'a good description. So, perhaps we should start from when you first met.'

'Alright,' she agreed, 'it was in the spring of 1988 in Paris. I was there on holiday and Anthony told me he was working there and had been since his return from Nigeria.'

'As an accountant?'

'That's what he said.'

'And you didn't believe him?' picking up on the slight nuance in her voice.

'I did at first,' she said, 'but later I began to have doubts.'

'Why?'

'Well,' she explained, 'for an accountant he did rather a lot of travelling. I mentioned this to him once, but all he said was that he was carrying out audit work for a number of his firm's overseas clients.'

'Did you ever meet the people he worked for?'

'I don't believe I would have;' she said, 'I was only in Paris for a week and I never went back there, but it was the evening before I returned to London. Anthony and I had been having a drink in the bar of the Mercure Paris Monty Opéra Hotel where I was staying when the senior partner of his firm came into the bar.'

'Can you remember his name?'

'I can, yes; it was Nicholas Anout. A typical Parisian I thought at the time; ultra-smart, a trench coat draped across his shoulders and oozing in super-confidence. I remember thinking at the time he looked like Lord Lucan, without the moustache, but with a similar smooth elegance. I'm sure you've seen the type I mean, Mr Spencer?'

'Many times,' he smiled, amused by her description, 'we have them in London too, of course, but I always think you can easily distinguish the Frenchman from his English counterpart.'

'How right you are.'

'Do you think you would recognise him again?'

'I might,' she said hesitatingly, 'although it was almost twenty-five years ago. A long time and he was a good ten years older than Anthony which would make him in his late fifties now.'

'We may or may not be able to trace him, but if we did and for whatever reason he should deny employing your late-husband, what you've just told me could be important to us. Such a suggestion is purely hypothetical, Mrs Johnson, but in such an event, would you be prepared to support us?'

'I wouldn't be too happy,' she sighed, 'but I would, I'm sure, feel that I had to. This whole business, Mr Spencer, is too serious for me to merely shrug off because I didn't want to commit myself.'

'Thank you,' Philip said, 'I appreciate that. You said a few minutes ago he was the senior partner, did you ever hear the names of any of the others?'

'No, Anthony seldom discussed his work, or any of his colleagues. Also,' she went on, 'after we were married he left the firm and returned to England. I had a flat in Peckham at that time and we stayed there until we went out to Zambia in 1992.'

'And during this period, was he working in London?'

'He worked freelance from home.'

'I see,' Philip nodded, realising this was going to make their task of finding out what Anthony Johnson had been actually doing then even more difficult, 'and the travelling; that continued?'

'He was away quite a lot, yes; mostly in Europe and only for a few days each time.'

'Probably explains why we haven't been able to fill in those years.'

'I haven't been much help, have I?' she said apologetically.

'I wouldn't say that,' reassuring her. Although she had only given him the name of one of Johnson's associates, it remained to be seen where that might lead, 'we know more than we did ten minutes ago, Mrs Johnson. Your late-husband was apparently a very secretive person, but given time, we will unravel the part of his past which we believe is crucial to us in satisfactorily concluding our investigation.'

'Mr Spencer?'

'Yes?'

'You said on the phone you had read Mr Hutton's report.'

'I had, yes,' he said, 'and I expect it all came as something of a shock to you -'

'- I can't tell you,' Kate interrupted, 'how I felt when he told me, I really cannot. My aunt, you know, was an honest woman and if she had found out, she would have been distraught, also,' she added, 'she would have been extremely angry.'

'And justifiably so.'

'What I was wondering,' she said, 'is why the Foreign Office have become involved in the theft, or I should say the recovery, of those pieces; are you treating this case as part of your enquiry because of any possible link with Anthony?'

'It is too early to say, or even conjecture,' he answered, impressed by her logic. Kate Johnson was an extremely intelligent woman; he had already realised that when he had first met her, 'but,' he continued, 'I would be surprised if Anthony Johnson had been involved. There is a much wider issue here, apart from what happened in Samriboi, and this is why we have to follow-up on every lead we get, however irrelevant it may turn out to be in the end.'

'I recognised the name of the antique dealer who sold the figurines to my aunt, Mr Spencer.'

'Did you?'

'Yes,' she smiled, 'no doubt you're wondering how I knew. It's quite simple, actually,' she explained, 'the weekend before last, Steven and I were staying at "The Smugglers" in Taunton when Pamela Brookes, who had been married to Norman, came into the restaurant with her husband. She introduced him to us as Gregory Smythe-Jones.'

***

By late Tuesday afternoon, Martha was in Departures at Schipol Airport, waiting for the six o'clock British Airways flight to Heathrow to be called. Alex had been alright the day before when she had approached him as soon as he had arrived in the office and to pre-empt any comment he may have made to the short notice, she quickly concocted the tale of a reunion party in London for some relatives on her father's side of the family who had arrived unexpectedly from Australia. He had merely nodded his acceptance of her explanation, saying it would be good for her to get away for a few days. She had been a bit taken aback, prepared for him to remind her of the inevitable accumulation of paperwork waiting for her when she got back to work, but when she thought about his manner now, she realised he had been like that for several days; abstracted, as though there was something bothering him. Not that he would tell her if there was; she had enough on her own mind without worrying about anyone else's problems.

She only had hand baggage which meant she could go directly through Customs and into Arrivals. She wasted no time in hiring a car at the AVIS desk and once she had collected it from the long stay car park, made her way out of the airport and on to the M3 motorway. She had a long drive ahead of her and wanted to reach where she planned to spend the night before the light failed, not being too familiar with the route and concerned in case she should take the wrong exit from the motorway.

Dusk was beginning to fall by the time she finally arrived and had pulled into the front forecourt of the hotel. She had already reserved a room, gratified to find she wasn't too late for a meal in the restaurant. Apart from some toast before leaving for the office in the morning, she hadn't eaten all day. Since hearing about Anthony, food had been very low on her agenda, but now, to her surprise, found she was hungry. She ordered their lemon sole with garlic and parsley butter, new potatoes and baby carrots and a half bottle of *Macon-Péronne*. As an aperitif, she asked for a campari and soda. Over the years, since the divorce, Martha had grown used to her own company and in many respects often preferred the life-style she had made for herself. It wasn't that she didn't have friends, because she did. Also, she'd had a number of affairs, but all the men she'd had a relationship with so far, fell short of what she was looking for. She had been kidding herself of course, she knew that, but was still unable to stop comparing each of them to Anthony. It's like the Cole Porter song Frank Sinatra used to sing, she thought: "I've got you under my skin; I've got you deep in the heart of me, so deep in my heart that you're really a part of me ....." and as the words came back to her, Martha experienced again the sharp pain of her loss, doing her utmost to re-surface and to just enjoy the moment. Tomorrow will be different, she promised herself, taking a sip of her campari.

***

'British Telecom has come back to us this morning with a rather surprising result from John Brookes' phone call, Philip.'

'Yes?'

'It was made from a subscriber's telephone number in Amsterdam,' Charles said, 'and you may not be all that surprised to hear the name of the subscriber is Martha Jacobsen.'

'Why would she have gone through all that subterfuge of pretending to be someone else, Charles; have you any ideas?'

'Not really,' he admitted, 'but it does seem odd behaviour. How would she have explained that if Pamela had still been at her old address, I wonder.'

'Perhaps she knew, or guessed, that Pamela would no longer be there.'

'But,' Charles put in, 'she wasn't to know that John Brookes would have telephoned Pamela and told her about a woman called Pat James trying to get in touch with her.'

'That's true;' Philip agreed, 'all I can say is I think she's up to something. If she was planning to be in England for a few days she could very well be here already. Do you know, Charles, I don't like the sound of this.'

'Do you think this wanting to meet up with Pamela has anything to do with Johnson's death?'

'I would say that's more than likely.' Philip answered, remembering how intense Martha Jacobsen had been when she was telling him about the affair she'd had with him, brief though it had been.

'You mean she blames Pamela for the break-up of the relationship. More than ten years is a long time to harbour such, probably unfounded, grievances.'

'That's what concerns me. Wanting to see Pamela has to be a spur of the moment decision and it's possible that Johnson's murder has acted as some sort of catalyst.'

'I see what you mean,' he agreed, 'I think we should put out some feelers here. I suggest we contact Immigration at this end and Reservations at Schipol Airport. If there's nothing, we can telephone her ourselves, either at Bakker & Bakker or at home.'

'That's fine; meanwhile to avoid raising any false alarms, perhaps for the present we hold back in contacting Pamela Smythe-Jones.'

Charles dialled the number of Head of Immigrations at Heathrow on his direct line and Philip could tell by the grim expression on his face that the news wasn't good.

'We were right,' replacing the receiver, 'A Miss Martha Jacobsen arrived at Heathrow at seven-thirty last evening.'

'So we've missed her.'

'It looks like it;' Charles said, 'and where she has gone can only be guesswork.'

'I know, although if we continue to think along the lines we have been that the reason behind her visit is motivated by wanting to see Pamela, she may have made her way to Taunton.'

'That's a reasonable point, Philip, and when you consider she has Pamela's new surname, also that she is living in the Taunton area, she could have managed to find the address.'

'It probably wouldn't have been all that difficult.'

'I don't see we can do anything further at this stage.' Charles said, 'Up to now, this has all been conjecture on our part; we have nothing to substantiate what we have been saying about her intentions.'

'I know.'

'You won't have had the chance to go through your in-tray this morning, Philip, but when you do you'll see a copy of the case notes on the mugging of the real Clive Edwards from Police Headquarters in Paris. It arrived yesterday after you'd left the office to meet Kate Johnson.'

'Anything interesting, Charles?'

'I'm not sure, but there could be. Apparently,' he said, 'a man was charged, but the case was dismissed through lack of evidence. Although the police were fairly sure he was guilty, it was the person they believed who was behind the mugging they were more interested in. His name is Nicholas Anout and according to them a slippery character, officially describing himself as *entrepreneur directeur*, which I suppose in our language would mean a Jack of all Trades, and succeeding to outwit the authorities for a number of years.

'Kate Johnson told me yesterday that she first met Johnson in Paris and at that time he was working for a man called Nicholas Anout. She only saw him once, but from the way she described him he sounded a bit of a spiv. Also,' he added, giving him a wry smile, 'he reminded her of Lord Lucan.'

'Well, well, this could indeed be what we've been looking for. Did she say what sort of business he had?'

'Not exactly, I don't think she really knew. Not surprisingly perhaps Johnson didn't tell her much about his work, just that when he was in Paris at that time, he was working as an accountant for the senior partner of his firm, namely Nicholas Anout.'

'Did Johnson continue working for him after they were married?'

'She said he had resigned by then and moved back to London and worked as a freelance accountant up until the time they went to Zambia, but that could have been a lie.'

'He could still have been working for Anout.'

'It's a possibility.'

'A dual personality,' Charles said dryly, 'prior to 2002 he was known as Anthony Johnson and from then onwards as Clive Edwards, continuing to being known as Anthony Johnson to Nicholas Anout. He may have lost touch with Anout.'

'I wonder whether Nicholas Anout is still living in Paris.'

'Why do you say that?'

'Mainly because of his track record; perhaps he has had reasons for steering clear of Europe. I've been thinking about those oriental figurines; they were stolen in Singapore and presumably passed on to Lenny Yeung who organised their delivery to Gregory Smythe-Jones via Johnson perhaps – somewhat convoluted I must admit.'

'No, go on, Philip.'

'*If*,' Philip emphasised, 'there is a link-up between Nicholas Anout and Lenny Yeung, it is possible Anout may have left Paris -'

'- and now be in Singapore.' Charles finished for him.

'Yes,' he nodded, 'I'm remembering that other flight ticket.'

'You've a point there, Philip; Johnson could have still been working for Anout without Lenny Yeung's knowledge, unless he was going on to Singapore to meet someone else.'

'But whoever it was, Johnson obviously didn't want Lenny Yeung to know. A bit far-fetched I suppose.'

'Not necessarily; when you consider what we've learned about Johnson, he was no doubt capable.'

'He must have lived a charmed sort of life.'

'In what way?'

'Well, as far as his assumed identity of Clive Edwards, it took ten years for him to be found out.'

'You could say, Philip,' Charles smiled, 'a cat has only so many lives.'

'True.'

'I've also been considering Gregory Smythe-Jones in all of this.' Charles said.

'So have I. Kate Johnson asked me whether we were tying Johnson in with those figurines. Incidentally, when she saw the receipt which wasn't until she handed it over to Reginald Hutton, she recognised the name of the antique dealer who sold them to her aunt.'

'Really?'

'She and Seven Robertson were introduced to him over a week ago. This was when they were spending the weekend in Taunton and Pamela and Gregory Smythe-Jones came into the restaurant.'

'Life moves in a strange way sometimes, doesn't it, Philip?'

'It certainly does.'

'Going back to Gregory Smythe-Jones,' Charles said, 'it would be best if we got New Scotland Yard to interview him. What do you think?'

'I think the same. We don't want Smythe-Jones to get any inkling that we suspect him of any involvement he may have with Lenny Yeung; not yet, anyway.'

'In respect to Nicholas Anout, we should try and trace his whereabouts now, in fact anything else we can find out about him.'

'Another search.' Philip commented dryly.

'Yes, this investigation is turning into one long game of "Blind Man's Bluff"!'

***

The car was still out there; a dark-red saloon, parked up on the grass verge directly across the road from the house. Pamela had first noticed it shortly after Gregory had left for the station around nine and it had remained in the same position all morning. She was too far away to make out whether it was a man or a woman behind the wheel, but whoever it was could only be interested in their property; they had no immediate neighbours along that relatively quiet stretch of road, most motorists preferring to take the more direct route in and out of the town, but if they were planning a robbery they were going about it rather obviously, in broad daylight as well, and after a while dismissed it from her mind, deciding it was possibly an estate agent eager to increase his sales portfolio. It wouldn't have been the first time since Gregory and she came to live in the area when they had received unsolicited and unwanted calls from over-zealous house agents.

The gardener had brought in some chrysanthemums and she was in the hall arranging them in a vase when the front door bell rang, the sudden noise startling her and making her jump. Ever since she had read the piece in the paper a week ago she had been jittery, anticipating another visit from Philip Spencer. It was therefore with some trepidation, taking a deep steadying breath in an effort to quell her rising anxiety, she walked over to open the door.

'Martha Underwood!' she gasped, staring in astonishment at the woman she had known in Samriboi and never expected to see again. 'What on earth are you doing here and how did you find out where I lived?'

'I wanted to see you, Pamela,' Martha said quietly, 'and it wasn't all that difficult to find out where you were.'

'I suppose you had better come in now you *are* here.' Pamela said, unable to display even pretence of being gracious. She had always known

189

that Martha disliked her and had ridiculously blamed her for breaking up the relationship she'd had with Anthony and as she led her into the house, couldn't think of one valid reason why Martha had gone to such lengths to actually come and visit; it just didn't make any sense.

'Thank you, Pamela,' Martha smiled, a smile which didn't reach her eyes.

'Would you like some coffee?'

'No thank you; I won't be staying long.'

'Really? So, why are you here, Martha? I would like to know.'

'Would you?' another smile hovering for a second and one Pamela didn't like and as she looked at her more closely she felt there was something very wrong with her. She had never known her all that well and on thinking back to the Samriboi days Pamela couldn't recall having a conversation with the woman. Anthony had told her he had slept with her, pointing out in his eloquent way, that it had meant little to him and could hardly have been described as a meaningful or long-lasting relationship. Pamela hadn't been interested in any other liaisons he may have had; they had meant nothing to her, but as she looked at Martha now, standing in the middle of the library, the same room she had taken Philip Spencer, she began to wonder about her state of mind. Whether Anthony had been telling the truth or not was neither here nor there, but perhaps Martha's interpretation of what had transpired between them years ago, had meant considerably more to her. If this was the case, Pamela failed to see that it was any concern of hers. If Martha had some deep-rooted emotional problem, well so what.

'Yes, I would, Martha,' Pamela answered, 'you must admit this visit is somewhat out of the blue.'

'I don't need to tell you the real reason,' she said slowly, 'but let's say I was curious about the sort of life you were leading now.'

'But why?' genuinely puzzled, finding the exchange not only meaningless, but bizarre. Here she was, in her own home, and being subjected to this, starting to regret inviting her in. Pamela was not accustomed to being put at a disadvantage; she had always maintained an air of aloofness, a disinterest of becoming embroiled in other people's problems. It had been the same with Anthony; she had been aware of his social hang-ups, but they had been of no interest to her.

'Does your husband know about Anthony?' Martha asked her.

'You mean about him being murdered in Amsterdam. Gregory and I read about it in 'The Times',' she added.

'I don't mean about his death. I was referring to the affair you had with him; does he know about that, Pamela?'

'Gregory has never shown any interest in my life before we met, Martha. Of course he knew what happened to Norman.'

'And what did happen to him?'

'You know as much as I do about that, Martha,' she answered slowly, at the same time trying to fathom out what the woman was leading up to, 'the official verdict in Samriboi was that Norman was shot by one of the locals who broke into the bungalow.'

'Anthony and I met the day he had the car accident. I don't suppose he told you that.'

'Why should he have? The last time Norman and I saw Anthony was on the Saturday night at the club. I don't remember him being around after that.'

'We both know that's not true.'

'I believe I've had enough of this haranguing.' Pamela said quietly, 'what right have you to come here. What's the matter with you, Martha? Don't you think your behaviour is bordering on the extreme?'

'The reason we met that day was because I asked him to; I had hoped that once you and Norman left Samriboi, we could get back together again.' she said, as though she hadn't heard her, 'And do you know what he told me?'

'I'm not interested; surely this conversation was between you and Anthony and nothing to do with me.'

'That's where you are wrong, quite wrong. He told me that you and he would soon be going back to England. Together.'

'Nonsense. Absolute nonsense.'

'Is that what your husband will say when I tell him?'

The ormolu clock on the mantelpiece chiming the hour broke the silence in the room. Was this what she wanted; revenge, a mad form of retribution which may have lain dormant for over ten years and then, learning about Anthony, it had all been too much for her to handle. Of course she was lying. Even if she had seen Anthony on the Wednesday, he would never have told her about any of their plans; that would have been entirely out of character. Far too much depended on their carefully thought-out scheme where secrecy had been the key to it succeeding, which it had up to now.

'Do you really think my husband will listen to what you have just said?'

'I would say he would;' she answered, 'at first he may not believe me, but I will have sown the first seed of doubt in his mind.'

'That's wicked!'

'Not as wicked as being involved with murdering my husband, Pamela.' and without saying another word, she pushed past her and walked back into the hall.

'Just a minute;' scarcely trusting her voice. She couldn't remember ever having been so angry and knowing that Martha had no grounds for making such a remark did nothing to lessen the way she was feeling. The woman was unhinged, Pamela was sure, desperately trying to think of a way to prevent her taking her outrageous statements any further, 'why are you in such a hurry, Martha; I thought you wanted to talk to Gregory.'

'Oh, I do, but I'll be back later; probably this evening.'

'Is it money you want, Martha?'

'To buy my silence, you mean?'

'If you wish to put it like that, yes, but my reason for suggesting this is because I don't want Gregory upset. This marriage means a lot to me which may surprise you and I don't want any of your malicious meddling to create waves.'

'Alright, I'll go along with you, Pamela, but how do you know I won't speak to someone else; the police for example or to the newspapers. I'm sure they will listen to what I have to say.'

'Whether they do or not, doesn't bother me all that much, but I don't think any of them will take you seriously. You have no evidence to support your suspicions, also you will be a blackmailer, remember. Nobody has a very high esteem for people like that.'

'Perhaps not.' but the dismissive way she shrugged her shoulders was enough for Pamela to realise she had her exactly where she wanted; she had already achieved what she had set out to do this afternoon by placing her so-called cards on the table and emerging from the confrontation with a cash reward.'

'I would want the money in cash.'

'That can be arranged, so,' she asked, 'how much?'

'Fifty thousand.'

It was a lot, but Pamela didn't demur; it would be worth it to get rid of the woman. Also, she still had her own bank account which meant Gregory need never know she had made such a large withdrawal.

'Alright, Martha. It's too late to do any banking today. You had better tell me where to meet you as I don't want you coming back here.'

'I suppose it had better be in town, then.' she said with obvious reluctance, 'There's a café next door to The Castle Hotel -'

' – is that where you're staying?' interrupting her.

'Yes.'

'I much prefer the lounge bar in The Castle.' Pamela said. The hotel wasn't one she and Gregory went to, although she had been in two or three times since moving to Taunton and from what she could remember, the majority of customers were tourists, reluctant to bump into anyone she knew and being placed in the awkward position of having to introduce Martha to them.

'Incidentally,' Pamela asked as she opened the front door for her, 'how are you going to explain your new-found wealth to Luke?'

'Luke and I divorced eight years ago.'

'I would say, Martha, he's had a lucky escape; I don't think he would have liked being married to a blackmailer.'

Pamela stood on the top step and watched her walk down to the car, at the same time making a mental note of the registration number. It wasn't until she started to drive away that she saw the car rental sign in the rear window. There could be a simple explanation why Martha had chosen to hire a car. Not that it mattered, she thought, going back inside the house.

It didn't take her long to wonder whether she should have handled the situation differently, but her main concern had been to prevent Martha talking to Gregory; offering her money was the first idea she could think of, but now, as she weighed up other possible options, she was beginning to question the wisdom of her decision. She could have dismissed Martha's threat and pre-empted any further visit by telling Gregory exactly what had been discussed this afternoon, but it was too late now; he would be bound to take the blackmail issue as a sign of her guilt, proof to him that Martha had been telling the truth. Pamela felt sure this would strengthen any growing suspicions he may be having about her. She had no illusions about her husband; Gregory was a shrewd and calculating businessman; the material evidence of the extent of his success was apparent. No, she decided, she had to think of another way; she was loathe to allow Martha Underwood to get away with this. Blackmailing after all was a criminal offence and at this point in her reasoning she thought of one person who could extricate her from this dilemma, but she would have to be clever. Not dissimilar to venturing into the lion's den she thought, taking the card Philip Spencer had given her from her wallet and dialling his telephone number.

Chapter Thirteen

He was shown into the same room he had been in the last time he was here and, as then, she offered him coffee which again he refused. She had been unable to conceal her surprise, or her dismay, when she had opened the front door to him. Pamela Smythe-Jones was not as clever as she apparently thought she was. Devious certainly, but not clever. She had overlooked the fact that part of his training was to instantly recognise any sign of being manipulated as he'd done when she had phoned him.

She must be aware she was under suspicion, also the likelihood of him returning, but in an attempt to pre-empt a further visit and re-direct his focus on to someone else, she had instead brought Martha Jacobsen into the picture, but all Pamela had achieved was to strengthen his belief that she had been involved in her husband's murder. What she had done by phoning him had been a dangerous decision to make. By agreeing to Martha's attempt to blackmail her and not deciding to tell him, Pamela could have given Martha more ammunition.

Philip had spoken to Martha the evening before. Immediately after Pamela's call he had driven down to Taunton and booked into the Castle Hotel. Martha had been in the lounge bar when he went in and one look at her expression told him a great deal; she wasn't only displeased to see him, she was furious. He had spent no more than half an hour with her and while she admitted, without much prompting, that she had made an attempt to blackmail Pamela, this hadn't been accompanied by any sign of regret of having been found out and certainly none of remorse. He couldn't make her out, he'd found it impossible to believe the reason she had given for making the trip to Taunton.

"I wanted," she had said, "to make her suffer and the only way I could think of doing this was to threaten her by telling her husband about what happened in Samriboi."

"And do you know? Can you say with any authority," he had answered, "what *did* happen?"

"Of course I have no proof," she had snapped back, "but I am positive that Pamela Brookes, as she was then, is as guilty as hell! The woman is a schemer and a manipulator."

"Harsh words."

"So they might be," she had retaliated, "but I believe they are justified. Pamela *used* Anthony; she wasn't in love with him."

"When I spoke to you, you gave no hint you knew of his death in Amsterdam the week before."

"That's because I didn't know. I only heard on Saturday; the barman at the Krasnapolsky told me."

"Were you aware Anthony Johnson had assumed another identity after he left Samriboi?"

"I did as a matter of fact."

"The barman wouldn't have known, Miss Jacobsen, so how did you find out?"

"Does it really matter?" exasperation in her voice.

"It might."

"It was when he called into the office; I overheard our receptionist refer to him as Clive Edwards."

"This was on the Monday and yet, a week later when I met you, you made no mention of this."

"Why should I have?" she'd shrugged, "As far as I knew, Anthony was alive and although I was annoyed with him, it didn't make any difference; I still loved him, Mr Spencer. Nothing could have altered that."

"Even although he may have been a murderer?"

"That, as far as I'm concerned, is questionable."

"In what way."

"You appear to have overlooked the person who would have been quite capable of shooting Norman. It was Pamela Brookes who had wanted to escape; she wanted to escape from a marriage she was utterly bored with, not that she would ever have married Anthony of course. You only have to look at the affluent life style she has; Anthony could never have provided her with that."

"You do realise these are potentially slanderous remarks, Miss

Jacobsen?"

"Quite honestly, Mr Spencer, I don't care!"

It was then Philip decided there was nothing to be gained by continuing to talk to her. Her explanation for blackmailing Pamela didn't ring true. If Martha's main objective had been, as she had described it, to make her suffer why, according to what Pamela had told him, had she been so quick to agree on the figure of fifty thousand pounds. It didn't make sense. Surely, Philip had reasoned, she could have simply phoned Gregory Smythe-Jones and told him; in that way, the end result would have been more effective. The more he thought about her behaviour, the more he was starting to seriously question her sanity. As he had watched her, she hadn't looked much different to when he had last seen her in Amsterdam, except for a slight nervousness in her manner which could have been her reaction to being caught out, but now and again as he had been talking to her, her attention had wavered, giving him the impression she wasn't hearing everything he was saying. Whether Martha Jacobsen was mentally disturbed, only a psychiatrist would be able to determine.

"Miss Jacobsen," he had said to her, "I would suggest you don't get in touch with Mrs Smythe-Jones again."

"Why should I; it would be pointless now."

"Furthermore, I think it would be advisable if you were to leave Taunton."

"You don't have to concern yourself, Mr Spencer," her voice full of contempt, "I'll be on my way back to Amsterdam on Friday morning."

He hadn't seen her again and when she hadn't been in the restaurant at breakfast time, he thought it likely she was avoiding him.

'I must say, Mr Spencer,' Pamela Smythe-Jones was saying, 'I didn't expect to see you today; I thought you would be fully occupied dealing with Martha Underwood.'

'Attempted blackmail, Mrs Smythe-Jones, while undeniably a serious offence, does not come within my province, unless it bears any relevance to the investigation I am currently involved in, which is, as I told you, primarily a murder enquiry.'

'That's all very well,' she drawled in her Sloane-like voice, 'but what do you intend to do about her?'

'I have no intention of doing anything about her,' Philip said, 'I've already spoken to her and listened to what she had to say. It is entirely up to you, Mrs Smythe-Jones. If you are prepared to press charges of attempted blackmail, I suggest you contact the police.'

'I'll think about it.'

'I would like to ask you some further questions about the night your husband was killed -'

'- for goodness sake, why?' she interrupted, 'I've told you all I know.'

'Mainly, they concern the times you arrived and left the club that night.' he said, ignoring her outburst, 'I have spoken to most of those expatriates who were in the club, all of whom were already there before you arrived and they remembered when you came in and when you left, but there appears to be a discrepancy in those times you gave me.'

'A discrepancy?'

'Let me recap,' Philip said, 'although you didn't actually give me the time you arrived in the club, you did say that you and your husband had your evening meal at six-thirty as you were in the habit of doing and as soon as you had finished you left for the club, therefore I think I would be right in saying you would have arrived there around seven-thirty at the latest. Would you agree?'

'I suppose so,' shrugging, 'as I said to you before I can't remember exactly.'

'According to some of the others it was eight forty-five that evening.'

'That's not true! They're lying!'

'I can always get written and signed statements to verify this, you know.'

'It doesn't make any difference to me; they would still be lying, Mr Spencer. Anyway,' she went on, 'how can they possibly be so certain after all this time?'

'Let's talk about when you left the club.' he persisted.

'As I've said, it was late, after midnight.'

'That is not what I've been hearing, Mrs Smythe-Jones; more than one of the people I've been talking to told me you didn't stay long, no more than an hour in fact.'

'Rubbish! Once again, they're lying!'

'Can you give me any reason why they should be?'

'I haven't a clue, probably because they don't like me.'

'Would this have been because of your affair with Anthony Johnson?'

'You have no right to ask me such a thing; no right whatsoever.'

'Under the circumstances, I have every right. Up to now, my questioning has been carried out on an informal basis, Mrs Smythe-Jones, but should I decide to formalize this, I can assure you I will.'

'It would still only be my word against theirs, so it would be up to you who to believe.'

She was at it again, provoking him, pressing him, but he wasn't going to be placed in the position of taking that further step. Not yet. There was, he felt, still a long way to go, considerably more ground to cover. Later, it would be up to the courts to decide whether she was guilty of being an accomplice in her husband's murder. Meanwhile, there was a bigger issue here, that of smuggling on an international scale and he wasn't finished sifting through Johnson's shady past. There seemed to be no doubt that he killed Norman Brookes, but he still needed proof and he strongly believed by continuing to talk to those people who had been in Samriboi at the time, he would find it.

'Did you read about Anthony Johnson's death in 'The Times' last week?' Philip asked her as he was preparing to leave.

'I read about a man called Anthony Johnson having been murdered in Amsterdam' she answered, 'but quite frankly I didn't believe the article was referring to Anthony whom we knew in Samriboi; he died in a car accident.'

'Even although your late-husband's name was mentioned?'

'Propaganda.' accompanied by another dismissive shrug, 'Unlike most people, Mr Spencer, I don't believe everything I read in the newspaper, even in one as prestigious as 'The Times'. In my opinion, the purpose of the article was to place the blame for what happened to Norman on to Anthony Johnson. A neat conclusion to a case which had been unresolved for many years and presumably had remained open.'

'While I can't accept your theory,' he told her, 'I can confirm that Anthony Johnson did not die in the accident. He returned to England the following morning, subsequently changed his name and was in fact murdered while in Amsterdam recently.'

'How extraordinary, Mr Spencer.'

'I would like to return to that night again.'

'This is all becoming rather tedious.' she sighed.

'I'm sure it is. However, I interviewed Mr and Mrs Richardson while they were together but everyone else was seen individually and they were all agreed on when you were in the club, therefore, unless you can give me a credible explanation for these time differences, I will have no alternative but to treat this as an indication that you will be giving me a false statement.'

'For goodness sake,' the drawl more exaggerated; her whole manner verging on the theatrical, 'you'll have to remind me of those times again, Mr Spencer.'

'Your arrival, according to my witnesses, being eight forty-five, shall we say from when you finished your evening meal, a space of time would have been at least three quarters of an hour –'

'- not as long as that.'

'I would think so.'

'Well, all I can suggest is that perhaps we took longer than usual over our meal. Also, Mr Spencer, when I told you we started dinner at six-thirty, I didn't necessarily mean exactly at that time. It is far too long ago for me to remember.'

'Alright,' he nodded, 'how do you explain the larger gap of time from when you left the club after spending no more than an hour there, until you contacted the police at the time officially recorded of ten minutes past one; a period of approximately three hours?'

'That has to be wrong; it couldn't possibly have been.'

'Mrs Smythe-Jones,' Philip persisted, 'if independent and unrelated witnesses tell me that you arrived at eight forty-five and left after no more than an hour, I am inclined to believe them, so,' he continued, 'where did you go after you left the club?'

'I told you, I went home; back to the bungalow.'

'And discovered your husband had been killed?'

'Of course.'

'How long did it take you to drive home?'

'Ten minutes.'

'Right, if you left the club around ten you would have reached home by ten minutes past.'

'I suppose so.'

'Then what did you do?'

'What *do* you mean?'

'Did you wait almost three hours to inform the police or did you get in touch with anyone else?'

'I didn't speak to anyone until I reached the police station.'

'I am aware the bungalows were not equipped with telephones, Mrs Smythe-Jones, therefore presumably you had to drive there.'

'That's right. While I still don't believe I stayed in the bungalow for almost three hours before reporting Norman's death, you have to understand, Mr Spencer, the shock of finding him the way I did was dreadful. My first instincts were to run out of that bungalow and put the sight of him lying slumped across the desk, the back of his shirt covered with blood, right out of my mind, but of course I didn't. It's true I did take a while to calm down and to stop shaking, I think I may have passed out for a few minutes, I don't know, but when I eventually went out to the car I was in such a state of shock I wasn't in any fit state to drive.'

'So, what did you do?'

'I remained there, sitting inside the car, for what seemed an age, but I really have no idea how long it was before I felt able to drive into the town and speak to someone at the police station.'

'But, when you were questioned by the Zambian authorities, you led them to believe you had only just discovered his body. Why didn't you tell them the truth, Mrs Smythe-Jones?'

'Because I was ashamed of the way I had behaved. It had been cowardly of me. I didn't want Norman's family to know how I had reacted.'

'I see,' he said, 'and you would be prepared to sign a written statement supporting this?'

'I have no objection, Mr Spencer. I'll sign it.'

***

Gregory had seen the silver grey BMW turn into the drive from his rear view mirror, having passed it only seconds before. Pamela hadn't mentioned she was expecting anyone, certain it couldn't be one of her friends so early in the day and hoping it wasn't the man from the Foreign Office again, remembering how upset she had been after she'd read that piece in the newspaper, although she had insisted she hadn't been. He was approaching the station now and, pulling into the car park, decided to put any further conjecturing to the back of his mind, knowing that if the driver of the BMW was Philip Spencer, Pamela would be well able to answer any more questions he asked her.

He had only been in his office for twenty minutes when Ellen buzzed through from the showroom to say Inspector Hugh Bannister of New Scotland Yard had come in and was asking to see him.

'Any idea why, Ellen?' he asked her, stalling for time. Gregory did not like surprises; they worried him. He preferred to be in full control and for whatever reason this Inspector Hugh Bannister had for calling unexpectedly, it couldn't be good and of course he had no alternative but to see him.

'Sorry, Gregory,' she answered, 'he didn't say.'

'Alright, Ellen,' he said, preparing himself, 'you'd better show him in.'

Inspector Bannister was a tall thin man in his mid to late forties, Gregory reckoned; his donnish appearance made more pronounced by rimless glasses.

'How can I help you, Inspector?' Gregory asked, gesturing towards the small conference table, deciding it would be more conducive to whatever the man had to say.

'Mr Smythe-Jones,' he said, 'the reason I'm here is in respect to a sale you made of four oriental figurines.'

'Yes?'

'I have the receipt you gave the lady at the time she made the purchase.' passing the receipt across to him.

'Six years ago,' he commented, noting the date, 'I would have to check my records to make sure, although I must say the receipt appears to be one of ours.'

'Is the hand-writing yours, sir?'

'Not mine, no; it does resemble my assistant's.'

'You're not sure?'

'One cannot be too careful, Inspector,' Gregory pointed out, 'forgeries do occur quite frequently in this business and as New Scotland Yard is involved, presumably there is something wrong.'

'These four figurines, Mr Smythe-Jones, have been formally authenticated as being part of a private collection and were stolen a few months before they were purchased by Miss Campbell.'

'Stolen property! Are you saying that Gregory's Antiques have handled stolen property?'

'Once you have shown me the entry on your records of the sale, I will be in a position to answer that.'

'I see.' Tight-lipped, he walked over to the desk and switched on the computer. He remembered only too well Lenny giving him those figurines. He had been in Hong Kong making selected purchases of embroidered silks and tapestries for an Asian theme he was planning and Lenny had suggested he included the figurines, saying they should fetch a good price for anyone particularly interested in ivory and porcelain pieces of that style. As usual, he hadn't asked him where they came from and as a precaution had not included them in any stock inventory. This had been, as far as he was concerned, the main risk of any transaction between Lenny and him and up to now there had been no comeback.

Gregory scrolled back to the year 2006, displaying on the screen all the sales made during May and there they were; the first of May, two ivory and two porcelain figurines sold to Miss Campbell.

'Here is the entry, Inspector.' he said, swivelling the screen round for him to see for himself.

'Right,' he said, 'and what sort of stock system do you have, sir?'

'We always have a physical stock check each year, although all purchases and sales are entered into the computer system.'

'Do you and your assistant conduct the stock checks?'

'Oh, no; my accountants always do that as part of their annual audit.'

'Well, it would appear that those four figurines were sold from here, Mr Smythe-Jones.'

'That's dreadful, Inspector. This sort of thing has never happened in my business before.'

'Do you have the receipt for when you bought these items?'

'Afraid I don't; you see, I was in Hong Kong on a sales trip in the April of that year. Mostly, I was purchasing embroidered silks and tapestries and as those figurines caught my eye I bought them in the hope they may appeal to anyone interested.'

'And you didn't receive any receipts?'

'For the silks I did, but not for the figurines. I actually discovered them in one of Hong Kong's night markets and didn't get one.'

'Are you in the habit of making purchases for the purpose of selling them from such an unorthodox source?'

'No, I'm not, Inspector.'

'I've seen your showroom,' he said, 'and found it most impressive. Do you have regular customers?'

'There are a number of people who often come in and have a look round. Usually, they are looking for something in particular and invariably they make a purchase.'

'Do you operate a client base, sir?'

'I never felt there was any need.'

After he had gone, Gregory remained at the window looking down at the street below, watching as Inspector Bannister emerged from the building and with long strides reached the traffic lights at the pedestrian crossing. He went over in his mind everything that had been said. There had been questions Gregory had wanted to ask him, but had held back, not wanting to display any sign of alarm; the most important one being, why, what should be a straightforward enquiry to establish where he'd bought those figurines, be carried out by one of New Scotland Yard's senior officers? Should he be reading more into this, he wondered. Should he now give Lenny a ring? Gregory wanted to speak to him in any case about the figurines, but perhaps it was time Lenny was told about Philip Spencer.

'There have been a few worrying developments, Lenny.' Gregory said to him as soon as he came on the line, not wasting any time on unnecessary preamblings.

'Just how worrying, Gregory?'

'That remains to be seen, but I think you should know what's been happening here.'

'Fire ahead.'

'First of all, do you buy the English 'Times'?'

'Occasionally, but not for a couple of weeks; why?'

'There was a piece in last Wednesday's edition which in many respects is apropos to what you had been telling me about Clive fixing the car crash in Africa.'

'Really?'

'Yes, the journalist had certainly done his homework,' going on to relate as much as he could remember from the article, 'so,' he added, 'you could say as far as Clive's assumed new identity was concerned, that the cat is well and truly out of the bag, but to come to my point, Lenny, ironically, not only did I know the man who was shot, but he was Pamela's first husband.'

'Extraordinary, Gregory,' he said, 'but where does the worrying part come in?'

'Frankly, I don't know whether to be worried or not, but a few days before 'The Times' ran the piece, Pamela had a visit from someone from the Foreign Office; Philip Spencer he's called, and he was asking her about the night when Norman was killed, also about the rigged car crash.'

'What day did she get this visit?'

'A week past Monday,' Gregory said, 'she didn't tell me at first; it wasn't until she read that piece in the paper on the Wednesday morning. She had been concerned about my reaction if she told me she'd had this visit from Philip Spencer.'

'Understandable enough, Gregory. Anyway,' Lenny went on, 'I'm glad you've told me. I don't think we need concern ourselves over what happened all those years ago in Zambia, but what we should be considering is just how close Philip Spencer is in reaching any incriminating conclusions which could affect both of us.'

'I know.'

'I had a call from my co-director at Bakker & Bakker telling me he'd had a visit from him.'

'He gets around, doesn't he?'

'Let's hope he doesn't get too close for comfort, Gregory.'

'That aptly brings me to my other reason for calling you.'

'Yes, go on.'

'You remember the four ivory and porcelain figurines I brought back with me from Hong Kong?'

'Yes, I do, a few years ago though.'

'Six, Lenny. Well, this morning, an officer from New Scotland Yard was here. Apparently, they have been authenticated as having been stolen a few months before you handed them over to me.'

'Good God! This has never happened before!'

'I know, Lenny. When I heard, as you can imagine, I was taken totally off guard, which meant I had to think pretty fast.'

'What did you tell him?'

'Well, when he asked to see a receipt for their purchase, I concocted the explanation that I had been to Hong Kong on a sales trip, which of course was true, and that I had discovered the figurines in one of their night markets and the stallholder didn't give me any receipt.'

'Neat. Do you think he believed you?'

'Hard to say, but if he didn't, I don't suppose there's much he can do about it.'

'What about our other transactions,' Lenny asked, 'have you recorded those sales you've made?'

'No, I've always kept those separately, not on the computer system, and they have always been made to personal contacts I've built up over the years. On reflection, it's a pity I hadn't held on to those pieces until I had a buyer, but I didn't.'

'I wouldn't blame yourself, you know, Gregory.'

'I know, but -'

'- you're concerned there could be a link between this and what Philip Spencer is trying to unearth?'

'Yes,' he admitted slowly, 'I am.'

'There's no point, Gregory; worry is a killer.'

'A psychological attitude, Lenny.'

'Perhaps. Not that I want to add to any of the stress you may be going through at the moment,' he said, 'but there are too many background noises for my liking; we have to be circumspect here, especially where this Spencer guy is concerned. There is a possibility, only a possibility mind you, that Cecelia may have been followed during the time she was in London.'

'Why do you say that?'

'She told me when she came back that she'd had two encounters while she was away. In Amsterdam she was approached by someone purporting to be Peter Prescott and then when she arrived at Heathrow he spoke to her again. I don't know whether this was actually Philip Spencer or not, but either way, it sounds as though she was tricked into telling him where she was going, namely Russell Square. As you know, she was staying at the Hotel Russell -'

'- and you think she could have been seen talking to me in the lounge bar?' he interrupted.

'Again, Gregory, I don't know. However,' Lenny continued, 'if you should be asked at any time whether you had seen her there, I suggest you say you were old friends and had met up for a drink while she was in London. Incidentally, for the record, Cecelia came from London originally and lived there up until the time she came to Hong Kong about twenty-five years ago.'

'Alright; that shouldn't be too difficult.'

'Good, and I'll prime Cecelia to say the same if she should ever see the man again, or anyone else if it comes to that.'

***

Number thirteen The Mews was one of six mock-Georgian town houses, the cobbled street tucked neatly and unobtrusively behind Norwich cathedral. Philip had phoned Harry Knight before leaving Taunton, deciding he could be helpful in providing him with what he needed to disprove Pamela's statement. Six o'clock was chiming somewhere in the distance as he pulled up outside the house and walked up the short paved path to the front door.

'Mr Spencer?'

'That's right;' Philip said, 'I appreciate you being able to see me, Mr Knight.'

'No problem; as I mentioned on the phone, I finish work early on a Thursday, but,' he added, opening the door wider, 'come in.'

Philip followed him across the hall and into the kitchen; ultra-modern with honey-toned Italian floor tiling; mustard and cream fitments; a long pine-wood table in the centre of the room with matching high-backed chairs and a cream roller blind at the sash window overlooking the River Wensum at the back of the mews.

'Would you like a beer, Mr Spencer?'

'Please; just what I need after that long drive.'

'I bet,' opening the fridge door and taking out a couple of cans, handed one to him, 'here you are;' he said, 'I've often wondered why that first beer at the end of the afternoon always tastes better than any of the others.'

'So have I,' Philip smiled, 'probably feel you've earned it.'

'I don't know,' he grinned, 'but I certainly work a lot harder here than I did when I was in Zambia.'

'I've been talking to a number of people who were there at the same time as you, Mr Knight,' Philip said, 'and they all described to me what the expatriate life was like out there.'

'I take it they're all back in England now?'

'Yes, that's right, although Mr and Mrs Richardson only returned a couple of weeks ago.'

'Bill and Mary; they were real colonials, you know; they'd been living in Samriboi a long time. Also,' he added, 'Bill played a good game of snooker.'

'He mentioned he'd had a game with you on the night Norman Brookes was killed.'

'I thought he may have done. He was always rather sceptical about that business and now, of course, learning that Anthony did a disappearing act at the same time, it would seem he wasn't all that far away from the truth.'

'They've all told me about that evening in the club which has helped me to formulate some sort of idea about the sequence of, for instance, the various times everyone arrived and left.'

'I see,' Harry nodded, 'well, I'll do my best to remember as well.'

'If you would.'

'If you'd asked me before I met Norman's brother the other week and reading the piece in 'The Times', I would probably have had some difficulty, but since then, I've been thinking and beginning to wonder what really must have happened. I can't remember the actual date, Mr Spencer, except that it was a Wednesday, about a week before Christmas. I didn't get to the club until eight-thirty, even a few minutes later, I don't know, but I'd been playing squash after work and had gone home to change and have something to eat. The squash club was attached to the mine company's offices and although I worked for the bank, I was able to get my membership.' he explained.

'I understand Pamela Brookes arrived very soon after you did.'

'She did, yes. Within minutes I think.'

'Had you noticed her driving behind you?'

'No, I didn't actually, but I suppose she must have been.'

'Terry Price has drawn up a rough sketch of where you were all living.' taking Terry's map from his pocket and passing it across the table to him.

'Yes,' Harry said, looking at it, 'it's pretty accurate too.'

'That's good. Am I right in saying you would have had to pass the Brookes' bungalow on your way to the club?'

'Oh, yes; there was no other way, because turning to the right out of the crescent would have merely taken me round all the other bungalows, so I naturally turned left and then right towards the roundabout in the direction of the club.'

'I understand, and did you notice if there was any car parked outside their bungalow when you went back to change and when you left for the club?'

'Only Norman's.'

'How long do you think it took you to change and have your meal?'

'It was only a snack, but I would say about three quarters of an hour at the most.'

'Alright, and you spent some time talking to her when she arrived, didn't you?'

'Yes, but not for long. Pamela didn't stay more than an hour and by then the Richardsons had joined us and that was when Bill and I had our game of snooker.'

'And after the game, Mr Knight?'

'Bill and Mary went home and I had a couple of drinks with Terry and his wife and the three of us left the club at the same time which was about eleven-thirty.'

'When you drove into the crescent -'

'- sorry to interrupt, he apologised, 'but it's just occurred to me Pamela's car wasn't there so she couldn't have gone home as she said.

Mind you,' he added, 'I suppose it's possible she may have gone somewhere else.'

'Have you any ideas where?'

'No, I haven't, but I'm sure you've learned by now that she had earned herself something of a reputation in Samriboi. It was quite obvious to us, except for poor Norman of course, that she was having an affair with Anthony, but she may have been involved with someone else.'

'We'll find out, Mr Knight.'

'Do you suspect she may have had something to do with any of this?'

'We have no proof at this stage.' Philip said, sensing that Harry Knight was sufficiently intelligent to realise he was unable to say anything further.

'Anthony would have needed help to leave Samriboi that night, but I do appreciate your position. Your task must be like trying to put a jigsaw together, Mr Spencer.'

'And made more frustrating by finding some pieces missing.' Philip finished for him.

Later, having booked into The Premier Inn' in Duke Street, he gave Charles a ring, wanting to tell him where he was and that he would be back in London the following morning.

'Any progress, Philip?' Charles asked.

'Not a great deal, except I now have a signed and written statement from Pamela Smythe-Jones which differs considerably from what she said before in that in a rather obvious effort to wriggle out of the position she'd found herself in with respect to the time she arrived and left the club, she has said she and her husband probably took longer than usual over their evening meal, and that she actually found his body much earlier, but was unable due to her shocked state, to call the police.'

'Not much of an alibi.'

'Exactly, and this is why I decided to drive here as I wanted to speak to Harry Knight. And this was where Terry Price's sketch came in useful.'

'Yes?'

'As Harry's bungalow was next to the one the Brookes had, he would have had to drive past it each time he went anywhere and Pamela's car wasn't outside when he went back home after work and prior to going to the club.'

'Interesting.'

'It is, isn't it; especially as everyone I've spoken to was in agreement that she arrived only a matter of minutes after Harry.'

'That suggests she would have had time to drive Johnson back into the town after he'd rigged the crash.'

'She could always explain that away by saying she had been somewhere else immediately after her meal and before arriving at the club, but it's interesting to note that as the place where the car was found is just off the road to Ndola, we now know thanks to Terry's sketch, that if she had been there, she must have been unlucky enough to turn into the Samriboi Road only minutes after Harry joined it from the crescent which could explain the short space of time between when they arrived at the club.'

'That sounds feasible, Philip. A pity he hadn't noticed her driving behind him though.'

'I know, and if he had, he would have been bound to see whether she had a passenger.'

'Did Harry Knight see her car parked outside the bungalow later that night?'

'No, according to him it wasn't there.'

'Quite damning for her if she should be called to the witness box; she would have to do some quick thinking to get out of that one.'

'She might say she'd been with someone and didn't get back to the bungalow until much later.'

'Because of her promiscuity, you mean?'

'Yes; Harry only reiterated what most of the others have been saying about her behaviour around the town.'

'All in all,' Charles said, 'it does appear that the cards are rapidly stacking up against her.'

'They do, but then when this case eventually reaches the court room, it will be in the hands of the legal profession.'

'Were you able to see Martha Jacobsen when you were in Taunton?'

'Yes, I spoke to her last evening and this is another reason why I'm phoning you, Charles. I don't altogether believe her explanation for trying to blackmail Pamela. Martha was insistent that it was to make her suffer by telling her husband about what had happened in Samriboi. Martha Jacobsen is an extremely bitter woman and yet she had been quick, too quick in my opinion, to meekly settle for the money; in other words to back-off.'

'She sounds somewhat unstable, Philip.'

'I believe she is; she told me she would be returning to Amsterdam tomorrow morning. I'd like us to make sure she is on the flight.'

'We'll see to that, Philip.'

'That's good and I should be back before eleven in the morning.'

Chapter Fourteen

Martha had no intention of flying back to Amsterdam the following morning. She did, however, book out of 'The Castle Hotel', choosing instead, a smaller one away from the centre of the town. She needed to plan what she would do next, somewhere quiet without any likelihood of being disturbed by either Philip Spencer or Pamela. She hadn't liked his manner the other evening and the way he questioned her was tantamount to an interrogation. More or less ordering her to leave Taunton and not to make any further contact with Pamela had rankled. It wasn't as if she was under arrest, for God's Sake; she was free to go anywhere she pleased, with or without his approval. And she would; she would leave when she was ready and not before. It would appear Pamela, in her vamp-like way, had hoodwinked yet another susceptible male. From the moment Philip Spencer had walked into the bar, Martha realised she had been set up. Pamela had tricked her into believing she would go along with her, but she must have contacted him as soon as she had driven away from the house and he, presumably hot-footed it down to Taunton for the sole purpose of putting a stop to any blackmailing. How smug she must be feeling; one telephone call to Philip Spencer to do her dirty work for her; her husband would continue to know nothing about what had gone on in Samriboi; also, she would have got rid of her blackmailer. If anything, Martha's resolve to deal with her had intensified; she had to think of a way, this time foolproof, of how to destroy the woman who had cast such a spell over Anthony.

It wasn't until later in the day when she was in the hotel bar that the idea came to her; it was so incredibly simple, she wondered why she hadn't thought of it before. Taunton had more than one daily newspaper and even if Pamela didn't buy a copy someone in the area would and if they were to read something, however ambiguously written, to discredit her reputation that would be sufficient to achieve the result Martha wanted. Pamela Brookes was first and foremost a snob, very much aware of her social standing and, presumably now living as she did, would have made a number of acquaintances sufficiently interested in her, particularly concerning her past. It was of no concern to Martha that she wouldn't be able to see for herself the impact such an exposure would have on Pamela, but she was confident it would be effective in reducing her elevated standing in the Taunton community, including hopefully to create a rift in her marriage. Even if her husband accepted whatever lies she would presumably come up with, there would always be an element of doubt in his mind. That would be sufficient, Martha felt, to avenge Anthony's death.

She took 'The Times' cutting from her bag, smoothing out the creases caused by the constant folding and unfolding she had subjected it to since Saturday. Reading through the piece again, picking up on every nuance, one in particular literally jumped out at her, continuing to have the ability to enrage her: "..... and up to the present time it is understood that there is no valid explanation .....". It sounded to her as if Anthony was being used as a scapegoat. In Martha's opinion, it was of no consequence who actually pulled the trigger that night. Was this the way a previously unsolved murder case was being finally wrapped up, she wondered bitterly. Did the journalist, Guy Ford, really know what he was talking about? Had he actually been to Samriboi and seen for himself where Anthony had crashed his car? She very much doubted it. Martha knew exactly where the ravine was; she'd passed it numerous times on her way to Ndola. If Anthony had driven there and rigged the accident which seemed to be the general consensus of opinion, it would have been impossible for him to reach Lusaka without help. Someone had helped him and who other than the woman he had been having an affair with. Pamela Brookes. Why else was Norman shot on the same night?

Martha returned to Samriboi and like the reel of an old movie she followed each sequence of events throughout that day, from the morning when she had been playing tennis with Peggy to when she and Luke went back home from the club. For days from when she'd heard the Brookes would soon be leaving Samriboi she had begun to hope that she and Anthony could get back together again, but as soon as she had spoken to him that afternoon, realised there had been no substance in them; he had not lost his obsession for the woman. When she arrived at the club on the Wednesday evening, she had been glad Pamela hadn't been there and somehow she managed to act naturally chatting to Peggy and Terry when really she had felt like weeping. When Pamela hadn't appeared until later she assumed she must have been with Anthony, but she'd been wrong. It had been ten when she and Luke went home but Pamela had already left the club by then. This could mean she had driven Anthony to Lusaka; she would have had time as Martha heard the following day it had been around one in the morning before the police arrived at the Brookes' bungalow. She tried to remember whether Pamela's car had been there when Luke and she had driven into the crescent, visualising now the front of their bungalow. There had been a light on, not from the lounge, but from one of the rooms at the side of the building. Norman's car had been there; she was positive about that, but there was an empty space next to it where Pamela usually parked. The reason it hadn't been there was because she hadn't return from Lusaka, although remembering how long it took to drive there, she would have been hard-pressed to do the return trip in the time. She could have taken him as far as Kabwe though, Martha thought, and if so she knew where he must have spent the night; it would have been at 'The Tuskers Hotel'. 'The Tuskers' wasn't the only hotel in Kabwe, but most of the people she had known in Samriboi had stayed there at one time or another, so she was probably right. Pamela Brookes thinks she is so damn smart, Martha murmured under her breath, but she isn't. It needed someone who had lived there to have been able to work all that out; Philip Spencer wouldn't have, that's for certain. Why should he; for all Martha knew he probably didn't even suspect Pamela as being involved. He would need proof and where was he going to get that? Yes, Pamela had covered her tracks well, therefore all the more reason to expose her for what she is and for what she did to Anthony. Taking out a notebook from her bag, Martha began to draft out what she was going to send to the editor of Taunton's main newspaper.

It rained heavily during the night; thunder rolling over from the Bristol

Channel, preceded by flashes of lightening illuminating the room, making further sleep impossible. The end of the Indian summer, she thought, turning her back to the window and pulling the duvet over her head, not sorry to be leaving soon. Once she had sent off the email, Martha decided she would make her way back to London. She found Taunton claustrophobic, but then, she had always preferred cities. Even living within the tight expatriate community of Samriboi hadn't been as bad as this town; she had always been able to fill her days with the knowledge that their stay was only temporary. In the beginning, they had been good years, but it hadn't taken long before the disillusionment had set in, brought about mainly by the sheer tedium of everyday life, punctuated periodically on her part by short trips back to London. Meeting Anthony had added to her growing disenchantment, both with her marriage and being more or less forced to meet up with the same friends each day when the general conversation lacked any real depth or interest. She had allowed herself to become insular, but she'd hoped that Anthony would change all that. Finally, when Luke and she returned to England, Martha recognised she no longer wanted to stay married to him. Those had been difficult weeks leading up to the divorce with Luke stubbornly opposing every reasonable request she had made in the terms of the settlement, as if she was hell bent on extracting as much money as she could from him. By the time the divorce came through she had made up her mind to return to Amsterdam. It hadn't taken long to settle back in her home country; she found a job which she enjoyed, made new friends and was reasonably content with the way her life had turned out. That was until recently; seeing Anthony again had spoiled everything for her; once more he was occupying her mind. Perhaps she thought she would feel differently once she had dealt with Pamela Brookes.

By midday she was ready to leave. The rain had continued intermittently through the morning, but by the time she pulled away from the parking area in front of the hotel, a pale watery sun was breaking through grey clouds. Soon, Taunton was behind her. Progress was slow with heavy traffic all seemingly going in the same direction towards the

M5. It wasn't until she joined the motorway she was able to put her foot down and maintain a steady speed, overtaking many of the trucks she had seen earlier. She was in the slip road leading to the first service station when the brakes failed. She was unable to reduce speed, the car rapidly losing control, zigzagging towards the car park, going into a spin on the wet tarmac and crashing into the side of an articulated truck parked fifty metres away by the perimeter fence.

***

Philip called into Charles' office as soon as he returned to London; it had been a miserable drive for most of the way, especially on the motorway, with a combination of rain lashing against the windscreen and spray from the stream of traffic, predominantly trucks, heading in the direction of the city, making visibility poor.

'Good, Philip, you're back safely;' Charles said, 'you made good time in spite of the weather.'

'I listened to the weather forecast last night so thought it best to make an early start.'

'Well, you were right to be concerned about whether Martha Jacobsen would have been on her flight to Amsterdam this morning; she had a reservation for nine o'clock, but didn't turn up at Heathrow.'

'Therefore it's anyone's guess where she is now.' Philip said, although not all that surprised. She would have to surface at some point he thought philosophically.

'Presumably she will eventually be returning to Amsterdam,' echoing his thoughts, 'and as soon as she turns up at Heathrow, Immigration will let us know.'

'Mind you, Charles, it's what she is up to at the moment that bothers me. I've no way of knowing whether she took my advice or not; she may have left Taunton on Thursday not wanting to see me again.'

'She may have done. Do you think she realised you were staying at the same hotel?'

'I would say so; a woman as innovative as she undoubtedly is would have made it her business to find out.'

'You're probably right; from how you've described her she does seem to have a knack of causing trouble.'

They were interrupted by the buzz of Charles' internal phone, Philip watching him as he pressed the button, some second-sense telling him this could have something to do with their enquiry. Charles' secretary had seen him come into his office and she wouldn't be interrupting him unless she considered it sufficiently important.

'Yes, Alison,' he was saying, 'that's right, put him through.' at the same time picking up the receiver of one of the other telephones, 'Good morning, Guy.' he said, looking across at Philip, a quizzical expression on his face. This would be the journalist, Guy Ford, Philip worked out, intrigued to find out why he was calling.

'Well, well,' Charles said, after replacing the receiver, 'as you've probably realised, Philip, that was Guy Ford from 'The Times'.'

'I thought it might be.'

'He had a call from the editor of one of Taunton's newspapers a short while ago. Apparently, an email came through earlier this morning from someone calling her or himself P. James and the context of what this person wanted them to print was too hot for him to handle. Guy will be sending this through by teleprinter within the next couple of minutes, so we'll be able to read it for ourselves.'

'Martha Jacobsen.' Philip said.

'Sounds like it, yes; Pat James was the name she used when she phoned John Brookes. Not very clever of her.' he added grimly.

'I agree, another sign perhaps of how unhinged she's become. Did Guy give any indication why the editor should have contacted him?'

'Mainly because he'd read Guy's piece in 'The Times' the other week and I rather think he trusts Guy's integrity. He wouldn't have wanted it to fall into someone else's hands, especially as very broad hints were made in the email which would be detrimental to the Smythe-Jones who are, apart from being extremely wealthy, much-respected in the Taunton area.'

Alison came into the office at that moment, giving Charles a couple of sheets of A4.

'This message has just come through, sir; I've made an extra copy; you'll both be able to read it at the same time.'

'That was thoughtful, thank you, Alison. Do you think you could rustle us up some coffee?'

'Of course.'

Charles passed a copy over to him: 'This should make interesting reading, Philip.'

"Apropos to the article in 'The Times' (Murdered Man was Imposter, Wednesday 26th September), when it was obliquely suggested there was "a certain relevance" in the murder of Norman Brookes to the disappearance of Anthony Johnson in Zambia ten years ago, I would strongly challenge this implication. While evidence has now proved conclusively that Anthony Johnson did change his identity on his return to Europe, any further aspersions to his character can be little more than conjecture.

"The article was biased against a man who may or may not have been guilty. If it now, after several years, transpires that the murder of Norman Brookes was not carried out by a local gang as decided at the Inquest, Mr Ford should be asking himself why Anthony Johnson would have gone to such lengths as to shoot Norman Brookes; he would have had nothing to gain, even although rumours have indicated he had been having an affair with the wife of the murdered man, but these were only rumours.

"Only one person was responsible. Only one person would gain and it certainly was not Anthony Johnson, but then, dead men can't talk. There is another factor which should be taken into consideration; Norman Brookes' widow re-married within a matter of months after his death and is now living in considerable luxury in Taunton, thus disproving the existence of any strong romantic bond there may have been between her and Anthony Johnson, indicating that any suspicions attached to him for having been responsible for the sudden demise of Norman Brookes on the same night he had decided to leave Zambia as dramatically as he had, are not only unlikely but unfounded. P. James."

'I'm not surprised the editor wouldn't touch it,' Philip remarked dryly, 'surely she didn't really expect him to, Charles?'

'Who knows,' Charles shrugged, 'but even if it didn't reach the print stage, the damage had been done; the editor would have known immediately she was referring to Pamela Smythe-Jones.'

'Even although her name hadn't been mentioned?'

'I would think so; as you know, Philip, Taunton is a relatively small town, not like London where nobody knows or cares what anyone else is doing, far less about what they had been or done in the past. In comparison, they are a parochial lot and if this had been published,' he added, tapping the copy on the desk, 'you can be sure there would have been many who would have done their best to find out.'

'Pamela would, even now, still be considered an outsider.'

'That's right. As far as the editor was concerned, he would have access to discover who Norman Brookes had been married to; he may have been sufficiently interested to have done this at the time he read Guy Ford's article.'

'No wonder he said it was too hot to handle.'

'Too true; Gregory Smythe-Jones would have been down on him like a ton of bricks.'

'He could afford to.'

'At the moment, Philip, he can, but who's to say what will emerge from these enquiries into his activities.'

'Going back to this email,' Philip said, 'I think we can say Martha Jacobsen is responsible.'

'Yes, one final stab at Pamela Smythe-Jones before she returns to Amsterdam.'

'I still think she's behaving irrationally. If she does go back, she won't know whether it will be printed or not.'

'I know,' Charles agreed, 'but either way she will have sown the seed I suppose, but as you say, not rational behaviour.'

'You know,' Philip said slowly, 'I've been thinking.'

'Yes?'

'Somewhat far-fetched, although not entirely unreasonable to suggest Pamela shot her husband and not Johnson.'

'That's always a possibility, Philip. A lot depends on just how close the pair of them were; perhaps not so much Pamela's feelings towards him, but we don't know, and never will, how besotted he was by her and he would have to be to shoot her husband in cold blood like that.'

'Once again, in the final analysis, the courts will decide. If she is taken into custody, it would be virtually impossible to charge her with murder -'

'- because, as Martha Jacobsen said, dead men can't talk.'

***

The fatal accident at the Taunton Deane service station was on the six o'clock news; Luke Underwood, having called into the "Sherlock Holmes" for a drink after work, remained at the bar and as far away as possible from the television screen. He had a dislike of his leisure moments being interrupted by the outside world, namely a depressing reminder of what was all too often mainly doom and gloom. He missed the first part of the announcement, but hearing Martha's name mentioned pulled him up with a jerk. Unable to believe what he was hearing, he moved closer to the screen:

"........................ the body of the woman was identified this afternoon by her sister, Mrs Audrey Park," the studio announcer was saying, followed by the cameras zooming into the service station presumably shortly after the accident happened. The area, which appeared to be one of the car parks, had been cordoned off with tape, a group of white-faced onlookers being interviewed by a reporter in the foreground and behind him, the wreck of a dark red saloon car. Luke couldn't see the make; not that it mattered, he had no idea what Martha would have been driving. There was no mistake though; it had been Martha alright. If he'd had any doubts, as soon as he heard Audrey's name mentioned, he knew for certain. The camera zoomed into the reporter, blotting out the mangled heap of metal: "it's too early to say at this stage," he said, "what caused the crash. Some of the people here whom I've spoken to are all agreed that the car had seemed to be totally out of control; it had not reduced speed as it entered the parking area, causing considerable panic among those in the vicinity of its path until, miraculously without further damage, had finally collided with the articulated truck, which the driver may have done her best to avoid, but without success ...."

Luke couldn't bear to hear any more and turning his back on the screen, returned to the bar. So, he thought, she's gone. The woman he had been married to; had once loved. He was finding it hard to absorb the stark fact of the absolute finality of it all. He should give Audrey a call; the two sisters had never been close and he had only met her a couple of times, but he had liked her. He didn't have her address or telephone number, but that was no excuse. It was the least he could do, but deciding to wait until the following day; she would have quite enough to do, without hearing from an ex-brother-in-law. There was one person he could talk to though; Terry would understand why he needed to offload some of the shock he was feeling.

He waited until he was home before giving him a ring. As always each evening Luke bought the 'Evening Standard' and as soon as he read the headlines, wished he hadn't. Exercising his willpower, he didn't read what they had to say, realising it was unlikely to differ from what he'd already heard on the news. He didn't have to be told it had been a spectacular fatal accident at the Taunton Deane Service Station as the headline boldly proclaimed.

'Luke,' Terry said, 'I hoped you would call.'

'You've seen the six o'clock news then?'

'I have, yes, but I couldn't be certain it was Martha.'

'Oh, of course, you mean about the surname?'

'Yes, so it was her?'

'It was Terry. Martha reverted back to her maiden name of Jacobsen after the divorce and, like you, when I heard I couldn't believe it, but as soon as I heard Martha's sister mentioned, I knew for sure.'

'Sorry, Luke,' he said sympathetically, 'how are you feeling?'

'Numb, actually. Just numb. I mean, as you know, I haven't seen or heard from her for years, not since the divorce in fact and when she told me she was going back to Amsterdam to live.'

'Well,' Terry said, 'there's nothing you can do, Luke.'

'I know and to be honest, I don't want to do anything. Even the thought of feeling obliged to give her sister a ring is too much at the moment. I'll probably feel differently tomorrow, at least I hope so.'

'It can't be easy for you and it's pointless me telling you not to dwell on it.'

'Thanks, Terry. It's just so bloody final, that's all.'

'I know.'

***

'Who is Lenny Yeung, Gregory?'

'Lenny?'

'Yes, he phoned about ten minutes ago, said it was urgent. He wants you to call him back.'

'Alright, I'll do that, Pamela,' he said, shrugging off his jacket and draping it over one of the kitchen chairs, 'meanwhile, why not open a bottle of wine and don't look so worried, Lenny is an alarmist; I've known him for years and he is inclined to over-react.'

'But who is he, Gregory; you haven't said.'

'He's my Hong Kong supplier, darling.' he explained briefly, going into his study to make the call.

Pamela didn't usually question him about anyone who phoned, but since Philip Spencer's visit the day before her nerves had been on edge, expecting that every time the telephone rang it would be him. It had been bad enough seeing him again without being subjected to more questions although she did think she'd handled the situation as well as she could having had no pre-warning that she would have to go over again those differences in time. Obviously, she had underestimated his terrier-like tenacity and he'd been spot-on when he had suggested the reason why the others hadn't liked her was because of her relationship with Anthony; not that any of them could substantiate what they were thinking. They had been basing what were no more than narrow-minded suppositions on tittle-tattle; it wasn't as though Anthony and she had been caught in any compromising situation. All of this conjecturing brought her full circle back to Martha; by her vindictiveness she had arrived too close to how Norman had been shot and how Anthony had been able to get away from Samriboi that night. If, heaven forbid, the case was brought to court and Martha was called to the witness box, she didn't need any imagination to realise how the prosecuting lawyer would use that. It didn't bear thinking about, but this wasn't just something she could ignore; Martha remained a threat. Pamela had a nasty feeling that her hastily put-together plan to over-rule her had failed and the fact that Philip Spencer was not going to do anything about the attempted blackmail was not a comforting thought. Martha was still in a position to attack her from another angle, therefore nothing had changed.

Pamela had spent the rest of the morning after Philip Spencer had gone, worrying about what she should do about Martha. By midday, she'd had enough; she couldn't stay indoors a moment longer, she had to get out. She would try and find out whether Martha was still in Taunton, dismissing that she may have already left and returned to wherever she came from. Pamela had little to go on; she could remember the make and the number of the car she had been driving and that she had been staying at 'The Castle', and driving into Taunton, she had pulled up outside the hotel. There was no sign of the car in the parking area, but that didn't necessarily mean she'd booked out. Pushing open the door, Pamela went inside, walking over to the reception desk.

'Good morning, Mrs Smythe-Jones.'

'Good morning, Sally,' Pamela forced a smile; the downside she thought of knowing so many people in this town, 'I'm looking for an old friend of mine,' she fabricated, 'Mrs Martha Underwood; I believe she's staying here.'

'When was this, Mrs Smythe-Jones?' pulling the register towards her.

'I think she must have booked in on Wednesday, Sally.'

'There was no-one of that name, although we did have a Miss Martha

Jacobsen, but she booked out this morning.'

'Oh, she must have changed her name; it's some years since I've seen her. I'm sorry I missed her, Sally, but thank you for your help.'

'It's a pleasure, Mrs Smythe-Jones.'

Disappointed, Pamela returned to the car, but she wasn't ready to give up yet. For Martha to have gone to such lengths to make the trip to Taunton presumably to confront her, Pamela didn't believe she would have paid any attention to whatever Philip Spencer may or may not have said to her. For him to have arrived at the house when he had, must indicate he had driven down from London on the Wednesday shortly after she spoke to him. He would have booked into 'The Castle', and once Martha realised he was staying at the same hotel, this would probably have been sufficient to make her want to book out and perhaps, Pamela reasoned, move to another one in the town. Rather like looking for a needle in a haystack she thought and was on the point of abandoning a pretty hopeless task when she saw her car.

'Everything alright, Gregory?' she asked him when he came back into the kitchen, handing him a glass of chilled Sauvignon.

'Yes,' he said, taking the glass from her, 'a slight hiccup, that's all, but nothing that can't be corrected.'

Was Gregory like her, Pamela wondered, raising her glass, did he have his own secrets, ones he couldn't share with her. There were times when she found it difficult to understand her husband, although over the years they had been married, she had learned to read and interpret any sudden change in his expression and this evening was no exception. Lenny Yeung may be one of his suppliers, but whatever he'd had to say to Gregory was not, as he had so casually expressed, as a slight hiccup. She knew it would be pointless for her to ask him anything further; goodness knows she had enough on her own mind to contend with.

'Do you know, darling,' she said, 'what you and I need is a holiday.'

'I think you may be right, Pamela,' surprising her with such a positive response; normally he would make the excuse it would be impossible to get away from the business for any length of time, 'did you have anywhere in mind?'

'I hadn't really thought, but somewhere warm.' wanting to say as far away from here as possible.

***

Philip didn't learn about the accident until he saw the news on television at nine. Immediately, his mental antenna was on alert. Unless the car Martha Jacobsen had been driving was defective, he couldn't accept it had been an accident, therefore he reasoned, she had either staged a rather spectacular suicide or someone had deliberately decided to bring her life to an abrupt end. It took only a matter of minutes for him to find out which police headquarters was handling the enquiry, relieved to hear the case had been passed from Taunton to London, the reason being he was told by an Inspector at Taunton that as the deceased sister lived in Swiss Cottage this would make it easier for her to quickly identify the body, which he had added, had been carried out by her at fifteen hundred hours that afternoon. Philip hadn't relished the idea of driving back to Taunton; at least it was contained in one central spot and if it turned out to have any connection with their own investigation, it would simplify further enquiries they would have to make.

By nine the following morning, Philip had both the mechanic's and the pathologist's reports. He was not too surprised to read the accident had been caused by the main screw in the steering column having been loosened. They stressed this had not become loose through maintenance neglect. Attached, was a copy of Avis' last full maintenance on the vehicle, the date being three weeks earlier. To further convince the mechanic who carried out the check, two of the small screws securing the outer casing of the steering wheel housing were found lying on the floor below the dashboard where they must have rolled.

The pathologist's report was relatively straightforward; death had been instantaneous, the impact of the crash concertinaing the front bodywork of the vehicle and throwing the driver on to the windscreen, resulting in a broken neck and cracked frontal cranium.

'Good morning, Philip,' Charles said, coming into his office, 'I see you've got the reports; where would you suggest we go from here?'

'A good question, Charles,' Philip said, shuffling the papers on his desk, unable to come up with anything positive; this turn of events had thrown his line of thinking in respect to where his enquiries had been progressing into a temporary void.

'I think I know how you must be feeling,' Charles said, 'and if it's any consolation I feel the same; it's as if the rug had quite literally been pulled out from under our feet. However,' he went on, 'I don't know about you, but after reading the mechanic's report, I can't help thinking of one person most likely to have instigated the crash.'

'Pamela Smythe-Jones.'

'Quite, but the question is, while she may have had the opportunity, would she have had the expertise. What do you think?'

'As to that, I don't know. I won't be chauvinistic and say most women would lack the technical know-how, but somehow she doesn't strike me as the type of female to spend much time with her head under the bonnet of her car, but then as we know from experience, appearances can be deceptive.'

'Apart from the fact she was married to Norman Brookes and lived with him in Zambia for a few years and is now married to Gregory Smythe-Jones, that is about the extent of what we do know about her.'

'Sketchy, isn't it?' Philip agreed, 'I'll put out a search this morning; see what transpires. Perhaps John Brookes will be able to point us in the right direction; tell us, for instance, what she had been doing before she met his brother.'

'Yes, he should be able to help. Of course he's going to assume we're considering her as a suspect, but that can't be helped. We have to move on.'

'He won't know about Martha Jacobsen though; the name if he heard it would have meant nothing to him.'

'That's true, not many people in England would have either, Philip. Even Hugh; he only knew about the name she had elected to call herself when she contacted John Brookes.'

'All of which means that, for the time being, hopefully we can keep this murder from the press. Goodness knows, Charles, we need a bit of breathing space. I'll also get in touch with Forensic; they may have been able to get a clear set of fingerprints from around the steering wheel.'

***

The Brookes Estate was six miles south of Norwich, the grounds separated from the road by a six-foot stone wall, backed by a line of elms, their leaves already beginning to change colour. The double gates to the property were open, the gravel drive leading up to the front door of what looked to Philip as being a converted farmhouse; the building, two-storey, stone-built, tall sash windows and at the side, jutting out towards a fenced paddock, an extension had been added, giving the house a lop-sided appearance.

John Brookes must have heard him as he was standing at the top of the flight of steps as Philip pulled up, quickly coming down to introduce himself.

'Lovely place you have here,' Philip said, shaking hands, 'and far from the maddening crowd.'

'Takes a bit of handling,' he smiled, 'it's been in the family for generations;' he explained, 'in my grandfather's time it was run as a farm, but not anymore; now, it's mainly a stud farm, with riding stables which is my wife's domain.'

'Sounds idyllic compared with the frenetic life in London.'

'I don't know about idyllic,' he laughed, 'anyway, let's go into the office; I've arranged coffee and some sandwiches for us.' leading the way over towards the annexe.

'You mentioned on the phone, Mr Spencer,' he said, once they were inside and he had poured out two mugs of coffee, 'you wanted to learn something about Pamela's background.'

'Yes, that's right,' Philip nodded, stirring his coffee, 'since starting the investigation into your brother's murder, I've interviewed a number of the people who were in Samriboi at the same time. As we are rather hampered by the fact that this happened a number of years ago, plus the distance between here and Samriboi, we've had to try and built up a picture of what living over there was like.'

'You will, of course, know about Pamela's affair with that chap, Anthony Johnson?'

'Yes, we do.'

'I read about his recent death, Mr Spencer.'

I thought you may have done. You see, Mr Brookes, in the course of our enquiries, further developments have occurred. These are not directly concerning your late-brother, but his wife's name continues to crop up. I apologise for not being more specific -'

' – no, no, Mr Spencer, I understand. You have a job to do and I respect that and I can assure you that as far as Pamela is concerned I am completely unbiased. Since reading that article, I've had to face the grim reality of the possibility she may have helped Anthony Johnson on the night Norman was killed. What I'm trying to say is, whatever the outcome will be and she is culpable, it won't come as any great shock. I'm sorry to say I am unable to be charitable towards her.'

'I understand what you mean and in similar circumstances I'm sure I would feel the same.'

'So, what do you actually want to know about her, Mr Spencer?'

'First of all, her family; did you ever meet any of them?'

'I met them for the first time when she and John were married and then a few years later I bumped into her brother.'

'Were they married in Norwich?'

'Yes, they were; she'd lived there all her life apparently. I heard her telling my mother she'd gone to Wessex Lodge, a girls' school in Norwich.'

'Is this an independent school?'

'Yes, it is; her father was one of the top surgeons at the hospital in Norwich.'

'Are her parents still alive?'

'No, they died quite tragically, actually; they were holidaying with friends in the south of France and their yacht capsized. There were no survivors, Mr Spencer; this happened shortly before she and Norman went out to Zambia.'

'What did she do after she left school?'

'From what I could gather, I don't believe she did a great deal. She is a fairly secretive sort of person, but from what little she did say, it sounded as though she tried her hand at a number of jobs; some secretarial work and modelling I think and after a while she left Norwich and went down to London to live and that's where Norman met her.'

'Not in Norwich, then?'

'No, probably because he didn't move in the same circles as she did, but he'd been in London on a course at the London School of Economics and they met in, of all places, a night club. Ironic really, because Norman was definitely not the night club type, but some of the other chaps on the course had persuaded him to join them that night.'

'If I could go back to when you found the coroner's report, Mr Brookes.'

'Of course.'

'I understand this was among some other papers belonging to her.'

'Yes, that's right, but there was nothing else of any importance;' he replied, 'old theatre programmes, train timetables and flight tickets, even her old passport.'

'What did you do with it all?'

'I suppose I should have thrown most of it out,' he shrugged, 'but it didn't seem right somehow, after all, it belonged to Pamela, so I put it into a box file. I have it here, actually,' he added, getting up and going over to a metal filing cabinet, pulling open the bottom drawer and taking the file out, 'there you are;' handing it to him, 'I'll expect you will want to have a look through everything.'

'I would, yes; there might be something of interest to us, but if you don't mind, I'll take it back with me. I'll give you a receipt of course.'

'Oh, I'm sure that won't be necessary;' he smiled, 'I can't see Pamela coming back for it.'

'Probably not,' Philip agreed, 'if it had been important to her she would have taken it with her when she left. You mentioned her brother earlier, Mr Brookes.'

'Yes, Eddie; he's a few years older than Pamela and when I last saw him it sounded from what he was saying that he had done quite well for himself.'

'What line of business?'

'He served his apprenticeship as a motor mechanic when he left school and before he was thirty he owned half a dozen garages in the area, also a large car hire business in the centre of Norwich. We went for a drink and he told me how he had always been mad keen about cars and even in his early teens had loved nothing better than taking old bangers to pieces to find out how each part functioned and then he'd put them back together again.'

'It takes all sorts, eh?' Philip commented.

'It certainly does; he mentioned something else which somewhat surprised me.'

'Yes?'

'About Pamela, a very young Pamela, but Eddie said she would watch him for hours while he was doing all this dismantling, even did a bit of fetching and carrying for him. It's just that she never struck me as the type; I can't imagine her ever getting her hands dirty!'

Chapter Fifteen

Philip spread out the contents of the file John Brookes had given him; the passport he put to one side and all the receipts and various programmes dating before 2002 he returned to the file. The passport had expired the following year, the fifteenth of February. He found the first entry he was looking for; an entry stamp for Saturday, the 14th December 2002 at Heathrow, another one, three days later, on Tuesday the 17th at Orly Airport, Paris and the last entry made before the passport expired, on Thursday, the 19th at Norwich Airport. Among the other receipts around that time, there was nothing of any significance, except for a receipted bill from the Mercure Paris Monty Opéra hotel for the two nights, 17th and 18th December.

That was the same hotel where Guy Ford had first seen Anthony Johnson; why, of all the hotels in Paris, had she chosen that one, unless Johnson had suggested it to her before he left Samriboi and if that had been the case, it would indicate her involvement in what happened there. Had she been the one who supplied him with the pistol and had brought him back to Samriboi after he'd rigged the crash and later that night driven him to Lusaka, or somewhere relatively close to enable her to get back to the bungalow in time to contact the police? It all fitted neatly together, but because of the time factor, next to impossible to prove. There was a slim possibility that someone who had been working at the hotel in Paris at that time may remember seeing her, especially if Johnson had been a regular customer. Philip wasn't even sure whether it was worth following up on such a tenuous lead, but he had to try. It was only three o'clock; he could be in Paris by eight this evening, picking up the receiver and dialling Eurostar reservations.

Philip had stayed in a number of Mercure hotels in France, but never this one and immediately he walked into the lobby he liked what he was seeing: high ceilings, glittering crystal chandeliers, their light reflected in the guilt-framed wall mirrors, gleaming black and white floor tiles and contemporary furnishings. There were still times when he visited anywhere new he would think of Hilary, conjuring up in his mind what her reactions would have been. The bitterness of losing her the way he had no longer had the strength to overwhelm him in the same way as when she died; the bullet from a sniper's gun which had been intended for himself. Seven years ago and they had both been working for the Metropolitan Police and had spent the previous weekend planning their forthcoming wedding, but it wasn't to be. When these sad memories returned, although less frequently now, he was able to treat them philosophically, but he had been reluctant to consider a close relationship with anyone else and often doubted whether he ever would. He was well aware how sterile his life had become, his energies being focused entirely on work, but so far being incapable of acting any differently.

Within fifteen minutes he had booked in and taking his overnight bag to his room came back downstairs again. There were two barmen on duty in the lounge bar, one of them considerably older than the other, and working on the premise he may have been with the hotel for some time, Philip made his way over towards him.

'Good evening, sir;' he said, 'what would you like to drink?'

'I'd like a lager, please. Lovely hotel.' Philip added conversationally.

'This is your first visit, sir?'

'Yes, it is, although an old friend of mine used to come in here regularly. This was several years ago; you may not have been with the hotel then.'

'I've been working here since I left school; it's possible I might remember him. What was his name, sir?'

'Anthony Johnson.'

'Mr Johnson,' he repeated, 'yes, I do remember him and you're right, it was a long time ago. Mr Johnson used to come into the bar most evenings.'

'That would have been before he returned to England.'

'I thought he may have done, although I did see him again,' he went on quickly, reminding Philip of how openly informative barmen could be. They also made reliable witnesses he had found and invariably had good memories, 'this was about ten years ago, a few weeks before Christmas it was.'

'I expect he had his wife with him. Anthony and I had lost touch by then, but I heard he had married.'

'There was a lady with him; very glamorous she was, reminded me of Marilyn Monroe.'

There it was, the proof he'd been looking for. The woman would have been Pamela and they had met up in Paris, and as obviously they hadn't stayed together, Philip wondered why she had gone to the trouble of flying over to Paris to see him. Perhaps Martha Jacobsen had been right, remembering how emphatic she had been about Pamela's guilt. She had been insistent that Pamela had used him, recalling Martha's exact words "..... Anthony had fallen into her trap ....." Had Pamela promised him they would have a future together if he agreed to dispose of her husband, arranging to meet in Paris and this had been when she had told him their relationship was over? Could she have been so ruthless? If she had wanted out of her marriage, why not simply divorce him and then marry Smythe-Jones? Having met her twice, Philip had the distinct impression the woman was first and foremost motivated by her own social status which required money to achieve. The fact that Smythe-Jones was wealthy may not have been enough; he should find out whether Norman Brookes had made a will and considering the size of the Brookes' estate, it was more than likely. She would probably have been left well provided for, with perhaps a healthy personal income and not one she would have been prepared to forfeit to latch herself on to someone of Johnson's ilk. In other words, Philip caustically concluded, she had perhaps even before going to Zambia, set her sights considerably higher than a man who was not only married, but from when he left Zambia, no visible means of support. That, he thought, would not have suited Pamela Smythe-Jones one little bit.

'Are you dining in our restaurant this evening, sir?' he asked, returning from serving a couple who had come into the bar, 'I can reserve you a table if you are.'

'That's good of you, but as much as I'm sure I would find something I would like on the menu, I would really prefer an Italian meal tonight.'

'In that case,' he said, 'you won't be disappointed with the 'Bella Italia'; only a five minute walk away from the hotel.' he added.

Philip was half-way across the lobby towards the front door on his way to the restaurant the barman so enthusiastically recommended when, like a clip from a movie he hadn't seen for a while, he saw Hilary's old friend, Sophie Grant. She was standing outside the glass doors to the hotel's restaurant reading the menu and hadn't noticed him.

'Hello, Sophie.' Philip said, walking over to her.

'Philip!' swivelling round, a look of amazement on her face.

'How are you?' he asked, kissing her lightly on the cheek.

'I'm fine. It's lovely to see you, Philip,' she smiled, 'it is such a surprise after all this time, I can't remember just how long ago.'

'Neither can I. A lot of water has passed under the bridge since those days.' remembering how the three of them used to meet up on a Friday night for a drink when he wasn't on duty. It must be at least ten years ago and before Hilary joined the Force.

'I was so sorry when I heard about Hilary,' she said, placing a hand on his arm, 'and I apologise for not getting in touch with you at the time, but I knew how devastated you must have been and I suppose I didn't want to intrude. I'm sorry, Philip.'

'Thank you, Sophie, but you don't need to apologise. I always knew how much you both valued your friendship.'

'That's true,' she smiled gently and he could tell by her sad expression she was thinking back, 'since we were five years of age in fact; I don't know whether Hilary ever mentioned it, Philip, but it was on our first day at school, that's when we met and were placed next to each other in the classroom.'

'She did tell me and the reason for this was because of the initials of your surnames.'

'That's right; Graham and Grant, you can't get much closer than that.'

'Have you anything planned for this evening,' he asked her, wanting to spend a little longer with her; not to reminisce, but he genuinely wanted to know what she had been doing in the intervening years. He found her unaffected manner refreshing compared to the women he had been used to meeting; most of them focused on their careers to the exclusion of anything else, all of which made it difficult to ever really get to know them and find out whether there was more to their lives than boardroom meetings, seminars and brain-storming sessions.

'Not really; this is my last night here,' she told him, 'and I was looking for something on the menu which was a little different.'

'According to the barman, there's a very good Italian restaurant a few minutes' walk away from here; that is, if you like Italian food.'

'I love it.' she said spontaneously.

The 'Bella Italia' was, as the barman had said, close to the hotel and as soon as they went in he knew it was the right choice; apart from the appetising aromas of garlic and wine, the waiter who showed them to their table had greeted them with genuine Italian hospitality. Ceiling-high wall mirrors immediately gave the impression of the restaurant being larger than it was; coloured posters and prints, depicting the vineyards of Italy and the vivid blue of the Mediterranean; large red and yellow earthenware pots filled with flowering shrubs and playing softly in the background, guitar music.

'A piece of Italy.' Sophie said as they sat down and were handed menus.

'Have you ever been there?'

'My parents took me once, but I was far too young to appreciate the country and somehow I've never been back.'

'Too busy?'

'I suppose so,' she admitted, 'everyday life just got in the way, Philip. You mean to do something, but never get round to it. But what about you,' she asked, 'are you still with the Police Force?'

'I was seconded to the Foreign Office about six years ago.'

'More interesting?'

'You could say that,' he smiled, 'but I enjoy it.'

'Are you with MI6, then – sorry, I shouldn't have asked you that.'

'It's no great secret, not as it used to be, but unless it's necessary, I usually describe myself as attached to the Foreign Office, which is quite true of course.'

'I did think of joining the police, you know.' she said, 'This was when Hilary had been recruited, but instead I switched to a totally different type of career.'

'Sounds intriguing.'

'Not really; I studied fashion design at the college in Norwich and about five years ago I branched out on my own.'

'In Norwich?' he asked, having forgotten for a moment that Hilary and she had both come from there, although Hilary and her family had moved further south by the time she had been in her teens.

'No, in Winchester.'

'We're practically neighbours, then.' feeling inordinately pleased. 'Anyway,' he went on, opening up his menu, 'shall we order?'

'What do you think?' he asked her a couple of minutes later, 'it's an extensive menu, isn't it?'

'I know,' she agreed, 'it depends on how hungry you are, Philip, but I like the sound of the baked aubergines with the plum tomatoes and mozzarella.'

'I'll go along with that,' he said, 'good for a starter and for the main course; have you decided?'

'Well, somewhat spoiled for choice, although their *Merlazzo al forna* sounds good.'

'Pan-fried cod with puréed peas,' he read out, 'with raisins, spring onions and cucumber sauce. We'll have that, shall we?'

'Sounds alright to me,' she agreed, 'and shouldn't be too over-facing either.'

'And a bottle of *Chianti Malini* or if you prefer we could have the *Bianco di Pitigliano.*'

'I'm no wine buff, Philip; the *Malini* will suit me fine.'

Their meal lived up to expectations: the food was cooked to perfection and the waiter service was second to none. Philip couldn't remember when he had last enjoyed an evening so much; impromptu and totally unexpected.

'Would you like a desert?' he asked, when the waiter had cleared away their plates.

'I don't think so,' she said, leaning back in her chair, 'perhaps a coffee though.'

'How often do you come to Paris, Sophie?'

'About a couple of times a year, but I haven't stayed in the Mercure for a long time. It's a bit of a coincidence, you know,' she said, 'but the last time I bumped into someone else I hadn't seen for years.'

'Really?'

'Yes; it was ten years ago,' she explained, 'I got married that summer and we came to Paris for a pre-Christmas break. I reckon you could describe it all as a whirlwind romance and not unsurprisingly it didn't last.'

'I'm sorry about that.'

'I should have known better, Philip. I was twenty-five, not exactly a kid, but I was going to tell you about the person I saw.'

'Someone from your school days?'

'You're absolutely right,' she smiled, 'she was called Pamela Waterman when Hilary and I knew her; I did hear she'd married. I can't remember his first name, only his surname, which was Brookes.'

'Pamela Brookes. Now that was a coincidence.'

'Why; do you know her?'

'Yes,' he said slowly, 'I know her alright.'

'This is to do with your work, isn't it?' she asked, surprising him with her perceptiveness.

'The last thing I want to do, Sophie, is to spoil this evening by talking about something which you may find distasteful.'

'I think you know me well enough to realise I'm not like that, also, Philip, I would like to think of myself as a discreet kind of person, but if you don't want to say anymore, I'll understand.'

'Pamela Brookes is one of many people I've been interviewing recently in connection with a current investigation we are conducting,' he explained, 'and if I do elaborate, Sophie, you won't know any more than many other people I've spoken to over the last couple of weeks.'

'I see.'

'Would you mind telling me what you thought of her,' he asked, 'what I mean is I would like to learn as much as I can about her earlier years. All I know so far is that she was brought up in Norwich and has a brother called Eddie who owns a car hire business and a number of garages in the area.'

'Eddie was a few years older than her and I'm not surprised he's in that kind of business; even when he was still at school he was crazy about cars, it was all he could talk about. Pamela used to brag that he knew all about cars and had taught her how to dismantle one and then reassemble it.'

'Did you believe her?'

'Not at first, no but something rather odd happened; this was in our last year, one of our teachers had a bad car crash; fortunately she wasn't killed. We heard that her car had been tampered with, something about the steering column having been loosened. The police suspected this had been done while it was parked in the school grounds. They interviewed us all, but I don't believe they learned anything.'

'Not very pleasant for you.'

'No, it wasn't, and then a few days later Pamela went absent; this was right in the middle of the term and I didn't see her again until that time in the Mercure.'

'I suppose you all thought she had something to do with it?'

'Not really, Philip. We didn't think she would have been capable. But in spite of that incident, I have to say she wasn't very well liked.'

'Why do you think that was?'

'I don't know, but probably a lot to do with her manner. She was terribly spoilt and had more freedom than the rest of us at that age. Pamela never lacked boyfriends; she was what my mother would have described as boy-mad, but she had a habit of poaching other girls' boyfriends, also she was secretive; we didn't like that.' she added.

'I'm beginning to get the picture,' he said, 'and having met her, I can't say I'm too surprised. When you saw her, she was with someone, wasn't she?'

'Yes, she was. I assumed it was her husband, but on reflection, perhaps he wasn't.'

'Why do you say that?'

'Oh, a couple of reasons; she didn't introduce him, which at the time I did think peculiar, even for her, also she made it very plain she didn't want to prolong any conversation we may have had.'

Philip didn't ask her much more. Although he was keen to gather together everything he could about Pamela, he didn't feel it fair to inflict this on Sophie. Even what little she had told him had been helpful; as far as Pamela's personality was concerned it would seem she hadn't changed since those earlier years, recalling Martha's bitter tirade, but perhaps the most crucial point was that he now had two witnesses; the barman at the hotel and Sophie, to support what Charles and he had suspected; Pamela had known Johnson faked the crash and made prior arrangements with him to meet up again in Paris, all of which went a long way towards the viability of charging her with aiding and abetting her husband's murderer. Ideally, to conclude this section of the investigation, he needed proof of her having driven Johnson either to Lusaka, or as Harry Knight had suggested, as far as Kabwe. There was a way round this which he intended to put into effect when he next spoke to her, but first he wanted to read the contents of Norman Brookes' will; it could provide the motive which up to now had only been based on supposition.

Their coffee arrived at that moment, and during the seconds he had been mulling over in his brain the ins and outs of the additional information he had, Sophie had remained silent, as if sensing he needed the space.

'Shall we finish off the wine?' he suggested.

'Good idea.' giving him another of her spontaneous smiles and, as he'd noticed before, her smile really did reach her eyes; they were very attractive eyes: grey-blue with astonishingly long lashes. He hoped he wasn't reading too much into seeing her again, not discounting she may already be in a relationship. He wondered, although only fleetingly, what Hilary would have thought.

'Hilary wouldn't have minded, Philip.' she said quietly, uncannily tuning into his thoughts and she was right; those years he had been with Hilary, although he knew he would never forget them, had faded into the past and now, when he thought about her, it was through an imaginative mist of memory and as he looked at Sophie and the way her eyes filled with unshed tears, he realised it was time to let the past go.

'I know.' for a second unable to trust his voice.

'Philip,' she said, 'I haven't been able to tell you all that much about Pamela; probably because I never knew her well enough.'

'You've given me more than you think, Sophie.'

'You see,' she explained, 'after we left school, as I said, I didn't see her again. From time to time I heard snippets about her from the friends I continued to keep in touch with after I left Norwich, but apart from her marrying that was it.'

'You didn't know she and her husband went out to Africa to live?'

'No, I didn't. I wonder how she adapted to life out there. I can't see her mixing with the expatriate community as no doubt she would have to if she wanted any kind of social life.'

'Apparently she didn't fit in very well.'

'Oh dear, poor Pamela.'

'You don't mean that, do you?' he grinned.

'Not really, Philip, but honestly, she was her own worst enemy; frequently falling out with people, mostly because of wanting to appear more important than anyone else. All I can say, her husband must have had a lot to contend with being married to her.'

'Sophie,' he said, deciding she should know about what happened in Zambia as, in time, it very likely would become common knowledge once the case reached the courts as he had no doubt it would, 'ten years ago, when you saw her in the Mercure, her husband had been dead for a week.'

'Good Lord!' she gasped, 'What happened to him?'

'He was shot dead in the bungalow where they were living in Zambia and the authorities were unable to find the killer, the official verdict being he was a victim of a local gang.'

'So, the man I saw her with couldn't have been her husband.'

'That's right.'

'I realise I shouldn't be asking you this, Philip, but I'm going to all the same; I think you know who he was.'

'Sophie,' unable to keep the smile from his face, 'I believe you are in the wrong profession; you should have been a detective.'

'Like Miss Marples?' she laughed.

'A very young Miss Marples.'

'Seriously though, Philip,' she said, 'I've been thinking about what you've been saying about Pamela's husband; do you suspect the man she was with as being responsible?'

'Most of the evidence we have does indicate that Norman Brookes was shot by him –'

'– and Pamela,' she interrupted, 'she must have known.'

'Yes,' Philip nodded, 'she must have done. There was an article in 'The Times' last week, Sophie. It was in Wednesday's edition; I don't know whether you saw it or not.'

'I may have done, although when I'm busy I am inclined to skim through the paper, only selecting pieces which catch my attention. What was it about?'

'It started off by mentioning the death of a British visitor in Amsterdam –'

'– yes, I remember. I didn't read it all, but there seemed to be some controversy over the man's true identity.'

'That's the one,' he said, 'it went on to mention that he had been presumed dead ten years ago as a result of a car crash in Zambia, which happened at the same time Norman Brookes was shot.'

'How dreadful. A bit of a mess, isn't it?'

'You could say that.' smiling at the understatement.

'Philip.'

'Yes?'

'When you said you knew the man who'd been here with Pamela, did you also know they would have been in the hotel together?'

'I had proof that she was staying at the Mercure, also proof that he had arrived in Paris a few days earlier, but I didn't know where he was staying.' he answered, again reminded of her sharp intelligence.

'So I gave you the proof you needed?'

'No, I already had that about fifteen minutes before I met you, but you have confirmed this for me.'

'You probably know what I'm thinking.' she said, her head on one side as she waited.

'Whether you'll be asked to appear as a witness should the case be brought to court?'

'I was, actually.' a small smile hovering on her lips, 'It would be an experience; I've never been in a courtroom before. I'm not being skittish, you know,' she said, 'although I wouldn't enjoy giving evidence against someone I used to know, I think I would consider it my civic duty.'

'I appreciate your frankness, Sophie. Shall we have another drink here or would you prefer going back to the bar at the Mercure?'

'Oh, the Mercure, I think. The short walk will do me good after that splendid meal. Thank you, Philip, it was lovely. I expect you lead a fairly busy life?' she added.

'At times, yes, but there's no set pattern. It all depends on what particular case I'm on, also how long they last.'

'I see. I was wondering whether we could meet in Winchester sometime. I would like to take you to one of my favourite restaurants in the town.'

'I'd like that very much.'

***

By Monday morning, having heard nothing further from Scotland

Yard, Gregory was becoming increasingly more confident that was the end of their enquiry. To him, it was simple logic. Those figurines had recently been valued; their valuer had recognised them as having been stolen and duly reported the matter to the police who, in turn, traced them as having been purchased from Gregory's Antiques, followed by him saying he had bought the figurines in Hong Kong and the question over their origin coming to an abrupt halt when they learned there was no receipt. His earlier concern of why Scotland Yard had been brought in no longer seemed all that significant with their continuing silence. What was more pressing was Lenny's worrying insistence about Cecelia's vulnerability and how he should make sure there was nothing to link his activities in Hong Kong to London. The indisputable fact Lenny was putting his own position as top priority rankled, making him question if after all these years he had misjudged his old friend's loyalty.

It was unfortunate Pamela had taken the call from Lenny on Friday, but that couldn't have been helped; Lenny was not to know he had been a little later getting home that day. She had appeared to accept his brief explanation, but he couldn't be sure. Usually, she wouldn't question him about anyone who called, but recently, ever since she had that visit from the chap from the Foreign Office, she had been behaving strangely, as though her mind was elsewhere. He hadn't asked her who had called at the house the other morning, assuming she would have told him if it had been Philip Spencer. Perhaps her suggestion they have a holiday was a sensible one; it had been months since he had taken any time off. Ellen was perfectly capable of dealing with the business; he had no qualms there, but he still hesitated, not quite understanding why. Over the week-end Pamela had further exacerbated this uncharacteristic indecisiveness of his by constantly talking about their holiday and asking him where they should go. The answer to that was he had no idea, but knowing Pamela, he was aware she wouldn't let the subject drop, but meantime, he had a full day ahead of him. Life used to be uncomplicated, he grumbled to himself as he made a start on opening the mail: a wife who occupied herself during the day and appeared reasonably content; eating out in one of Taunton's restaurants most evenings; a reliable housekeeper who made sure their house ran smoothly and efficiently and a gardener who needed no supervision, but now all of this taken-for-granted equilibrium seemed in danger of being eroded and this unnerved him.

Most of the post was routine; a couple of trade magazines, invoices, bank statements, circulars, nothing that needed to be dealt with immediately. Separating the bills from the rest of the correspondence and placing them in the invoice tray, a small white hand-written envelope which he had missed, slipped out from beneath one of the magazines and fell face-down on the floor. Picking it up and turning it over, he noticed the Taunton postmark. Wondering who could have sent it to his business address, he opened it and pulled out the single sheet of paper: "Why don't you ask your wife about Anthony Johnson?" he read. This was vindictive stuff, he thought in disgust. Obviously whoever had written those words must have a deep hatred for Pamela. Could that article last week have triggered this off, he wondered. If it had been sent from anywhere else than Taunton, he could have understood that someone, perhaps someone who had known Pamela when she was in Samriboi, had read the piece in 'The Times' and decided to make mischief. The fact it had been posted in Taunton didn't necessarily mean the person lived there; they could have been visiting. In Gregory's opinion, people who sent anonymous letters were sick, as no doubt this one was. He didn't see there was anything to be gained by telling Pamela; the wisest thing to do, he decided, was to forget about it. She had been upset enough over Philip Spencer's visit without this and, tearing the note up, he dropped the shredded paper into the waste bin.

The remainder of the day passed uneventfully and he was able to shake off the feeling of unpleasantness over the letter. He had a couple of meetings out of the office in the afternoon and managed to catch an earlier train back to Taunton.

'This is a surprise, Gregory;' Pamela greeted him at the front door, 'what sort of day have you had?'

'Not too bad, darling,' he said, kissing her, 'it's good to be home.' he added.

'I have a surprise for you,' she said as they went into the kitchen, 'it's about our holiday. No, don't look like that. I know I've been a pain this weekend going on and on about it, so I decided I would go ahead and book for us.'

'Not for long, Pamela, I hope.'

'No, only for a few days.'

'Don't keep me in suspense then; where are we going?'

'To Hong Kong, darling.'

'What!'

'Hong Kong; you don't mind do you?'

'No – no, it's a good idea. It's only that I expected somewhere nearer, that's all.'

'I realise you've been there before, but I haven't, Gregory.'

'I know, darling. So,' he asked, 'when do we go?'

'On Wednesday and returning here next Tuesday.'

'That's alright.'

'Really?' a slight frown appearing.

'Really. Tell me, what made you decide on Hong Kong?'

'Oh, that was because of the call you had from your supplier on Friday and then, this morning, I saw an advert in the paper for a seven-day trip.'

Well, Lenny, thanks very much, if you hadn't phoned the other day, Pamela and I might have taken our holiday in Spain or Italy and not practically on your doorstep!'

Chapter Sixteen

Norman Brookes had made generous provisions for his wife; his last will and testament was made out in 1999, the same year they went out to Zambia. Obviously at that time he hadn't known about her unfaithfulness, otherwise, presumably he would have made a number of changes, or it could have been he never got round to it and certainly he wouldn't have expected to die in the way he had.

She had been left an annual income of thirty thousand pounds, reducing by fifty per cent if she should re-marry, also full ownership of their villa in the South of France which John had told him she had sold before her marriage to Smythe-Jones for 2.5 five million pounds. She continued to own a twenty-five per cent share holding in the estate, refusing John's offer to buy her out. In a nutshell, Philip thought, Pamela Smythe-Jones was a wealthy woman in her own right, meaning such an inheritance could provide the motive they had been looking for. Soon, he would have to bring her in for questioning, but before then, he needed to go back to Norwich. He had found what Sophie had told him about their teacher's accident more than disturbing; it indicated that Pamela would have had the know-how and the capability to cause Martha Jacobsen's death, but as before, he lacked a motive. Disliking the teacher was not enough; if Pamela had been responsible there must have been something considerably more for her to go to such lengths. The woman could have died as a result of the accident, but she hadn't. Whoever had loosened the steering column of her car must have wanted the driver to be killed. For this reason he had to speak to the teacher; it was possible, while she wouldn't have known for certain, she may have some idea. Sophie had given him the names of both the teacher and the headmistress, which gave him the necessary starting point. The police report of the accident could wait; Philip was reluctant to approach them at this stage, wanting to continue making any enquiry about Pamela Smythe-Jones as unofficial as possible.

It was two in the afternoon as he approached Norwich and, following the road west out of the city centre, turned left at the crossroads and into Earlham Road, driving on for about half a mile until he reached the double gates to Wessex Lodge where the brass plaque inscribed with the school's emblem and motto: *Loyalty at all times*, together with the name of the headmistress, confirmed what he had hoped; Miss Eleanor Grainger was still there.

The school secretary personally escorted him to the headmistress' office with only a slight raising of eyebrows when he introduced himself.

Philip's first impression of Eleanor Grainger was that here was a woman well accustomed to authority, judging by the severe expression on her face when she shook hands with him.

'My secretary has informed me you are from the Foreign Office, Mr Spencer.'

'Yes, that's right;' handing her one of his cards, 'it's good of you to spare the time to see me, Miss Grainger.' watching her as she scrutinized it.

'You are obviously here in an official capacity.' she commented dryly, peering at him over the top of her glasses.

'I am, yes,' deciding to come straight to the point, sensing her impatience; certainly not into any social preambles, 'my visit, Miss Grainger,' he explained, 'concerns the car accident involving one of your teachers, Miss Margaret Hudson, seventeen years ago.'

'Oh, dear,' she sighed, visibly shaken, 'I had hoped never to hear that unpleasant incident ever mentioned again. That business was quite detrimental to the school, you know; in fact,' she went on, tight-lipped, 'three parents actually took their girls away; they objected to them being subjected to being questioned by the police. Not good at all.'

'It is my understanding,' Philip put in; 'the police were unable to trace the person responsible.'

'No, they were not; it's always been my opinion that as Miss Hudson wasn't fatally injured, they didn't put too much importance on how the accident occurred.'

'But she could have been killed, Miss Grainger; to tamper with someone else's property with the intention of harming them in any way is a criminal act.'

'Naturally I can't argue with that;' she said waspishly, 'but surely, as this happened so many years ago and fortunately Miss Hudson survived the crash, there is nothing to be gained by going over old ground, all of which leads me to ask, Mr Spencer, why have you come to see me?'

'For some weeks now,' Philip said, selecting his words carefully, gauging how much he should say to her, 'I have been involved in the investigation of a murder enquiry which up until a few days ago bore no relation to Miss Hudson's accident.'

'Yes?'

'Firstly,' ignoring her autocratic manner, 'and briefly, I would like to go back ten years when, in Central Africa and on the same night, a man was shot dead and another rigged a car crash, enabling him to fake his own death -'

'- there was an article in 'The Times' last week about this.' she interrupted.

'I thought you may have read it. However, as a result of new evidence which was emerging before the piece in the newspaper, both cases had been re-opened -' pausing for a moment, giving her the opportunity to say anything further but she remained silent, continuing to look at him, her grey-green eyes unblinking behind the lowered frames of her spectacles, and knowing he had her full attention, continued to explain, '- and in the course of our investigation a considerable number of people have been interviewed, including those who were at the time living in the same town in Zambia. Last week, one of them, a woman, died as a result of a car accident, the damage to the vehicle prior to the accident being an exact replica to what had been carried out on Miss Hudson's car.'

'It remains unclear to me, Mr Spencer,' she said, 'how you have made the connection. I wouldn't have thought in my, admittedly limited knowledge of such occurrences, that such a way of rendering a vehicle dangerously unroadworthy was not unique.'

'You're right, of course,' Philip conceded, 'but in this case it has transpired that another of those people questioned had, not only the technical ability, but originally came from Norwich and was here when Miss Hudson had her accident.'

'Mr Spencer,' she said slowly, sounding for the first time less confident, 'you obviously know the name of this person.'

'I do, Miss Grainger, but I am not in a position to reveal it, also I would remind you that these are enquiries only. I am not saying, or even suggesting, that whoever tampered with both vehicles is the same one.'

'I understand, but what you have said is rather worrying. I am first and foremost concerned, you understand, with the reputation and good name of the school; I don't want anything to tarnish that. It was bad enough all those years ago with the unwanted publicity, mostly caused by the press, without all of that being resurrected.'

'And it is for this reason I am conducting any enquiry I make as circumspectly as I can; to protect everyone's privacy. If I could return to Miss Hudson's accident for a moment, Miss Grainger,' he went on, 'you've already mentioned how three of the parents decided to take their daughters away from the school, but did you hear anything untoward, talk among the girls for instance, or your staff, which could have indicated to you who may have been responsible?'

'As for the staff, certainly not. If they had any views, as far as I was aware, they kept to themselves.'

'And the girls?'

'Oh, there were rumours, but that's all they were. I didn't give them any credence and I don't believe the police did either, that is if anyone had mentioned to them any suspicions they may have had, but you know what young girls are like.'

'I don't believe I do, Miss Grainger; perhaps you could enlighten me.'

'Over-imaginative, trying to out-do each other, especially if for some reason, they disliked anyone, but I've always found there is never much substance to what they've dreamed up.'

'Was Miss Hudson a popular teacher?'

'She *is* popular, Mr Spencer.'

'She is still with the school?'

'Oh, yes; she is a relatively young woman and even after her marriage a few years ago she stayed on with us.'

'I would like to see her, Miss Grainger, if that can be arranged.'

'I suppose you must,' she sighed, 'I'll just check to see if she's free at the moment.' pressing the intercom button on her desk.

***

Margaret Hudson had not been too forthcoming at first when he had talked to her, if anything, she seemed reluctant to discuss the accident. Such reticence, similar to what he had experienced with the headmistress, merely contributed to what he was beginning to suspect; namely, there had been an abrupt curtailment to police enquiries, although unwittingly, Margaret Hudson had provided him with what he needed to confirm this. He had used a different approach to the one with Eleanor Grainger; half-way through their conversation he had mentioned one of her ex-pupils, Pamela Waterman, as she had been then, asking her why Pamela had, following the accident, been absent for the remainder of the term. Her reaction had been instantaneous: "Her father, who was on the board of school governors," she'd said, "told Miss Grainger that Pamela was suffering from depression caused by post-examination stress."

"Would you have said she was a nervous type of girl?"

"Not in the least, Mr Spencer; quite the reverse, extremely self-confident in fact."

"I understand the police questioned many of the girls at the time of the accident."

"They did. I was still in hospital when they came here, but of course I heard about this later when I was back at work. Apparently, they wanted to know whether they had noticed anyone in or around the area where I usually parked my car. They also questioned the staff, but of course they hadn't."

"Going back to Pamela," Philip had said, "have you considered that she may have done; she may have known the person who tampered with your car and actually witnessed what he or she was doing? She may have been afraid to speak up."

"That hadn't occurred to me, Mr Spencer, but then if she had, why didn't she tell either Miss Grainger or the police?"

"But if she had, they would only have had her word for it."

"Does it really matter," she'd sighed, "after all this time? I wasn't badly injured, you know; slightly concussed and that's why they kept me in hospital for a few days, purely for observation purposes."

"Did she have a boyfriend?" the question throwing her; she hadn't expected his swift change of direction.

"Er -" she had hesitated, the colour leaving her cheeks for a couple of seconds, "- er – no, she didn't, not as far as I knew." and it was at that precise moment Philip knew she was lying.

"Did you, Miss Hudson?"

"Sorry?"

"Have a boyfriend around that time?"

"I did as a matter of fact."

"You may be finding these questions irrelevant, but I can assure you they're not; they are assisting me in building up a picture, an understanding of a person's personality and background and as I've told your headmistress, this is an enquiry only, and I am unable to elaborate on any findings or suspicions I may have, as everything must first be corroborated and found to be significant to that investigation. In respect to your accident, I believe there is only one irrefutable fact; you personally were targeted. I cannot accept that someone went to where the staff cars were parked and picked one at random. Am I making myself clear?"

By then, she had become quite pale and he almost felt sorry for the woman; it hadn't been his intention to cause her distress, but the invisible barrier he had felt he was up against had to be broken and, regrettably for her, she seemed to be the weakest link. She had taken a while to answer, but he waited, giving her the time she obviously needed.

"Have you read our school motto, Mr Spencer?' she had asked him.

"*Loyalty at all times.*"

"That's right. The staff all feel very strongly about that and it's for this reason I am finding it difficult to handle some of your questions. Anyway," she had continued, "I do appreciate what you've been saying and I understand your reasons, but all the same, I dislike telling tales about people and casting aspersions in any way, but you leave me with no choice and of course it is up to you to prove or disprove the importance of what I'm going to say."

"Thank you, Miss Hudson."

"The boyfriend I had at the time had been Pamela's. I know she was only seventeen, but appeared older than her years and I am only six years older than her. I had seen him with her a couple of times when he had picked her up from school in the afternoons and then one day when I was leaving, after all the girls had gone, he was waiting for me in his car. He drove me back into Norwich and well," she had attempted a smile, "our relationship began more or less from then onwards. We were together for about a year," she'd added, "and then we broke up."

"So," Philip said, starting to see what must have happened and as Sophie had told him, Pamela had a habit of poaching other girls' boyfriends. Also, Martha Jacobsen had insisted how Pamela had broken up her relationship with Johnson, but this time, so many years earlier, the tables had been turned. Pamela wouldn't have liked that, giving him yet another motive, "in essence," he went on, "her boyfriend left her and chose you instead. She wouldn't have been very happy about that."

"I don't think she was, Mr Spencer, but she never said anything to me. Anyway, she couldn't have hated me all that much, that is, if you're thinking she was responsible for my accident. Whoever did the damage would have needed the technical knowledge and as far as I knew Pamela hadn't and of course at that time she didn't even drive."

It was well after six when he finally pulled into the car park at Headquarters. The drive from Norwich had taken longer than usual; road works and heavy traffic for a good stretch of the motorway forcing him to reduce speed and by the time he reached London all he wanted was a refreshing cold beer and a meal, followed by an early night, but first he must make out his report in readiness for the meeting with Charles in the morning.

He was half-way through keying in the salient points of his talk with the two women when his internal phone rang.

'I wasn't sure whether you were back yet, Philip.'

'Only about ten minutes or so, Charles.'

'You must be tired.'

'More weary than anything else; I've known better stretches of motorway, today was particularly bad.'

'Why don't you call it a day,' he suggested, 'there's no rush to write up your report. I take it that was what you were doing?'

'Nearly finished it actually.'

'Have you anything planned for this evening? Charles asked.

'Just to relax; a beer and some good food.'

'How does Simpson's sound?'

'Sounds pretty good to me.'

'Fine. Judith is spending a couple of days with our daughter and her family,' he explained, 'and although she's left me some ready-made meals, I'd much rather eat out, so I'll give Simpsons a ring and reserve a table.'

Leaving their cars at Headquarters they took a taxi to The Strand. Simpson's restaurant was one of Philip's favourite: dark wood panelling; glittering crystal chandeliers; cream damask table-linen; silver service and piano music playing softly in the background all created a club-like atmosphere. They both chose the prime roast rib of beef with roasted potatoes and fresh vegetables and while they waited Philip had his lager and Charles a campari soda.

'I think we can now bring Pamela Smythe-Jones in for questioning, Charles.'

'I'm sure you're right,' he agreed, taking a sip of his campari, 'you obviously found today productive.'

'I did, although not from Miss Grainger, the school's headmistress, except for an impression of her reluctance to discuss the accident, but the response I got from Margaret Hudson gave me a possible motive which could be quite damning for Pamela. Apparently,' he explained, 'shortly before the accident, Pamela's boyfriend finished with her in preference for her teacher, Margaret Hudson, who incidentally is only six years older than her.'

'And given what we've learned about Pamela's behaviour when she was living in Samriboi, it does make sense.'

'I think so.'

'The pieces are beginning to slot into place, aren't they?'

'Yes, and as I said to you when I returned from Paris, we now have two witnesses to confirm that Pamela did meet Johnson on her return from Samriboi and that should be conclusive proof that she was involved in both her husband's murder and Johnson's disappearance from the scene.'

'You've done well, Philip,' he smiled, 'it's been a hard slog, I know.'

'I feel rather like a human yo-yo,' Philip grinned, 'I'm starting to know Norwich and Taunton quite well.'

'All we're waiting for now is the breakthrough we need to crack open this smuggling racket.'

'Any news from Derek yet, Charles?'

'He reported in this morning, but only to say that so far Cecelia Cunningham hasn't been seen in Lenny Yeung's company, which of course doesn't mean they are not in contact with each other. Derek is continuing to keep tabs on her and although she has been leaving every morning for her office in Central and returning to her apartment each evening, that seems to be the extent of her daily routine.'

'It looks as if that part of our investigation requires some nudging; otherwise it is in danger of going stagnant.'

'I couldn't agree more, Philip; have you any ideas?'

'Nothing specific, except that perhaps we should take a close look into the activities of both Lenny Yeung and Nicholas Anout if we can, but there must be a pattern somewhere as to how they conduct their businesses. I can't believe any nefarious transactions are made haphazardly. There's a keen, probably devious, brain here.'

'The question is who's the controller; Yeung or Anout?'

'One or the other,' Philip put in, 'there can't be two. The others in this scenario are, I would say, the puppets.'

'From what we've learned so far, I would suggest it's Yeung. Except for the barman in the Hotel Russell who clearly remembered seeing him, none of us have. All we do know is that the two men in Amsterdam and Gregory Smythe-Jones take instructions from him and Cecelia Cunningham of course.'

'I think you're right about Yeung; from what little we've heard about Anout, it sounds as if he is an opportunist, accustomed to ducking and diving. Where is he now? Apparently, it's many years since he lived in Paris, probably quickly vacated the scene when things got too hot for him after Clive Edward's murder. When you think about it, Charles, it is only because of the possibility that Johnson may have continued to work for him, that we believe he is involved in the big picture.'

'He just might be, Philip.'

'Why do you say that?'

'Nothing definite of course, more's the pity, but I was thinking about that extra flight ticket Johnson had to Singapore.'

'That's been bothering me as well,' Philip admitted, 'but I haven't come up with any rational explanation why he was going on there instead of back to London.'

'Neither have I,' Charles said, 'and you know how I dislike coincidences.'

'Yes?' intrigued, waiting for him to elaborate, knowing he wouldn't be disappointed; he had long respected Charles' unbiased reasoning, so unlike himself. Charles didn't think or act on hunches and intuition didn't figure in his make-up.

'Well,' Charles said, 'I'm working on the premise Johnson had continued negotiating with Anout, at the same time cheating on Lenny Yeung. Although, Philip, it could be more than that; returning to what I said a couple of minutes ago. Coincidences. All of which brings me back to those figurines.'

'I see where you're coming from,' Philip nodded, 'they were actually stolen in Singapore and if we believe half of what Smythe-Jones has said, made their way to Hong Kong. We know there is a link between him and Yeung, via Cecelia Cunningham, also we believe that she was Johnson's replacement, at least as far as Amsterdam and London were concerned. I think we can safely assume these places were Johnson's territories. Perhaps they had extended to include Singapore,' he suggested, 'I can't see Lenny Yeung going over there to collect them.'

'No, neither can I, Philip. All somewhat convoluted, but credible all the same. It does make me wonder though, whether Johnson didn't bring them over to England which would make Smythe-Jones' explanation pure fabrication.'

'But if Johnson had,' Philip asked, 'why not fly straight to London from Singapore and cut out Hong Kong?'

'I can make a couple of suggestions,' Charles said, 'if Yeung is the controller perhaps for reasons of his own he preferred to see them first. Can you remember the time difference between the robbery and when Smythe-Jones sold the figurines?'

'I'd have to check, but I think it was about six weeks.'

'We don't know how long Smythe-Jones had the figurines until he sold them, but we could possibly find out. This would mean a closer inspection of his records.'

'Also his passport; he may not even have been in Hong Kong when he said he was.'

'Well, he was rather caught on the hop when Hugh Bannister turned up. He wouldn't have been expecting that, which could mean he conjured up an explanation on the spur of the moment.'

'In order not to throw any direct suspicion on Lenny Yeung?'

'Possibly.'

'What was the other suggestion you mentioned, Charles?'

'That those four figurines were not the only items stolen; there could have been more, not necessarily the same. A police report would have been made out at the time of the robbery; could make interesting reading.'

'It would be even more interesting if Nicholas Anout's name cropped up again.' Philip remarked dryly.

'That's true. When do you propose to formally question Pamela Smythe-Jones?'

'Sooner rather than later. I'll make arrangements for the interview room to be made available at Taunton's Headquarters for tomorrow. She won't like that.' he added, chuckling.

'Not good for her image among the local community, eh.'

'I think I should call in at 'Gregory's Antiques' first, apropos to what we've been saying.'

'And I'll get someone to find out all they can about the robbery; all we know so far is when it happened and that the figurines were stolen from Sir Desmond Bevington's private collection. There might have been a spate of burglaries around that time and there is always the chance that rumours may have been circulating in the area.'

'There was no break-in mentioned in the police report which could be considered odd if you take into account where Sir Bevington had been living.'

The wall clock was softly chiming eleven when Philip turned the key in the front door of his apartment in Belgravia and going inside, he noticed the green light flashing on his answering machine. Pressing the switch, Sophie's voice immediately filled the hall: 'Hello, Philip,' she was saying, 'I wanted to give you a ring to say how much I enjoyed the other evening and to thank you again for the lovely meal. I realise you must be busy at the moment and may find it difficult to take any time off, but how about this Saturday; I'll understand if you can't. Bye.'

The apartment felt strangely silent after he'd switched off the machine. He did want to see her again. Very much. It had been a long time since he had heard such warmth in a woman's voice. Not since Hilary. Perhaps, he decided, dialling the number Sophie had given him, it was time to let go, tuck away those memories of what he thought of as his other life; the years he had known and loved Hilary. During those dark weeks and months which followed her death he had never thought for one second he would ever be able or even want to fill the terrible void of losing her, but now, it was as though at last he was emerging from a long black tunnel and one he'd used to cocoon himself against the real world, a world in which he had no longer felt comfortable.

'Sophie,' he said as soon as she answered, 'I hope I haven't woken you, but I've just this minute come in.'

'No, Philip, I wasn't asleep, and I'm glad you phoned.'

'I'd had every intention of having an early night, but Charles Harper suggested we have a meal together, my boss by the way.'

'You must be on good terms then.'

'We are, yes, but I don't suppose you'll be surprised to hear we spent almost the entire evening talking shop.'

'Tiring.'

'Normally it would have been, but for some reason I'm less tired now than I was earlier in the evening, having just driven back from Norwich.'

'Did you visit my old school?'

'I did actually,' unable to keep the smile from his voice; she really must be the most perceptive person he had ever known.

'I expect it looks exactly the same as when I was there. Who did you see, Philip?'

'Miss Grainger –'

'– Good Lord, is she still there? I thought she would have retired ages ago!'

'She didn't look as if she was ready for retirement yet; she's quite a formidable lady.'

'We all used to call her Battle; behind her back of course.' she laughed.

'She probably knew all the same,' laughing with her, 'and after having met her, I think I would have called her that when I was a kid.'

'You went to the school to ask her about Miss Hudson's accident?'

'I did, but I mentioned no names, especially not yours. Anyway,' Philip went on, 'I didn't learn any more from her than I knew already; she was quite reluctant to talk about the accident.'

'Probably because of the school's reputation.'

'That's the impression she gave me.'

'So, it was a wasted trip, Philip?'

'Not exactly,' unsure whether he should say much more. It wasn't that he didn't trust her integrity, because he did; he was concerned about bombarding her with anything she may find unpleasant.

'I'm asking too many questions.' interrupting his thoughts.

'No, you're not,' reassuring her, 'it's just that I don't think it's fair to lumber you with too many details of this case, Sophie, parts of which are pretty grim.'

'I'm not the squeamish type, Philip and since Saturday I've been thinking over what you told me, in particular about Pamela and if she is involved in any of this, I feel very strongly she should be brought to task.'

'There is a lot more to it, but I'd like to think we are nearing the end of the investigation. Mostly at this stage, frustratingly, it's only theory and suppositions, with a smattering of solid facts. But, as far as that accident is concerned, although Miss Grainger had nothing much to add, Margaret Hudson eventually opened up.'

'She's still there as well; some things never change, do they?'

'It must sound weird to you hearing these names mentioned.'

'It does; suddenly seventeen years doesn't seem such a long time after all.'

'Anyway, your old teacher, who isn't really old, was married a few years ago, but is, apparently, still referred to as Miss Hudson. Did you know she is only six years older than Pamela?'

'Is she really; I hadn't realised. When you're seventeen, anyone over twenty-one is ancient!'

'True,' he chuckled, 'she did tell me about a boyfriend she had at the time of the accident had shortly before been going with Pamela -'

'- you mean he dumped her for Miss Hudson?'

'Sounds like it.'

'Pamela would have hated that!'

'Margaret Hudson had ruled Pamela out as being responsible because, to her knowledge, Pamela wouldn't have had the technical know-how.'

'But, according to Pamela, she did.'

'Incidentally,' Philip said, 'I had already learned about that before you told me on Saturday.'

'So, it hadn't been idle bragging on her part.'

'Look Sophie, I don't want to keep you on the phone for much longer; it's getting late, but you mentioned when you rang about Saturday.'

'Yes, that's right; I'd love to see you again, Philip. Do you think you will be free?'

'At the moment it looks as though I will be, but I have to warn you that may change, so I hope you'll understand.'

'Of course I will; and if you can't, Philip, there will always be a next time, won't there?'

Chapter Seventeen

HONG KONG

Cecelia couldn't be sure when she first realised she was being followed; it hadn't been the same person each time which only added to her confusion, but the man who was standing outside the second-hand shop a few yards from her office and appearing to study a display of faded black and white postcards of old Hong Kong, had been there before. This had been on the previous Wednesday and now, as then, as she walked towards the taxi rank, he moved away and, with his back to her, carried on along Pedder Street. She didn't know whether to be concerned or not and so far hadn't considered it sufficiently important to tell Lenny, not that he could do anything. Whoever it was, she reasoned, would give up; it wasn't as if they would have learned much: each morning, except Sunday, she had walked down to Pedder Street from her apartment in mid-levels, lunched at the same little restaurant next door to her office and in the early evening made her way back home. She hadn't seen Lenny since the day she came back from London, more than a week ago, and since then her social life had been zero; in other words, a pretty dull existence, but she had taken Lenny's warning seriously and had been acting as naturally as possible. She had been expecting him to call for the last few days to confirm the trip to Singapore he'd told her about, but so far, nothing.

There had been a typhoon warning earlier and it was now raining heavily; not a steady downpour, but torrential, unrelentless; vicious sprays of water bouncing up from the fast over-flowing gutters and soaking her feet, and as always when it rained, an available taxi was a rarity. Why was it, complaining irritably to herself, and trying to keep her head and shoulders dry with what was proving to be a totally useless umbrella, that these drivers had such an abhorrence for admitting damp passengers; didn't they realise that the longer people had to wait for a taxi the more damp they became.

She had to wait a good ten minutes before she reached the head of the queue and one came along. Before stepping inside, she looked back down Pedder Street to see him joining the taxi rank and then wishing she had resisted the impulse; what she had seen unnerved her, not something she was accustomed to feeling, always considering she was in full control of her life and answerable to no-one.

'Glenealy Street, number eleven, please.' she instructed the driver in her limited Cantonese which she had learned primarily for taxi drivers, although one look at his disgruntled expression in the mirror, conveyed his contempt, but she had grown impervious to a Chinaman's reaction; she was a foreigner, or as they described westerners, a *guilo* and not expected to understand their language. They were waiting at the traffic lights at Queen's Road Central when her mobile rang and ignoring the flash of irritation on the driver's face, pressed the switch.

'Cecelia,' Lenny said, 'where are you?'

'On my way back home,' she told him, intentionally not saying his name, 'in a taxi at the lights at Queen's Road Central.'

'Right, get him to take you to Le Tire Bouchon in Graham Street; do you know where it is?'

'Yes, I've been there before.'

'Fine, 'I'll be there.'

It was fortunate she knew where the restaurant was and able to direct the driver with only a couple of turn rights and turn lefts until she saw the small French restaurant tucked neatly and unobtrusively between a herbalist shop on one side displaying a selection of Chinese dried goods and herbal remedies: ginseng; dried fish, abalone and shark's fin, and Chinese teas. Normally, when the weather was fine Cecelia had seen the older members of the family playing mah-jong in the open doorway, and on the other side of the restaurant, Wing On, the tailors, had their business where large hand-written posters in the window, written in English, promised to make a shirt in twelve hours and a suit in forty-eight. Paying the driver, she stepped out on to the pavement, ducking to avoid a cascade of rainwater flowing from a broken drain pipe above her head, and opened the door to the restaurant.

She had always liked Le Tire Bouchon and wondered, as she adjusted her eyes to the subdued lighting, why she didn't come more often. The place was recognised as being Hong Kong's original French restaurant; a classic-style interior, comfortable, even cosy ambience, booths separating the tables adding intimacy and seclusion from other diners.

'Cecelia.' Lenny called out to her. He had chosen a table at the far end of the room and she hadn't seen him at first.

'Hi, Lenny.' she said, walking over and sitting down.

'Hi.' giving her one of his rare smiles, 'Everything alright?'

'I'm not sure,' taking off her jacket and putting it on the seat next to her, 'but I think I'm being followed.'

'This evening?'

'Yes, when I came out of the office, but he wouldn't have known I was coming here. I've actually seen him before, and like that evening, he was there again.'

'Would you recognise him if you saw him again?'

'Probably.'

'So,' Lenny insisted, 'what happened; did you manage to get rid of him?'

'Nothing *happened*,' she emphasised, 'as soon as I appeared, he moved away down Pedder Street, although as I was getting into the taxi, he'd returned and had joined the taxi rank and, as I've said, there was no way he could have known I wasn't going straight home as I have been in the habit of doing recently.'

'Fair enough, Cecelia; I'm being ultra-cautious at the moment. It sounds as if this Peter Prescott, not that I believe it's his real name by the way, remains much to the fore and as I said to you last week we must be circumspect.'

'I understand, Lenny.'

'I knew you would,' he said, beckoning to the waiter, 'however, whatever these people are up to I am determined it's not going to disrupt my business; we have work to do, Cecelia, and I'm depending on your support, more than ever since Clive went.'

The waiter came over to their table with the menu and the wine list, curtailing for a few minutes anything further being said. Lenny ordered a bottle of *Merlot* to accompany their meal of chicken and liver paté and *beauf bourguigon* and while they were waiting for their food to arrive, two aperitifs; a *kir royalle* and a dry martini.

'Lenny?' she asked, raising her glass, 'Why do you think they are so interested in my movements?'

'The answer is simple,' he said, 'their aim is to try and trace me. You see, Cecelia, up to now, although they may suspect my involvement in the various recent -' pausing for second, - recent activities, they've never seen me, therefore they have no idea what I look like, especially here in my own habitat.'

'Oh,' smiling at his dry humour, 'you mean because you're Chinese?'

'Quite. That in itself, provided I remain in Hong Kong for the present, should be an excellent disguise.'

'But, they know about you?'

'Undoubtedly, yes, but I don't believe enough to identify me. They know my name and that of the business, but they won't know my home address.'

'Can you be certain?'

'Yes, Cecelia, I can. As far as any Hong Kong records are concerned it's in Garden Road in Mid Levels; an apartment I bought several years ago, but I have never lived there. I'm telling you this,' he explained, 'because I want you to realise there are certain – for want of a better word – drawbacks to the work.'

'And for anyone who should be working for you.'

'Yes and each of these people must possess a strong sense of self-preservation which I believe you have, Cecelia.'

'Thank you.'

'Oh, it's not a compliment.' he said, his expression typically inscrutable.

'These people you talk about,' Cecelia said, lowering her voice, although there was no-one sitting at the table next to them, 'are they

MI6?'

'I would say so.' the expression unchanging.

'They are highly skilled and trained individuals, Lenny.'

'I'm sure they are, but they are still human beings, Cecelia; men and women, both sexes are not infallible.'

And neither are you, Lenny, she wanted to say, but of course she didn't. Presumably he knew what he was doing. She wasn't all that concerned about herself, after all, she reasoned, as far as she was concerned she wasn't doing anything unlawful. She had no idea, and didn't want to know, where the various items she either delivered or collected came from, or whether they were illicit or not. Nobody in the publishing firm knew she also worked for Lenny. As she was freelance, she could select her own hours and as she spent most of her time there six days a week, this meant any time she took off was never questioned. An open-ended contract and it suited her.

'You look thoughtful.' he said, taking another sip of his martini.

'I was wondering when you want me to go to Singapore.' she lied.

'Ah, yes,' he nodded, putting his glass back down on the table, 'I'd like you to fly over there on Friday; can you manage that?'

'No problem.'

'I've pre-empted your agreement,' he said, taking a couple of envelopes from his pocket and passing them across to her, 'this one,' he went on, pointing to the smaller envelope, 'contains your return flight tickets: Friday morning, the nine o'clock flight, arriving at Changi Airport at ten minutes to one, and returning here Sunday, midday. I've made a reservation for the Friday and Saturday at the Mandarin Oriental in Raffles Avenue as usual.

'And you want me to meet Nicholas?'

'That's right. He'll be in the hotel's main cocktail lounge at six-thirty on Friday. This other envelope is for him, Cecelia.'

'Okay,' putting them both into her bag.

'He'll give you a small package which you'll bring back with you. I suggest you put in the baggage you'll be checking through. Any problems with that?' he asked.

'It isn't drugs, is it, Lenny?'

'No, Cecelia, I can assure you it isn't. I would never compromise you with any of that stuff. It will contain a few pieces of antique jewellery which later I want you to take on to England, but not yet, very likely next week. I would like to make sure we no longer have these people breathing down our necks first. I don't want you bumping into Peter Prescott again; a second visit so soon after your last would be tempting providence.'

***

'I think I've seen Lenny Yeung, Charles.'

'That's a first, Derek;' Charles said, 'up to now, apparently no-one else has. How sure are you?'

'Not absolutely,' Derek Insole said, his voice echoing long distance, 'but this evening, around seven, Cecelia Cunningham left her office as she has been doing each day and hired a taxi. She's always gone directly to her apartment in Glenealy Street, but -'

'- she didn't this time.' Charles interrupted, hoping this was what they had been waiting for.

'No; I had already phoned ahead to the guy I had positioned outside her apartment block, this was as soon as she got into the taxi and he phoned back when she didn't turn up.'

'I see, and -?'

'I'd taken a note of the driver's number; it didn't take long to contact him and he was quick to say he'd dropped his fare at a restaurant in Graham Street, not all that far from where she lives, actually.'

'And you went along there, Derek?'

'No, I got someone else, the reason being I think she may have noticed me outside her office. Anyway, she was in there with a Chinese guy and he heard her refer to him as Lenny.'

'That's something, Derek.' Charles said, 'Anything else?'

'There was, yes. He handed over two envelopes to her; she only opened one of them which contained a couple of flight tickets, one to

Changi Airport and a return back here -'

'- Singapore.' Charles said, taking a sharp intake of breath.

'Interesting, wouldn't you say?'

'Indeed it is. I don't suppose your officer heard when she was going?'

'Afraid not, only the words Changi Airport. They left soon after that; she went first and he followed about five or six minutes later. In fact, my man was able to take a photograph of him while he was waiting for a taxi.'

'Excellent.'

'I'll be sending an image through to you shortly.'

'Alright, Derek, and were you able to put a tail on him?'

'Sorry, it wasn't possible, Charles. We're in the middle of a massive storm tonight and as you've been to Hong Kong you'll know how scarce these damn taxis can be then.'

'Don't I just.'

'I haven't been in touch with Reservations yet, but I'll do that next. Once I find out the time of her flight, do you want me to continue to have her followed, Charles?'

'Please. Have you someone else, apart from the officer you've just mentioned?'

'Yes, the same one who was outside Yeung's place in Garden Street, where incidentally he didn't arrive after he had left the restaurant.'

'Not to worry, Derek; this is a start to finally tracking the man down. Keep in touch.'

***

Lenny had meant what he had said to Cecelia: his determination not to allow anyone, MI6 or otherwise, to disrupt the way he conducted his business was paramount to him. Lenny was single-minded and self-motivated and had been since his teens. He couldn't recall a time when he hadn't striven to be 'top dog' and it was probably for this reason he had never married. There had been no shortage of women over the years; all of them fully focused and dedicated to their careers. He had lost count of the evenings he had been subjected to hearing about their various achievements and confrontations they were apparently experiencing on a daily basis and all the time oblivious to the opulence surroundings of some of the Island's most exclusive restaurants to which he'd taken them.

In comparison, having a meal with Cecelia was a pleasurable experience. She made no demands and seldom talked about herself which he appreciated. He had known her for a long time, but with Lenny there was a wide line between them emotionally and one he would never cross; she worked for him and to a degree he trusted her, mainly because he'd never had any reason not to. He had found what she had told him this evening disconcerting and wondering now how much longer it would be before he was recognised. Whoever was behind the search for him was persistent and Lenny didn't think he would give up. It hadn't been too clever of Gregory to have displayed those figurines in the way he had and, in retrospect, Lenny couldn't think why he had deviated from the way he normally sold any pieces he had sent through to him. Gregory never told him the names of these buyers of his, only that they were all private collectors, hand-picked by him and, under normal circumstances, those pieces wouldn't have been re-sold, but remained in the family. Perhaps, Lenny thought, it was unreasonable to blame Gregory for the swift chain of events resulting as soon as the figurines were seen by the valuers, but all the same it should not have happened. As usual, grumbling under his breath, it looked very much as though he was left to pick up the pieces, remembering an old proverb he had learned at school: "For want of a nail, the shoe was lost; for want of a shoe, the horse was lost; for want of a horse, the rider was lost; for want of a rider, the message was lost; for want of a message, the battle was lost; for want of a battle, the Kingdom was lost" stifling a shudder of apprehension, and hoping it wasn't an omen.

It was still raining heavily when he left the restaurant and, for once, Graham Street was practically deserted. Undecided whether it might be better to walk along to Pedder Street to find a taxi when, surprisingly, one came along, the wheels causing a spray as it drew up alongside him and, instructing the driver to take him to his apartment in Causeway Bay, leaned back in his seat which felt uncomfortably damp through the thin fabric of his jacket. Like most Cantonese, he hated rain, especially at night when the sound muffled out the normal and familiar cacophony of Hong Kong.

By the time they reached Causeway Bay and his taxi had turned into Hing Fat Street leading off from the top of Causeway Road, the storm had abated and he was able to reach the main door of the building without getting another soaking. The night porter greeted him cordially, pressing the button for the lift which would take him up to his apartment on the fourth floor.

Although he had explained to Cecelia about his property in Garden Road he had chosen not to tell her the Causeway Bay address, considering it best she didn't know should she have the misfortune to meet another Peter Prescott and be tricked into revealing where he lived. Lenny had tried to build up what he realised was no more than a smokescreen, but better than nothing. He was in no doubt MI6 were on to him and would only have the Garden Road address which wouldn't be any help to them. As an added precaution, Lenny had for some time, had possessed two passports; both in the name of Yeung except for the difference in the first names. He had no qualms about using Yeung twice, working on the premise that Yeung in China was as common as Smith in England. His real name was William Leonard Yeung and it was this passport, one which was issued to him when he was granted British citizenship, he used normally. The other passport in the name of SimonYeung now and again came in useful. He had first starting calling himself Lenny while he was at London University and continued to do so when he returned to Hong Kong after graduating and as a form of insurance if he should ever need a quick change of identity, managed to obtain this one, mainly thanks to Nicholas' contrivances. He doubted now whether Gregory even remembered when he was called William. For all he knew, that could have been his second Christian name and that he simply preferred to be called Lenny. Not that it was all that important, he thought, as the lift glided to a silent stop outside the door to his apartment.

Although late, he didn't feel like going to bed, knowing he would find it impossible to sleep. Making himself some lemon tea, he took it with him into the lounge and switched on the television, but there was nothing on any of the channels of any interest, turning down the volume to mute. Apart from the Tiffany lamp on the table beside him and the flickering screen, the room was in darkness; the full-length curtains his maid had already drawn before she left earlier in the evening shielded him from any outside intrusion. He needed this quiet time to think, to make contingency plans in the event anything should go wrong. Lenny was a realist in spite of his outward appearance of confidence. The 'what if' situation could have been created for him personally, he thought cynically, taking a sip of the tea, immediately feeling, as he swallowed, the soothing effect from the warm liquid with the slight tangy flavour.

His first concern was Gregory, feeling he could be the weakest link. In spite of Gregory's assurances that he kept all records regarding everything he received from him separate from the running of his business, may not be infallible if New Scotland Yard decided to make a return visit for the sole purpose of looking further into his records. This had been last Thursday and when he spoke to him the following day to find out whether he would be interested in the antique jewellery, he had sounded less stressed out, but it was now Wednesday and he had heard nothing further from which could mean there was nothing to report. It would still be afternoon in England and pulling the telephone towards him, dialled Gregory's office.

He recognised the voice of his assistant as soon as she answered, having spoken to Ellen Boyle several times over the years.

'Good afternoon, Mr Yeung,' she said, 'although it must be almost midnight with you.'

'That's right; it's been a long day,' Lenny answered, 'Could I speak to Gregory please, Ellen?'

'I'm sorry, Mr Yeung, but he isn't here.'

'That's alright; I'll try him on his mobile.

'I don't think he will have it switched on because he'll be airborne probably for at least another nine hours.'

'Where is he going, Ellen?' trying to keep the annoyance from his voice: it was hardly the woman's fault if Gregory had decided to make himself absent in this clandestine fashion.

'He and his wife were booked on this morning's nine o'clock flight to Hong Kong, Mr Yeung; I thought he may have told you.' she added hesitatingly.

Hong Kong! What the hell was he playing at? Could he really be so stupid and misguided to put his head in the proverbial noose? And without letting him know either! A whole gamut of indignations spun through his brain, each one vying for position, but none of them made any sense.

'How long will he be away, Ellen?' keeping his voice level, not wanting her to realise the strength of his reactions.

'They'll be back next Tuesday. I think it was very much a spur of the moment decision to take a holiday,' picking up on his vibes, 'in fact,' she added, 'Gregory told me his wife had planned it all; apparently she had never been to Hong Kong before.'

'Well, Ellen,' he said at last, 'I must admit I am surprised, but this means I'll be able to meet up with him here.' mentally calculating when they were likely to arrive the following morning, 'Did Gregory mention which hotel they will be staying in?'

'He did; it's the Mandarin Oriental.'

The Mandarin. It could have been worse, Lenny thought; it could have been the Excelsior which was practically next door. It just meant he would have to keep away from the Mandarin's 'Captain's Bar' for the next few days; his favourite place for a drink at the end of the day.

'Good choice.' he said.

'It seems a lovely hotel, Mr Yeung; I've seen pictures of it. Very luxurious.'

'One of Hong Kong's best.' Lenny said before ringing off.

There had been no trace of envy in her voice. Ellen Boyle, he reckoned, was one of the world's workers, reasonably content with her lot. He doubted when she did have a holiday, she would go any further than Spain or Portugal. Not for her, flying off to the Far East and being pampered for two weeks in an exclusive hotel with swimming pool and other recreational attractions.

So, he thought, taking his half-drunk tea into the kitchen, in a matter of hours Gregory and his wife would be arriving and there was not one damn thing he could do about it. He would get in touch with him of course; he would have to. To anyone unfamiliar with Hong Kong, Lenny knew they found the place vast, never silent, restaurants, bars and nightclubs open late, and always, the pavements thronged with people of all nationalities, but to someone like himself, born and bred here, it was a village; scarcely a day went by when he didn't see someone he recognised and the last thing he wanted was to turn a corner or walk into a bar and come face to face with Gregory.

It wasn't until he was in the bedroom, hoping to catch up on a couple of hours of sleep, he realised that, apart from the obvious inconvenience of Gregory being here, he may be doing him a favour. It meant that now he could take those pieces of jewellery back to England with him, which would avoid any possibility of Cecelia experiencing a repeat performance of what she went through the other week. She would be flying over to Singapore on Friday, as they had discussed this evening, and returning on Sunday morning; he would arrange to meet Gregory, hand the jewellery over to him before he took his flight back on Tuesday. He wouldn't like it, but that was just too bad. He'd taken stuff back to England with him before, so in Lenny's opinion what would be so different.

***

Gregory was in the 'Captain's Bar', having ordered a lager, when his mobile rang. Lenny's number was illuminated on the display panel and, thankful Pamela was still in their room, he pressed the button.

'Gregory; Lenny here.'

'Hello, Lenny.'

'What the hell are you thinking of, Gregory? Coming to Hong Kong of all places!'

'I can explain.'

'There's no need. As you've no doubt realised, I've spoken to Ellen.'

'Of course. I should have told you, I suppose.' he admitted.

'You're damn right you should have.' the tone of his voice making him cringe. Gregory had never known Lenny to be so angry.

'Look, Gregory,' Lenny was going on, 'you're here now and nothing can change that, but I would like to say not too wise on your part, my friend, not too wise at all. However, now that you *are* here, I suggest you take the jewellery back with you next week.'

'Just a minute, Lenny; that wasn't part of the agreement.'

'Precisely, but you've left me with little choice.'

'What do you mean?'

'Unwittingly or not,' Lenny said, obviously making an effort to control his temper, 'your presence in Hong Kong at this time could be putting me in a very compromising situation, also yourself, Gregory. I'm surprised you didn't consider that. You are aware as well as I am, that we are currently, not to put too fine a point on it or exaggerate the outcome of what's been happening recently, under close scrutiny by the authorities, and by authorities, I mean MI6.'

'Everything has quietened down over the last few days; I haven't had any further visits.'

'Don't be so damned naive! We're not only talking about those figurines, we're talking about the whole picture here, Gregory. Can't you see that? There's far too much at stake here for either of us to become complacent. And, for your information, Cecelia is still being followed and that, quite frankly, worries me.'

'Oh.'

'Is that all you can say? And there's another thing, Gregory, your business.'

'What about my business?' genuinely puzzled, not understanding what he could mean.

'By coming away,' Lenny said, 'you have left yourself wide-open.'

'How? Ellen is in charge and she's more than capable of handling the business.'

'And if anyone turned up again from New Scotland Yard, Gregory, and asks to have another look at your records – no, I'll rephrase that – demand to look at your records, how would she handle that? Eh?'

'That won't happen.'

'My God, how I wish I had your confidence which is, in my opinion, tantamount to blinkered complacency.'

'Don't you think you're worrying needlessly?'

'I do not! Anyway, Gregory, I hope you've got the message loud and clear. Enjoy your stay and I'll see you on Monday evening at six in the 'Captain's Bar. Alright?'

'Alright.'

'Good.'

Gregory was thoughtful as he switched off his mobile. Lenny had been right in what he'd said. In retrospect now, he really shouldn't be here, but what could he have done in any case; Pamela had made all the arrangements and he felt he had to go along with her, not to have done so would have only alerted her into thinking he had something to hide, which of course he had. What a bloody mess, he thought, taking a long deep sip of his beer.

***

'Nicholas.'

'Hello, Lenny; how are you?'

'Could be one hell of a lot better,' Lenny said caustically, 'I didn't mention this to you the other day when I rang, but those oriental figures you sold me six years ago have been causing me a considerable amount of aggro.'

'How?'

'Don't come the all innocent with me, Nicholas. As you know, I never question your sources, but for God's sake, man, I did trust you – I didn't expect them to be listed as stolen property.'

'I had no idea, Lenny.'

'I'm sure you didn't, Nicholas.' anger turning into sarcasm; so much easier with a man like Nicholas Anout. Also, Lenny realised, nothing would be gained by continuing to berate him; years of lying low, switching countries to avoid arrest and extraditing himself from sticky situations had all given Nicholas an impenetrable veneer, Lenny was well aware when he was slap up against a barrier which he, even with all his well-honed skills, wouldn't be able to break through. Often, he had seriously wondered why he continued to deal with him, but always he came up with the same answer: Nicholas was the man who could supply him with exactly what he required. If he had an outlet, as he had now with Gregory, for selected pieces of antique jewellery, Nicholas was the man who would invariably know where to find them and, with him being in Singapore, where he had lived since that debacle in Paris, was ideal; this saved him from putting himself in a too vulnerable position, with Cecelia acting as an intermediary. There were always risks in what he was doing, Lenny never under-estimated those, but this way he could organise and ultimately control the various transactions.

'You might not believe this, Lenny,' Nicholas said, 'but those figurines were bought at auction here and if I remember correctly, they were in a job lot, oriental artefacts they were described. There was nothing else of any significant value, so how they ended up there I do not know.'

'Okay, okay, I hear what you're saying,' and not believing a word of his too pat explanation, 'but the main reason for phoning you was to let you know that Cecelia will be arriving at Changi Airport on the Singapore Airlines flight at twelve-fifty on Friday afternoon. Don't meet her as you normally do, Nicholas. She'll make her way directly to the Mandarin and she'll meet you in the cocktail lounge at six-thirty. I trust you are *au fait* with all of that?'

'Fine, no problem. You're being extra-cautious, though, Lenny.'

'I have to be and without going into any great detail, there's always the possibility she may be followed.'

'Is this part of the aggro you mentioned?'

'Too true, my friend. However, as they say, it's business as usual.'

'She's obviously aware of your current situation.'

'I'll correct you there, Nicholas, it isn't only *my* current situation; it's *ours*, but yes, as much as she needs to be.'

'Alright, Lenny.'

'She'll be bringing you the payment for this consignment in US dollars as usual.'

'Thank you, Lenny and I've already packaged the pieces, also I'm going to include a rather attractive blue agate cameo broach which you might be interested in, should fetch a fair bit to a collector.'

'An antique?'

'Of course, although to be accurate, it's described in the trade as a non-estate antique, but I've always thought that to be something of a misnomer, haven't you?'

'I'm no expert, Nicholas, so you'll have to explain.'

'Neither am I, Lenny, believe me, but I spoke to someone recently who is, and he told me it means the jewellery once belonged to someone and not necessarily to an estate as such, but my point is, surely if it's an antique it must at one time have belonged to someone.'

'Very profound, Nicholas.' Lenny found himself smiling; Nicholas was incorrigible and as a number of times before he found it impossible to stay mad with him for long.

Chapter Eighteen

'Gregory's Antiques' didn't open until nine-thirty. Philip had already put in an hour at Headquarters, completing the report he had started the day before and tidying up his desk which was showing signs of him not spending a great deal of time in his office over the last couple of weeks. The last of their good summer had gone, followed this morning by an autumnal chill and already the trees along the Embankment were beginning to look forlorn, their almost naked branches reminding him of the cold months ahead.

He paused outside the antique shop for a moment to look at the window display, not that there was a great deal: a small oblong table in a dark highly polished wood, the bow-shaped legs in gilded bronze and intertwined with enamel flowers and leaves. On the centre of the table, a set of ten crystal liqueur glasses and decanter, the stopper multi-faceted and pyramid in design. The only other item was a chair, or according to the discreetly placed card, a *fauteuil*; high-backed, upholstered in rich tapestry in muted shades of dark blue and red. The overall effect was, he had to admit, although somewhat too elaborate for his taste, elegant, very French and undeniably pricey and, pushing open the door, he went inside.

'Good morning, sir, can I assist you, or would you prefer to browse?'

He hadn't noticed her at first, his eyes taking a few seconds to readjust from the brighter light outside.

'Good morning; as much as I would like to look round, I'm here to see Mr Smythe-Jones, if he is available.'

'Mr Smythe-Jones is on holiday at the moment and won't be back until the beginning of next week. Is there anything I can do to help you?'

'I'm not sure,' Philip answered slowly, at the same time trying to assimilate what she'd told him, wondering if there was anything significant about Smythe-Jones being away or not, 'you say he's on holiday?'

'Yes, he and his wife are spending a few days in Hong Kong. They only left this morning as a matter of fact.' unwittingly telling him exactly what he wanted to know.

Hong Kong. Why on earth should they be going there? If, he decided, he was going to be given any answer to that, he would have to introduce himself; otherwise it was doubtful whether he would be able to get any further, taking out one of his cards. As he expected, as soon as she read it, her manner altered and he didn't miss the quick flash of alarm, also the way her hand shook slightly as she gave the card back to him.

'I don't understand,' she said at last, 'but is your visit – official, Mr Spencer? I would like you to know,' she went on before he had time to answer, 'I've worked for Mr Smythe-Jones for almost thirty years – as his personal assistant.' she added.

'I see, and your name, Madam?'

'Ellen Boyle; Miss Ellen Boyle.'

'Well, Miss Boyle, to answer your question;' he said, 'I am here in an official capacity, although the questions I had hoped to ask Mr Smythe-Jones were routine; they concern part of an enquiry we, at the Foreign Office, are conducting.'

'Is this something to do about the oriental figurines, Mr Spencer?' surprising him by the naive way her mind was working. Ellen Boyle, he was thinking was a woman devoid of any guile, where being cunning or deceitful would be totally alien. Looking at her now and taking in the knee-length black pin-stripe skirt, the no-nonsense cream silk blouse with the Margaret Thatcher bow, even to the single strand of pearls, that to her, fashion hadn't moved on since she was a young woman. How far, he wondered, did her loyalty extend to the man for whom she had worked for so long. This could soon be tested.

'You knew about the figurines, Miss Boyle?'

'I did actually,' she said and perhaps fortuitously for her, a couple came into the shop, followed almost immediately by a young woman with a briefcase in one hand and in the other what appeared to be promotional posters, recognising the enlarged photograph of the Royal Victoria and Albert Museum.

'Will you excuse me for a moment, Mr Spencer,' she said, making to move over towards the couple who had remained indecisively by the door, but I must attend to these customers.'

She was obviously running the business on her own; it would appear, he thought, walking over to a large glass cabinet displaying antique jewellery, that for all Smythe-Jones' wealth there must be an element of meanness in his character, or was his reluctance to employ additional staff an indication of maintaining a tight control of the business, making it easier for him to conceal any dubious activities. Thirty years was a long time to work for one employer and no doubt from when he had interviewed her, Smythe-Jones had considered Ellen Boyle possessed the qualities he wanted; steady, reliable and willing to prove her worth. She wasn't married which could imply she had absorbed herself in the work she was doing, Gregory Smythe-Jones, the husband substitute, being the central pivot to her life. Perhaps not as fanciful as it might sound, watching as she explained the history of a set of Victorian miniatures. Meanwhile, the girl, her body language conveying barely controlled impatience, had moved closer to them and he watched, amused, waiting for her to interrupt, but she didn't; with a polite nod to acknowledge her presence, Miss Boyle continued to discuss the merits of the miniatures, pointing to the spider-thin embroidery on the tiny canvases of black satin. Not as meek as she at first appeared, Philip decided.

No more than five minutes and she was back, the sale completed and carrying one of the rolled-up posters.

'I'm sorry about that, Mr Spencer.' she said, putting the poster down on one of the tables and joining him at the display cabinet, 'I see you're admiring our range of antique jewellery; most of it is of European origin and some of the finer ones are from the Far East, Japan mainly.'

'Very impressive, Miss Boyle. Now, if I may, I'd like to go back to what I was saying.'

'Of course, Mr Spencer. You were asking about the four figurines, weren't you?'

'Presumably Mr Smythe-Jones has told you they had been stolen.'

'He did, yes. He was terribly upset, you know. You see, that sort of thing has never happened before.'

'I understand you made the sale?'

'Yes, that's right. I remember the lady very well; she told me she had been collecting pieces of that nature and when she saw those four she decided they would be a perfect match for the others she had in her home in Scotland. I've been wondering ever since the officer from New Scotland Yard came to see Mr Smythe-Jones what had happened to her. Obviously they must have been valued professionally, but somehow she didn't strike me as the sort of person who would have been too concerned about their value.'

'You're probably right. Sadly, she died, Miss Boyle and bequeathed them to her niece and, not sharing her aunt's love for oriental artefacts of that kind, she decided to sell them.'

'I see,' she said quietly, 'and of course it would have been necessary to have them valued first.'

'Mr Smythe-Jones explained to the officer how he made the purchase during a buying trip to Hong Kong.'

'I know.'

'However,' Philip said, wanting to give the impression he had no more questions to ask, 'I will have to wait until he has returned; as I mentioned, the questions I have to ask are routine and surely a few more days won't make all that much difference to us at this stage in our enquiry. I apologise for taking up so much of your time this morning.'

'That's alright, Mr Spencer.' accompanying him to the door.

'You have a really splendid display, Miss Boyle,' conversationally, 'and from what I've seen most of the furniture must have come from the Far East, unless of course,' he added, Mr Smythe-Jones purchased them in this country.'

'Some, yes,' she explained, 'but as you say, the bulk of the Far Eastern furniture and tapestries, although purchased at auction were shipped over from Hong Kong, over a number of years. Before then, we only sold European antiques.' she added.

'Really? And have you always used the same shipping company?'

hoping he hadn't said too much, but he needn't have worried.

'Oh, yes, we've been with Bakker & Bakker right from when we branched out to include antiques from that part of the world.'

'Bakker & Bakker,' Philip repeated, affecting a casualness he certainly didn't feel, 'not a Chinese company, then?'

'No, Mr Spencer,' opening the door for him, 'they're Dutch, but have a branch in Hong Kong.'

Waiting for a taxi to take him back to Headquarters, Philip mulled over what he had learned. While hearing that the Smythe-Jones wouldn't be back until the following week what Ellen Boyle had told him far outweighed the temporary setback. Once again, the name of Bakker & Bakker had been mentioned. Another link, and a strong one, between Yeung and the Smythe-Jones. Dare he hope that the net surrounding the key suspects in this double enquiry was closing in? Right from the start when Hugh had passed on to Charles what John Brookes had told him, it had felt like two steps forward and one back; even this morning or, more accurately, especially this morning.

Charles' secretary told him Charles was at a meeting, but he had left a note for him.

"Philip," he had written, "I phoned Sir Bevington's office and made an appointment to see him tomorrow late morning and have booked the first Eurostar. Singapore police have been back to say there was a spate of Embassy robberies around the time of Sir Bevington's, perhaps he can throw some light on all of this."

Grateful to Charles for going over to Paris which meant he could concentrate on the third section of this expanding enquiry; namely, Martha Jacobsen's murder. The only way he could do this was to drive down to Taunton again. With the Smythe-Jones' out of the way, he didn't have much choice. A lot depended now on what Derek was going to come up with and then perhaps they would be able to move in and wrap up the whole business. Before leaving the office, he telephoned the Castle Hotel to reserve a room for the night and scribbled a note for Charles to tell him where he was going. Collecting the overnight bag which he always kept in the office to save him wasting time in going home first, he took the lift down to the ground floor, checked out and walked across to the car park.

***

Dejà vu, Philip thought, pulling up outside the Castle Hotel exactly as he had done a week ago and walking up the short flight of steps to the front door. The same receptionist was on duty and as before greeted him with a friendly and natural smile which he found refreshing after being confronted more times than he cared to remember by the disinterested haughtiness of her city counterparts.

'Good evening, Mr Spencer; it's nice to see you again.' turning the register round to face him, 'Just your name and car registration number, sir, that will be enough.' and reaching up to the board behind her for the key to his room.

He filled in what she had asked for, at the same time glancing across to the facing page, seeing his entry for the previous Wednesday and memorising the registration number of Martha Jacobsen's car.

'There you are, sir,' handing him his key, 'we've given you the same room.'

'That's fine, thank you.' picking up his bag, 'Incidentally,' he said, 'last week you had a guest staying here called Miss Martha Jacobsen –'

'Oh, dear,' she said, a hand going instinctively up to her mouth, 'that poor woman. I heard about the accident when I came off duty that day. Was she a friend of yours, sir?'

'Not exactly,' he answered obliquely, 'it was just that I recognised her name in the register.'

'You did know about the accident?'

'I did, yes.'

'What a dreadful thing to happen to her and to think I only saw her the day before.'

'You mean on the Thursday?'

'Yes, she actually booked out that morning quite early.'

'That explains it, then. If she hadn't, I'm sure I would have seen her at breakfast.'

'I've thought since that perhaps she moved to another hotel for the night as the crash was at the Taunton Deane Service Station which is only on the outskirts of the town.'

'We'll never know.'

'No, sir, we won't. A friend of hers called into the hotel on Thursday afternoon asking for her.'

'Really?'

'Mrs Smythe-Jones, she's one of our regular customers, often comes into the restaurant with her husband. She told me she had heard Miss Jacobsen was staying here and was hoping to meet up with her.'

'I daresay she will have heard all about it by now.'

'I'm sure she will have. Taunton isn't a large town and news spreads very quickly, especially when it is as tragic as this.'

Once in his room, he took out his notebook, turning to the last page where he had jotted down the names and addresses of a few hotels close to the town centre. Before leaving London he'd had no clear plan of what he was going to do once he reached Taunton, except over the last couple of days it had become important to him to make every effort to find out where Martha Jacobsen had spent Thursday night. What the receptionist had so readily told him was yet another indication of Pamela's guilt. Why had she decided to get in touch with her? He couldn't think of any credible explanation, but there had to be one. Looking at those addresses again and checking them against a map of the town centre he'd brought with him, he noticed that although there were eighteen hotels and guest houses in and around Taunton, there were very few as central as The Castle. Working on the premise she would have chosen a smaller one where it was unlikely Pamela and her husband would frequent, he decided to walk along and find out.

He drew a blank at the first one; the Bedford Hotel; they'd had no guest called Martha Jacobsen staying there last week and apart from a slight raising of eyebrows from the middle-aged receptionist when he showed her his card, the name didn't appear to have registered with her, or perhaps she just had a bad memory.

The second hotel, a few hundred yards further along, was closed for renovation and had been since the first of September, but the receptionist at the Brampton in a quiet cul-de-sac behind the church told him that Martha had spent last Thursday night there.

'Is there something *suspicious* about what happened to Miss Jacobsen?' she said, lowering her voice dramatically.

'Why should you think that, Rosemary?' having noticed her name tag pinned on to her jacket.

'Well,' she hesitated, 'you being with the Foreign Office, I mean.'

'I am here in an official capacity,' Philip said, 'and in a way you're right. However,' he went on quickly in an attempt to put her at her ease; the last he wanted was to start any rumours flaring up, recalling what the receptionist at The Castle had said about the people of Taunton, 'when an accident of this nature occurs and the person was already known to us, as a matter of routine we must look into how and why it happened.'

'Oh, I see; well,' she smiled nervously, 'I think I do.'

'You see, the lady had booked in here on Thursday and as I had been talking to her the evening before in another hotel in the town where she had been staying, I have to ask a few questions which are routine ones and nothing for you to be concerned about.'

'What do you want to know, Mr Spencer?'

'Only how she spent Thursday evening; whether she went out for a meal or ate in your restaurant, for instance.'

'I don't think she went out, not before nine anyway.' she said, 'I had just come on duty when she arrived on Thursday morning and I was still here then and I know she was in our restaurant when I left.'

'And her car, Rosemary,' he asked, 'did you happen to notice where it had been parked?'

'I do actually. As I've said, I had just come on duty and I saw her from the window.' pointing to the window directly opposite to the desk, 'This was when she drove into the car park, parking it near the entrance and as it was in the space next to mine, I noticed it was still there when I went home.'

'You're sure it was the same one.'

'Oh, yes; I had already seen the Avis sticker in the rear window when she drove in; it had a Heathrow Airport address on it and when she was booking in she mentioned she would be driving back to Heathrow early the following morning. She had already left the hotel when I came on duty the next morning and later when I heard about the police being called in that night, I did wonder whether she had been disturbed by the noise. Apparently, quite a few of our guests were, one or two even complained.'

'What was the problem?' immediately alerted, his dislike of coincidences to the fore.

'Oh,' she smiled, 'it turned out to be nothing really. A guest had seen someone loitering in the car park and phoned down to the night porter; by then, whoever it was, had gone although he still gave the police a ring. They checked all the vehicles parked outside, but there was no sign of any of them being broken into.'

'Perhaps the guest had been mistaken,' Philip suggested in the hope of encouraging her to elaborate, 'an over-active imagination perhaps.'

'I don't think so, sir. The lady is one of our residents; we all know her well and she was positive someone was out there. You see,' she went on, 'she's a light sleeper and being a warm night she had left her window open. She told Edward, that's the night porter; she heard a clicking noise like a car door opening. At first when she looked out everything appeared as normal, but as she stood at the window, for at least five or six minutes she thought, she noticed what at first seemed like a dark shadow, but then realised it was someone in the car park, walking close to the hedge.'

'How could she have been so certain; it must have been dark out there?'

'It would have been, yes. We have a lantern above the front door, but it only lights the area around the steps; it doesn't extend to where the cars are parked.'

'She must have good eyesight.' Philip said.

'She probably has, sir,' Rosemary said, 'but she heard footsteps, which was what decided her she wasn't mistaken.'

Philip's mobile rang as he was walking back to his hotel and sure this would be Charles, he pressed the 'on' switch.

'Hello, Philip,' Charles said, 'still working?'

'I'm finishing now,' Philip said, 'I feel in need of some light refreshment, followed by a hearty steak.'

'Sounds good to me,' Charles laughed, 'I'll be glad when Judith gets home and I can start eating something that hasn't been pre-cooked.'

'I read your note, Charles, so it will be an early start for you tomorrow.'

'That's true, but I'm hopeful the talk with Sir Bevington will clear up a number of points. Anyway, Philip, I've had a call from Derek; it looks as if events are starting to move over there.'

'That's good; it's about time, isn't it?'

'I know; up to now it has been very much the waiting game for him, but Cecelia Cunningham met up with a man she was overheard to call Lenny.'

'Great.'

'Also,' pausing for a second and Philip could tell he was smiling; Charles was always like this when they were balanced on the edge of what they felt was the breakthrough they wanted, 'he handed over a couple of flight tickets to her. Derek has since checked with Reservations and she is booked to fly to Singapore on Friday morning, returning to Hong Kong on Sunday midday, Hong Kong time.'

'So, she's on the move again.'

'Yes, Derek is arranging to put a tail on her. It won't be easy of course because we don't know where she'll be staying in Singapore.'

'I realise that,' Philip agreed, 'and if it is Anout she's meeting this probably explains why he has succeeded in not being caught.'

'That's right, but I think it's safe to assume she'll be carrying something back with her. The big question is, Philip, do we let her get through Customs in the hope of seeing what she does next.'

'Off the cuff, Charles and in view of what I've discovered today, I would say we let her go through.'

'Yes?'

'Gregory and Pamela Smythe-Jones left for a few days holiday in Hong Kong earlier today.'

'Well, well.'

'It could be, only a guess of course, but a possibility all the same, he might have something on him once they arrive back at Heathrow on Tuesday and, if he has, we'll have got him.'

'A bit foolhardy of him going over there at this present time, wouldn't you say?'

'I would say so, Charles. I spoke to Ellen Boyle this morning; she's his assistant, and she obligingly informed me that they always used Bakker & Bakker to ship larger items, such as furniture, rugs and paintings from Hong Kong.'

'Now that is interesting. Very interesting in fact.'

'It makes the search of 'Gregory's Antiques' all that more crucial, but in view of what you've told me, Charles, we'll have to delay that until the Smythe-Jones are actually winging their way back here, otherwise it may alarm the whole lot of them.'

'I'll go along with that. At least,' he went on, 'we have a few days breathing space. Shall we meet up tomorrow when I get back from Paris? I might have something to add to what is fast resembling a very large can of worms.'

***

'If you would like to come this way, Mr Hastings, I'll take you along to Sir Bevington's office.

Charles followed the woman, her low heels making little sound on the carpeted corridor, until she stopped at a door halfway down and opening it, gestured for him to go in. They were in a small vestibule; comfortable with softly upholstered sofa and chairs, a long oval coffee table with a folded copy of that morning's London 'Times'; a nostalgic reminder of

England in the heart of the Parisian capital.

The door to an inner office opened and the man, who could only have been Sir Bevington, emerged and strode quickly towards him.

'Good morning, Mr Hastings,' he said, shaking hands vigorously, how are you?'

'I'm very well, thank you, Sir Bevington.'

'I'll bring in some coffee, Sir Bevington,' his secretary said, 'or would you prefer tea, Mr Hastings?'

'No, coffee would be perfect.'

'Thank you, Annabel. Do sit down, Mr Hastings; this room is far more amenable than my office. I'm sorry to say I'm not the tidiest of men and I have never grown accustomed to all this paperwork. So much for computers and the promises of a paper-free desk!'

'You're right,' Charles agreed, 'there is more of it than ever these days.'

They waited until the coffee arrived, spending the few minutes discussing what was no more than trivia: the weather, soaring prices in both Paris and London, and the dubious merits of public transport in both cities. He was easy to talk to, probably Charles thought, from spending a career being convivial, hosting embassy receptions. Sir Bevington was tall, over six feet, broad-shouldered, with a shock of thick white hair and a rather impressive handlebar moustache.

'I apologise for not formally thanking the police in London for returning the figurines; most remiss of me, but believe me, Mr Hastings, I was most grateful to have them back. Never thought I would ever see them again, certainly not that they would turn up in England.'

'I've read the Singapore police report,' Charles said, 'and apparently your robbery was not the only one around that time.'

'That's quite right; there were three others, Mr Hastings.'

'I understand that although a list was made of everything stolen, only you agreed to make your theft official and when the figurines were taken to the valuers resulted in them being identified. If you had decided against them being officially listed, the chances of you having them returned to you would have been extremely unlikely.'

'I see, fortuitous for me in that case. Mr Hastings,' pausing for a second and looking at Charles closely, 'on the phone yesterday, you told me you were with the Foreign Office; am I correct in thinking that in your particular case this means you're working for MI6? The reason I'm saying this is because there must be considerably more to warrant you making the journey specifically to talk to me about the theft of those figurines.'

'You're right on both counts, Sir Bevington; I am with MI6 and have been for a number of years. My colleague, Philip Spencer, and I are currently conducting an investigation which at first only concerned two incidents which happened in Africa a decade ago, but over the last couple of weeks has mushroomed to incorporate crime on an international scale. There are key figures involved, although two of them continue to elude us. One of them lives in Hong Kong, the other, well,' Charles shrugged, 'he could be anywhere. We have his name, nationality, which is French, although he hasn't lived in France for a number of years. We don't know what he looks like, but we do have a witness who met him once and believes she would recognise him again. Up to now, we have no proof, but we believe he may be living in Singapore.'

'My goodness.'

'When I mentioned crime on an international scale, Sir Bevington, I was referring to illicit goods being transported to and from Europe and the Far East, some of which had been acquired illegally.'

'Like my figurines?'

'Quite.'

'What a convoluted business.'

'I have known less complicated cases.' Charles dryly commented, 'but we are nearing the end of the investigation, a number of loose ends to clear up and then we should be ready for concluding the case, also to a final showdown., One of the questions I wanted to ask you is, do you know why only you agreed for the theft of your figurines to be officially listed?'

'Oh, dear,' he sighed, 'this is where it becomes somewhat awkward.'

'Yes?' encouragingly.

'All robberies, Mr Hastings, were carried out under the Embassy roof, so to speak. These people were colleagues of mine and we were accommodated in apartments within the British Embassy. The robberies all occurred during the same week when there had been functions laid on for visiting ambassadors. The guests, who were all formally invited, were living and working in Singapore. Members of the senior Embassy staff were there each evening. Security was always tight, you understand, and more especially when we had foreign dignataries. There had been no sign of any of the apartments having been broken into. They had all been empty at the time, our wives being with us in the main part of the building, also nothing had been disturbed and, each time, only relatively small items were taken, but each were of a high value. Naturally enough, we all talked amongst ourselves, speculating on how the robberies were carried out.'

'And did you have any ideas?'

'Not at first, but once we had recovered from the anger and the shock of knowing that someone had entered our homes with the sole purpose of stealing from us, we started to rationalise. I can't remember which one of us pointed out that whoever it had been knew exactly what they wanted and were able, without leaving any traces, to open cabinet doors and extract items which would fetch good prices either on the open market or to a private collector who would have had no intention of selling them on for gain.'

'So, what you're saying is, that he must have known you all -'

'- yes,' he interrupted quickly, 'and had actually been in our apartments before.'

'What about maids?'

'We didn't think it was likely. You see, these women had been working for the Embassy for years. They had been hand-picked, their backgrounds vetted. It would have been more than their jobs were worth, also they would have found it impossible to get further work. They would have lost face, Mr Hastings, together with bringing shame to their families.'

'I understand. Presumably you all compared notes as to who had been invited into your apartments?'

'Yes, we did and there had been surprisingly few. I think probably the reason for this was that we spent a good part of the week, including often weekends, when we were on official duty, either hosting or entertaining Embassy guests, that in any free time we were inclined to do very little personal socialising. What I meant by this being somewhat awkward was that it became clearer and clearer to us that it must have been someone whom the Embassy considered worthy to be invited to attend any of their functions. It wouldn't have sounded good at all, if we started naming names; do you understand what I mean, Mr Hastings?'

'I can, Sir Bevington. Nobody likes casting aspersions; it would be all too easy to make a mistake and, whatever the outcome, everybody who had been invited to the Embassy or worked there, of course, would feel they were under suspicion.'

'That's exactly what we thought and no doubt this was the reason my colleagues decided not to pursue their report, although I never asked them why.'

'Amongst yourselves, did you have any suspicions?'

'Nothing definite,' he answered slowly, 'and it would be a trifle caddish to pinpoint someone for the simple reason you didn't take to him.'

'First impressions.'

'Are most lasting.' Sir Bevington finished for him. 'A truism perhaps.'

'And very often are the right ones. Anything you decide to tell me, Sir Bevington,' Charles said, 'will be treated confidentially, but I have to say will be discussed with Philip Spencer. And I do appreciate your reticence.'

'Well,' taking a deep breath, 'the man I'm talking about came from Belgium. He was in finance apparently, had his own advisory business. I don't know how long he'd been living in Singapore, a number of years I think, and then about seven, maybe eight years ago he became a regular guest at many of our cocktail receptions and formal dinners. He was a good friend of Lord and Lady Harper who had arrived from Hong Kong around that time. I'd guess he would have been in his early fifties then.'

'What didn't you like about him?'

'It was his manner really; it quite literally set my teeth on edge. A bit too smooth for my liking. It was nothing he would actually say, but he had this patronising way of talking down to people, not an attractive trait. If you asked me to describe the man, all I could come up with is that he looked like Lord Lucan.'

'And his name, Sir Bevington?'

'Simon Brel.'

It wasn't as if Charles expected to hear him say Nicholas Anout, but he had to admit to feeling disappointed. It was always possible he had changed his name, but it was a slim chance and, as Sir Bevington had said, you couldn't go round thinking the worst of people merely because you didn't like them. Hard to tell whether he had moved any further or not. At least now he had a better idea of what life must have been like living at the Embassy and had worked out a rough plan in his mind how the robberies could have been planned.

'Just one last question, Sir Bevington,' he said, 'you would have had an address for him, wouldn't you?'

'Oh, yes; he'd been staying in a service apartment south of the river, but I heard he had moved away and I don't remember seeing him again. This would have been five years ago, round about the time I took up my position here.'

Charles thanked him for taking the time to speak to him and was halfway to the door when Sir Bevington stopped him: 'I'm intrigued to learn how my figurines found their way to England, Mr Hastings.'

'Some of it is conjecture on our part,' Charles told him, 'but we believe they were handed over to someone acting as a courier and taken to Hong Kong. From there, we do know they were then taken on to England and displayed in an antique shop in London. That part can be confirmed, although whether they were collected by the antique dealer or, as he has informed us, purchased on a street market in Hong Kong, is questionable. The figurines were then purchased by a lady not long after they arrived in England and she took them home with her to add to her collection of oriental figurines of a similar type. A few weeks ago, she died, her estate passing on to her niece who, deciding to sell the figurines, took them along to a firm of valuers in London. You probably know the rest.'

'My word! What a story! Quite amazing, rather like a jigsaw puzzle.'

'That's an excellent description of our work, Sir Bevington.'

Before leaving Paris Charles made a quick call to Headquarters and hopefully, by the time he arrived back they would have had time to check out what he wanted to know. It had been when Sir Bevington had mentioned that Simon Brel had been Belgian he began to consider the possibility that Brel and Anout could be the same person; this being reinforced by Sir Bevington's description of him: "...... a bit too smooth for my liking," he had said and adding that he reminded him of Lord Lucan, which tallied with what Kate Johnson had said. Certainly Brel was a Belgium name, but that was no proof; they only had what the barman in the Mercure in Paris had told Guy Ford that the man who had been talking to Johnson was French, snowballing from then onwards with Johnson introducing him to Kate. If, as they suspected, Anout had supplied Johnson with his replacement passport, a change of his own identity with supporting documents would be child's play to the man. Ever since Philip and he had heard his name mentioned they had been stymied by the fact up to now they hadn't been able to find out something more substantial about him. It could be perhaps they had been focusing too much on Yeung and, consequently, overlooking possibly the main supplier.

It didn't take long for one of the officers to get back to him and within minutes of arriving at Saint Pancras, Charles knew he had been right. Headquarters had run two checks. There were three men called Simon Brel around the same age as Anout; two of them resided in Belgium and neither of them had been living in Singapore at any time in their lives, the third, born in Belgium, moved to Rome in 2000 and apart from return visits to Belgium had made no other overseas trips.

The second check was considerably more revealing. It transpires that Nicholas Anout was born in Paris in 1956 where he lived until he left France to live in Singapore in 2002, but the interesting fact was that although his father, Matthew Anout, was French, his mother came from Belgium, her maiden name being Simone Brel. It would appear from Immigration that no-one called Simon Brel had either entered or left Singapore during the last twenty years. So, Charles thought with some satisfaction, the visit today to see Sir Bevington had not been wasted time and, provided they found the man, they could pull him in for questioning having sufficient to build up strong evidence against him. It would of course mean they would have to re-open the burglary case in Singapore, but he couldn't think of any other way round this. Perhaps Philip would have some ideas when he saw him later.

Chapter Nineteen

By Friday midday it became apparent there would be no let up, no sitting back until the Smythe-Jones arrived at Heathrow Airport on Tuesday and no weekend leave. Although disappointed he wouldn't be able to make it to Winchester on Saturday, Sophie assured him she understood and as she had said the other day, there would always be another time. Charles and Philip were kept informed via Derek of what was happening in Singapore. The officer he had assigned to follow Cecelia Cunningham had phoned through to Hong Kong a little over an hour after their plane had touched down at Changi Airport to tell him he had managed to find out where she was staying. It was too much to expect he would be able to keep a constant surveillance on her movements, but there was always the chance, provided she was unaware of being followed, he might be able to see whether she met anyone while she was there. A second officer would take over from him at Hong Kong International Airport on Sunday from the moment she cleared Customs, Derek to be advised immediately by them if she was carrying any illicit items.

'In theory,' Charles said, 'it sounds a neatly co-ordinated plan, but unfortunately not foolproof.'

'I know; too much supposition, but I can't think of a better one.'

'Neither can I, Philip. There's not much we can achieve here at present; we're relying on Derek to take us up to the point where, if we can't nail Anout, we should have sufficient on Smythe-Jones. When will you be picking up the search warrant for 'Gregory's Antiques?'

'Hugh is organising that; they'll be there as soon as they open on Tuesday morning. As far as the search on Bakker & Bakker's establishment is concerned, because of the sensitive nature of Derek's position in Hong Kong he won't be making his presence known to any of the shipping staff including Yeung if he's actually in his office, instead, he's arranged for a couple of officers from Interpol to go there; this will be at three-thirty in the afternoon Hong Kong time and, allowing for the one hour difference between here and Amsterdam, two of our men will arrive at Bakker & Bakker at ten-thirty in the morning.

'A good strategy, Philip, which should result in them all being taken unawares and no chance to warn each other.'

'It is something of a gamble, I admit, but if it achieves nothing else it should give them a good shake up. I will be very surprised if we don't unearth some discrepancies.'

'Incidentally, something of interest has come to light. It only came through this morning, but Immigration has confirmed that in 1993, a William Leonard Yeung applied for and was granted British Citizenship.'

'Did he indeed? I don't suppose we should be all that surprised; thousands of Hong Kong people were doing the same in the years leading up to the handover in 1997; enabling them to establish another residency as a 'just in case' precaution. He already knew England well, having been educated here; it was probably a natural choice for him.'

'Perhaps he's been hoist with his own petard.' Charles commented dryly.

'Well, it certainly makes it considerably easier for us knowing that if and when necessary he can be extradited to Britain, and no amount of strings he may attempt to pull in Hong Kong will help.'

'True. And what about Pamela Smythe-Jones? I realise you've been stymied this week with her going off on this trip to Hong Kong.'

'I know and it looks as though I will have to continue holding back until her husband has been dealt with.'

'One thing at a time, eh?'

'Yes, that's right. It's rather a unique situation when husband and wife are both suspects in two separate crimes. In some respects hers is a fairly straightforward matter while Smythe-Jones' offences, primarily because of the involvement of others, is complicated and until we get the reports of the searches, both here and in Hong Kong, we won't know the full extent. A lot depends on what he may be carrying and if he is we will be in a position to take him into custody pending investigations into his business records. It's going to be a bit tight synchronising those reports within the requisite forty-eight hours.'

'All these varying factors do appear to have come to a head rather quickly, wouldn't you say?'

'I would, yes; for these few weeks we have been able to more or less take our time and systematically follow up on leads, but now, well,' Philip shrugged resignedly, 'whoosh! We're having to move rapidly, but I can't say I'll be sorry to get the whole business tied up.'

***

Singapore Customs phoned Derek to report that Cecelia Cunningham had six pieces of antique jewellery in her possession, all of it undeclared and unaccompanied by the required licence. The bag had been checked through by the passenger when booking in at Changi Airport and, as instructed, she was not intercepted, nor were the items confiscated by the airport authorities. There were two matching bracelets in gold and sapphire, an enamelled gold and amethyst pendant and three dress rings; a single ruby, pearls in a gold and silver setting and an emerald set in platinum. Derek now had the proof that these had been acquired during her visit to Singapore as Customs at the Hong Kong International Airport had already confirmed when she had left on Friday there was nothing contained in her luggage which contravened customs' regulations.

Derek received a call from the officer who had been tailing her since she left Hong Kong on the Friday to say she hadn't been on her own when she had arrived at Changi Airport on Sunday morning, coming into Departures accompanied by someone who closely resembled the description he had been given of Nicholas Anout. Apparently, he had held back while she checked in and it would appear by their manner towards each other they were, to quote the officer, more than good friends.

By the time the plane touched down in Hong Kong at midday, Derek had arranged for a relief officer to station himself outside her apartment building in Glenealy Street on the off chance she may go straight home. The officer who had been on the same flight phoned Derek at twelve-thirty to say he was now in the same queue as Cecelia Cunningham waiting for the airport express. This was the tricky part, Derek thought, knowing from experience that for him to continue to follow her once she reached Central would be unlikely. He couldn't help but feel disappointed that they had been unable to find out who she must have met in Singapore. It was too easy to jump to the conclusion it was the man she had been with at Changi.

It was eleven in the morning in London when he phoned Charles: 'Good morning, Charles;' his voice crackling with static, 'sorry, the line's dreadful.'

'Perhaps it will clear,' Charles said, 'but I can hear you well enough.'

'I've just had a call from the officer who's been outside Cecelia Cunningham's apartment for most of the afternoon –'

'– so, she did go straight home, then?'

'Yes, she did. Anyway, Customs in Singapore confirmed earlier this morning that she had several pieces of antique jewellery in her luggage which she must have taken collection of while she was over there, but about an hour ago she left her apartment and he was able to follow her. Fortunately, she didn't take a taxi, but walked the relatively short distance to the Botanical and Zoological Gardens where she met up with a man who sounds as though he might be Lenny Yeung. The officer managed to photograph them both as she handed over a package to him which, of course, may or may not contain the jewellery. However,' he went on, 'we did have a stroke of luck.'

'Yes?'

'There's a taxi rank outside the main gates of the Gardens and the officer, having decided to take a stab at trying to find where the guy was heading for, managed to stand next to him and when a taxi drew up overheard the address he gave the driver. I'll be arranging for someone to check it out and if it does turn out to belong to Lenny Yeung, he will have done a good day's work.'

'He certainly will have; this is indeed the breakthrough we've needed.'

'I hope so,' Derek said, erring on the cautious side, 'as soon as I've seen the photograph, I'll send it through to you, Charles, also a list describing the jewellery and then you'll know what to be looking for when Smythe-Jones turns up.'

'You and your officers have done well.'

'We still don't know who gave her the jewellery, but there is something else.'

'Yes,' listening while Derek told him about a possible relationship between Cecelia and Anout, if indeed it was Anout she had been with.

'Well, well,' he said, 'this should be something we can use. We're getting closer, Derek. Someone may talk.'

'Perhaps.'

'I think they will.' confidently, sounding as though he meant it, but Derek was inclined to agree with him. He had often learned that when people find themselves in tight corners if they felt threatened in any way, they would say or do anything to extract themselves from blame, 'and the Smythe-Jones, Derek?' Charles prompted.

'As far as I can make out, they have been doing all the usual tourist things, nothing out of the normal. Each time I've seen them they've been together and unless his wife is *au fait* with what he's up to, I would say he hasn't met up with Lenny Yeung yet.'

'Perhaps he will soon; tomorrow is his last day before they come back to England.'

'I know. Customs have already received their instructions, Charles, and if he is carrying anything he shouldn't, they will let me know immediately.'

'That's fine, then it will be up to us at this end to pick up from there.'

Derek was only too aware there was little time left now before the Smythe-Jones left and if their theory was correct in that he would be taking the jewellery back with him, any meeting between him and Lenny Yeung must be imminent. Was he right in assuming his wife knew nothing about what was going on? The fact that the woman was not exactly squeaky-clean herself didn't prove a thing either way, although he had a gut feeling Smythe-Jones was acting on his own, but again nothing to substantiate this.

Since the Smythe-Jones had arrived in Hong Kong there had been a set pattern to their days; either sightseeing or shopping, often taking the Star Ferry across to Kowloon, making it easy for following them, the officer always managing to take advantage of the excellent cover given by the ever-present crowds thronging the streets and not once, apart from shop assistants and bar staff, had they spoken to anyone else, not even to other tourists like themselves. Each evening, when they had returned to the hotel, they had a pre-dinner drink in the Captain's Bar and this evening, their last day in Hong Kong, was no different, except Pamela wasn't with him.

Derek, without turning round, watched the reflection in the smoke-glass mirror behind the bar as Gregory Smythe-Jones, walking past him, went over to one of the tables. It was almost six-thirty and the bar was beginning to fill up with office workers from Central, together with a smattering of tourists, the mens' faces flushed with too much sun or perhaps too many bottles of Tsingtao and the women carrying an assortment of glossy carrier bags displaying the names of the exclusive fashion houses: *Balmain, Jean Paul Gaultier, Chanel* and *Issy Miyake*, each designer name vying for prominence. There was only one free table remaining and Derek fully expected him to take it, but instead, he walked to the next one and without hesitating sat down. Here we go, Derek muttered to himself. Virtually at the eleventh hour. The man he had joined had his back to the room and from where Derek was standing looked like a dozen others: short black hair, slim build and the regimental dark business suit. Taking his drink with him, he walked over to sit at the vacant table.

'I trust you and your wife have enjoyed your stay, Gregory.' Derek clearly heard him say as he sat down, deliberately positioning himself where he had a view of the bar and the open doorway as though waiting for someone, but not before looking at him. It only needed a quick glance, affecting indifference, to see he was Asian and comparing him with both photographs he had seen of Lenny Yeung, he bore a strong resemblance, even discarding that to most westerners all Chinese men looked alike.

'Very pleasant, but I'll be glad to get back tomorrow.'

'Understandable I suppose under the circumstances.'

'Yes, Lenny, it's those circumstances which I am finding difficult to live with.'

'Don't you think you're dramatising the situation, Gregory?'

'I don't think so. I told you when you rang on Thursday I was not at all happy about acting as courier. This was not what we planned.'

'You seem to have had a lapse of memory.'

'What do you mean?'

'This won't be the first time you've taken anything back with you. I admit it hasn't happened often, but I have my reasons for not sending Cecelia.'

'Alright, Lenny; I hear what you say, but I am taking a risk after all.'

'We are all taking risks, my friend. Don't believe you have the monopoly on that.'

'Anyway,' Gregory said, 'Pamela will be joining us shortly, perhaps you'd better let me have the stuff.'

'She doesn't know then?'

'She damn well does not and I don't want her to know either.'

'Your decision of course, Gregory, but what I'm doing is being cautious here,' he said, 'you'll collect the package from the cloakroom attendant -'

'- who's being dramatic now?'

'There are too many people in here, besides the man is on my payroll.'

'How will he recognise me?'

'No problem. He's already spotted you. Haven't you ever noticed that when there are no customers in there, he invariably stands outside the door? Oh, and Gregory,' he added as Gregory got to his feet, 'don't neglect to leave a couple of dollar bills; it will be expected.'

***

A frantic Alexander Van Ommeron dialled Lenny's office number at midday on Tuesday only to be told by his secretary that he wasn't taking any calls. She wouldn't even tell him whether he was in his office or not which further exasperated him and only served to increase his mounting panic. His hands were shaking as he re-dialled, this time Lenny's mobile number, but that also proved hopeless; the simple explanation, for one reason or another, he was not available. He took a deep breath, leaned back in his swivel chair and looked at his depleted office: his computer and all the back-up discs had been taken, also the contents of his filing cabinets and desk diary. There had been four officers from the International Police waiting for him in the outer office when he had arrived that morning and had been quick to proffer their search warrant. He was conscious of his white-faced receptionist, as she sat rigidly behind the desk and when he spoke to her had visibly jumped, dragging her eyes away from the four of them.

'There's nothing to worry about, Sonia,' he told her, 'this is purely a routine inspection. If there should be any calls for me,' he added, 'just tell them I'll phone back later.' Even as apprehensive as he was, Alex had the presence of mind to realise that it was possible Lenny may call and he was the last person he wanted to speak to with the officers within earshot.

'Yes, Mr Van Ommeron.' but he could tell by her wary expression she wasn't convinced.

They had followed him into his office, one of them firmly closing the door behind them and systematically began making a cursory check through the various computer menus and sub-menus, scrolling back through weeks and months of transactions, before closing down the computer and telling him they would have to take most of his records away in order to conduct a more thorough check. During all the time they were in the office they gave no explanation of the reason behind their visit and when he had asked, they had been non-committal, except to say they should be in a position to return everything by the end of the week.

After they had gone Alex buzzed through to the outer office, asking Sonia to bring him a coffee; he felt in the need of an injection of caffeine to steady his nerves before speaking to Lenny, anticipating in advance what his reaction would be, but now, if anything, the situation was worse.

For some inexplicable reason Lenny was non-contactable.

***

In the offices of 'Gregory's Antiques', Ellen Boyle was doing her utmost to remain calm with her innermost thoughts in turmoil. Mr Bannister from New Scotland Yard had been waiting outside the shop when she turned up for work that morning, but this time he wasn't on his own; he had two other men with him whom he introduced as being officers from his department. Once inside, he showed her what he described as a search warrant for the business premises. It was not as though he was impolite in any way, quite the opposite; he was going to great lengths to reassure her there was nothing she should concern herself about, although she couldn't help thinking that this couldn't possibly be true. He appeared to know that Gregory was away, but maybe Mr Spencer told him, being ignorant of any form of police procedure and rapidly becoming more confused by what was happening. For the first time since she came to work for 'Gregory's Antiques' she felt quite inadequate and unable to handle the situation as well as she should. Ellen Boyle was the type of woman who lacked any natural inquisitiveness, entirely incurious, always placing great pride in her work, dedicated to making sure the business ran smoothly and, here she was, practically incapable in Gregory's absence to cope without literally falling to pieces. It wouldn't have been so bad if she had been able to get in touch with him, but that was impossible; he and Pamela would now be more than half-way through their flight from Hong Kong. It did occur she could call his lawyer, but just as quickly rejected the idea as being too precipitous without Gregory's agreement. She watched as one of the officers sat down in front of the computer and without asking her for the password, was into the system within seconds. Obviously a computer expert, she decided, experiencing a small stab of apprehension. She may be described as not being worldly-wise, but Ellen was not entirely blinkered when it came to her employer. Although she really didn't have anything substantial to support doubts she may have about the extent of Gregory's professional honesty, it was something she had come to realise over the years and blindly accepted, excusing her weakness that this knowledge, for what it was worth, did not concern her, but ever since Mr Bannister had been to see Gregory about the oriental figurines, she had felt uneasy. For a while, Ellen had, in her spare time, made a study of different categories of antiques, reading up all she could, spending time at the British Library and as soon as she had seen the figurines Gregory had brought back from Hong Kong, she had realised their value and was finding it hard now to believe he had picked them up from a market stall, but never having visited Hong Kong, she had no idea of whether this was considered normal out there or not, making every effort to dismiss such suspicious thoughts she may have. And, now, the man from New Scotland Yard was back again and she was powerless to prevent him checking through their records.

They didn't stay so long, about a couple of hours and when they were leaving he took her to one side, while the other two went ahead.

'I do apologise, Miss Boyle,' he said, 'for this disturbance, but I can assure you it has been necessary.'

'I suppose it must be, Mr Bannister, 'but I don't know what Mr Smythe-Jones will have to say when he gets back this afternoon.'

'At the risk of sounding repetitive,' he smiled apologetically, 'I am sure there is no need for you to unduly concern yourself. We will, of course, be talking to Mr Smythe-Jones as soon as possible. By the way,' he added, his hand already on the door handle, 'when there are deliveries, in particular from overseas, were you responsible for booking them into the system?'

'Oh, no,' she was quick to answer, feeling more confident; this was familiar territory, 'Mr Smythe-Jones always did that. You see, as he was the one who placed the order, he wanted to make certain at first hand that everything was as it should be.'

She watched him as he rejoined the other two officers out on the pavement and walking briskly away in the direction of Bond Street. She hadn't found his words encouraging; she was more worried than ever, not necessarily about herself, but of Gregory's reaction when he heard, closing the door and going over to the small desk she had at the far end of the shop, busying herself between customers and to when she could give him a ring, but at the time their plane would have touched down at Heathrow she was in the middle of serving and when the sale was completed, she was further delayed by a couple coming in to enquire about a pair of fifteenth century pen and ink drawings they had seen in the window. It was therefore after five when she finally had the shop to herself and, taking advantage of the lull, dialled Gregory's mobile number, waiting with trepidation for him to answer. Nothing. No dialling tone, only silence. He couldn't have switched it on again after they had landed; that was the only explanation she could think of. She would try again later, she decided, only partially relieved at the slight reprieve.

***

The initial reports started coming through to MI6 Headquarters at midday where they were analysed and collated. As the Cathay Pacific plane approached the runway at Heathrow, preparing to touch down before taxiing to a standstill, Philip, having briefed Customs, was in one of the interview rooms waiting for Gregory Smythe-Jones to be shown in.

He spent the time going over the reports and the summarised notes Charles and he had made. There were four in total, the one on the search carried out on Lenny Yeung's apartment in Causeway Bay arriving last. Up until then there had, disappointingly, been nothing positive to suggest he was criminally involved in either Alexander Van Ommeron or Gregory Smythe-Jones schemes.

Interpol checks on Bakker & Bakker Hong Kong over a twelve-month period of all shipments to the associate company in Amsterdam and 'Gregory's Antiques' in London tied in exactly with their incoming shipping documents, but by the time both Charles and he had read the final report, not only were they at last able to put together the whole of what would appear to be an extremely lucrative scam, but it revealed the names of others who were involved and up to now had merely been on the periphery of their enquiry. They now had the proof they needed; each and every person was directly linked to Lenny Yeung and contributed to the case they were building up against him. He was undoubtedly the kingpin, the pivot of the organization and they were confident, once they broadened their investigation, more evidence would come to light. It transpired that his company, Bakker & Bakker in Hong Kong, was run along orthodox lines, suggesting it was more than likely acting as a front for his other activities. He was using one of the rooms in his apartment as an office: his desk, facing the full-length plate glass window overlooking Causeway Bay and across the water to the skyscrapers of Kowloon, held only his computer and a desk diary. A tall intricately carved Chinese cabinet in polished teak conveyed its true purpose once the door was opened. The safe, with the central combination lock, looked incongruous in an otherwise ordinary room, even with the computer placed symmetrically on the centre of the desk it could still pass as a study, but as it had been disguised as something quite different, gave the place a more official, even sinister, appearance. Interpol had no difficulty in entering the computer system, but deciphering the combination took them a little longer. There was no money inside, no pile of bank notes in different currencies, and no documents, legal or otherwise. Instead, each of the shelves were stacked with a mixture of arts and crafts, some of it modern Asian pieces and Chinese country antiques, and several pieces of antique silver tableware. One of the shelves contained jewellery, predominantly antique, much of it in jade and opal, and a silk-lined box of precious and semi-precious stones. Furthermore, at the back of one of the shelves, Yeung had kept a number of old diaries going back as far as the late nineties. Significant as all of this was, the most instantly damning for Lenny Yeung was his current diary. Clive Edward's name had been entered throughout the year, together with the dates when he went on courier assignments, the last ones being on Monday, 17th September when he flew from London to Amsterdam and when he should have been travelling on to Hong Kong on the Wednesday. Cecelia Cunningham's name was also entered. She had made a number of trips to

Singapore since January, also the dates when she flew to Amsterdam on Thursday 27th September, her ongoing flight to London on the Saturday, returning to Hong Kong on the Monday morning. A bonus was the record of those contacts Clive Edwards and Cecelia Cunningham made in Amsterdam, namely Jan Jansen and Cecelia's meeting with Gregory Smythe-Jones in London. The last entries Yeung had made were her flight to Singapore the previous Friday, her meeting with Nicholas Anout and her return to Hong Kong on Sunday, all of which gave them sufficient to pull in Lenny Yeung, his co-director, Alexander Van Ommeron and Gregory Smythe-Jones. Data in the computer system would take somewhat longer to scrutinize due to the volume of entries, although Interpol, having been alerted about the possibility of finding Nicholas Anout's name mentioned, quickly spotted the name in a file entitled 'Sources', together with his address and mobile phone number in Singapore, both of which Charles said he would check. The officer leading the search of Yeung's records had then scrolled back six years and was rewarded by finding that Cecelia Cunningham had made a trip to Singapore on Saturday, the 1st of April 2006 and, once again, had met up with Nicholas Anout, returning to Hong Kong the following day. Suspecting a similar pattern to the way Yeung conducted his business, he had located the relevant diary of that year which revealed, as Gregory Smythe-Jones had said, he had been in Hong Kong around that time, but more importantly, had seen Yeung the day prior to him returning to London on Tuesday, the 4th April. This was truly the 'icing on the cake', Philip thought, replacing the sheaf of papers in his briefcase as the door to the interview room opened and Gregory Smythe-Jones, followed closely by a customs' official, walked in.

'This is outrageous! I demand to know what is going on!'

'Please sit down, Mr Smythe-Jones,' Philip said, keeping his tone level and watching him as, without saying anything, he grudgingly pulled out a chair and sitting down heavily, a deep frown creasing his forehead. Philip nodded at the official who, interpreting the gesture, left the room closing the door quietly behind him.

'Mr Smythe-Jones,' Philip said, once he had told him he was with the Foreign Office and not missing the quick flash of alarm which appeared across his face, proving perhaps that his wife must have told him about at least one of the visits he had made, 'those items of jewellery you brought from Hong Kong and attempted to pass through Customs this afternoon were not accompanied by the required documentation, therefore you were contravening legal airport regulations. That, in itself, is a serious offence which could carry a heavy fine as well as the items being confiscated. However,' Philip continued, surprised at not being interrupted, but he remained stolidly seated across the table from him, 'we have strong evidence that, not only is this not an isolated case on your part, but you are evading the law on a wider scale in the conducting of your antique business.'

'What the hell is that supposed to mean?' jumping to his feet, the chair scraping on the wooden floor, his face flushed with indignation.

'Mr Smythe-Jones,' he warned, 'this interview is a preliminary one and is not being recorded, but if you prefer to get in touch with your lawyer and for him to be present during further questioning, I would be agreeable in bringing this meeting to a temporary close, although it will have to be resumed at police Headquarters.'

'I haven't decided yet,' belligerently, 'and what about my wife, Mr Spencer?'

'What about your wife, Mr Smythe-Jones?'

'She must be worried seeing me being dragged along here.'

'Your wife will be waiting for you,' Philip told him quietly, 'and then you can explain to her why you were approached at Customs.'

'I didn't like your inference about my business affairs.'

'I can assure you it was no inference. We are in the midst of conducting a major crime investigation involving the smuggling of valuables in and distributed around Europe, some of the items which are in fact stolen property. It is our task to seek out the perpetrators and to draw a permanent stop to these illegal activities. Your name has occurred too many times during the course of this investigation, so much so, that this morning we had no alternative but to conduct a search of your business premises –'

'– you what!' but this time remained seating, 'that is an imposition. I wasn't even there! I wasn't even in the country!'

'The timing of the search, together with other searches carried out today, was not made randomly and I would remind you that we were quite within our rights in doing so.'

'I just cannot believe this!'

'Perhaps it might be wise for you to give your lawyer a call.'

'I don't see why I should; my records are in perfect order.'

Of course he was bluffing. He must know he was rapidly losing ground and yet he persisted in what could only be a flimsily held together belief that he was going to emerge unscathed, deciding to take a tougher line with him.

'Our evidence proves differently. However,' Philip added, standing up, 'I would ask you to accompany me to New Scotland Yard and you will still have the opportunity to get in touch with your lawyer if you should change your mind.'

'It would seem,' almost sneering, obviously trying to control his temper, 'I have no choice, but first I must speak to my wife.'

'Of course. She can either come with us or, if you prefer, arrange to meet you later.'

'That would be best; I don't want her driving all the way down to Taunton.'

Pamela Smythe-Jones had an indecipherable expression on her face when Philip saw her; it was impossible to tell the extent of her concern, except she looked paler than she had the last time he saw yet, but whether any concern was for her husband was debatable. She pointedly avoided looking at him, but waited until Smythe-Jones walked up to her, placing a hand on her arm. He couldn't hear what they said to each other, but after a couple of minutes, she leaned up, giving him a light kiss on the cheek and walked, without looking back, towards the exit.

A driver from New Scotland Yard was waiting for them when they reached the pavement outside the airport terminal and led the way to the reserved parking area for police vehicles. The journey into London was a silent one; for the first time Gregory Smythe-Jones looked uncomfortable. As well he might, Philip thought, glancing at the man seated next to him and wondering whether he would decide to call his lawyer once he heard of the results of the search and was told there would have to be a full official stock-take. Surely he wouldn't be foolish enough to continue to hold out, insisting there was nothing amiss with his business records. Even he, with all his arrogant confidence, would know when he was losing.

***

As the car taking Philip and his passenger entered Victoria Street, the impressive glass-fronted building of New Scotland Yard now in sight, Cecelia was dialling Nicholas Anout's number in Singapore, one she knew off by heart. It was after midnight, late to be calling him, but he had to be told. There had been a message on her answering machine from Lenny when she arrived from attending a publishing dinner which had gone on longer than usual and with more glasses of wine than she was accustomed to she wanted to go straight to bed, but she couldn't ignore the flashing light on the machine. Lenny hadn't said much, but enough: "Cecelia;" his voice breaking the silence of the room, "this is serious. I've just spent the last few hours being grilled by Interpol. Don't know what is going to happen now, but I want you to destroy any records you may have linking your name with mine. Also, delete this message. Will be in touch." She had done exactly what he'd asked; there was now no evidence of any connection between them. There were some old diaries with dates of meetings they'd had and the flights she had made on his behalf, also her current diary, all of which she tore up, dividing the shredded pieces of paper between two bin bags. Finally, she deleted his name and contact numbers from her computer.

Nicholas answered immediately and hearing his voice had a calming effect, a respite from the turmoil in her brain although realising it was unlikely she would get much sleep for the few hours left until morning.

'Cecelia, *ma chère*,' he said as soon as he heard her voice, 'what is wrong; you sound distraught.'

'I've had a message from Lenny; he'd left it on my answering machine. It was to say he'd been held for questioning by Interpol –'

'*Mon Dieu*! Where is he now, Cecelia? Have they taken him into custody?'

'I don't know, all he said was he didn't know what was going to happen, that it was serious and for me to destroy anything which might link my name with his.'

'And have you done that?'

'Yes, but what about you, Nicholas?'

'Don't worry about me, *ma chère*; at least if anyone does turn up here I will have been warned, but it's you I am concerned about. Do you feel up to facing them if and when they should contact you?'

'I think so.'

'They're ruthless, Cecelia. They won't let up. I should know.' he added and she could hear the bitterness in his voice. She was aware of his past; those years in Paris, the shady deals he'd been involved in, also latterly in Singapore where he'd fled after a particularly nasty business which had almost gone drastically wrong for him. She had no illusions about him and she had long ago accepted his background. Their relationship was an unusual one. They were lovers, and had been for more than eight years, almost from the first time they met when she had been in Singapore on one of her Asian courier assignments for Lenny. Although they often spent months apart, a special bond had developed between them where neither of them made any demands on the other, both of them reasonably content with the way things were.

'I do not like to think of you over there and possibly being subjected to all this aggravation; more than anything I would like you to come here, but now is not the right time. It's more than possible Interpol will have your name and if you should turn up at the airport they will have been alerted.'

'You really want me there with you, Nicholas?'

'*Naturelement.*' without any hesitation, his concern instantly reassuring, but at the same time she wasn't certain whether she wanted to do that. Living in Hong Kong for so long had become a way of life to her; she had a lovely apartment in a quiet part of mid-levels, and even without what she earned from working for Lenny, the income she received from the publishing firm was more than sufficient to provide her with what she needed.

'I would have to think about it, Nicholas,' she said, 'I would feel I was letting Lenny down, besides,' she went on, 'the situation for him may not be so dire.' metaphorically crossing her fingers.

She lay awake for a long time going back in her mind to those earlier years from when she had been with Anthony through to the present and wondering for the first time in her life whether it was her destiny to associate with men who had decidedly shady backgrounds. Perhaps. She had finished with Anthony as soon as she learned he was married and even now, she didn't believe it was anything noble on her part, realising she had always had an abhorrence for men who cheated on their wives and it was possibly the reason why she had never married, thereby avoiding such a deception. As she was drifting off to sleep she wondered why she hadn't mentioned to Nicholas she had been followed for the last couple of weeks which quite possibly might have included the time she had spent in Singapore last weekend, but suddenly it didn't really seem to matter all that much. Whatever will be, will be ......

Chapter Twenty

Philip spread out the signed statement on the table, aligning it with the tape recorder, and looked at the woman facing him. She had lost none of her haughtiness and affected indifference since he had seen her the evening before when she had been told they were keeping her husband in custody while a thorough check was carried out on his business records, including an official stock-take. If anything this morning she was even more Sloane-like and disdainfully aloof, as though what had been happening didn't affect her. She was either a good actress or considered her husband to be innocent of any charges which may be made, also impervious to the fact that there was only a matter of hours before the decision would be taken whether he was guilty of receiving stolen goods and manipulating figures in his records to greatly reduce his tax liability, both of which were criminal offences and depending on what the courts decided punishable by prosecution, possibly a prison sentence.

'I don't see there is anything to be gained, Mr Spencer, in bringing me in here; I know absolutely nothing about my husband's business.'

'Mrs Smythe-Jones,' Philip said quietly, 'The reason you are here has no connection with your husband's business.'

'Really?' eyebrows raised as they had been before, which by now he had interpreted as her way of prevaricating and, as then, he had no intention of playing games, confident he had sufficient evidence and knowledge to bring this official interview to a satisfactory conclusion.

'This interview,' he continued as though she hadn't spoken, 'will be conducted along official lines and will be recorded, but first I would ask whether you wish to get in touch with your lawyer, which you have every right to do and for him to be present.'

'Of course not. I see no need. Whatever you accuse me of, Mr Spencer, I know I am innocent.'

'As I've said, it is your prerogative. If you should change your mind I will bring the interview to a temporary halt until his arrival. Is that clear?'

'Yes.'

'Good, then we'll begin.' switching on the recorder, 'It is ten-fifteen on Wednesday morning, the 17th October, 2012. There will be two parts to this interview; one, concerning the murder of your first husband, Norman Brookes, in Zambia on the 18th December, 2002, and the other, the murder of Martha Underwood (née Jacobsen) on the 5th October 2012.' hearing her sharp intake of breath as soon as he mentioned Martha Underwood's name and picking up the statement, read it out to her, 'Do you wish to make any changes?' he asked.

'No, I don't. What I've said is as accurate as I could possibly be. I shouldn't have to remind you it was a long time ago.'

'Right. Since last talking to you, Mrs Smythe-Jones, I have received signed statements from a number of people who were in the club on the night your husband was killed, all of which do not agree with the times you have given me. Also, I have a further witness who has stated you were not at home when you said you were, namely around ten past ten that night, which makes your explanation of the three hours before you called the police as unacceptable, so where were you?'

'If these so-called friends have all agreed that I left the club before ten, I must have been home. I didn't go anywhere else.'

'Didn't you?'

'Where would I have gone, Mr Spencer?'

'When I first spoke to you on Monday the 24th September and asked how well you knew Anthony Johnson you told me he wasn't a personal friend.'

'He wasn't, he was just another expatriate. There were so few of us; we needed to talk to *someone* when we were doing our best to socialise.'

'I suggest Anthony Johnson was more than a mere acquaintance, Mrs Smythe-Jones; I would suggest you and he were in a relationship, in other words, you were lovers.'

'That really is laughable!'

'Is it? Why then, did you meet him in Paris shortly before Christmas in 2002? Before you say anything, I would point out that I have two witnesses to say you were with him.'

'Everyone has a double, Mr Spencer, or so they say.'

'There are indisputable facts and ones that we must accept; your husband was shot dead on the same night Anthony Johnson faked the car accident and left Samriboi. He could not have accomplished this on his own and whoever helped him must have been someone he knew extremely well. Would you not agree?'

'I suppose so.'

'Were you that accomplice?'

'Why on earth would I have got involved in anything so – so criminal?'

'You haven't answered my question; were you his accomplice?'

'Certainly not.'

'I have interviewed a number of people,' Philip continued relentlessly, wondering just how long she would hold on to what she'd said so far, just how tough was she, 'and from what they have said, indicates your involvement in the planned murder of your husband.'

'You will have to prove it then, won't you?' for the first time her southern counties' accent slipping. Was this a sign she was weakening?

'There is an alternative scenario, Mrs Smythe-Jones.'

'Do tell me.'

'That Anthony Johnson did not shoot your husband; you did, and the pair of you arranged together for him to escape, fake his death and if and when the case ever re-opened he would be blamed for the murder.'

'I – I didn't shoot Norman.'

'Who did then? Think carefully before you answer.'

'Alright,' the word coming out as a sigh, 'Anthony did. I never did anything wrong, you know. Alright, I gave him Norman's gun. I drove him to the ravine and then back to Samriboi and later I took him to Kabwe. After that, well, I don't know what he did.'

'We'll leave it there for the present, Mrs Smythe-Jones and have a short break before continuing. The interview,' he added, 'is temporarily terminated at quarter past eleven on the morning of 17th October 2012.' switching off the tape recorder.

***

They had literally thrown the book at him and for the first time in his life he was finding it impossible to extricate himself from what was happening. Lenny Yeung was a perfectionist; meticulous in the way he conducted his business and private life, neither of them encroaching on the other. Never once had he deviated; if he made a plan, there was no u-turning, no doubting he may be on the wrong course. To him, that was unthinkable. As far back as his university days, he had mapped out how he intended to achieve what was all-important to him; total independence, answerable to no-one with the freedom of choice, all of which required money and a great deal of it. And here he was, being escorted personally and officially to England and to God knows what. When he received the call from his manager at Bakker & Bakker, telling him officers from Interpol, equipped with a search warrant, had arrived at the offices, although he had been concerned, even alarmed, but not to any great degree. He knew they would find nothing amiss among any of his records there; the order books accurately agreed with all shipments made, sales invoices tied in with revenue received and banked. He was more angry than anything else; not with himself, but with Gregory. Although he didn't know whether they were looking for anything specific, he was confident they would go away empty-handed. But when, an hour later, the concierge buzzed up to him in the apartment, all that confidence took a complete nose dive. He was well and truly cornered, powerless to refuse entry to the officers, also with no time to make even a superficial attempt to hide or destroy the evidence. From then on, he had been on a downward spiral; his activities, his secondary and more lucrative business, were laid bare. Realising he had been unwise to believe his address in Causeway Bay would be a safe haven made no difference; if Gregory had not put those damn figurines for open sale, this would not have happened. Gregory had fouled up. He had been primarily instrumental in jeopardising, perhaps destroying, what he had striven for and achieved.

As their plane began its slow descent, these bitter thoughts were uppermost in his mind. As always, Lenny only considered his own situation, having little or no regard for others, even Gregory whom he had known since prep school. They had been eight years of age when they first met; boys from diverse backgrounds; Gregory, a product of an English middle-class family, his parents, both lawyers, with no real interest in him, handing him over to the care of a succession of au pairs, while he, Chinese, born and brought up in Hong Kong by a loving, but strict grandmother as is usually the way in China when the parents pursued their careers with the sole aim of providing a better lifestyle for their children.

In spite of these differences and occasional school boy squabbles, Gregory and he had remained friends, a friendship which continued when they were both at London University and by the time he had returned to Hong Kong they had already established a business relationship. And what now, mentally shrugging and glancing sideways at the man seated next to him. Derek Insole, MI6, based in Hong Kong, English, possibly from the south, late thirties and that was all he knew about him. The man was giving nothing away, providing no indication what else they had managed to dig up which would pull him any further into the quagmire of suspicion he was under. The official questioning at Police Headquarters where they had taken him from his apartment, once the charges had been laboriously put to him, routine police procedure, culminating in the only real surprise that afternoon, in being told the case would be conducted in London. Lenny had enough sense to realise he had no choice and after a brief word with his lawyer who agreed for one of his partners in the London office to handle his defence should the case reach the courts, Lenny capitulated, but with reluctance. Round one to them he had decided caustically, determined to do his utmost to outwit them.

During the intervening hours from the moment he came on board the previous evening he'd had sufficient, perhaps too much, time to think, methodically placing everything they had come up with in their order of importance to him, although the bulk of it so far had been heavily veiled by officialdom; they only told him what *they* wanted him to know which was, in essence, operating a courier service between Hong Kong and Europe of goods with no supporting documentation of origin, a number of which had been listed as stolen. Secondly, although not necessarily in that order of importance, his connection with Nicholas Anout. Immediately his name had been mentioned yesterday Lenny had a strong impression they would be pursuing this, which meant he would have to exercise considerable caution. He could either tell them all he knew about Nicholas and the names of his various contacts in the Far East, or he could play down any dealings he may or may not have had with him. To take the first option would have definite repercussions. While he could shop him, Nicholas had equally as much on him.

It would seem from what they said, they had given Alex a good going over and as he had suspected and repeatedly warned him, his auxiliary set of records were not so cleverly concealed, a child of ten with basic computer skills could have found them, not that he was one to talk, remembering how speedily his own records had been uncovered. Although they had no proof he had any involvement with how Alex conducted his business, the fact of him being a co-director made him legally liable, thereby adding to their growing list of charges. And then there was 'Gregory's Antiques' and the results of the search carried out there, once again coming back to Gregory and his involvement with him. It would seem that Jan Jansen had not been left out of what was becoming more like one big round-up, ironically and perhaps predictably, bringing Clive back into the picture. And last, but certainly not least, Cecelia. They would be bound to pull her in for questioning and whether she was strong enough to hold out remained to be seen. So much for him warning her to dispose of any evidence of his name, he thought cynically, and inwardly cringing, remembering when they had found the old diaries which he should have got rid of years ago. And there was the added dilemma of providing them with any explanation, written or otherwise, of the contents of the safe which of course he couldn't.

All in all, not good, he concluded, fastening his seat belt in preparation for landing at Heathrow and looking out at a scene as gloomy and dismal as his thoughts; dawn was about to break, the sky, dark grey and thick with heavy rain clouds, and as they touched down, it started to rain, splashing against the window and bouncing off the tarmac.

***

'It is midday on the 17th October 2012,' Philip said after switching on the tape recorder again. Pamela Smythe-Jones, apart from accepting some coffee half an hour ago, hadn't changed her position or her expression of contrived detachment and the more he silently studied her he was certain that that was what it was; an attitude she had decided to adopt, an attempt to step mentally outside of her immediate surroundings. The vibes he was receiving were almost tangible and didn't fool him. She was worried alright, reminding him of a rabbit caught in the glare of a car's headlamps on a lonely dark stretch of road with nobody to come to her rescue.

Before re-commencing he had asked her once more whether she wanted her lawyer to be present, but as then, she refused, accompanying this with a withering expression under half-lowered eyelids.

'The last time I spoke to you, Mrs Smythe-Jones was on Thursday the 4th of this month after receiving a call from you the previous day to say you'd had a visit from Martha Underwood who attempted to blackmail you. You agreed to meet her the following day in the lounge bar of the Castle Hotel where she was staying. Is that correct?'

'Of course it is.'

'And I told you I had already spoken to her advising her not to see you again. But it would appear that after I left you on the Thursday, you went into Taunton, to the hotel, asking for her.'

'Did I?' she drawled.

'You tell me, Mrs Smythe-Jones.'

'Why should I have, Mr Spencer? I had nothing to say to the woman.'

'You were recognised by the receptionist in The Castle.'

'Well, you only have her word against mine, then, haven't you?'

'Martha Underwood was still in Taunton, having moved to another hotel.'

'Really? You do surprise me; why on earth should she have done that?'

'There could be one or two reasons,' he said, 'one of them being to avoid seeing you again. She knew her attempt at blackmail had failed and she would still have had another day before she needed to be back in London for her flight on Friday morning.'

'I don't see what any of this has got to do with me.'

'I believe it has everything to do with you, Mrs Smythe-Jones. When the news of her accident reached the press later on the Friday, there was no mention of how or why the accident happened, but following the mechanical check on her vehicle it was discovered it had been severely tampered with, which after a few miles rendered it virtually useless.'

'So?' rudely this time, a reaction he wasn't unhappy with.

'This damage could only have been done on the Thursday night when the car was parked outside her hotel.'

'These things happen. Probably drunks coming out of the pub at the corner of the road; I've heard it's a rowdy place.'

'Where were you on Thursday evening, Mrs Smythe-Jones?'

'Me! You suspect *me* of being responsible! This is outrageous; I don't know the first thing about cars!'

'I repeat,' Philip said, ignoring her outburst, 'where did you spend Thursday evening?'

'I can't remember, probably at home.'

She was stalling. She hadn't been expecting that. She should have done, of course, but it only illustrated the extent of her arrogance.

'You said just now you have no knowledge of cars.'

'Well, I don't.'

'It is my understanding you know a great deal. You learned at a very young age how to render a car not only non-roadworthy, but potentially dangerous.'

'Nonsense!'

'I have a reliable witness to support what I've said. Also,' he went on stolidly, 'I would like to remind you of an accident which occurred to one of your teachers at Wessex Lodge. Her car had been tampered with in precisely the same way as Martha Underwood's had been; fortunately your teacher was not killed, but she could have been.'

'Coincidence.'

'I don't think it was any coincidence. I think the damage was carried out by the same person.'

'You think *I* did?'

'Put it like this, Mrs Smythe-Jones, at the present moment there is no evidence to consider anyone else as a suspect. However,' he persisted, 'to return to the Thursday again -'

'- what a waste of time all of this is!'

'That remains to be seen.' calmly, not rising to her escalating temper, 'Martha booked into the hotel during the Thursday morning, parking her car in the front forecourt. During the evening, someone was seen out there in the parking area and gave a reasonably good description of the person. It's for this reason, it is important to know where you were on that evening. Perhaps you've remembered?'

'Not really.' shrugging, 'One week night is very much like any other. It's often quite late by the time my husband gets home from work; we're inclined to do all our socialising at the weekends.'

'I would remind you,' Philip said, that this interview is being recorded.'

'I haven't forgotten!'

'What time does your husband usually get home?'

'Around seven.'

'And you are always at home when he arrives?'

'Of course.'

'Hopefully, his memory is better than yours. Mrs Smythe-Jones. He will surely remember whether you spent the whole evening at home.'

'Why don't you ask him?'

'I will, in due course. How did you know there was a pub in close vicinity to the hotel?'

'Sorry?'

'A few minutes ago you mentioned there was one at the corner of the road.'

'Well, there is, isn't there?'

'I suggest after you left The Castle having been told that Martha

Underwood had booked out, you had the idea she may have changed hotels, assuming perhaps she hadn't finished what she had set out to do. It would seem her sole purpose for blackmailing you was to prevent her talking to your husband. The warning I gave her, that was all it was, may not have had any effect; she may have planned a different approach. In other words, Mrs Smythe-Jones she still remained a threat to your marriage.'

'As a matter of fact I had made up my mind to tell him all about Martha's visit.'

'And did you?'

'Not yet.'

'This happened almost two weeks ago, I would have thought you would have had plenty of time, especially as in the interim you have both been on holiday and probably spending more time with each other than usual.'

'I didn't want to worry him.'

She was doing her utmost to parry everything he threw at her with, so far, only one slip-up in that she must have known which hotel Martha had chosen. He recalled seeing the pub and as she had said it was on the corner of the road, but he rather doubted her flimsy suggestion of it having the reputation of being rowdy. It had struck him as a quiet part of town, well away from the centre.

'I would further suggest,' continuing from where he had left off earlier, 'that once you had driven away from The Castle, you made an attempt to find where she had gone. It could have been pure chance you hit upon the right hotel.'

'You don't know what I did! If you really want to know, I drove back home!'

'So you admit you did call in at The Castle?'

'No, of course, I – well, I didn't.'

'You spotted her car in front of the Brampton Hotel –'

'– and if I did, how on earth would I have known it *was* her car?'

'You would have noted the make, possibly the number, when she called to see you the day before. On the Thursday you went along to the Brampton Hotel later when it was dark and carried out the damage which resulted in the fatal accident the following day.'

'You have no proof.' she snapped, looking directly at him.

'On the contrary, Mrs Smythe-Jones, I have sufficient proof to place you under arrest -'

'- you cannot do this!' the words exploding from her, followed by her chair scraping on the floor as she jumped up, both hands palm down on the table facing him, every line of her body rigid with rage.

'Sit down please,' waiting while she dragged her chair back to the table and did as he told her, 'I duly charge you, Pamela Smythe-Jones with the murder of Martha Underwood on Friday, the 5th of October 2012, also with aiding and abetting in the murder of Norman Brookes on Wednesday, the 18th of December 2002. This interview is now terminated at half past one on Wednesday afternoon, the 17th October 2012.

***

'Sophie's Designs' in the centre of Winchester; a street in the ancient city tucked away behind the cathedral and next to Winchester College, but nowadays the focal point for shoppers tired of the stereo-typed predictability of High Street shopping and seeking something a little different, was immediately eye-catching in its understated elegance which appealed to him. Philip stood for a minute or two before going in, wanting to absorb the atmosphere in a part of Winchester he had never visited before, wishing now he had taken more time off to explore. Work, he thought wryly, had for far too long, ever since Harriet died, predominated over leisure time. He dared to hope since meeting Sophie again that that may change.

The front facia of the shop, painted royal blue, blended in well with its neighbours; a fine arts gallery on the left and a hand-made jewellery shop on the right. In the centre of her window Sophie had positioned an old-fashioned Singer sewing machine, reminding him of the one his grandmother had owned and how fascinated he had been as a young lad watching as with both feet on the ironwork treadle plate she had nimbly and with apparent ease sent the treadle working to produce perfectly formed stitches on the length of cloth she expertly guided along below the needle. The only other display piece was a dressmaker's dummy with a swathe of scarlet and silver-threaded fabric draped around the padded shoulders. The whole effect was charming, impatient now to go into the shop and surprise her.

He wouldn't be able to spend much time with her before having to get back to London. The meeting the previous day with Charles and Derek had lasted longer than any of them had expected and when he finally reached home it was too late to call her, but he did want to see her, even if only for a few hours. It had been Charles who had suggested he should fly back with Derek when he returned to Hong Kong on the late night flight. There wouldn't be much happening in London in respect to the two cases with the preliminary court hearings still a week away. They had come up against a drawback in that according to the authorities in Singapore, Nicholas Anout was no longer residing at the address they had for him, having apparently moved out the day before, and not surprisingly the number for his mobile was unobtainable, although Passport Control had confirmed he was still in the country. All of this had given Charles the idea of how they could make a final attempt to try to locate him before the preliminary hearings.

'We all realise,' he had said, 'that Anout is a tough nut to crack, but I think this is where we can use Cecelia Cunningham to flush him out.'

'You think she is his Achilles heel?' Philip had asked him, finding it difficult to accept Nicholas Anout had one.

'Everyone has one.' Charles smiled, uncannily reading his thoughts, 'It's knowing where to find it; that's the tricky part. So, Philip,' he went on, 'Pamela Smythe-Jones put up a good fight today?'

'In respect to Martha Underwood, yes, but it didn't take long for her to capitulate on what she had previously stated on her part in that business in Samriboi, although it was a matter of saving her own skin. Of course we don't know whether she will convince the prosecution. She is so accustomed to getting her own way, I don't believe for one second she thinks anyone would disbelieve her.'

'She shouldn't be so sure.'

'I know, Charles, but either way, she is guilty of culpability whether she pulled the trigger or not.'

'What's your personal opinion, Philip,' Derek had asked him, 'do you think she could have shot him?'

'I would say she would be capable of doing so, but I believe Anthony Johnson fired that gun alright. I would say her relationship with him was of no consequence to her; she wanted out of a marriage which no longer suited her and had probably metaphorically lined up Gregory-Smythe-Jones to take his place; a man of social standing, wealthy and in a position to provide her with the lifestyle she wanted. To have actually carried out the act of murdering Norman Brookes in cold blood signifies to me that Johnson's feelings for her ran very deep indeed. He took a risk, she gave him the great heave-ho and went off and married Gregory Smythe-Jones, Johnson changed his name, although not his identity and, we can fill in the rest.'

'Some plot.' Derek remarked dryly.

'Some woman.' Charles added.

They had spent the remainder of the meeting discussing the more complex and convoluted case of smuggling on a grand scale, fudging annual returns and adjusting business records to avoid paying further taxes plus a general misappropriation of funds; the three of them agreed the courts would take several weeks before reaching their final assessment and conclusions. Philip hadn't seen Lenny Yeung the previous day when he had been escorted to New Scotland Yard from Heathrow, although Derek told them when he arrived at Headquarters Yeung had refused to say anything further until his lawyer was present which would be this afternoon with Derek conducting the interview.

Meanwhile, with his hand on the door handle of 'Sophie's Designs', he was taking a few hours off and looking forward to every minute of spending it with her.

Chapter Twenty-one

HONG KONG

Hong Kong's Sympathy of Lights greeted them as their taxi approached Kowloon; the spectacular sound and light show along the waterfront, the exteriors of the city's major buildings aglow with a myriad of vivid colours, the piercing lights and laser beams reaching across the harbour.

'Fantastic, eh?'

'Quite breathtaking.' Philip agreed, marvelling as he did each time he came to Hong Kong, the sheer magnitude of everything: the skyscrapers reaching up to the sky; the dark outline of the Peak an ever-present backcloth to the Island and the sheer density of the stream of traffic and the people. A city which was never still.

'Shall we call into the office first, Philip, before we call it a day?'

'That's okay by me,' he agreed, 'there could be something for us.'

'There should be,' Derek said, 'it's always the same with these long haul flights, isn't it? I don't know about you, but I feel I've been in limbo for days.'

Within minutes their taxi turned into Hankow Road, pulling up outside Pauline Chan Jewellery. The suite of offices MI6 had been occupying for a number of years was on the first floor of the building above the shop, the door to the stairs leading off from the small vestibule. Derek keyed in the code number and the door swung open, locking automatically behind them. Philip had been there a number of times and was familiar with the layout, following Derek along the labyrinth of narrow corridors until they reached his office.

'I'll arrange for some coffee,' he said, pressing the buzzer on the desk, 'that should keep us going until we have something more fortifying.'

There were a number of reports on his desk and sifting through them he pulled one of them out, together with the accompanying tape.

'This could be it.' he said, glancing up at him.

'They should have been able to get something from Cecelia

Cunningham's calls.' Philip said, and hoping they were not going to be disappointed. A bugging device had been fitted to her phone on Tuesday and this was the first time either of them had had a chance to listen to any calls she may have made or received.

Derek slipped the tape into the recorder and, using the printed report as a guideline, they waited for it to start.

'The first message,' Derek said, reading out loud from the report, 'was one which came through on her answering machine on Tuesday in the late afternoon, although she didn't take it until eleven forty-five that night: "Cecelia;" the man's voice, Derek silently mouthing the name of Lenny Yeung, reached them clearly, "this is serious. I've just spent the last few hours being grilled by Interpol. Don't know what's going to happen now, but I want you to destroy any records you may have linking your name with mine ......"

Twenty minutes later, she made a call to Singapore to tell whoever answered about Yeung's message, adding that he had instructed her to destroy any evidence which would link her with him. "And have you done that?" "Yes, I have, but what about you Nicholas?" "Don't worry about me, *ma chère*; at least if anyone does turn up here I will have been fore-warned, but it's you I'm concerned about ....."

Only two more calls had been made by her, both to Bakker & Bakker; the first on the Wednesday and the second the following day, each time, asking to speak to Lenny Yeung. She took a second call from the man calling himself Nicholas later that day telling her he had changed both his address and mobile phone number and passing these on to her.

'There you go,' Derek grinned, switching off the machine, 'That was exactly what we've been waiting for.'

***

SINGAPORE

After talking to Cecelia on Wednesday, Nicholas realised that Lenny's silence was ominous and could only mean one thing; he had been taken into custody. She had mentioned Interpol and that did concern him although he made an attempt to play down the possible significance which could affect him and this was something Nicholas was not prepared to tolerate. Moving out of his apartment in Orchard Road and purchasing another mobile phone were only the first contingency steps in widening the gap between him and the law, an exercise with which he was well familiar. His new apartment, similar to the other one he had vacated, was a service one and in another part of Singapore. Ideally, he would have preferred to leave the country, but recognised the folly of such a move. Also, he had meant what he had said to Cecelia; he wanted her here with him even if this could result, should she decide to leave Hong Kong, in further endangering his own position, but being pragmatic, decided to face that problem if and when it should arise.

The person who really worried him was Lenny. They had always conducted their business transactions on a formal footing, neither of them truly trusting the other. Lenny's attitude over those figurines had irritated him and he hadn't been fooled by his affected protestations. Lenny had known all along, right back to the beginning, that not everything he sold on to him had been acquired legitimately, therefore somewhat late in the day to be putting up this sort of innocent front. But then, Lenny was like that. It was as though he shrouded his whole life in a veil of mystery, giving the impression he was next door to bloody perfect, when in actual face he was far from it. Lenny Yeung was as crooked as he was. But, perhaps, with what was happening at the moment he had the upper hand. Lenny was on the verge of being banged up while he remained free, at least to move, albeit within the limited confines of his adopted country.

Something or someone, Nicholas decided sourly, not happy with the way he was thinking, had triggered off this catalogue of events which, if he wasn't careful, was in danger of running out of control. Ever since Anthony hadn't turned up at Changi Airport last month he'd had the gut feeling he hadn't heard the last of him. He had first met Anthony in 1987. He had only recently completed his contract in Nigeria and without any definite plans of what he was going to do next, decided to spend some time in Paris. Anthony had only been twenty-five then, but from the way he was talking it was plain he had learned very quickly how to survive, more importantly, he possessed a devil-may-care attitude in his primary objective which was to make money which he firmly believed in his somewhat naive and blinkered way would pull him up and away from what he used to describe as his humble beginnings. Anthony was, and probably still is, Nicholas thought, an inverted snob; always attempting to attain what was in essence the unachievable, but he had proved useful to him over the years. Anthony continued working for him during the time he spent in Zambia, successfully sourcing a steady supply of locally-mined diamonds and emeralds and for this he was paid well. When Anthony called him a few days before he made his dramatic exit from Zambia and said he was on his way back to Europe, saying it was essential for him to change his identity, he had taken it for granted he would be able to arrange it for him, which he did. At a cost. Not in monetary terms for Anthony, but the resulting debacle over the botched-up job of arranging it, resulting in him having no alternative but to vacate Paris.

Nicholas had no address for him, only a mobile number and after a couple of attempts of trying to call him he gave up. If Anthony was in some sort of trouble, the last thing Nicholas wanted was to become embroiled. The coincidence of both Anthony and Lenny being uncontactable at the same time was not lost on him. Surely it was too far-fetched to consider they knew each other? Could he possibly be working for Lenny as well? If he was, Lenny would know him as Clive Edwards, not Anthony Johnson. The more Nicholas tossed this idea around, the more he thought it just might be the case, all of which brought him to the person who may know. Cecelia. She had been working for Lenny for the last eight years and would possibly know the names of any of his other couriers.

He was on the point of calling her when his mobile rang. It must be her, he thought, picking up the phone; she was the only one he had given his new number to so far. The surprise in not hearing her voice was immediately outweighed by a shiver of apprehension. He didn't even consider it could be a wrong number, the build-up of tension over the last few days having honed his normal reactions to the unexpected.

'Mr Anout?'

'Yes.' he answered automatically, too late to realise his mistake.

'My name is Philip Spencer, Mr Anout; I'm from the Foreign Office in London.'

'The Foreign Office.' he repeated, stalling for time.

'Yes, that's right. I'm conducting an investigation concerning an international matter and would appreciate if you could spare the time for us to meet.'

'I'm sorry, Mr Spencer,' Nicholas said, at the same time attempting to reign in his runaway thoughts and control his panic, 'I have absolutely no idea why you should want to see me. Perhaps you would be kind enough to explain.'

'I will of course be more explicit, but I prefer this to be on a face to face basis. I'm staying at the Majestic Hotel, Mr Anout, which I understand is quite close to your apartment; I'll be in the lounge bar at midday.'

'Just a moment,' Nicholas said quickly, sensing he was going to end the call, 'how will I recognise you?' aware of how pathetic that must sound.

'You won't, Mr Anout, but I believe I will recognise you.'

***

HONG KONG

As each day went by Cecelia was becoming increasingly more agitated. It was now Saturday and she had heard nothing further from Lenny. She had tried repeatedly to call him on his mobile, also at Bakker & Bakker, but received no response from either; the mobile seemed to be out of action and his secretary, whom she had always disliked, was unforthcoming, merely saying in her irritating sing-song voice that Mr Yeung was unavailable. Aware she was still being followed and had been since coming back from Singapore on Sunday didn't help, the thought now occurring to her they, whoever they were, could have known she had gone to Singapore and may even have been watching her while she was there. She'd had a call from Nicholas on Wednesday evening giving her his new address and mobile number, proving in spite of making light of his own situation, he had taken her warning seriously. As he had said to her, if the authorities had been able to get hold of the knowledge of his whereabouts, it would now be useless information to them. "I did this as a precaution, Cecelia," he'd said, "Lenny may not have had my name on his records, but I considered it best and especially for you if you decide to come here." She had then told him about being followed, but he hadn't sounded too surprised. "They're a pretty thorough lot, you know," he'd reminded her, "and if they are MI6, well what more can I say?"

"That they won't give up." she had finished for him, her unease intensifying.

"Quite."

She had spent the remainder of the week absorbing herself in work in an attempt to keep the rising panic at bay, but it didn't. She had made no plans for the weekend and the thought of the empty hours until Monday morning was not a comfortable one. A couple of her colleagues suggested she joined them for a drink at midday when they closed the office, but she declined, inventing instead something about already meeting a friend for lunch. She knew she would find it impossible to be sociable; also she didn't want anyone to notice how worried she was. Somehow, Cecelia thought, switching off her computer and clearing her desk, she had to get through this time. Nothing would be achieved if she started to fall to pieces, wondering where all her customary self-sufficiency had gone. Perhaps she wasn't as tough as she always considered herself to be.

He was out there again; the same man she had seen before, standing in exactly the same position affecting an interest in Thomas Wong's permanent display of ancient postcards, but instead of walking away when she appeared, he came straight over to her.

'Miss Cunningham,' he said unhesitatingly, giving her no opportunity to deny it or even to ignore him, 'I'm from London's Foreign Office,' handing her a small white card, 'and I would like to ask you a few questions in respect to an investigation we are currently working on.'

She glanced at the card; it appeared to be authentic, but how did she know he wasn't bluffing. His name was, apparently, Derek Insole, also there was a professional smoothness about him which reminded her of Peter Prescott. Lenny had suggested he could be from MI6; perhaps, she thought, all their officers came out of the same mould.

'Shall we go along to Staunton's for a coffee,' he suggested, once again pre-empting her, 'more comfortable than standing around here, also less noisy.' he added, beginning to move away in the direction of Staunton's wine bar and café, placing her in the insidious position of having to go with him.

Staunton's was only a short distance away and one she had been to many times; a Mediterranean-style café and unanimously voted to be the best people-watching spot in Hong Kong. Cecelia knew the area well, but wished she was accompanying anyone rather than a man from the Foreign Office. By now, as he pushed open the door to the café, she had resigned herself to being subjected to a line of questions, any of which could be a trap, reminding herself to be on her guard and not slip up the way she had with Peter Prescott. It had already occurred to her that this Derek Insole wanted something from her, something perhaps the Foreign Office had been unable to extract from anyone else they may have talked to, the obvious assumption being it must concern Lenny. Indeed, she thought, who else?

'It's possible, Miss Cunningham,' he said, once they were seated and the coffee had been brought over to them, 'you may be able to help us.'

'In what way, Mr Insole?'

'That does remain to be seen,' he answered obliquely, 'but first I would like to establish a number of points, primarily your relationship with a man called Lenny Yeung.'

'Lenny Yeung.' she repeated slowly, playing for time. Was this the first trap, she wondered. Did he actually know she had anything to do with Lenny, or was this his way of finding out? Chances were that he did know, meaning again she had no choice. 'I have known Lenny for a number of years' he's an old friend whom I meet now and again.' she said.

'Are you employed by him, Miss Cunningham?'

'I work for a publishing firm, Mr Insole, as I am sure you will already be aware.'

'On a full-time basis?'

'Very much so.'

'Does your work involve much travelling outside Hong Kong?' he asked and at that precise moment she knew what he was leading up to; he knew damn well she did and with this realisation it went a long way to prove that Peter Prescott was also with the Foreign Office. So, it would seem that Lenny had been right.

'A fair bit,' she admitted, selecting each word carefully, 'I'm in the sales and marketing side of the business,' she explained, 'and this means visiting potential customers to promote our titles.'

'Is there a particular area you concentrate on, Miss Cunningham?'

'Mainly in the Far East.'

'Europe?'

'Occasionally, but not very often.'

'When did you last see your friend, Lenny Yeung?' the slight change in the pattern of his questioning unnerving her. This was really and truly like walking on eggshells, she thought.

'About a week ago; last Sunday in fact.'

'Where was this, Miss Cunningham?'

He knew! Derek Insole knew where she had met Lenny! She desperately tried to think back to Sunday, right from the moment she had left her apartment in Glenealy Road and walked along to the Gardens. Lenny and she had arranged to meet on one of the benches in the Fountain Terrace Garden. Being a Sunday afternoon, it was more than usually busy with families taking advantage of the late summer warmth and at no time had she been aware of anyone taking any particular notice of her. Lenny had waited until she was seated before coming over. He hadn't stayed long; possibly he was too aware of the vulnerability of meeting openly where he could so easily be spotted. She wasn't sure whether he left the Gardens before her, but there was no sign of him outside the gate. In spite of her awareness of possibly being followed that afternoon, it would appear she must have been.

'We hadn't agreed to meet,' she said, 'it was purely by chance. I had taken a walk in the Botanical and Zoological Gardens which is not far from where I live and that's where I saw him.'

'By chance, you say?'

'Yes, that's right.'

'You were seen, Miss Cunningham; both you and Lenny Yeung. I'd like you to have a look at this photograph.' he added, sliding the print across the table towards her.

'Surely, Mr Insole,' she said quietly, reluctant to pick it up in case he would notice her hand shaking, such was the shock in literally seeing in black and white the evidence of not only being in Lenny's company, but in actually handing him the package, 'this – this blatant snooping is an infringement of my liberties.'

'Under the circumstances, I have to say that is debatable. You see, Miss Cunningham,' he explained, 'the magnitude of our investigation is such that anyone we consider to be involved, even remotely, has to be subjected to close scrutiny. That is the way we work, unpleasant for the recipient, but I can assure you necessary and quite within our jurisdiction as laid down by the law.'

'I am not aware of doing anything wrong, you know. Also, Mr Insole, you haven't told me anything about what you *are* investigating.'

'In the main,' he started to explain, 'it concerns, for the want of a better description, the acquisition, legitimately or otherwise, of items of considerable value and distributing them illegally from one country to another.'

'And you think Lenny is involved?'

'We not only think he is, Miss Cunningham, we have strong evidence to prove that he is.'

'You said earlier you thought I may be able to be of some help to you.'

'Although I have been asking you about your association with Lenny Yeung, I believe you are in a position to assist us in apprehending the second key figure in this scheme, possibly others.'

'How?' she asked, mentally struggling to shrug off her feelings of disquiet, intuitively realising who this second person was. It must be Nicholas. And she waited for him to elaborate, to mention his name, knowing in advance she was no match for him. It was obvious that Derek Insole's trained brain, as with Peter Prescott's, operated in a totally different way to her own. Any questions he had asked her in the last five minutes or so had all been contrived. He had already known the answers; he had known that her relationship with Lenny was a business one, remembering back to the evening she had met him in *Le Tire Bouchon*, wondering if, after all, Derek Insole had managed somehow to find out she had gone there. And what about her visit to Amsterdam and London? Presumably, if Peter Prescott and he were working together, Derek Insole would know about that and given their tenacity in keeping an eye on her, they very likely were aware of her meetings with Jan Jansen and Gregory Smythe-Jones. Were they 'the others' he had mentioned?

'I would like to go back six years,' he was saying, 'to March 2006 to be exact. We understand you made a visit to Singapore and during that visit you were given a package containing four oriental figurines; these you brought back with you to Hong Kong and handed them over to Lenny Yeung.'

'That isn't true!'

'Would you be prepared to say that in a court of law and under oath?'

'You have absolutely nothing to support what you've just said. Nothing; it is all pure fabrication.'

'We have proof you were in Singapore then.'

'I probably was, but I would have been there on behalf of my publishing firm.'

'And would your firm be able to corroborate this?'

'They may be, Mr Insole. What you must realise is that I work very much as a free agent for them. I have a contract of employment naturally, but it is an open-ended one. As I've already said, I'm involved in sales and marketing. My directors don't demand or even expect a blow-by-blow account of my working schedule. All they are interested in is a full order book. I am on expenses, within an agreed budget, of course, and although I always inform them when I'm away, they don't require any detailed itinerary.'

'I see. However,' he went on, 'on the occasion I'm talking about although you may, as you've explained, been on business, we have strong evidence to prove you did in fact take delivery of those figurines which incidentally had been listed officially as stolen property -'

'- I must object to the way this conversation is going, Mr Insole. You are now suggesting that I was in receipt of stolen property!'

'The man who gave them to you, Miss Cunningham, has long been suspected of having acquired them, but it is only recently that new evidence has turned up, allowing the case of the theft to be re-opened.'

'I know absolutely nothing about any of this.'

'You have met this person a number of times over the last eight years, Miss Cunningham, and on each occasion he has handed over to you certain packages which you, acting as Lenny Yeung's courier, have brought back to Hong Kong.' he said calmly and giving no impression he had heard her outburst. She knew she was on the edge of floundering, saying something which he would immediately pounce on, but had no idea of how to extricate herself from the position he had placed her.

'While I realise I don't need to tell you this,' he persisted, 'but the man's name is Nicholas Anout, although during this particular period he was calling himself Simon Brel.'

'Neither name means anything to me, Mr Insole.' So, she thought, feeling a tightness in her throat, making breathing difficult, they had done their research on Nicholas. One consolation though, he wouldn't be at the address they presumably had for him, but she must phone him. He needed to know about all of this.

'Going back to this print,' he said, once again unnerving her with the way he switched from what he had been saying, 'what was inside the package you gave to Lenny Yeung last Sunday?'

The question she had been dreading. Whatever she said would be wrong and would never coincide with what Lenny would tell the authorities when he would surely be asked, but she had to think of something. Anything.

'I had bought him a present.'

'Yes?'

'It was a plaited leather belt with a gold and silver buckle.' remembering Lenny had been wearing a similar one when they'd had their meal in *Le Tire Bouchon*.

'And yet you say you hadn't arranged to meet him on Sunday?'

'That's right, but I planned to call in with it later that afternoon.'

'I see,' he said for the second time and she wasn't fooled by the disbelieving expression on his face, 'to his apartment in Causeway Bay?'

'No,' too quick to correct him, 'Lenny lives in Garden Road, not very far from my apartment actually.

***

LONDON

Sophie was already there, in the lounge bar of the Strand Palace Hotel, when he arrived. She had phoned him shortly before he left Hong Kong earlier in the week telling him she would be in London for a couple of days attending the bi-annual Fabric Fair and staying at the Strand Palace.

The smile she gave him as he walked over to her table acted as an immediate fillip. The relentless build-up over the past three weeks had taken their toll, exacerbated by the inordinate amount of travelling and, as always at the end of an investigation as intensive as this one, a general feeling of anti-climax. They all had had their part to play and it would now be up to the legal profession to make the final decision over the destiny of the offenders. In respect to Pamela Smythe-Jones, both charges brought against her; namely, aiding and abetting in the murder of her husband, Norman Brookes, and being personally and solely responsible for the death of Martha Underwood, would be treated separately by the courts, and until such time as she was summoned, agreement was reached on Wednesday by the West London Magistrates' Court that she would be held in custody. Inevitably, with the public's interest and curiosity already whetted with the media's mention of Anthony Johnson, it didn't take long for her name to be recognised by more than one press reporter attending this initial hearing, resulting in the news reaching the front page of the following morning's newspapers.

Gregory Smythe-Jones had fared slightly better in that he had been allowed bail until the first Crown Court hearing which would include the charges against Lenny Yeung, Alexander Van Ommeron and Nicholas Anout, although once again his name attracted the attention by the media which didn't bode well for him once he returned to Taunton.

Nicholas Anout's somewhat desperate attempt to evade him the previous Saturday had failed, resulting in some significant findings, all of which contributed to his arrest and extradition to England the following day.

Philip had pre-empted him not turning up at his hotel by arranging, with the assistance of police headquarters, to be waiting outside Anout's apartment building in an unmarked police car, accompanied by one of their senior officers. They were not disappointed. Anout had emerged from the main door of the building shortly before midday, but instead of walking in the direction of the Majestic Hotel went the opposite way to join the queue at the taxi rank further along the pavement. Less than ten minutes later he had reached the head of the queue and had taken the next taxi which stopped alongside him. Not unsurprisingly, with their driver dextrously negotiating the midday traffic, they ended up outside Changi Airport, waiting only long enough for Anout to pay off the driver before walking a few paces behind him into the Arrivals Hall. They followed him to a Singapore Airlines check-in desk, both of them glancing up at the destination board. Bangkok – 1500 hours. Later, once they had apprehended him and taken him into custody, it transpired from speedy checks carried out by Philip's counterpart in Bangkok that Nicholas Anout had a residential address there, also he rented a suite of offices in the city's business area, trading under the nebulous description of a finance and investment executive, the resultant search revealing substantial and incriminating evidence of his various acquisitions in the Far East, including several pieces he had brought into the country from Singapore. He had even misguidedly recorded on his desktop computer, presumably for his own benefit, dates and addresses of each establishment, including half a dozen entries made during March and April of 2006, the three addresses all belonging to the British Consulate in Singapore. As Derek and he agreed when he returned to Hong Kong the following morning, not very sensible of Anout, but then perhaps he continued to believe he was untouchable and by keeping his records out of his adopted country gave him that assurance.

'How lovely to see you, Philip.' Sophie said, pulling out a chair for him.

'And you, Sophie;' leaning over and kissing her, 'and a bonus that you are in London which is surely worth a bottle of champagne.'

'So,' she said when the waiter had brought the champagne to their table and they had taken their first appreciative sips, 'Pamela made headline news yesterday.'

'She certainly did,' he agreed, 'and as you have probably gathered, our work is now complete on the two cases; the final decision on her fate will be in the hands of the courts.'

'I must admit I was somewhat surprised to read about the second charge made against her for the murder of Martha Underwood, although I don't suppose I should have been, given the nature of how the woman died. What I've been wondering, Philip, is whether there is a connection between both of those crimes; it all sounds so – so coincidental somehow.'

'You're right about there being a connection, albeit a rather tenuous one, in that both Martha and Pamela had an affair with Anthony Johnson.'

'In Zambia?'

'Yes, although expatriates in the same town out there and would be in each other's company regularly, apparently they weren't particularly friendly towards each other.'

'Ah,' Sophie said, 'I'm beginning to get the picture.'

'I thought you might.' Philip smiled, not in the least surprised at the speed in which she was reaching her conclusions.

'Well,' she said, speaking slower this time, obviously putting her thoughts in order, 'the first question I asked myself when I read about it was why Pamela would want to get rid of her; what possible motive would she have had. She must have hated her a great deal to go to such lengths and so long after she'd left Zambia.'

'And what did you come up with?' prompting her, impressed as he had been before by her logical thought process.

'Sorry to disappoint you, Philip,' she smiled, taking another sip of her champagne, 'but I can't think of anything. I've been remembering back to Miss Hudson's accident and if Pamela had been responsible she was only a teenager at the time and probably like most girls of her age saw everything from a highly emotional level, especially when it came to boyfriends, and made a rash decision for revenge. Oh, I don't know,' she shrugged, 'I know I'm not making much sense, but Pamela is a thirty-five year-old woman and I would say that normally, thirty-five year-old women don't go around killing other women out of adolescent-like jealousy.'

'You're making a great deal of sense,' he assured her, 'and what you're saying is actually spot-on. I know what was reported contained only the bare bones of the charges, but it won't be long before the press will have succeeded in extracting as much meat as possible, which of course will also be available to anyone sufficiently interested in attending the trial. You see, I spoke to Martha Underwood twice not long before her fatal accident; the first time was to find out as much as I could about what she and her fellow-expatriates were doing at the time of Norman Brookes' murder and Anthony Johnson's subsequent disappearance. The second time was as a result of a telephone call from Pamela telling me she'd received a visit from Martha, the sole purpose being to blackmail her.'

'Why?'

'A good question. If anything, having talked to Martha Underwood, she made no attempt to conceal her deep hatred for Pamela and I would not have been too surprised if she had resorted to violence in an attempt to remove Pamela, but instead, she had chosen another way by threatening to discredit her in the eyes of her husband, using the threat of blackmail as a lever -'

'- did she actually *know* Pamela was involved with Anthony Johnson in the shooting of her husband?'

'She had no proof, Sophie; she was only guessing, but such was the strength of her assumptions she honestly believed if she spoke to Gregory Smythe-Jones, it would be sufficient to sow the seeds of suspicion in his mind and, understanding Pamela's particular character, Martha also believed that would destroy her marriage to a man who has provided her with such a lavish lifestyle, and to many of the Taunton residents, an enviable one. What Martha didn't take into account was how her plan to blackmail Pamela could so easily be overturned.'

'Which it was.'

'Yes, with disastrous consequences; Pamela, while appearing to accept Martha's demands, immediately contacted me, presumably in the hope we would then focus our suspicions on Martha, thereby reducing, or even eradicating, our growing suspicions of her, but she must have felt there would always be the chance that Martha would carry out her threat and talk to her husband. In other words, Pamela was literally back to square one and on the night of the same day she talked to me she carried out the damage to Martha's car which resulted in the fatal accident the following morning at the service station only a few miles out of Taunton.'

'My goodness, Philip! What a jumble it all is; I really don't know how you've managed to unravel it all.'

'A great deal of spadework, some of it getting us nowhere, also a good team of dedicated officers.'

'You're too modest, Philip.' she said, laying her hand lightly on his arm.

'Perhaps you're biaised.' he smiled.

'Perhaps.' a teasing smile hovering on her lips.

***

Kate was waiting for Dawn to arrive at St.Pancras Railway Station. This was Dawn's first free weekend since she started working for the British Consulate and had surprised both Steven and herself when she had phoned them the evening before to say she would be on the Eurostar train arriving in London at six-thirty. It had been two months since they had last seen her and the first time since she took up her position at the Consulate as a translator and they were both looking forward to hearing about her new life in Paris. They had so much to talk about and Kate wondered whether the weekend would be long enough.

Exactly on time, the passengers filtered on to the platform, Dawn easily recognisable in the middle of them all by her glossy dark-brown shoulder-length hair and her cherry red wool coat and matching leather boots, the ones she had treated herself to shortly after graduating.

'Hi, Mum,' she called out, almost running towards her, weaving in and out of the other passengers, 'you're looking good!' hugging her tightly.

'You too, dear.' Kate laughed, realising how little her daughter had changed since she was a young girl, arriving home at the end of each term, reminding her, as then, just how much she had missed her.

'Steven,' Dawn asked, linking her arm with hers, 'is he still at work?'

'He should be finished now,' Kate said, looking up at the station clock, 'I said we'd meet him in 'The Moon' although I don't need to remind you it will be pretty hectic in there on a Friday, but we should manage to find a table.'

'We'll take a cab, shall we?'

'I was going to suggest that actually,' quick to agree, 'better than standing for ages at the bus stop.'

'I know,' Dawn said, 'I've always thought it odd when you consider how many buses there are in central London, that the one you want always seems to be the last to arrive and then usually behind at least three others and you have to make a mad dash to catch it.'

'I suppose Paris is the same.'

'Oh, Mum, Paris is a lot worse; believe me! It's always busy, not just at rush-hour!'

'You're enjoying it though?'

'I am, yes; it's taken a bit of getting used to, but I'm making friends and really enjoying myself.'

Steven was in 'The Moon' before them, having succeeded in finding a free table, fortunately well back from the packed bar area.

'Hello, Dawn,' he said, kissing her, 'you're looking well; it's great to see you. Your Mum and I were delighted when you called to let us know you were coming.'

'I was going to surprise you, but I thought it best to let you know; you may have been going away this weekend or something.'

Once Steven brought their drinks over, Dawn told them what it was like working within the confines of the Consulate and how very different from what she had expected.

'Not too 'stuffy' for you?'

'No, Mum, not in the least. In many respects, quite laid back; they're a friendly lot and that includes our superiors and,' she added, 'I like the man I'm immediately responsible to. I suppose you would describe him as coming from the 'old school', Steven.'

'Hey, young woman,' Steven chuckled, 'I trust you're not implying -'

'- no, Steven,' she grinned, 'but you know what I mean. His name is Sir Desmond Bevington, not at all standoffish and really easy to talk to. Apparently, he's spent many years working in the Far East, his last posting being in Singapore and hasn't been in Paris all that long.'

'Sounds an interesting chap.' Steven commented and Kate could tell by his expression he was enjoying the exchange of banter which Dawn was always quick to bring into her conversations with him.

'Oh, he is. You've just reminded me of something which happened about two weeks ago.'

'Yes?'

'It was Sir Bevington's birthday and his wife gave a surprise party for him in their apartment which is part of the consulate building. It was all very informal: embassy officials and their wives, translators like me and quite a number of secretaries. I expect you're both wondering when I'm going to get to the point.' she smiled, her head on one side as she looked at them.

'The suspense is killing us.' Steven teased.

'Well, I'll put you out of your agony then. In their lounge, Sir Bevington had a large collection of oriental figurines; they were in a glass display cabinet and immediately I saw them I was reminded of those Aunt Eileen had. He saw me looking at them and told me he'd been collecting them for a long time, ever since he was posted out to the Far East –'

'– did you tell him about your aunt's collection?' Steven interrupted and Kate realised he was thinking exactly the same as her.

'I did, yes.' Dawn said, 'and then, this is the rather strange bit, he pointed out four of them which he told me had been stolen about six years ago when he was in Singapore and only that afternoon New Scotland Yard had returned them.'

'That's incredible!' Kate gasped; not so much that the figurines must be the same ones, but that Dawn was working for the man who owned them.

'Is it? What's wrong; you both look – stunned.'

'Before I tell you the whole story, Dawn,' Kate said at last, 'I'll explain, as you describe it, the reason for us looking stunned. I mentioned to you shortly after Aunt Eileen's funeral I had decided to auction off her furniture, pictures and more or less everything else in her house, except of course for your cheval mirror and the Queen Anne canteen of cutlery. It was Steven who recognised the possible value of her collection and I took them along to a firm of antique valuers which Mr Anderson had personally recommended. You can probably guess what happened after that.'

'The valuers recognised them as having been stolen; I say that because I once saw a programme on television about how they hold lists of certain stolen pieces in the event they may eventually turn up.'

'You're right.'

'What about Aunt Eileen's other figurines, Mum; they all looked very much the same to me?' Dawn, ever-practical, asked.

'All the others had been acquired legally by the antique firms and as you know how meticulous she was, she had kept all the corresponding invoices.'

'Aunt Eileen would have been furious.' Dawn said quietly, 'How she would have disliked what she would have described as the stigma of handling stolen goods. Ugh!'

'I'm sure you are right, Dawn,' Steven said, 'although I never met the lady, from what your Mum has told me about her character, I believe she would have reacted in that way.'

'There's been quite a lot happening over the last few weeks,' Kate told her, 'all of which we'll relate to you as far as we can in chronological order, but there is one rather odd aspect which has occurred.'

'What's that?'

'Not only has New Scotland Yard been involved,' Kate started to explain, 'but the Foreign Office also and it has transpired that the re-appearance of Aunt Eileen's figurines appear to have acted as some sort of catalyst. Would you not agree, Steven?' she asked, turning to face him.

'Absolutely; mind you,' he added, 'those figurines aside, a great number of the various sequence of events right from the moment you happened to be looking in the window of the Ceramics Centre may have taken an entirely different turn of direction, but that is perhaps something we're not likely to ever know.'

'You mean if I hadn't seen Anthony's reflection in the window that afternoon, the final outcome may not have been the same?'

'I wouldn't say that exactly,' he answered slowly, 'from what we've learned from Philip Spencer – he's with the Foreign Office, Dawn;' he explained to her, 'there were already moves afoot to bring things to a head, but what you were able to provide him with Kate, in the way of crucial background information, not forgetting the infamous – and mysterious – Nicholas Anout, must have helped them considerably.'

'Nicholas Anout;' Dawn put in, 'that's a French name, isn't it?'

'Yes, he's French alright. When we get home, Dawn, we'll show you the report in Thursday's 'Times'. It means, once you've read it, you will be starting more or less from the end, but at least hopefully, your Mum and I will be able to fill in the blanks for you.'

'All I can say,' Dawn said, looking at them both, 'my life in Paris seems extremely dull compared to what's been happening here!'

Other titles by Margaret Alty:

Tangled Web – ISBN: 978 1 84549 422 3

Jenny – ISBN: 978 1 84549 442 1

Camouflage – ISBN: 978 1 84549 478 0

The Last Orange – ISBN: 978 1 84549 560 2

A Meadowbank Mystery

Murder in Meadowbank –ISBN: 978 1 84549 494 7

Double Act –ISBN: 978 1 84549 537 4

Murder After Hours –ISBN: 978 1 84549 579 4

A Gathering of Crows –ISBN: 978 1 84549 594 7

All published by arima Publishing.

www.ingramcontent.com/pod-product-compliance
Lightning Source LLC
Chambersburg PA
CBHW051231260626
47162CB00002B/371